Dunnegan's Cottage

MacKay Series
Book Two

NORA WEIRICH

ISBN:PB: 979-8-9917834-0-8

ISBN:HB: 979-8-9917834-2-2

10 9 8 7 6 5 4 3 2 1

First Edition December 2024

For my family

&

the heritage that gives me inspiration.

Prologue

"They're out there!" He shouted, "We gotta kill 'em all!"

"Gavin, there's no one out there!" Sam Watson reasoned. Keeping a wary eye on Gavin as perspiration soaked through his clothes and erratic body movements made worse by the uncontrollable twitching. *He's high as a kite*, Sam thought, *what the hell did he get ahold of this time?* "What did he take?" Sam demanded of the others in the room.

"Hell, I don't know. Maybe he got ahold of some crystal meth someone made in their bathroom or heroin that was cut wrong." Jason offered. "I don't know. He went out on his own a while ago, and when he came back, he was like this."

"They're coming! See 'em? Sons-a-bitches. I can wipe 'em out now! All the son'-a-bitches. Don't know who they're dealin' with!" Gavin shouted again while looking out the nearest window; a dark-haired woman sidled up next to him.

"Gavin honey," Cheryl pleaded, rubbing her hand up and down his back. "You need to calm down, baby. There's nobody there. Nobody knows we're here. We're safe."

"Get away from me!" Gavin snarled, backhanding the woman with enough force to propel her across the small room. She slammed into the wall and slid awkwardly to the floor.

"Goddamnit, Gavin! Get a grip!" Sam shouted and crouched down to guide Cheryl up. He eased his arm under her arms and helped her to stand. "Are you alright?" he asked as she rubbed the back of her head.

"Yeah. I think so. This isn't good, pal," she said softly.

"No, it sure as shit isn't," Sam whispered. "We certainly don't need this now. We're too close to the end."

"Go ahead! Help the whore to her feet. You and her been screwin' behind my back anyway!" Gavin accused. He moved to the table picking up the Glock 45 and pointed it toward Sam and Cheryl.

"You start shooting off rounds with that thing, you asshole, and somebody is gonna know where we are." Sam ground out through clenched teeth. "You're high! And you're going to screw up this whole operation!" Sam warned as he moved Cheryl behind him. "Now put that damned thing down before you hurt someone."

"Oh, I'm gonna hurt someone alright. First you two," he smiled, "and then I'm gonna deal with those sons-a-bitches outside."

"There's no one out there, Gavin!" Jason yelled

"Now who's gonna be first? You?" He waved the gun in the general direction of the couple across the room, zeroing in on Sam. His vision was becoming blurry, and his hand shook violently. "Or her? Eeny-meeny-miny-moe." He slurred the old childlike phrase and the gun fired on the last word. Gavin turned and raced out the door, Sam made sure the bullet didn't hit Cheryl, Jason or more importantly the small girl curled on the floor in the corner of the small cabin.

"Protect her!" He told Cheryl, referring to the young girl. Getting the nod, he high tailed it in pursuit. *We need that asshole,* he seethed, *or we won't know where the drop is.*

Sam paused for a millisecond to let his eyes adjust to the inky black woods surrounding the cabin. He listened to the void for a direction to head. Sam could hear Gavin running in front of him panting heavily. Deciding that Gavin had just run straight out of the cabin Sam followed suit. Running as best as he could in the heavily dense underbrush, while trying to track the asshole ahead of him. The haphazardness of Gavin's trouncing about, disturbed the quiet eeriness of the wood that surrounded them. Footsteps, breaking twigs, and the occasional rage induced shout seemed to come from every direction. Sam finally stopped to listen and all he could hear was his own labored breathing.

"Bastard!" he whispered. The woods, heavy with moisture, made the air thick and oppressive. He could no longer hear Gavin at all, as he looked around it occurred to him that he couldn't see the lights of their cabin anymore. Realization hit him; he was lost in the woods and had no idea how to get back. As he stood still, trying to get his bearings, he heard what he *thought* were the first raindrops splashing on the ground cover.

"Perfect." he hissed. "That's about all I need." He bent down, hands on his knees trying to relax his breathing and felt a stabbing pain at his side. Then stood and reached his hand in under his jacket to press against where the pain was getting stronger. His fingers came out of his jacket wet and sticky. Blood. It wasn't rain splashing the leaves on the ground. He could smell it now. He was bleeding all over the place. "Shite!" he said. Gavin's gun had found a mark after all. *Apparently, me adrenaline kicked in,* he thought. But he didn't know how long it would last. He was already feeling woozy, and the pain was getting worse.

Knowing he would need medical care but had no clue which way to go. Sam looked up and tried to see the moon, but the canopy of the trees blocked his view.

"Well, Gavin wanted a place deep in the woods where no one would find us. Or the operation. And tha` s wha` he got." He mumbled. "Just walk. Eventually ye'll get ta a road. If ye donna bleed ta death first!"

He walked for what seemed like hours and miles. His legs were getting tired, and he was feeling weak from blood loss. It was getting darker if that was possible in the black wood. Real raindrops began to sift through the trees. "Yeah. Tha` s what I said before. 'Perfect!'" Before long, rain came down heavily, as he was walking blindly, using nearby tree trunks for support. He stumbled and fell but staggered upright again and kept moving. *I could be walkin in circles,* he thought. But kept walking. *If I'm movin,* he thought, *I'm no` dead.* Walking for hours and convinced he *was* going in circles. Noticing it was getting lighter he realized the sun was coming up. The rain had subsided, and he could hear rushing water to his left. *A creek,* he thought. *Follow the current and ye should be able ta get oot o` the woods. Or maybe, ye've walked ta the ocean, ye sorry bastard,* he thought. He could feel himself getting increasingly weaker and his vision was becoming impaired. Suddenly he broke out of the woods and came to a red shale dirt road. Sam raised his gaze and saw a small house down the road and stumbled toward it.

"Must find help." he thought, or maybe he spoke aloud. He wasn't sure anymore. "Need help." He walked as far as he could and collapsed behind the SUV parked beside the small grey house he had seen in the distance.

Chapter One

Megan Dunnegan looked out of her kitchen window smiling at the happy sound of rushing water. Thanks to the overnight rain, water was slapping against the rocks in the creek bed as it rushed down to the lake. She had a lovely view of the back of her property from the small single door window. Washing up breakfast dishes wasn't much of a chore, when she could gaze out the window and watch the seasons change before her eyes. Just as she was about to return her attention to the dishes, she spotted a man staggering down the red shale dirt road.

Drunk, she thought to herself. *Every year, at least one camp counselor parties too much.* She groaned inwardly. Turning her attention back to the breakfast dishes. Finishing, she turned and surveyed the main room of the cozy two-bedroom cottage. She loved it here. She had grown up coming to the Rileyville farm to spend her summers.

Her ancestors came over from Ireland in the 1860's to settle in Pennsylvania on the three hundred-sixty-eight-acre farm. Since then, the farm had been passed from father to eldest son down through the generations. After her father Patrick retired, he broke with tradition and turned ownership over to Megan and her brothers Nathan and Morgan.

Nathan, the eldest, a film director who lived mostly in New York. Because his job took him all over the world he mostly stayed in hotels when he was on location. However, there were a lot a projects happening in Vancouver, so there he had a small two bedroom apartment. Morgan, who played the middle child like a champ growing up, was a plastic surgeon and lived in Beverly Hills where he had his offices, because, as he said, "that's where the money is!" Her parents had always wanted to retire to the farm. Patrick was a "putterer" as his wife called him. He liked to fix things and there was always plenty to keep him busy on the farm. He also liked to work with wood and building things. Her parents built a lovely rambling house at the top of the Rye Lot and Patrick had a pole barn put up near the house for all his woodworking equipment. In the end there was a shop that even the master carpenter Norm Abrams himself would be proud of.

The family homestead's main house was an impressive eighteen room Victorian. When the brothers came with their families, that's where they stayed. It was close to the lake and had a huge yard for the kids shaded by two ancient silver maple trees. The "Big House," as it had been dubbed by all, had always been available for use by all family members who come for weekends and extended vacations, summer, and winter through the years. Everybody used the old place. Cousins, aunts, and uncles, in addition to Megan's brothers. It was a family place. That's the way it had always been and that's the way Megan and her family wanted it to stay.

But for Megan, the little grey cottage on the other side of the lake road was the draw. It was small, compact, and cozy. And she loved it. She made the move from New Jersey, and now lived in the cottage full time.

Megan's friends in Jersey had tried to talk her out of relocating. Telling her she would be bored and isolated. But she knew different. She loved the farm, the little village of Rileyville and the town of Honesdale. It was peaceful. The people were friendly, always there if you needed anything, and a good deal of them had known her all her life. It was a comfortable area and comforting as well. And when she moved to the farm, she was looking for just that, comfort, and caring people whom she could care for. So, she came home to Rileyville and opened her own Family and Geriatric Practice.

Including herself, Megan had two other doctors on staff. All three of them were licensed for Adult Family Practice and Pediatrics, but she was the only one who specialized in Geriatrics. She had seen the growing need for geriatric care years before, when her grandmother spent her final years suffering from dementia. That's when she decided she would do all she could to help patients and their families deal with the diseases of aging.

She glanced at her watch. "If I don't get a move on, I'm going to be late." Looking to Max, her beloved Great Dane, "Let me start the car and I'll be right back to get you, ok?" Smiling at the large beast she grabbed her purse, keys, and medical bag, on her way out the front door. She glanced up the road but could see no sign of the counselor from earlier.

"Must have stumbled his way back to the camp to sober up." She chuckled as she shut the front door. Megan walked down the large flagstone porch, built by her Dad and Granddad years earlier, to the side of the cottage where her Jeep Wagoneer was parked. When she rounded the corner of the cottage, she saw the counselor who had been staggering down the road, lying face down in the grass behind the SUV.

"Holy shit!" She muttered. Not knowing the guy or his character she approached carefully.

"Hey kid, are you ok?" But he made no sound. "Hey kid?" she said louder, and still he made no movement or gave any inclination that he had heard her. "Passed out cold." She threw up her hands. *Now what do I do?* She thought. "Well, what am I gonna do with you, face down in the grass?" she asked the unconscious youth. Suddenly he shot up with a burst of energy and managed to get himself to a kneeling position. He looked up at Megan. *This is no kid*, she thought to herself, *this is a grown man. Ought to have better sense.*

"Hospital." He managed to whisper and fell backwards.

Momentarily stunned, Megan hesitated for a second before her instinct kicked in and he was no longer a potentially dangerous stranger, he was a patient in need of help. She rushed to the back of the car and knelt beside him. One look at the front of his shirt and she dug into her purse to locate her cell phone and dialed 911.

"911 emergency response, what is your emergency?" the operator said.

"This is Dr. Megan Dunnegan." Megan gave the dispatcher her address and directions to the farm. "I have a man down with an abdominal wound. There appears to be considerable blood loss. My cell number is 570-555-4622." Before the operator could say anymore Megan ended the call.

She touched the seemingly unconscious man's shoulder and said, "Lie still, the squad is on the way. I'll be right back" She ran back to the cottage, swung the door open and rushed for the bathroom linen closet. Gathering several boxes of packing gauze and towels. Max came to attention the moment she ran into the cottage. Being at tune to her his body was rigid and on guard.

"Stay here Max." She told the pup while snatching the blanket off the sofa and charging back out the door to the man on the ground.

She knelt next to him and gently peeled back his blood-soaked shirt to reveal the wound. "This is a bullet hole." She said, while lifting him slightly on to his side looking for an exit wound. "Straight through." she murmured. She applied pressure and began to pack the wound to stem the flow of blood. As she worked, she talked softly, knowing that, although he may not understand her, in most cases, the sound of another person's voice usually helped calm most patients. "Looks like this is more than three hours old," she said as she struggled with his limp body to get the pressure bandage secured. "Provided the bullet didn't hit anything important on its way in or out, it would appear; your major problem is blood loss." She worked quickly and then covered him with the blanket to help avoid shock. She reached for one of the towels and began to wipe the sweat and dirt from the man's face. His eyes fluttered open, and he looked at her.

"Hospital." He forced out.

"Yes. Shh, I've called 911. The ambulance is on the way. Just lie still and try to relax."

He tried to reach into his pocket, but his strength was sapped. Megan moved his hand away and reached into his inside jacket pocket, finding it seemingly empty. However, as she felt more deeply in his pocket, she found a slit in the lining. As she reached in, her fingers touched leather. Megan got ahold of it and gingerly pulled it from its hiding place. It looked like some sort of wallet. She looked to him for approval to open it. He closed his eyes and nodded weakly. It wasn't a wallet; in fact, the whole thing was no bigger than a business card and no thicker than a cardboard box flap. It was his official identification. On one side of the thin leather billfold was a gold embroidered shield and on the top flap was the man's picture, name, and the initials FBI across the top.

"Secret." He breathed.

She looked back into his opened eyes, but had no time to ask the obvious question, as the screaming ambulance came barreling down the road with the volunteer paramedics right behind.

Megan backed out of the way, allowing the paramedics to take over. She closed the ID billfold and slipped it into the back pocket of her scrubs. When the paramedics got the patient on the gurney, the driver asked if she was going to follow them to the hospital. Megan told them she would and without further delay all parties got into their respective vehicles.

Wayne Memorial Hospital in Honesdale was twelve miles north of the cottage. Megan removed the man's ID from her pocket and dropped it into her purse and asked Siri to call her office. After explaining briefly to Jess, one of the other doctors at the practice, what had happened, she asked if Jess would cover while she went to the hospital.

"Of course, I will. Take as long as you need and if things get hectic here, I can call Sara to come in. I know it's her day off, but a doctor never *really* gets a day off." Jess's smokey chuckle always made Megan smile.

"Thanks, Jess. I'll get back to you later this morning."

"Don't mention it." Pushing the button on the steering wheel, Megan ended the call.

Megan concentrated on the situation at hand. *What in the hell was an FBI agent doing out here in the secluded hamlet of Rileyville, and how the hell did he get shot?* Her mind was spiraling.

"And why didn't I hear it?" Suddenly she remembered Max. "Oh shit! Max!" She called Jess back. "Jess, can you go to the cottage, get Max, and take him to the office? He was supposed to come in with me today and I forgot all about him."

"Sure, boy you've done it now! He's gonna be pissed." She laughed.

"Yeah." Megan chuckled, "Give him some treats, and the car ride will make up for it."

"Good thing I have Nancy's Suburban today. That dog wouldn't have fit in my car. I will never understand why you got a Great Dane when you had such a small car."

"Well, he was just a puppy when I got him, but it didn't take me long to realize how fast he would grow. That's why I went and traded that one for this sucker. Listen, I need to go, we're getting close; I'll call you later." She ended the call, turned into the doctors' parking, across from the emergency room entrance. The paramedics wheeled the gurney through the double automatic doors, directly into a treatment area. While the EMTs told the on-duty doctor the status of their patient Megan walked up to stand next to the gurney.

She felt a tug on the bottom of her shirt, and she looked to the man whose badge identified him as Donavon Mackay, gesturing her to come closer. She leaned down and put her ear close to his lips.

"Please," he whispered with effort.

"Shh, you need to," she was cut off by his next words.

"Please do'na leave." He pleaded. Megan looked into his eyes and saw fear as they began to glaze over from loss of blood and shock. Unable to help herself, she took his hand and gently squeezed.

"I'll stay," she said and was surprised at the strength of his grip on her hand. "I promise I won't leave." The doctor startled her when he spoke, she jumped. "Holy shit!" she stammered.

"I'm sorry, Megan. I didn't mean to startle you," he said as he read from the preliminary chart the EMT had handed him. Dr. Bob Winston was in his late fifties and had not one gray hair on his head. He was tall with broad shoulders and looked more like a linebacker for the Philadelphia Eagles than a doctor.

"That's ok, Bob. What do you think?" she asked as the nurses cut off Mackay's shirt and removed Megan's field bandage to reveal the wound.

"We could have used you in our MASH unit in The Gulf War. This is a damned good field job." Bob told Megan as she smiled and looked back into the face of their patient. *Nice face*, she thought to herself. "We'll give him something to make him as comfortable as possible. You were right. It's a bullet wound. Looks like it went clean through. We'll have to make sure nothing was damaged internally on the way through, but the wound is far enough to the left that he should be fine. I've ordered a surgical team to take him up in a few minutes. Are you staying?" Megan nodded. "Do you know this guy? He's lost a good deal of blood and will likely need a transfusion."

"No, I don't. I found him collapsed behind my SUV this morning."

"Well, we'll have him typed. It's tough when we don't know any medical history. Allergies. Stuff like that."

"Yeah." Megan said vaguely, then remembered the ID and federal badge she had stuffed in her purse. "I do have…. Wait a minute!" She reached into her purse. Surely, they could contact the FBI for medical records. She placed her purse on the side of the gurney and searched inside for the badge. As she started to offer the black leather billfold, a nurse came into the treatment room, drawing the doctor's attention away from Megan and the patient. At the same time, Donavon Mackay's hand seized her wrist.

"No!" came Mackay's raspy voice.

"What? No, you don't understand. We can call for your medical records." She explained.

"Ye canna give um me badge." He whispered.

"Why the hell not?"

"... blow me cover. If ye... tell them me name... Sam Watson ... no allergies." The strain of talking was beginning to show on his face.

"What?"

"Please. I'm beggin` ye...lass's life... identity... secret." And with that he passed out.

Good God, she thought to herself.

"I'm sorry, Megan. Now what were you going to say?" Bob Winston looked down at the man lying on the gurney. "Ah I see he finally conked out." He noticed when she made no response.

Megan stood staring at the unconscious man on the gurney, trying to take in what he had just said to her. Suddenly realizing, the doctor had been speaking to her. "I'm sorry. What?"

"I asked what you were saying to me before Sally came in."

"Oh, nothing. However, while you were talking to Sally, Mr. Watson was able to tell me his name and that he has no allergies." Bob locked eyes with her, waiting for more. "Sam. His name is Sam. Watson. Sam Watson. No allergies. That's all I got. When are you taking him up?"

"Right now." He said as two orderlies and the nurse Sally came into the treatment room. "Just to confirm, you are staying right?"

"Yeah. I'll stay. I told him I wouldn't leave. Actually, I have some patients in-house. I can make rounds while he's upstairs." She handed him her card. "Here. My pager and cell numbers are on this. Can you keep me posted? I've gotta check in with my service here and the office in Rileyville." She stopped not knowing why she had told him all of that. "Please keep me posted." She repeated. *For God's sake,* she mentally berated herself, *you are a trained medical professional, trained to handle all kinds of emergencies. Get a grip!*

"Are you sure you don't know this guy, Megan?" he chuckled.

"Yes Bob, I'm sure I don't know him." She ground out. "But I *did* find him unconscious and bloody behind my car, so I have somewhat of an interest in his situation." She said with more frustration than was *probably* necessary, so she smiled and squeezed his arm. "Sort of makes me feel a little more of a responsibility."

"You didn't shoot him, did you, Dr. Dunnegan?" Dr. Winston grinned and raised his eyebrow.

Megan turned as she headed for the E.R. reception area. "No. I save all my target practice for smart ass doctors." She grinned back and waved high in the air.

"Give them a couple of hours up there." He laughed and returned her wave.

"Yeah." She mumbled, as she watched Mackay being wheeled to the elevator. His words replayed in her mind, *A lass's life, Secret identity.* She walked to the Nurses station and told them to get word to the O.R that she wanted to be paged when Mr. Watson was out of recovery. "I'm going over to Turkey Hill to get a pack of cigarettes and a soda—"

The nurse never looked up from her desk while cutting Megan off. "This is a smoke free campus, ma'am," Repeating the words drummed in with the enthusiasm of an irritated employee. "And Smoking is *prohibited* on hospital grounds." Then she looked up to see it was Dr. Dunnegan she had spoken to and paled. "Oh, Dr. Dun—"

"*After* that," Megan cut in and continued, "I'll be somewhere in the hospital making rounds"

As Megan crossed Main Street to the Turkey Hill gas station her mind raced. FBI? FBI? In Honesdale? As soon as she was back outside, she ripped off the wrapper, withdrew a cigarette, lit it, and took a long satisfying drag. She had been an on again/off again smoker for years, mostly in times of stress. Megan knew this was a wasteful purchase.

She would likely smoke less than half of the pack then throw the rest away. "Oh well." She said as she made her way back to the hospital and spent the next ninety minutes seeing patients. When her pager vibrated, she went to the nearest in-house-phone and punched in the numbers.

"This is Dr. Dunnegan."

"Dr. Dunnegan," came a woman's voice, "this is Lauren from the nurses' station in the ER."

"Yes."

"Dr. Otis just called down from the O.R., Mr. Watson will be out of surgery within the hour and should be in recovery about forty minutes. You'll be able to see him then."

"Thank you." She smiled and hung the receiver back on the wall unit.

An hour later Dr. Sam Otis Chief of General Surgery was briefing Megan. "The bullet had gone into Mr. Watson's abdominal area on the upper left side. Missed anything that could cause real damage."

"Thanks Sam." Megan smiled feeling oddly relieved with the news.

"We'll keep him here for a day or so for observation. However, he's going to be laid up for a few days after he leaves here. He's lost a great deal of blood. And will have to stay in bed for several days to rest and regain strength."

"Uh-huh." She nodded.

"Does he have any family in the area? Friends?"

"I don't know. I doubt it. I believe he's here...on business"

"Bob Winston said he's a friend of yours." Referring to the ER doc.

"What?" Megan was stunned.

"Winston says he's a friend of yours. If he has nobody else, he can stay with you, right?"

"Are you out of your mind?!" she shrieked, then looked around as people turned to stare at her. Speaking more softly, "I have no idea who this man is or how he got shot in the first place! And you want me to open my home to him? You have *got* to be insane to think I would allow that."

"Bob Winston said he was a close, *personal*, friend of yours. And I might add, I'm glad to see you're stepping out more, Megan."

"STEPPING OUT!" Megan had to lower her voice again.

"Yes, it does this old heart good. To see—"

"Bob Winston needs to..." she took a deep breath. "Look Sam, I don't know this man. I've never seen him before this morning, when I found him, face down, behind my car, with a bullet hole in his gut."

"You didn't shoot him, did you?" he chuckled.

"Did Bob tell you that too?" Throwing her hands up in frustration.

"No. Is it true?" the older man leaned closer and spoke more softly. "Did you shoot him, Megan?"

"No. I didn't shoot him. I don't even know who he is." Then she smiled when she noticed the twinkle in his eye. "But I'm thinking of shooting a couple of doctors."

"Well," Sam Otis shrugged, "if he doesn't have any family and nowhere to go when we kick him out of here, he'll be on the street. We can only keep him here for a day. Two at the most. Damned insurance companies.

"We should all retire and let the insurance companies treat and prescribe for patients. One of these days, people won't even bother with doctors. They'll just call the damned insurance companies, list their aches, pains, and injuries, and let the damned insurance company prescribe over the phone. I could play golf seven days a week, and I'd never have to pull on another pair of rubber gloves or scrub my arms until they're raw." He stopped and looked at Megan's semi-glazed eyes, and then he grinned. "I guess you've heard my opinion before, haven't you? Well. Now, as to your young man."

"Sam, he's not—"

"Yes, yes. So, you said. It doesn't matter. We simply don't have the extra beds to house him for more than a day or two. Busy season, ya know. All he needs is a place to rest and rebuild his strength. And since you are a doctor, you can care for him if he needs anything."

"You're nuts!"

"Maybe, but he is awake and asking to see you. Are you sure you don't know him?" Megan opened her mouth, but Sam raised his hand in his defense and chuckled. "Oh and the troopers are here, and they want to see you too."

"WHAT! Why?" All she wanted to do was leave and never come back.

"Troopers. Over there, by Recovery. Gunshot wound. Requires troopers. Want to talk with you. Right over there." He pointed to the two Pennsylvania State Troopers leaning against the wall next to the Recovery room.

"Good God!" Megan muttered.

Sam smiled and threw his hands up in the air. "You found him." He laughed. "Let me know what you decide about caring for the sick and wounded." And he walked away chuckling.

Megan approached the troopers.

"Troopers, you wanted to see me?" Megan smiled at the pair.

"Dr. Dunnegan?"

"Yes"

"Megan Dunnegan?"

"YES!" she said through clenched teeth.

"Ma'am, We understand you discovered one Sam Watson suffering from a gunshot wound, this morning?"

"Please call me Dr. Dunnegan or Megan not ma'am. And yes, I discovered Mr.Watson."

"Were you acquainted with Mr. Watson before this morning?"

"No."

"We have to ask you, Dr. Dunnegan, did you shoot him?"

"No! I didn't shoot him. I don't even know him. I've never seen him before and if I never see him again, it'll be too soon. But the next person who asks me....Look. I don't know him. I never saw him before this morning. I saw him while I was doing dishes. He was staggering down the road. I assumed he was a drunk. Then when I went out to my car, he was laying on the ground. I called 911. I administered emergency medical attention. The ambulance arrived and brought him here. That's it. That's all I know."

"You asked to be notified when he was out of surgery."

"He was lying on the ground behind my car with a hole in his gut. Wouldn't you want to know what happened to him after something like that?"

"You're going in to see him now?"

"Yes I am."

"We may want to speak with you again later, doctor."

"Fine." She walked away and through the Recovery room doors. "Did I 'shoot him?'" she muttered.

She walked cautiously into the room where the man in question was laying in a bed. His head was elevated slightly, and he seemed to be sleeping. She took the opportunity to get a gander at what he looked like. He had short cropped blond hair with some hanging loosely over his forehead. His skin was bronzed from the sun, and he had a well chiseled and defined physique. She picked up the chart stuck in the slot at the end of the bed and opened it to read. When she looked up from the chart, he was staring at her. He had jade green eyes. Like deep pools. *Eyes like the Scottish actor Ian Mackay.* she thought.

"Hi. How are you feeling?" she asked.

"Like I ha` been shot, lassie. I canna thank ye enough fer savin` me life, and fer nay tellin` the doctors who I really was." *His brogue is thick and sinfully delicious,* she thought.

"Don't mention it, and just for my own peace of mind," she moved to the head of the bed and lowered her voice to avoid being overheard by anyone who might be nearby. "why didn't you want me to tell the doctor who you were?" she took a breath, "and why were you shot?"

"I told ye, there's a lass whose life depends on no one knowin` who I really am." He winced as he moved. "What's yer name?"

"Megan Dunnegan. Do you have family here?"

"Nay, me family is in Scotland. Why?"

"Your doctor was just telling me that you can only stay here for a few days at the most and then you have to go home or wherever you're staying at the moment. You'll need to rest and regain your strength. You'll have to stay quiet and confined for several days to heal. Then it will take a month maybe two before your completely healed"

"No family and I havna a place ta stay either."

"Are you really with the FBI?" She asked as she helped to adjust the pillow behind him and elevate the head of his bed a bit more.

"Aye, in a way. I work wi` them from time ta time." He looked up into her face and saw kindness, but a certain amount of weariness too. "I promise ye, lass I'll do ye no harm. I'm one o` the good guys. But I canna go back ta where I was stayin. Can ye help me find a room where I can park meself while this bloody hole heals up?"

She eyed him closely and remembered what Sam Otis had said. *"He'll be on the street". My God,* she thought, *can I really be thinking of letting him stay with me?"* "I have a really big dog, who is *very* protective."

"Beg pardon?" He smiled.

"I have a big—"

"I heard tha` part darlin, I was wonderin what prompted ye ta say it."

"I suppose you can stay with me for a few days."

"Why would ye do tha`? Ye hav'na any idea who I am. I could be a mass murderer or rapist." He couldn't believe what he was hearing.

"Are you?"

"Nay, lass." He smiled weakly.

"But you do have a hole in your side," she paused for a moment "and I have a gun if you get out of hand. I am an *excellent* shot." She gave him a pointed stare. "I'll be back in a day or two to pick you up, until then. Get some rest." She turned on her heel, he stopped her with his words.

"Thank ye lass, I am indebted ta ye, and since we're gonna be livin tagether I think we can be on a wee less formal basis. My name is Donny."

She smiled and turned to leave the room again but stopped when she reached the door. "We're not living together. For reasons I don't even understand myself, I've agreed to house you until you're strong enough to look after yourself. Oh... Here." she reached into her pocket and pulled out his ID and badge billfold. "Do you want this back now?" he nodded, and she handed it to him. "Someone from downstairs will be up later with whatever personal effects you had with you when you arrived. And there are two state troopers in the hall who want to talk to you. Are you feeling up to seeing them?"

"Aye. Send them in."

She reached for the door handle and turned to look at him. "And by the way, if ANYBODY asks, I did *not* shoot you!" she said and left the room.

As she walked down the hall, she couldn't believe what she was doing. He was right. He could be a raving lunatic. "I'm the one who's a raving lunatic!" she muttered. She met Sam Otis in the hall and told him she would pick up Mr. Watson when he was released from the hospital.

He smiled and thanked her. "We Sam's have to stick together!"

When she left the hospital, she returned to Rileyville and her office. She had to talk to someone. Jess, she thought, Jess would talk her out of this ludicrous idea of hers. "Although it wasn't really *my* idea in the first place." She muttered. As Megan drove, she dug in her purse for the pack of ultra-lights she had purchased. And decided that she would be better served to go home and have Jess come there. There at least she could smoke and have a drink while she went over the predicament, she had gotten herself in. But Jess had been covering for her all day, and Max was at the office, so she guessed she better go there.

Chapter Two

"And don't you worry, Cathy, when Sean here laughs, he's not in 'some kind of a delirium'." Dr. Jess Andrews smiled reassuringly. "He's just a very healthy, happy baby boy." Jess watched as the new mother dressed her baby and then chucked the baby's chin. "Don't you have a lucky mommy? She has such a sweet little boy?" She walked them to the front door and held it open for the young mother. While Jess held the door open, she noticed Megan's Wagoneer pulling to a stop at the intersection next to the office. "You take that little dumpling home and enjoy every smile and gurgle."

"I feel so silly!" Cathy murmured.

"Nonsense! That's what we're here for. I'd rather have a false alarm than ignore something that could be potentially dangerous. You call us anytime you need anything." Jess rubbed the boy's back and smiled.

"Thank you, Jess. I will."

Jess watched Megan park and get out of her car as the relieved mother buckled her baby into the car seat. Megan reached the door Jess was still holding open "What are you doing here?" Jess asked her as soon as Megan was close enough. "I thought you weren't coming in today?"

"You won't believe what I have done. Where's Max?" Megan sighed as she walked in through the door.

"Max made his rounds of the exam rooms and is now resting in your office, and what *have* you done?" Jess and Megan smiled at the few last patients of the day as they walked through the waiting room area, past the closed exam rooms, and down the hall to Megan's office at the rear of the building.

Megan's office wasn't particularly large. She had never been very interested in big or fancy. However, what the room might have lacked in size for the practice owner, it made up for in character. Behind Megan's desk was a large bank of double-hung windows that went floor to ceiling. She felt it was important for nervous or worried patients and their family members to have a relaxing view during consultations in her office.

She had purchased the old 1803 house and converted it for her practice. The building fronted the narrow two-lane road that section into crossroads, locally referred to as "the corners." The house sat on the edges of a densely wooded lot until Megan purchased it. The property hadn't been properly cared for in years. The space beside the house was cleared for parking, and the area directly in the back of the building was partially cleared and the trees trimmed. She had planted native wildflowers that bloomed from spring through late fall, along with huckleberry bushes and fruit trees for wildlife to feast on when they wandered through the woods. During the winter months, when snow covered the landscape, it appeared like a wonderland. It was this view that could be seen from her office. Quiet and restful.

On the side wall of her office, she had floor-to-ceiling windows installed that overlooked the small paddock she had seeded with soft green grass. This is where Max could spend his days when she brought him to the office with her. And next to the paddock is a larger grassy yard where the children in the upstairs day care center could play outside when the weather permitted. When these windows were open as they were now, a lovely breeze swept in, bringing unpolluted mountain air and the delectable scents of wildflowers and fresh pine.

She had the wide pine plank floors restored throughout the house, along with all the original moldings and doors. The old glass doorknobs had been scraped of decades of paint and now sparkled in the sunlight. Her office used to be what they thought was the parlor, which accounted for the high ceilings. The walls were painted a cool light blue, and the doors and trim free of paint gleamed like the floors. Her white birch desk that she had unearthed in the barn attic on the family farm, just over the hill, had been restored and refinished. She loved her office and was here in the tranquil space she'd created when she wasn't with a patient.

Megan opened the door and was substantially welcomed by Max, her two-year-old Great Dane. "Oh, Max," she laughed as he stood on his hind legs, draping his front paws over her shoulders. "Thanks, kiddo. I could use a hug about now." She reared her head back and ruffled his uncropped ears while he slathered her face with his big wet tongue. "I missed you too, you big baby."

"He only does that with you." Jess chuckled. She closed the door behind her and eased into one of the chairs opposite her associate's desk. "Now what have you done? Tell mother all."

"Well," Megan hardly knew how to begin explaining the decidedly odd situation into which she had become involved. "Get down boy."

She nudged the big dog down on all fours and rounded her desk. Reaching into the top drawer she pulled out a moist towelette to wipe her face free of dog kisses and sat tiredly in her plush executive chair. It was the only "modern" piece of furniture in the room. "It's been a hectic day, to say the least. Odd really. I don't really know where to start."

"You can start by telling me calmly why you needed to go to the hospital this morning."

"Well, I was doing up my breakfast dishes and I saw this kid staggering up the road drunk. Or I thought he was drunk. Then when I went out to get in my car, the kid was passed out on the ground behind the car." She looked over to Jess sitting across the desk. When Megan stopped talking, Jess raised her eyebrows, waiting patiently for the rest of the story. "Only he wasn't a kid, and he wasn't drunk. He was a grown man, and he had a gunshot wound in his gut." Jess remained silent, so Megan continued. "I called 911. They came and took him to Wayne Memorial. I followed. When we got to the ER, he was in and out of consciousness, but asked me not to leave him, so I stayed."

"Why?" Jess leaned forward in her chair. She was a tall, very slender woman in her early thirties. Her blond shoulder length hair pulled back into a ponytail rested on the back of her neck. She wore little to no makeup and her chiseled features sometimes made her appear all business and rather stern. However, to her patients, colleagues, and friends, she was a soft touch for a sad story, a defender of individual rights and a devoted confidant. She had an infectious sense of humor but had no qualms about offering her opinion concerning a situation, a person, or a topic of discussion. She and Megan had only known each other a few years, but they had come to respect and depend on each other.

"I don't know exactly. Maybe it was the way he looked. Helpless and ...wounded."

"You've seen helpless and wounded before, Dearie."

"Yeah, well, I've never had one lying unconscious behind my car before. And maybe I felt guilty for thinking he was some silly kid who didn't know when the party was over. I don't know why I agreed to stay. Anyway, they took him up to the O.R. The bullet was a pass through, and they x-rayed and sutured him"

"Internal damage?"

"No. No serious damage. Too far left."

"Who worked on him?"

"Sam Otis."

"Good."

"Yeah. He's a good doc. He knows his business, but he wants to know everybody else's. He told me how it went in the O.R., and then what do you think he said?"

"I give up?"

"That they can't keep the guy for more than two days. Too short on beds and then I get his opinion of insurance companies. Short version."

"Too bad I sorta like the long version. More animation involved in that one." Jess grinned.

"Yeah, well, anyway, then he tells me the guy will have to have someplace to recoup when they kick him out, and Sam wants me to take the guy in at my place!"

"He didn't?" Jess laughed out loud and shook her head. "That guy's got balls of steel." She continued to chuckle for several minutes until she looked back at Megan and sobered quickly. "You told him where he could stick his suggestion, right?"

"Of course, I did!" Megan got up and turned to stare out the big window with her back to Jess. "At first." She looked around and saw the shock and disbelief on Jess's face.

"Excuse me?" Jess gaped, it was rare to see shock on her friend's face, but she saw it now. "Explain, please?" Was all Jess could muster.

"Well, the … 'shootee' asked to see me. And I went down to recovery and spoke with him... and the next thing I knew, I was telling him he could stay with me after he was released from the hospital."

"Are you out of your FUCKING *MIND*!? This joker could be a psychopathic murderer or—"

"I know." Megan cut her off. "Actually, that was his response when I told him he could stay. I don't know why I said he could, but I did." She dug in her purse, withdrew a cigarette, and desperately wanted to light it, but sighed and put it back in her purse.

Obviously, there was more to this. Jess thought. She knew Megan well enough to figure out there was something she wasn't telling. "Who is he?" she asked. "And do we know who the 'shooter is?"

"No. Hell, Sam Otis and Bob Winston, both asked if I shot him. Sam even went so far as to tell me he was glad to see me 'getting out more'. The damned troopers even asked if I shot him." She threw her hands up in the air, and Jess couldn't help but smile at the mental picture those conversations had created. "He goes by the name Sam Watson." Megan needed to be careful in this area. She had no idea whether or not what Donny had told her in the hospital was true. Nor did she have any idea why, in the name of God, she believed him, but she had to admit, for some reason, she did believe him. *Well, I must,* she reasoned, *or I would never have agreed to this ridiculous … anyway, if it is true, I'm not going to endanger a little girl's life by divulging what he told me.*

"What do you mean 'he goes by the name Sam Watson'?" Jess was getting closer to the edge of her chair. "You're telling me the guy had a bullet hole in his gut." She starts to tick off the events that were relayed to her. "You're not sure he's telling you his correct name, and you let him, and Sam Otis talk you into letting him stay in your house with you?!" She was incredulous. "I think you're the one who needs looking after. By a professional!"

"He had a wallet and driver's license, and it said his name was Sam Watson." Megan turned back to the window. *Jess is right*, she thought. *What the hell am I doing? I have no idea who this man is. What if he's lying about the girl? Why do I believe him?* "Before he's released from Wayne Memorial, I'll make sure I know all about him." There was a knock on the door and the office manager peeked in to let Jess know her next appointment was here.

"Ok. Be right there. Thanks, Liz." Jess rose and went to where Megan was standing. "Listen, my friend. Let's not do anything stupid, please, until we have had a chance to find out a little more information about this Watson guy. Ok?"

"Yeah. I mean no. I won't. I promise." She watched Jess cross the room and open the door. Then Jess turned back to Megan with her hand on the doorknob.

"Laying behind your car early in the morning with a bullet hole in his gut. You *didn't* shoot him, did you kiddo?" Megan glared at her and sat down in her chair. Jess was chuckling as she closed the door behind her.

Megan's first thought was to call the FBI and find out for sure if Donny Mackay was who he said he was. But if he *were* telling her the truth, would the FBI divulge information about an undercover agent? *And if his story is true, would my interference jeopardize the little girl's life further?* She wondered. *What if I go to the hospital and demand that he tells me the whole story or he can just end up on the street,* she mused.

"I wish I still had his badge." she told Max, who was watching her intently; "I could've threatened to call the FBI. or show it to the hospital if he didn't come clean." She looked down at Max, who groaned. "Yeah, I know. Dumb idea. Well, how about I just go and talk to him?" Max stood and laid his head on her lap. "I'll be careful sweetie, I promise, and *if* I let him come home with me, and he tries any funny business, I give you permission to rip his throat out. However, if that happens, keep the mess confined to the carpet. It's easier to replace than sanding the hardwood floors." Max raised his head, and his tail was instantly in motion as he once again slathered her with doggie kisses. Megan laughed out loud at the show of affection and ruffled his ears. She looked down at her watch. "Come on, big boy. If we blow this place now, I can do the tough talk at Memorial and still have time to stop in at Beth's Hometown Kitchen in town for dinner. I think this is even prime rib night. What do ya say?"

"AAARRROOOFFF!"

"Yeah, sounds good to me too. Come on."

She left her office and made the rounds with Max in tow, to say hi to all the patients and staff. At the broad cherry wood curving staircase, she headed up the steps to the second floor, where the in-house daycare center was located. As soon as she and Max hit the top of the staircase, the children ranging in age from two to six years came racing to Max. Megan and Amanda laughed as the kids wrapped their arms around the large dog. He loved every hug and ear tug.

"How're we all doing up here?" She had to speak loudly to make herself heard over the children's laughter. She smiled as the children and Max raced off to the carpeted play area. "How are things going up here today, Amanda?"

"Wonderfully, the kids love it when Max is here. And they enjoy it so when you bring him up to visit. I put him out in the paddock this morning so he could run; the kids loved watching him."

"I know, he loves to be with the kids, although he can't stay any longer today. I've gotta head back into town, so I need to take him home."

"Well, if you wouldn't mind letting him stay until the kids leave, I would happily take him back to the cottage for you."

"Oh, that's so sweet of you, but I need to go home and change anyway, so I think it would be better that I take him with me. He's been here all day anyway. Thank you, though. Max, come on boy!" she sang down the hall. Once Max was back at her side, she said her goodbyes to the kids and Amanda and promised to bring Max back tomorrow.

When Megan walked into her cozy cottage, she felt like she could take her first breath of air since this morning. She sank onto the sofa and slumped back against the cushions. Max climbed up beside her and laid his head in her lap.

"You'll have to stay here, buddy, while I go to town." She told him. "I'd take you with me, but I'm not sure how long I'll be." The big dog raised his head and looked at her with huge, sad blue eyes. "I'm sorry baby, I don't want to leave you but, I've gotta get some answers."

"Mmmmmmm." Max groaned.

"I'll bring you back something from Beth's; how's that? Want me to bring you a Polish omelet? Or a Honesdale Burger with cheese?"

"AAARRROOOFFF!"

"Ok. Now get off me. I need to check the voicemail."

Megan checked her messages. One from her brother, Nathan, said he and his wife Angie would be up with the kids for the weekend. She smiled at the thought of seeing them. She finished her messages and went to her bedroom to change her clothes.

Her bedroom was one of the additions that had been built onto the small cottage over the years, along with a master bath. Her great-grandfather had built the original building as a garage in the early 1900's. Then, her grandfather converted it into a living space and used it for summer rentals. Her mother and father took over the cottage in the mid 1980's for their own summer use, added onto the building as the family grew. When Megan moved into the cottage full time, she hadn't made any real changes to the room with the exception of the bed linens and curtains. Her mother has an abnormal fondness for purple and lilac, which Megan never understood. The room was large enough for a king size bed which was fortunate because Max always ended up in the bed with her. When Max was a puppy. Megan thought it was cute to have her pup sleep in bed with her, but as Max grew, Megan found she had less and less room in her own bed. Eventually, she gave up trying to keep him off the bed and purchased a king. There was a small closet in the back corner of the room and a large double dresser under the open pass-through into the kitchen dining area. It was a comfortable spacious room and had a relaxing feel with its soft yellow walls and pale green linens. The best part of the room were the divided light double French doors at the foot of the bed. They opened to a view out over the deck to the back yard and beautiful marsh garden her father had created. Beyond that was the private sixty-acre spring fed lake that was part of their farm.

The weather was still hot, and Megan was dressed in her scrubs, so she stripped off her sweltering clothing and replaced them with a pair of jean shorts and a bright peach t-shirt. She took her long red hair out of the clip and ran her brush though. She slipped on some sandals and left the bedroom. After giving Max fresh water and food, Megan was out the door and on her way to town for her talk with Mr. Donavan Mackay.

Donny sat in bed and tried to remember the last time he had been careless and gotten hurt on the job. He couldn't. He had also never been so careless as to get a civilian involved. However, he was fairly sure he owed the lady doctor his life. Without her help that morning, he would more than likely have laid there on the ground and bled to death. He wasn't sure why he asked her to stay once they reached the hospital. He assumed her compassion as a physician was the reason she agreed to stay. The big question was, "Why in hell did she invite me ta recuperate ta her home." He said aloud, shaking his head in wonder. "Either she's the kindest wooman, or the most reckless. I canna decide." He mumbled as he struggled to force one more bite of the mess he'd been served as his evening meal.

"Hey, how's it going?" The nurse asked as he breezed in the doorway. "Want to check your dressing here for a minute." He moved the tray table down the bed a bit, looking for signs of fresh bleeding on Donny's gauze bandaging. Then, to Donny's dismay, reestablished the tray table holding what Donny felt was the sorriest excuse for edible offerings that he had ever encountered. "There you go, Mr. Watson. Sorry to interrupt your dinner."

"Don't be." Donny mumbled. The nurse smiled.

"Yeah. I know. Pretty sad, isn't it? But the hospital has to be careful with seasonings for patients. Be nice if we had a five-star restaurant down there, wouldn't it? The night nurse comes on in about fifteen minutes; you'll like her. She's a lot prettier than I am." He said. "Your doctor will be in soon to see you before he leaves for the day."

There was a knock on the door, and Donny and the nurse watched as a gorgeous woman walked into the room. Donny's eyes traveled up her long slim, well-shaped legs, past the jean shorts and tiny waist to her tantalizing breasts where his eyes lingered for a few seconds. Finally, he moved his gaze to her face and spectacular violet eyes. The only person he had ever heard of having violet eyes was Elizabeth Taylor, and he always thought they were contact lenses or camera trickery. As she moved closer he noticed her thick fiery red hair falling about her shoulders.

"Hey, doc. Off duty now?" The nurse asked.

"Hi, David. Yes. Off duty for the day." Megan gave the nurse a cordial if brief smile and then returned her eyes to Donny's.

Nurse David cleared his throat and swung his gaze back and forth between his patient and the off-duty doctor. "Yeah, well, have a nice evening, both of you and I'll see you in the morning Mr. Watson." And with that he slipped from the room unnoticed by either Donny or Megan.

"How are you feeling?" Megan asked as she placed her purse on the tray table beside his dinner tray. "Hello?" she said when Donny remained silent.

"Uh, Aye, I'm feelin` ok." He couldn't believe this was the same woman from this morning.

"What's wrong? Are they giving you pain meds?" She smiled, "You look loaded."

"'Doc?' Doctor Dunnegan?" He almost blinked as he tried to recover his wits. "I'm sorry fer starin`, I didna recognize ye when ye came through the door."

"Oh, that's ok. I was in my scrubs this morning; a lot of people don't recognize their own doctor out of uniform. Although technically, I'm not your doctor." She smiled. "Besides, this morning you really weren't in any condition to notice what people look like." She took a deep breath. *Ok, now it's time to get down to brass tacks*, she thought. She pulled one of the visitors' chairs closer to the side of the bed. "So, you said all your family was in Scotland. Is there anyone you would like me to get in contact with? Let someone know where you are?"

"Nay," he eyed her closely, he could always tell when an interrogation was forthcoming. *Especially* when the would-be interrogator was a woman. "I told ye, I canna let anyone know who I am."

"Ok. And why is that again?" she leaned back into the chair and waited for his response. When no immediate response came, she continued. "Look, chum. I don't want to belabor the subject, but I figure I basically saved your butt this morning if not your life, and if we're going to be roommates for the next few days, I figure in all fairness, I'm entitled to some details."

"What do ye want ta know?" He sighed.

"First, how did it go with the troopers?"

"Fine."

"And? If this is such a big secret, what did you tell them?"

"I told them we had a wee bit of a lover's quarrel."

"You did WHAT?!!" Megan stood abruptly, knocking her chair back a few inches.

Donny's eyes sparkled as his mouth grew to a wide grin. "Nay, Megan, is it?" he reached out toward her. "I'm only havin` a bit o` fun wi` ye, lass. Please sit doon again. I told the troopers the truth. What did ye expect?"

"My name is Doctor Dunnegan. I'm not here for you to have a 'wee bit o` ' fun with. And I'd very much appreciate your telling *me* the truth." Frustration was beginning to get the upper hand, "Look, I have agreed to let you stay in my house while you heal. From a *bullet* wound, I might add, and I think I deserve to know what the hell is going on!"

"I told ye tha` —" he began, but was cut off.

"I know what you said earlier; I want to know, what little girl? Where is she? Why did you get shot? *How* did you get shot? Where is the girl now? And why are you even involved if you only 'help' the FBI *on occasion*."

"Anythin` else?" he smiled as the freight train of questions poured from her.

"Why don't you start with those first." Megan pulled the chair back to the side of the bed and sat down. She relaxed her shoulders and leaned back into the chair.

"Aye, well, I'm sorry, but I canna tell ye everythin` ye want ta know, other than what I've already told ye." Holding up his hand to forestall the oncoming argument, he continued "I had ta tell the troopers so they wouldna be trailin` me, gettin in the way and or blowin` me cover. I canna tell ye fer many reasons. The more information ye have, the more involved ye become and the greater chance o` danger ta ye. It's enough for ye ta know that I'm one o` the good guys. Aside from tha` I'm no goin ta tell ye more."

"Now wait just a goddamned minute!" She was seeing red.

"Well, I'm glad to see you young people getting on so well." Megan and Donny both whipped their heads toward the door to see Dr. Bob Winston standing in the doorway smiling. "And how does the patient feel?" He strolled over to the bed and pulled the chart. He glanced down at Megan. "Hello Megan."

"Bob. And we're *not* 'young people'! At least not the kind of young people you're talking about." She stood, grabbed her purse from the tray table and walked purposefully to the door. Before leaving she stopped and looked back at Donny Mackay. She lowered her voice and locked eyes with him. "Either you tell me what I want to know, *Mr. Watson*, or when they kick you out of here on your ass, you can set up housekeeping at the curb."

"Here now, wait a minute." Bob half laughed. He had known Megan long enough to know how stubborn she was, and that she usually meant every word she spoke. "It would appear that I came in at a bad time. Why don't you two finish up, and I will check back in the morning. Huh, how's that?"

"Works for me." Donny smiled and looked to where Megan was still standing with her hand on the door handle. From over ten feet away, he could see her violet eyes darken in anger. *She has every right ta be angry*, he thought. After all, she had offered him a place to recover from his wound without knowing how he was shot, why or by whom, and he was refusing to give her any information. Normally he would have immediately said no to Megan's offer of temporary shelter. Bullet hole or not. But it would be better for him to lay low while he recovered some of his strength. There was no point in going back on the job if he wasn't in top form. And to be honest with himself, he enjoyed sparring with her. She had fire and what Agatha Stuart would call, "sass".

Bob smiled at Donny and made his way to the door. "Now go and play nice with the other kiddies." He smiled at Megan and ducked out of the room.

"Now listen, lassie,"

"Stop calling me that." She tried to get a stranglehold on her temper. She didn't know what was going on. She rarely allowed anyone to get under her skin this way.

"What? Lassie? Why? What's wrong wi` it?" he arched his eyebrow.

"Lassie is a dog, not a woman. My name is Megan Devlyn Dunnegan." She turned toward him but kept her station by the door. Donny tried to hide his grin.

"Devlyn? I like tha` what would ye like me ta call ye la..." he stopped before forming the word but saw her begin to instantly stiffen. "I'm sorry. It's a wee habit. In Scotland, all young girls are lassies. Even some of the old ones are referred to as lass by loved ones. I promise tae be more careful o` the amenities. Now what would ye like me tae call ye?"

Dr. Dunnegan, she thought to herself. "You may call me Megan if you like." She stood so straight her back could've been made of steel.

"Well then, please, come o'er here, Megan, and let's start over." Trying to keep his chuckle to himself. "I'll try and explain a little better aboot meself if ye like, but understand I canna discuss the case wi` ye, no` yet anyway."

"I guess I'm going to have to take what I can get for right now." She sighed and returned to her chair next to the bed. "Ok. Are you married?"

"Cuttin' ta the chase, huh? Nay, I've ne're been wed." her smiled and Megan noticed what a nice smile he had. "Are ye?"

"No, I'm not. Do you have any children?"

"Dinna, I just tell ye I wasna're wed?" he asked as his eyebrows shot up.

"Hey, being unmarried doesn't necessarily mean you don't have children."

"Nay, I do'na have children either." He arched his eyebrow. "Do ye?"

"No, I don't. How old are you?"

"Old enough." He murmured.

"Oh, are we sensitive about our age?" she snickered. "How long have you been in the States? And how long have you been in the criminal business"

"This time o'er a month. What kind o` dog do ye have?" He wanted to change the subject for a while. Noticing her questions were cleverly going back to his case. *Smart woman*, he mused

"A Great Dane." She looked down at her watch. It was getting late, and she needed to go if she was going to get to Beth's to pick up dinner. "Listen, I have to go. Get some rest, and I'll try and come back tomorrow." She picked up her bag and turned to the door.

"Do ye like children?" Donny asked her before she reached the door.

"Yes, I do," she paused and gazed back at the man in the bed. He looked so powerful and weak at the same time. "Why do you ask?"

"Just wonderin`." He shrugged. "I hope me nay tellin` ye what ye're wantin` ta know willna be offendin` ye, Megan," the moment he said her name a jolt of electricity shot through her. Every hair tingled and every nerve heightened. "It is really safer tha` ye do'na become involved. I hope ye can understand." He was sincere in his words, and she knew it. She didn't know how or why, but she trusted him.

"I hope you understand that I haven't given up." She looked him straight in the eyes. "It's a small cottage, Donny. Close quarters. There's not much nightlife in Rileyville, and conversation is pretty much a mainstay recreation up there. Get some rest and I'll see you tomorrow. Good night." She smiled and escaped his view.

Donny returned her smile, but as soon as she was gone he was already feeling the loss. *This is daft!*, he told himself. *Ye need ta get a grip on yerself, Donny boy.*

"Ye got a job ta do, this is nay the time ta be getting` foolish ideas aboot a pretty country doctor." He scolded himself. "Get yerself ta sleep and forget what e'er fool notions ye ha` goin` on in yer brain." He closed his eyes and tried to block out her face and the lavender scent that lingered in the room in her wake.

Megan stood with her back to the door trying to shake the sensation that she had just experienced. *This is too weird*, she told herself. *Why do you trust him?* "Forget it and go eat a decent meal" she said aloud. She pushed herself away from the door and left the hospital saying hello to people she knew on the way out. *It's a small town*, she thought to herself. *If there's criminal activity going on, somebody will know something.* She stopped at Beth's Hometown Kitchen for a fast dinner and to pick up the promised burger for Max. Maybe she'll hear something of the local gossip, before heading back to Rileyville.

As soon as she walked in the door of the cafe, the scent of cooking foods captured her appetite and set her mouthwatering. She realized how hungry she was. Had she eaten at all since breakfast? All of a sudden, Megan was so hungry she could almost taste Beth's Prime Rib in garlic sauce before she even sat down at the counter.

Chapter Three

By the time Megan let herself into the cottage that evening, she felt she had been hit by a truck, then back over to make sure that job was done properly. She sank down into her cushy sofa and leaned back into the cushions to reflect on the day she had survived. Never in her life had anything like this happened to her, and she wasn't sure what to make of it. She wasn't completely confident she was doing the right thing in allowing Donny Mackay to stay with her once he's released from the hospital. "Well, the deed's done, Maxie old chum. How about a nice, chilled glass of wine?" The dog followed her to the kitchen where she unwrapped the burger and dropped it in Max's dish, then poured herself the promised wine. Max grabbed up the burger in his mouth and followed Megan out the back door and onto the deck.

"I've put my foot in it now, haven't I?" she asked Max who was sitting next to her on the deck watching the sun set over the lake behind the vast scenery of trees. "Logically, I can't think of any plausible reason I trust him, but, I think I do. It's too bad I can't take you in to the hospital to look him over." She gave the big dog a scruff behind the ear. It was amazing how in less than twenty-four hours her life had been turned completely upside down by one man.

Suddenly her hip began to buzz. Realizing that she hadn't taken her beeper off her waistband, she removed it now and looked at the number.

"What the hell?" She left the deck and going to the phone on her bedside table dialed the hospital. "Yes. This is Dr. Dunnegan, I was paged."

"Yes, Dr. Dunnegan," said the operator. "I will put you through."

Megan waited while she was connected to whoever had paged her. She couldn't understand it. She worked as an on-call doctor for the hospital from time to time, but she wasn't on call tonight. Finally, the other line was answered.

"Megan?" came a man's voice.

"Yes." *Why do I know that voice?* She thought, then, it hit her and her stomach went into knots. "Donny?"

"Aye."

"How on earth did you get my pager number?" She sat on the corner of the bed. *I can't seem to escape this man at all today*, she thought.

"I have me ways." He chuckled. "I was callin` to see how ye were gettin on." *Oh, now tha` sounded dense*, Donny scolded himself.

"How I was 'getting on'?" she narrowed her eyes. "What do you want, Donny?"

"I do'na like hospitals." He stated.

"Ok," *yeah, well*, she thought, *who does?* "I'm sorry to hear that. I guess you should have thought about that before you got yourself shot." She smirked.

"Isna like I planned it." He defended and then smiled at her quick wit. "What are ye doin` now?"

"I *was* sitting on the deck enjoying the peace and quiet of the evening sunset set with Max." *What the hell does he want?* "Why?"

"I'm bored." He sighed.

"Excuse me?"

"Bored, I'm bored."

"Read a book, watch TV. Is that why you had me paged? You're bored?"

"Aye. I find that I like talkin` wi` ye."

"You don't even know me. If you're that starved for attention, why don't you talk to some of the nurses?" *This is nuts*, she thought.

"Och, all they want to do is fill me up wi` drugs and look at me wound."

"They're nurses. That's what they do. Did Doctor Winston come back to see you?" she asked before remembering that Bob said he wouldn't be back until morning.

"Nay. But one of the nurses said I might be oot o` here in the morn." He waited to hear her reaction.

"*Tomorrow* morning?"

"Aye."

Shit, she thought. "Well let's wait and see what Doctor Winston says when he sees you. Listen, I need to hang up."

"Wait," not knowing what he could say to keep her on the phone.

"No, now listen. I have had a long exhausting day. I get up in the morning, and find a man shot in the stomach, lying on the ground behind my car. I'm asked by the doctors and troopers over and over again if I'm the one who shot him. You won't tell me any of the particulars of how you were shot. I find that somehow I am going to house you until you're healed. I'm tired. I don't want to talk to you or anybody else. I want to sit here and watch the sunset and enjoy my wine in peace and quiet." She growled. "And now you want me to sit on the phone and shoot the breeze as if we were old friends?"

"Ye're the one who invited me ta stay wi` ye lass." He had to admit she had a point. "And as far as the troopers are concerned, I told ye tha` they know what happened and they won't be hassling` ye anymore. I have explained why I canna tell ye what's goin` on. In fact, I might ha` told ye ta much already. Besides, I thought tha` we could try and get ta know each other better."

"Mister Mackay," Megan sighed, trying to control her frustration. "I appreciate your predicament, and please don't take this the wrong way. But quite frankly, I have had all I can take of you for one day. I need to sit back and decompress and regroup before I can deal with you again."

"Ye sound a wee bit miffed, luv." He grinned.

"*Miffed?*" *Is this guy a nut, or is it me?* Megan asked herself although she too, was finding it hard not to smile at this point.

"I'm sorra. I dinna know what else I can say ta ye. I know this has been hard on ye, but please remember *I'm* the one wi` a hole in me belly."

"That you won't tell me how you got!" This was becoming so frustrating she was beginning to find the whole ordeal almost comical.

"I promise tha` one day I will explain everythin` ta ye Megan." He soothed.

There it was again, the moment he said her name her whole body began to tingle. Knowing he would not let her off the phone until he had what he wanted, she decided to go with it. *At least*, she thought *I might be able to get a little more information concerning his background.* "Ok, you said your family is in Scotland. Do you have siblings?"

"Aye. Five brothers and two sisters." He settled back into the pillows.

"You're the youngest no doubt."

"Nay. There are three younger than me. Me brother, Ian and me sister Emily, and Steven. Do ye have brothers and sisters?" Wanting to know everything he could about her.

"I have two older brothers. They're both married now. How about yours?"

"Two o` me brothers are wed, and one is soon on his way." He smiled.

"How long has it been since you've seen them or been home?" She had by now slipped on her head set and was back out on the deck with Max.

"I was in Scotland four months ago on assignment and was able ta see just aboot all o` the family. I was in Philadelphia before I came here and saw me younger brother Ian and his lass who will become his bride soon if me brother has anything ta say aboot it."

"Wait, you said your younger brother's name is Ian? Ian Mackay? The actor?"

"Aye he is, do ye know his work then?"

"Yes, I do. Huh! Well, isn't that something? So, he and, what's her name? Madison Danaher are an item after all. Oh, that's nice. I'm glad the media has finally left them alone."

"Aye so are the rest o` us." He remembered the way the press hounded poor Madison and how she handled it with grace and poise. *Ian ha` got a good one there,* he thought and smiled "I take it tha` you had the misfortune ta have read aboot the ordeal in the papers then?"

"Yeah, and you know what? With everything that's going on in the world nowadays, you would think that the press would have better things to do than hound celebrities and who they may or may not be dating and about their personal lives. At times it makes me sick to realize what the modern media has stooped to, especially when it comes to twisting the facts of a tragedy. Just to sell more papers or magazines or a thirty second spot on the television. It's all about the bottom line though, doesn't it? Making as much money as possible, no matter who they have to bulldoze to get their story in the end." She took a breath. "How can you be related to Ian Mackay and still have such a secret job?" She was hooked, *this is getting interesting,* she thought.

Donny grinned as he listened to Megan get all fired up. *Ye and Ian's Maddy would be thick as thieves.* When Megan cleared her throat Donny swatted away the wool and answered the lass's question. "Ian is a verra private person. He's ne'er allowed his family ta be subject ta the press. What else would ye like ta know lass?"

"How does one become a secret agent?" Megan gestured with her hands not knowing what else to call him.

"Long story. People are touched by tragedy in life every day. And I'm willin` ta go ta any lengths ta see justice done." There was a somber tone to his voice and Megan wanted to know more. But decided not to press the issue, for now. *It appears I'm going to be stuck with him for a time. I can quiz him all I want later.*

"How long have you been in the, I don't know what to call it, *the business.* Sounds like the mob." She took a sip of her wine noticing how warm the air was even after the sun had set. She stood and took the grill lighter and lit the tiki torches on the deck rail to repel the bugs. Not that they really did their job, but as her mother said, *"They give such a lovely ambiance."*

"A long time. I entered the military service when I was twenty, completed me two-year hitch and ended up where I am today."

"With the FBI?" she asked

"There ere a lot o` agencies wi` all kinds o` initials, lass. Some work tagether, some dinna. I am called in ta work on.....lets just say they call me when there is nay another avenue ta travel."

"Does your family know what you do?"

"Ta some degree, as I said I was in Scotland on assignment, and me involvement was made public ta some."

"So, you're just as secret with them as you are with me?"

"Tha` s the right o` it, luv. I canna and willna put anyone in danger if I can help it. And lettin` the cat oot o` the bag so ta speak would do tha` verra thing."

"If what you do is so dangerous then why do it? Do you have a death wish or are you a thrill seeker?"

"Why do ye no` ha` a man in yer life?" Desperate to change the subject Donny asked the first thing that came to his mind, surprised at what came out.

"That was direct! Quite a change of subject Donavan Mackay." She laughed.

"Sorry luv, but it's me turn ta ask some questions o` ye." And he had to admit, he was more than a little interested in the answer

"Ok. What makes you think I *don't* have a man in my life?" she grimaced. "Never mind. I've never had a problem getting a date."

"I'm nay talkin aboot 'a date", lass. I'm talking aboot havin a man in yer life" Donny smiled to himself. *She's getting a wee bit defensive, aye?*

"At the moment I haven't time for personal entanglements. I have a practice to run and the family homestead to look after. I really don't have time for anything else."

"Why is tha` ?"

She took a sip of her wine. She had not planned to allow the conversation to go in this direction. She glanced down at her watch and even in the dark she could see it was well past ten. "Agent Mackay do you know what time it is? I need to go to bed and so do you."

"Ye dinna answer the question, luv. And what happened ta ye calling me by me given name?"

"I have to be at the office early in the morning. Get some rest and I'll stop by tomorrow to see how you're doing after I've finished seeing patients. Goodnight,... Donny."

"Good night Megan and rest easy."

Megan hung up the phone and sat on the deck for a short while before dousing the torches and going inside. While she was going through the cottage turning out lights, she thought about the conversation they had had. And she wondered if some personal tragedy had caused Donny to choose the path he had taken. *He said justice needed to be done. What could have happened that the proper authorities could not have done on their own?* She wondered. She remembered the warmth in his voice when he talked about his family and how abruptly he had switched the subject from his life to hers. *And while I'm thinking of it, why is everybody always asking me the same question or nearly the same question? What's wrong with my life?* She was busy, productive, and happy. She was doing exactly what she had always wanted to do. What was wrong with that?

"Hell, I don't know." She said to Max who had been watching her walk around in circles. "Just go to bed and forget about it." She went into her bedroom, pulled off her clothes, put on her pjs and slid in between the sheets to try and put the strangest day of her life behind her, if only for a few hours in sleep.

The following morning Donny lay in bed staring out the window. He was so deep in thought that he had not heard the door open.

"Hey man, how you feelin?" Came a man's voice from the doorway.

Donny whipped his head around and saw Jason Masters standing in the open doorway. "I'm great!" he sneered, slipping into a perfect American accent. "How do you think I am with a hole in my gut? And you?"

Jason was a tall lanky man with greasy dark hair pulled back into a ponytail. His pale arms were covered in tattoos as was most of his body. He continued into the room and closed the door quietly behind him.

"How'd you know where to find me?" Donny asked.

"Went down to that cafe at the 'corners' for coffee this morning. Couple of troopers were sittin there havin their obligatory donuts, talking about a gunshot wound. Figured it was you. What'd you tell 'em?"

"Nothing, As far as they're concerned I was walking through the woods and some crazy out of season hunter caught me with a stray bullet." This man made Donny's skin crawl. He couldn't wait to nail this piece of slime. "How's the kid?"

"Fine, she was kinda shook when you ran out of the shack after Gavin last night. Cried some, but I slipped a little something in her food and she shut up and went to sleep. She's ok "

"Whadaya mean 'a little something'?'" Donny raised forward in the bed, his eyes shooting daggers at Jason through his pain. "Christ! You didn't give her any of Gavin's shit did you?"

Jason backed away from the anger in Donny's voice and raised his hands in a defensive motion. "Hey, relax, man! I gave her a little of my own stash. I know it's good shit. I got no clue where Gavin gets his stuff. It'll kill him one of these days if he's not careful where he buys it. I just wanted to shut her up so I could figure things out. I know she's no good to us dead." Donny glared at the other man and leaned back against the pillows. "So, it's not hunting season. Did the cops really believe you?" he was twitchy and shifting his weight constantly.

"No reason not to. There's always some guy up here hunting out of season, or some farmer shooting at woodchucks. So they chalked it up to an accident. Anyway, wasn't any bullet to get, so they won't be able to trace it to anyone."

"Hey man, I'm really sorry about all this. If I had known Gavin was going to go off like that, I couldna put his lights out first, ya know?" Jason shuffled his feet around on the floor and found it difficult to look Donny in the eye.

Desperate for the safety of the thirteen-year-old hostage, Donny dismissed Jason's lame excuses. "He's an asshole and a loose cannon. If you don't get a handle on him, he's going to blow the whole deal and I've got money tied up in this one. Where is the kid now?"

"Tiff? She fine, Cheryl is with her at the shack. How long you gonna to be stuck here?"

"Another day or two, I think. Why?" Donny raised his eyebrow and squinted at the tall slime ball. "You try getting shot and see how fast you wanna get out of bed."

Jason straightened defensively "Hey, I already said I was sorry about the bullet. Don't tear into me. I'm not the one that put the slug in your gut." he rubbed his hand over his chin and sighed. Pulling up a chair he sat down and rested his hands between his knees. He was struggling to keep himself under control. "But you're right about Gavin. He *is* a loose cannon. Especially when he's hopped up. I mean the guy can't keep his hands off women. Age don't mean shit to him, and the girls aren't worth near as much cash if they're used. So, I've been thinking it's time to pack it in here and turn the kid over and collect." Jason didn't feel the need to inform "Sam" AKA Donny that Gavin was already back at the shack and had moved up the drop off per his own orders. Jason never liked the fact that Gavin always dismissed him when it came to making decisions.

"Good idea. When do we move and where do we take her?" Donny asked.

"I'll handle it. You won't be out of here in time, and I want to finish this tonight." Jason said.

"Not without me, chum. I already told you, I've got money in this, and I'll be in at the finish." Donny's anger flared again.

"Relax. I already talked to George. He's got the rest of the freight at the vacant Shulter warehouse in Scranton. Cheryl and I can get the kid there tonight and I'll get your share of the cash and be back here tomorrow morning. No sweat! Besides, I feel sorta bad about you gettin shot. Figure I owe ya." Jason fairly leaped out of the chair. He was so jumpy; it was obvious to Donny that Jason needed a fix. Donny would have loved to take him and Gavin down for the drugs, but there was a more important task at hand.

"What about Gavin?"

"Don't worry, man; if he shows up at the shack, I can handle him." He stood switching from one foot to the other. Jason was not a particularly good liar. As a child he twitched and moved his feet when he lied. Now as an adult and because of the drugs, most people had a difficult time knowing whether or not he was telling the truth because due to his drug use, he was in constant motion most of the time. But Donny saw through Jason's speech. During the months he'd been with the two drugged up men, he'd made a close study of the two of them and he knew who was in charge and it wasn't Jason. Jason was the weak link in the duo. He knew Gavin was the one making the decisions and he knew Gavin was the one who moved up the drop date. "Listen, I gotta get going. I need to get back and get set up to blow this place. We'll wait till it's dark and clear outta the shack. Won't take long to get to Scranton. Make the drop and collect." Jason smirked. "No problem! You relax and I'll see you in the morning." he paused with his hand on the door handle. "Ya know, you and me make a pretty good team. We think alike. Ya know? Ya might think about stickin with me for a while and we'll go south and see what we can scratch up down there. Ya know?" he grinned at Donny and was out the door.

This is the worst part o` the job, Donny thought to himself. Being around people who he despised and seeing what they did to each other and their victims and not being able to do anything about it or stop it until the time was right. But this job was more personal to him than any other. This was even more personal than the assignment in Scotland. Donny rested his head back in the pillow, and could feel his stomach lurch and the blood in his body begin to boil with anger and hatred. He *needed* to get these guys, he *had to make* it right, for *her*. He needed to make sure that what happened to her didn't happen to these girls. And he would give up his life to ensure the safety of these girls.

Donny closed his eyes and blew out his breath, then reached for his cell phone and punched in his contact number for the Federal Bureau of Investigation.

Jason walked into the shack to find Gavin packing up. In the corner of the room was thirteen-year-old Tiffany sitting on a cot , too drugged to notice the crumpled form of the woman laying in a pool of blood on the floor.

"W-w-what happened to Cheryl?" Stammered Jason.

"Didn't trust her anymore, She wasn't bein straight with me about what was going on between her and Sam. I don't put up with that cheatin shit. Doesn't matter, I was never gonna keep her around after the drop off anyway. By the way where the hell have you been?" Gavin never looked up while he spoke.

"I was hungry so I went to that little diner. While I was there the people in the place were talkin about a man who came out of the woods with a bullet hole in his gut. Said he was taken to the hospital and how some lady doctor saved his life. I thought it was Sam so I decided to have a look." Whether he was twitchy from needing a fix or not Gavin could always tell if he was lying. Jason learned early on in their association that telling Gavin the truth straight off was a better idea, he knew less pain that way.

"Was it him?" Now he looked up.

"Yeah it was. When you shot him the bullet went straight through. The story he told was that he was in the woods and caught a hunter's stray." He stopped there. He didn't want to let it slip that he told about the change in plans.

"I hope he dies. Come on, wrap this up and let's get the fuck outta here." They finished collecting what they needed for the drive to Scranton , carried the nearly unconscious Tiffany out to their van and drove away, leaving the dead woman on the floor of the shack.

Chapter Four

Megan dressed, ate, and was out the door with Max on her way to the office by six- thirty the next morning. Most of the patients on Megan's schedule yesterday came in to see Jess, but some had rescheduled for the next day. As a result, Megan's already full docket was now crowded. So, she decided she better get in early to get her morning paperwork out of the way before her first patient showed up. She needed to do some medication inquiries for a new Dementia patient, and look up some local support groups for the patient's daughter. As she made the short drive to her office, she went over everything she needed to get done during the day, and tried to estimate when she would get out of the office that evening. This was the daily undertaking she went through every morning, and she often wondered why she bothered, as she was never nearly accurate.

Megan parked in her usual spot at the office and pushed the button to open the rear way back door. Max leaped out of the car, and was at the door waiting to get inside by the time Megan had grabbed her medical bag from the passenger seat.

"I don't know what you're in such a hurry for, kiddo." She ruffled the big dog's ears before sliding her key into the door lock. "Do you see any other cars in the lot? We're the only one's here so far."

Megan walked through the office turning on lights and equipment, while Max made the rounds of the building with his nose to the floor. Within minutes he joined her in the mini kitchen behind the reception area where she was starting the first pot of coffee for the day. The office rule from day one was that whoever arrived first brewed the first pot of coffee and filled the tea kettle.

"Everything safe and secure, lovie?" she asked. Max loved going to work with his mom, and his presence was a big treat for the kids upstairs in the day care center. She reached for the electric tea kettle and smiled. The office staff drank gallons of coffee all day long, but her mother insisted she also have hot water available for tea. "Not everybody drinks coffee you know, dear." Megan mimicked. "Some people prefer a nice hot cup of tea." She smiled at the memory as she ran water from the tap into the kettle and plugged in the cord.

Normally the office manager was the first to arrive in the mornings, and she took care of all the messages and voicemail, but since Megan was first in this morning, she sat down to check the messages herself. While she listened, she made notes for herself, the receptionist and her associates concerning call-backs and appointments. When that was completed, she reset the voicemail and went into her office. Megan set to work on the medication list for the new dementia patient. She went through her appointment calendar for the day and pulled files for the patients she'd be seeing first. She did a fast check of her email, and then picked up her phone and punched in the number for the hospital, hoping to talk to Bob Winston about the recovering Donovan Mackay.

"Oh! Sam Watson." Megan said. "Damn!" she muttered. "I wasn't cut out for intrigue."

"Hi Megan, in to work rather early aren't you?" Bob asked when he picked up the call.

"Yeah, but given yesterday's events, I needed to reschedule some patients for today. I figured I better get in here early enough to clear up my paperwork or I'll be here till midnight. So, I'm calling about Mr. Watson. How's he doing?" Megan was relieved that she remembered not to use Donny's real name.

"Good. He could probably get out of here today, but I'd like to keep him one more day to make sure he doesn't have any negative reactions to the meds. Always tough when you don't have medical records."

"Yes, but he's awake now. He can tell you what you need to know." *What am I saying?*, she thought. "But I agree. Keeping him another day is a good idea. I have a full day here today, but when you make your rounds, can you tell him I'll try to be in to see him later this evening?" *Oh, why did I tell him that?* She cursed herself. *I need to think before I open my mouth.*

"You will, huh?" Bob chuckled, thank ye "Well that's nice."

"I'll need to speak with him if he's going to be staying at my house, Bob."

"Mumm-hmm."

"Goodbye, Bob."

"Goodbye Megan. And I will pass the message along to your young man." Megan could hear the laughter in Bob's voice and could picture the grin on his face. She wanted to deny the unspoken assumption again, but figured what was the point? She might as well be screaming into the wind. She sat looking at the phone after she replaced the receiver. "I don't know why he and Otis are so interested in my social life." She mumbled, then chuckled. *Probably because I don't have one,* she thought.

Megan moved toward the door when she heard Max trotting down the hall to her office. That could only mean one thing; people were beginning to arrive for the day. She glanced at her watch. Eight-thirty. She raised her eyebrows. She had accomplished a great deal in a short time. The office wasn't officially open for another thirty minutes. She could go up front and have coffee with the girls as they arrived.

"Hi Liz." She smiled at the Office Manager. "I checked the voice-mail for you and put a list on your desk."

"Thank you Megan, you know you don't have to do that." She smiled. Liz was twenty-three and working to put herself through nursing school. She was the first to apply for a job when Megan opened her practice. She was still in high school then, and was hired as part time receptionist after school. She was bright and learned quickly. It became apparent she could do anything she was asked, and noticed things that should be done before Megan did. Before long she had made herself vital to the smooth running of the office, and Megan promoted her to office manager/receptionist and raised her salary appropriately. When Liz graduated from high school, she bumped her hours to full time, and then took on the job of after-hour-on-call service in the evenings and weekends for extra cash. Megan had always been blown away by the young girl. Liz managed to go to evening classes at Wayne Memorial, and still handle her job at the office. She married her high school sweetheart the year before, and now was expecting their first child. She was a gem, and Megan was determined to keep her on staff hoping to one day bring her on as a nurse.

"I know, but I was here early. Besides, NOBODY could say you don't do your share around this place. So today is a tiny bit lighter for you. Have some coffee, and take a load off. How's Jimmy?"

Liz poured herself some decaf coffee and leaned against the wall. "Jimmy's good. Working overtime to make some extra money before the baby comes." Rubbing her large pregnant belly.

"Not much longer." Megan smiled remembering when Liz and her new husband found out they were going to have a child. Liz had asked Megan to be her doctor, and Megan told her she could be her primary care doc, but that she would be better served to see an OBGYN for the pregnancy.

"At least another month. Thankfully, I'll be able to work almost up until I deliver. Which reminds me, I need to put you down as the pediatrician, so you'll be notified by the hospital as soon as I deliver."

Megan smiled and rubbed Liz's swollen belly. "I'd be honored to take care of this little fella." She then lightly squeezed Liz's hand. "We'll see about you working clear up to delivery, missy. Even Wonder Woman needs to cut back sometimes."

Liz was ready to deny the need to cut back on her workload, until the side door opened, and Jess came in followed by Sara Compton, their other associate doctor.

"Morning ladies." Megan greeted both women. "Have some coffee before the rush starts. It's not everyday we have all three doctors in house and both Nurse Practitioners. It's going to be a busy day."

"You said it." Jess groaned on her way back to her own office to deposit her things before joining the group for the first cup of the day. "I could learn to hate Thursdays."

"But it does make the day go fast" Sara chimed in while she poured herself a mug of the fresh brew. She glanced out the side door window. "There's already activity in the parking lot."

When the wall clock was straight up nine o'clock, Liz went over and unlocked the front door and patients began to file into the office. Amanda came in with the second patient and ushered the first arriving children upstairs to the daycare center. It was a relaxed, friendly atmosphere. Everybody was on a first name basis. Liz knew instantly which patient was there to see Dr. Megan, Dr. Sara or Dr. Jess or which ones were there to see Jenny or Sharon the two nurse practitioners. The patients varied in age from small children and babies to the elderly. The older patients were a special treat to see as they usually brought; or sent in with their husbands, lovely containers of fresh baked cookies or some other sweet goodies, because according to one good natured lady who had known Liz and Megan most of their lives: "Those young girls don't eat enough to keep a bird alive over there. Cholesterol be damned!" She not only brought cookies or brownies, but she also occasionally accompanied her sweet treats with a big casserole of mac and cheese.

Megan saw patients all morning nonstop, and that's the way Megan liked it. She agreed with Sara. A busy day was fulfilling, and it flew by. She never rushed a patient, and all her patients knew this and appreciated the time she spent with them. Max spent the day upstairs in the day care center with the children of staff members and patients. Every once and a while Megan was with a patient she could hear the kids and Max running around upstairs and having a good time. When Megan would hear the laughing she knew she had made the right decision when she turned the second floor into a daycare for the staff's children and for patients who came in with kids.

At one o'clock, the office closed for lunch. Megan made it a policy that everyone has a long lunch, so she kept the office closed for two hours. That meant the office was kept open later two evenings a week, but patients who worked outside the home appreciated the accommodation because it meant they didn't have to take time from work if they needed to see a doctor. And it was no real hardship for Megan and her associates because they took turns staying in the evenings, and usually nobody was in the office much later than seven o'clock.

Megan walked her last patient of the morning to the front door and then turned to Liz. "Let's go over to the corners for a quick bite before it's time for the first applicant."

"I'm ready, and I'm thinking a BLT wrap would taste really good right about now." Liz said as she rose from her chair and grabbed her purse. Liz had scheduled two interviews during lunch for applicants to fill in while she was on maternity leave.

"Are you sure you don't mind sitting in on these interviews?" she asked Megan on their way out of the office.

"Of course not. I'm happy to help."

"Because I would really appreciate your input and feedback. You know I have a vested interest in my temporary replacement. If you don't get the right person, I'll come back after my leave and be faced with a mess! I certainly don't look forward to that.!"

"Can't say that I blame you. For myself, if we can find someone who can run the office a quarter as well as you do, we'll be lucky." She indicated Liz's purse. "You won't need that. We're effectively ruining your lunch, so I'll pay." Liz locked the door on their way out and they walked across the road and into the café for the fast lunch before returning to the office for the interviews.

The first applicant was a total disaster as well as the second. In fact the whole process took only a grand total of thirty minutes. Liz and Megan returned to the café across the road to sit and relax before the afternoon round of patients, when the second applicant left.

By five o'clock the daycare center was thinning out and Max had to come back downstairs. He made visits of his own going in and out of exam rooms hoping to find someone to pet him. All of Megan's patients were made aware of the dog when they first came in and those who did not want a visit from him would have the exam room door closed.

Jess and Sara finished with their caseload and went home. Megan still had one more little girl to see, and told the rest of the staff they could "pack it in.". There were no other patients scheduled for the day and she would close up. Liz wanted to stay until Megan was finished and help with the closing.

"You don't need to stay Liz. It's been a hectic day and you need to go home." Megan told her as she got ready to see her last case.

"NO way! I'm not leaving you here alone. See your patient and you and I will close the place down." Liz stood her ground and Megan knew it was pointless to argue and nodded in agreement.

When Megan walked her last patient out, Liz was in the background beginning to close up shop. As Megan waved goodbye to the little girl and her mother, a State Trooper cruiser pulled into the parking lot. *Oh God, now what?* She thought as she watched the uniformed men get out of the car.

"Can I help you Troopers?" She smiled

"Yes ma'am," stated the older of the two. "Have you noticed anyone strange around here lately?"

"Strange? No. Why?" She asked, looking the two men over. The older one was about five foot nothing, highly overweight and perspiring through his uniform. The other man was much younger. Much taller and well built. No more than thirty, if that. And he wasn't perspiring through his uniform. *Rookie,* Megan thought. He looked vaguely familiar, but she knew she had never met him, and assumed she had seen him around town at one time or another

"Well ma'am," started the older Trooper.

"Look, my name is Dr. Megan Dunnegan, please don't call me ma'am. And you are?"

"Sorry ma...uh, Dr. Dunnegan." Spoke up the younger of the two. "This is Trooper Hallet and I'm Trooper Mackay."

Mackay? She perked up. *Wouldn't a distant relative be a godsend?* "Do you live around here, Trooper Mackay?"

"What?" the young trooper was taken aback by the question.

"Are you from the area?" she bombarded him with questions. "Do you live around here? Do you have family here?" she asked.

"Yes...no...Uh. Yes, I live in the area. No, I have no family here." He looked at the attractive woman, but wondered why she was questioning him. He and his partner were the ones with the questions. *A verra odd lady*, he thought to himself. *Attractive, but verra odd.*

"Oh." She let out her breath that she hadn't realized she was holding in. "Well. Nice to meet you...both." She smiled. "Now what can I do for you?"

"Yes, ma...uh, Dr. Dunnegan. It's nice to meet you too. Uh, you see, Dr. Dunnegan," Mackay started, "There has been a disappearance here at one of the camps."

"Oh? I haven't heard anything about it on the news." She could feel her stomach go up in knots. "What kind, counselors going off together and getting lost?"

"No," Spoke up Hallet, "A little girl. Thirteen years old."

"From this camp?" Motioning behind her and up the hill toward the two camps that flanked her farm.

"No. But we're making the rounds of local doctors and businesses. In the way of a heads up. So people are aware. So to speak. In case someone would bring a young girl in for treatment. A young girl who looks terrified or especially nervous." The older Trooper explained.

"Trooper Hallet, *all* children are nervous when they come to the doctor. When did this happen, and why haven't I heard anything about it on the news?"

"We aren't at liberty to discuss the details of the investigation, Dr. Dunnegan,'' said Mackay. "But please be on the lookout."

"Do you have any photos of the girl that I might be able to look at?"

"Yes, ma'am. Here's one." Hallet pulled out a photo and handed it to Megan. The girl was pretty with long blond hair, blue eyes, and dimples. She had a bright smile and looked like she didn't have a care in the world. "Her name is Tiffany Bennett. She has been missing for two months. She was taken from a camp in New York State."

"New York? Have any other girls been taken?"

"We can't say now." Answered Mackay

"You can't say, or you *don't* know?" Megan shot back at the men. "May I make a copy of this to show the staff?"

"Yes." Stated Hallet.

Megan went back to the copier to make a copy and filled Liz in on what the Trooper had told her. She was also going to fill in Donny on what she had heard and demand he tell her what was going on. She had a bad feeling that he knew about this.

She went back outside and handed the photo back to the Troopers.

"If you hear or see anything, please give us a call. Here's my card."
Mackay handed her his card, and he and Hallet got back into their
cruiser and left.

Megan stood and watched the car pull aw*ay. FBI, she thought. "A
little girl's life depends on keeping my identity secret." he had said, she*
thought. Liz locked up the office door and followed Megan's gaze at the
disappearing Troopers' car.

"How terrifying for that poor girl." She said with her hand resting
comfortingly on her extended belly. "I can't even imagine how scared
she must be."

"What? Oh. Yes. It has to be a horrific experience for her. I hope they
find her alive, and castrate the bastards who took her." Megan said. She
punched the button on her key fob that opened the rear door on her
Wagoneer. Max leaped inside and laid down. Liz buckled herself into
her own car, and they waved to each other as they left the parking lot.

Megan let herself and Max into her cottage and closed the door.
Laying her keys on the kitchen table, she reached into her pocket and
drew out the Trooper's card. "Steven Mackay." She read. "'Little girl's
life depends on keeping my identity secret.'" She looked over at Max.
"What do you suppose are the chances that there are two Mackay's,
each involved in an investigation of two *different* little girls?" She decided she needed to talk to one of the MacKay's and now. Snatching up
her keys, she went out and got back into her car, turned the ignition,
and pulled onto Dunnegan Road.

Donny was sitting in the Geri Chair pushing food around on his plate when Megan walked purposefully into the room. Her expression suggested she was ready for a fight. And although he wasn't really interested in doing battle with her, he was willing to do anything that could help him avoid the mess sitting on the plate in front of him. He gratefully put his knife and fork down and smiled at her.

"Hello Megan."

"Good evening, Mr. MacKay." She crossed the room and stood in front of him.

"Are we back ta that ag—"

"Who is Tiffany?" She asked. After her visit from the state troopers, she was in no mood for fooling around with pleasantries.

"Tiffany?" he asked. "I dinna know." He hated to lie, but until he had heard that the girls had been rescued and the perps securely in custody, he had no choice. *How in the bloody hell did she hear about Tiffany*, he wondered. Her disappearance had been kept out of the press in the hope that with no publicity, it would be easier to recover her and the other hostages. Her parents had agreed, and the camp had been extremely relieved to avoid publicity. "Why?" *I need ta find oot what the lass knows*, Donny thought.

"I had a visit from some State Troopers at the office this evening. They're looking for a little girl who was taken from a camp over in New York State. Her name is Tiffany. I seem to remember you telling me that a girl's life depended on your secret identity. You wouldn't happen to know anything about this girl Tiffany would you?"

"State Troopers? Are ye sure they were who they said they were?"

"Here, one of them gave me his card." She took the card out of her pocket and handed it to Donny. As Donny read the card, she would have sworn she saw pure hatred flash across his face before he cleared his features and looked back at her. "What is it?" she said when he didn't speak.

"This is the man who came ta speak ye aboot the Tiffany girl?" He asked through clenched teeth and a tight jaw.

"Yes, why?" She was becoming alarmed. "Why? What's wrong?"

Just then the door to Donny's room opened and in walked his doctor, Bob Winston. "Well hello folks, I'm glad you're here, Megan. Mr. Watson, you are free to go."

"What?" Megan whirled around. "You said you were going to keep him another day for further observation."

"No, I said I would *like* to keep him, and I would have, but we're short on beds as it is *and* there was a big wreck down on 490." When Megan's face changed from frustration to concern, Bob held up his hand. "All injuries have been taken care of, but right now, we've got admitted patients on beds in the hall outside of the ER." he smiled at Donny/Sam. "So! Mr. Watson, you're free to go your merry way."

"But," Megan began to protest.

"Now," the smiling Dr. Winston interrupted, rubbing his hands together. "I'll have all the instructions you'll need before you take him home, Megan."

"No, I'm not ready for him! You told me you weren't going to release him until tomorrow, and I have nothing ready for him."

"Well, I wouldn't worry about that. Mr. Watson here seems like the patient sort. Besides, I don't imagine he's feeling up to raising a ruckus if he has to wait a bit while you sheet the bed." He looked back at Donny/Sam and grinned. "Are you son?" Donny grinned back. "So!" Bob continued. "Since I have already told you you're out of here, how are you feeling?"

"This is great news." Donny forced a laugh. "Isn't it Megan?" He looked up at his doctor. "I feel good. Thank you."

"Good!" Bob smiled. "Well I'll see you both in an hour. I'll also have your meds filled here at the hospital pharmacy. That way you both can go straight to Rileyville with no stops." And with that parting shot, Bob sailed out the door.

"Oh, how kind of you, Bob." Megan called after him. When he was gone, Megan looked back to Donny who was holding the now crumpled up card in his fist. "Hey, what did you do that for?" She asked as she snatched the crumpled mess from his hand. "I wanted to keep that in case I needed to call the cops."

"I'm a cop and there willna be a need ta be callin` *that* one." Donny growled shoving the tray table away from him, and made an abortive attempt to get out of the chair.

"Hey! Be careful or you're gonna do some damage. If you want out of the chair I'll help you." She placed her hand on his shoulder in an effort to keep him seated.

"I dinna need yer help." He snapped.

"The hell you don't!" She raised her voice and stood in front of him, blocking his exit from the chair planting her fists on her hips. "Now you listen to me, bub! Doctor Winston effectively released you from this facility to me. You're going to be staying in *my* house, under *my* care! Don't think you can talk to me that way, and get away with it. I don't take that shit from my staff, the hospital staff, or any member of my family! So back off!" She warned and continued. "Now if you've got some kind of gripe or something's bothering you, out with it! Don't give me attitude or I'll let the hospital kick you out of here on your ass and you can fend for yourself! Do we understand each other?"

Donny looked at Megan glaring down at him. He figured the last person who had spoken to him in that manner was Agatha Stuart when he and his brother had nipped some pastries from her bakery when they were kids. The lady doctor was right, of course. First, she saved his life. Then she stayed with him in the ER, and now she was allowing him to recover at her home. She really was, in his view, taking a huge risk. He would never allow one of his sisters to do what Megan was willing to do for him. *He* knew she didn't need to have any fear of him, but he also knew that *she* couldn't be absolutely sure of that. He was a total stranger with only his word and a set of identification documents, that if she knew how easily they could be forged, it would scare the bejesus out of her. She didn't know why he'd been shot, or by whom. He refused to tell her what his case was about, yet she was willing to open her home to him. *Aye, she's more than right,* he thought, *and I'm bein an ass.*

"Ye're right and I'm sorry luv." He bowed his head and then looked back up into her eyes.

"Thank you." Megan took a calming breath. "Now, would you like for me to help you get out of the chair?" In her mind Megan decided; for now questions about the card, the trooper and the girl would have to wait. The handsome Scot was being released and she needed to get him up, dressed and home. *Handsome Scot?* she thought. She looked down at the man sitting in the geri-chair. *Well, yeah, he is handsome. Good God!* She thought

"Aye, lass. I could use a wee bit o` help. Thank ye." He spoke softly.

One small victory for our side, she thought. "Now do you need help getting dressed?"

"Nay, I can dress meself, but I wouldna mind some help getting` up." He winced as he was assisted to his feet and walked to the bedside.

"Are you sure you can handle dressing on your own?" Megan asked as she struggled to keep the man standing. He was a great deal taller than she and with him leaning on her, she felt like he weighed a ton. However, with her arms around his hips and his muscles straining to support as much of his own weight as he could, she could tell that his strength was wearing thin.

"Aye, I'm sure. But can ye hand me the shirt and jeans from the closet?" he asked as he gingerly lowered himself to the edge of the bed.

Megan walked to the closet and reached in for the clothes folded on the shelf. "These are the same clothes you came in with?"

"Aye."

She pulled out the clothing and held each item up wrinkling her nose. "There's a bloody jacket and a pair of pretty gross jeans. That's it. You can't wear this stuff." She closed the closet door and went back to Donny.

"Well, luv I ha` no other clothes ta wear. They will ha` ta do."

"Can't you have someone bring—"

"Oot o` the question."

"Why? This seems so silly. Surely the..." she turned to glance at the door and spoke quietly. "Certainly your superiors know who you are and could bring you something decent to wear."

"I ha` no 'superiors' in the immediate area. Besides I do'na want anyone but the doctors ta know ye're helpin` me. I canna run the risk o` the wrong people gettin wind o` yer existence." He frowned

"Oh." This was not the response she was expecting. "Thank you."

"Yer' welcome." *I bet that was heard te say*, he chuckled to himself.

"Well," she cleared her throat, "if we can't retrieve your own clothing, we'll have to get you some new things." She took a step back and looked him over. "I can pretty much gather what your sizes are with one exception. Underwear."

Her bluntness caught him off guard. "I'm sorra?"

"I can take a run to Walmart and pick up some things for you." She picked up a napkin from his tray and the pen lying on the tray table and jotted down other items she should pick up. *Do I have clean sheets on the bed?* she thought. *I don't even have food in the house. Food, hell, I don't cook! I eat at the "corners". I wonder if they deliver?* She could have used another day. "I can pretty much figure out sizes for shirts and stuff like that, but I have no clue about men's underwear. Unless of course you'd like to spend your recovery in hospital gowns. I imagine I can borrow a few of those for your use since I am doing Winston a favor by taking you home now."

"It's a thrifty offer, thanks, but I prefer regular clothin`." He breathed.

She looked more closely at him when she noticed his breathing was becoming somewhat labored. "Why don't you lie down before you slide onto the floor?" He seemed to accept her help more readily this time as she helped him get back into the bed. It was obvious that the little bit of exertion had worn out what stamina he had left. When she had him settled and pulled the sheet up to his waist, she raised the head of the bed and adjusted the pillows behind his back.

"Ok, now. They're going to release you in an hour, so I need to go get whatever you'll need for the next couple of days. I realize I'm getting a bit personal, and I'm sorry if this embarrasses you, but let's have your underwear size." She picked up her purse and stood watching his expression change from disbelief to humor.

"Large." He smiled.

"Large? I need a size, you know like 34, 36, your waist size."

"I dinna wear briefs. I wear boxers and I need a large or extra large." He answered.

"You know, boxers are much better for men to wear than briefs." She said in her best professional tone while digging in her purse trying to find her keys. "You made the right choice."

"Thank ye, tha` s good since I canna wear briefs."

"Why not?" She challenged.

"They're tae small. I need lots o` room." He smiled as he watched her cheeks go from bright pink to crimson. "Ye're askin me aboot me undergarments wi` oot batten an eye, and yet ye blush at the answer." He grinned up at her. He looked straight into her eyes and the room was silent for several minutes while he waited for her to respond, but she didn't. She pulled her hand out of her purse and turned toward the door. "Oh, and lass?" he said. She stopped with her hand on the door handle and turned to look back at him. He smiled broadly showing straight white teeth. "I'm no` the least bit embarrassed."

"I never blush." She scowled at him and was out the door.

Chapter Five

I don't get it, Megan grumbled to herself while walking around the store grabbing at men's clothing. *Every time I try to get any information about or from this Mackay guy, something happens. Every time! It's uncanny. And not only am I being practically forced to house the man, but now, I'm buying his clothes.* She picked up three packages of lightweight pajamas with drawstring pants, a couple pairs of cotton lounge pants with elastic waistbands and six short sleeve t-shirts. "There." She said aloud. "That should hold him until he can get out on his own."

Then she came to the underwear section of menswear. So many styles, she blew out her breath. "*'large or extra large. I need lots o ` room'*" she mimicked. "He never mentioned his style preference. 'I need lots of room' she repeated. "Oh hell, who cares what style he likes? Go for the colors you like." She saw several packages of plaid boxer briefs. "Plaid!" She chuckled. "Perfect!" She grabbed several packages and threw them in her cart and as she turned to leave the department, she glanced up and saw an elderly lady staring at her. She could feel her face turn red and she smiled meekly at the woman and left the department.

On her way to the checkout she remembered that she had no food in the house. *Well, maybe a bag of Peanut Butter M&Ms, but he can't survive on those,* she thought. So she turned around and headed for the grocery section. "Now I'm supplying his groceries." she muttered. Before she got to the grocery section, she passed by the men's robes. She grabbed one and threw that into the cart. Then knowing the weather would begin to get chilly, she picked up a lightweight jacket, *without bloodstains,* she thought. "I hope he's recovered and gone before I have to get him earmuffs and snow boots!"

She stood at the checkout watching the cashier drag every item across the scanner trying to keep a bland expression on her face. *I sure hope the FBI pays him well,* she thought, *cause I'm not going to write this off as charity.* When the cashier read off the total Megan nearly fell over. *I will* definitely *be billing someone,* she thought as she swiped her credit card through the machine.

She parked in one of the spaces reserved for doctors at the hospital and rummaged through the plastic bags, transferring to one bag packages of pjs, socks, robe, a pair of knock-off Crocs, and boxer shorts. She looked at the package of boxers and grinned with satisfaction. Then grabbing a second package of boxers, she closed the bag and went into the building.

Megan entered Donny's room to find him sitting on the bed with his legs hanging over the side. "I'm "danglin," he informed her. "Under orders from the tall blond nurse."

"That's good. After being flat on your back for a couple of days, it's better to dangle your feet before getting right up out of the bed."

"Aye. Tha` wha` the blond nurse said. But she wasna willin` ta dangle wi` me." He grinned at her.

"You look a little better than you did when I left. Did they bring you your discharge papers yet?" She said as she put down the bag and her purse.

"Thanks. Nay they ha` no` brought the papers and wha` ha` ye got there?" He smiled.

"Oh well," she picked up the bag and began to hand him items. "You should be pleased to know you won't have to leave the Wayne Memorial sporting the stylish designer hospital gown. Here." She handed him the articles of clothing and watched in amusement as he examined blue knit pjs covered with the smiling M&M logo.

"Uh, thank ye. Aye, the gown doesna compare with these." he smirked. He picked up the package of boxers. "Are ye oot o` yer bloody mind?" He looked up at her.

"What?" she shrugged her shoulders. "You mean the colors? I know that tie die is a little wild, but I figured with your lifestyle it was a perfect statement." She smiled sweetly.

"It's no` the color I ha` a problem wi`, lass."

"Really? What then?" She answered with the best sincere interest she could muster.

"Did ye no look at the size when ye were pickin` them oot?" he handed her the package to inspect.

"What? Large. That's what you asked for." She handed them back "I'm sorry they didn't have that color in extra large."

"Megan," Donny was trying to decide if she was teasing or serious.

"Yes."

"These are *boy's* size large."

"I know." She smiled even brighter. "What? They're too big? You were exaggerating, right? That's what I thought. It's ok though. I knew you were embarrassed after all. I understand. It's only natural. Big strong secret agent, like yourself. So I got the next size down to be sure." She handed him another package that held size medium boxers adorned with Spiderman.

He looked at the two packages in his hands and then back to her bright violet eyes and warm smile. "Ye have a nasty sense o` humor, Megan Dunnegan luv." he grinned. "Did ye by chance happen ta get a pair o` *men's* shorts?"

Just as she was about to answer, the door opened, and a nurse came in with the discharge plan and medications. Twenty minutes later, all papers had been signed, the nurse had explained the medication schedule and an orderly had stopped in with a wheelchair. The orderly left the chair and promised to return when the patient was dressed, and ready to leave the hospital. As soon as the door closed behind the orderly, Donny looked at Megan with strained patience.

"If ye wouldna mind now, luv. I could get me clothes on if ye had shorts in yer bag a wee bit larger than these?" he gently waved Spidy in the air above his knee.

Megan burst out laughing. "If you could have seen your face!" she chuckled. "Yes, hold on." She dug into the plastic bag. "Most fun I've had in the last thirty-six hours." her voice trailed off. Then she dumped the bag on the bed, but the only thing that fell out were the knock-off Crocs. The room was silent for a few minutes as she stared at the red shoes. She raised her eyes to Donny. "I don't seem to have any with me." She whispered.

"Are ye tellin me ye..."

"I don't have them up here with me."

"What?"

"I'm sorry, I really thought I had them. I bought them. Honest, and I was sure I put a package in the bag." She lifted her hand and then dropped it to her side in apology.

"It was verra funny. I admit. Now wha` would ye suggest?" He asked, "Joke or no I assume ye know, I canna wear these." He held up the boys' pants and smiled.

"Commando, I guess. Until we get to the cottage, anyway." She tried but couldn't even get the sentence out without laughing.

"This in no` funny anymore, lass." Donny stated.

"Sure it is." Megan was obviously enjoying Donny's dilemma. Looking at his expression she couldn't contain her humor. She braced herself on the edge of the bed to protect her balance and drew a tissue from her pocket to wipe her eyes. She looked at Donny's unsmiling face and then blew her nose. "Oh, lighten up. You and every doctor in this place who has had any contact with you have had a field day at my expense for the last two days. It's only fair that I have my turn." She reached across the bed and began to take the clothing out of the packaging and remove the pins. "I have the correct size boxers in the car. When we get to the farm you'll be able to put on a pair. Do you need help getting into the pjs?" She asked, offering them to him.

"Nay I can do it meself. Would ye pull the curtain?"

"Sure." She smiled and pulled the privacy curtain around the bed. As Megan waited, she could hear Donny struggle with his task.

"I do'na imagine those doctors wander through the halls o` this facility wi` oot their drawers." He grumbled.

"You'd be surprised." She listened to him struggling to get dressed. Megan could hear his breathing becoming more labored and wanted to help him. However, she knew that if she charged behind the curtain, that would be a huge mistake. "Are you doing alright?"

"Nay," was his tired response.

She drew the curtain slightly back to find him sitting on the bed wearing the pj pants and holding the shirt in his lap. He looked defeated and cross.

"What's the matter, doesn't the top fit right?"

"I do'na know whether it fits or nay," he sighed, "I canna lift me bloody arm enough ta put the bloody thing on. This bloody hole in me side seems ta be limitin` me movement more than I thought." He looked at her with an unspoken plea for help and Megan gave him a sympathetic grimace.

"May I help you?" She closed the distance between them and assisted him with the pajama top. "Here." She said, "let's put your 'bloody arm on the injured side in first, and get the 'bloody' shirt settled over your shoulder...that's right, now duck your head into the neck. Easy. Good! Now slide your other arm in from the bottom and...pull the shirt down over your chest." She smiled, stepped back, and examined their joint handy work. "And there you 'bloody' are!" she took in his pale face. "How do you feel?"

"Like a wee lad wi` nay knickers on." Donny grimaced.

"I *am* sorry about that," she smiled, "But I assure you that I do have them for you in the car." She turned to look in the bag. "Now where are the Crocs? Ah! Here they are." She laid the ventilated plastic shoes on the floor and held Donny's arm for support while he slipped his feet into them. "Well, and you're ready to go. Rest a minute if you need to." Megan looked into his deep jade eyes and was temporarily submerged in them. Suddenly the door opened, and the connection was lost.

"Oh, I'm sorry," the unidentified nurse said, "I have the wrong room." And backed out.

"Aye, lass. I am ready ta leave this place, and I do'na care if ye've got the best bloody damn doctors in the world, I ne'er want ta see the inside o` this place again." He winced as he tried to reach his full height.

"I can see you're going to be a cheerful patient to have around." Said Megan just as the door opened again and the orderly entered the room. He walked to the wheelchair and put both hands on the handles and rolled it toward Donny.

"Hi, Mr. Watson. Your chariot awaits." He smiled

"My what?" Donny asked, slipping again into his perfect American accent. "There is no way I am leaving here in that thing."

"Don..." *Oh crap*, she thought. "Don't you think you'd be more comfortable in the chair, Sam? You can't even stand straight. You obviously need the chair. Besides, it's not like you have a choice. Hospital policy." She felt like she sounded flustered. *All these name changes,* she thought. *I'm just not cut out for this cloak and dagger stuff.*

"No I don't need that thing," Donny protested. "Please take it away."

"I'm sorry, sir." The Orderly explained. "But the doc's right. Hospital policy. If a patient has been admitted, they must leave via wheelchair."

"No, I don't want the damned thing. I don't need it and I refuse to ride in it." Donny's voice was getting louder, even though he was leaning more heavily on the edge of the tray table at the foot of the bed. He was definitely showing signs of fatigue, but obviously not willing to give in or give up.

Frustration was evident in the orderly's voice too. He was young and just trying to do his job. He didn't need this. "Please, Mr. Watson. I have to follow hospital..."

Megan listened with amazement as Donny and the young man in scrubs argued about the use of the wheelchair. She was also amazed at how easily Donny was able to completely mask his Scots accent.

However, she couldn't have the two of them yelling at each other on the surgical floor. Or any other floor for that matter. There were other patients to consider. Besides, if Donny Mackay didn't sit down soon, he was going to fall down.

"Hold it!" She said in a firm voice. "Enough!" She turned to the young orderly. "I understand you're just doing your job, kiddo, but you and I have both seen patients leave this facility on their own two feet." Then she moved her eyes to Donny who actually had the nerve to grin back at the orderly. "And *Sam,* we all understand now, that for whatever macho thing you've got going here, you don't want to ride in the chair. But the fact is, you need it. You've been standing for less than five minutes, I notice you can't do *that,* without leaning on the table. You're starting to sweat and it's a long walk to the car." She motioned for the chair to be brought closer. "So, get in the goddamned chair." She ordered.

Donny looked at her with narrowed eyes. He had thought for a second that he had won this skirmish. He could tell she wasn't going to back down, but he also recognized concern for him. He let out his breath and gingerly sat down in the chair. "Ok fine, sugar, but only because you're so pretty." He winked before she could say anything more.

Megan stood for a moment glaring at him. *THAT comment will be all over the hospital before I get my car unlocked,* she thought. She rolled her eyes at the orderly. "He's on pain meds." she said and glared at Donny. "Alot... of pain meds." She gathered his clothes from the closet and stuffed them into the supplied bag on the shelf.

By the time they got to the Wagoneer and Donny was comfortably settled into the front passenger seat, he was exhausted. Megan thanked the orderly for his help and his patience, and then rounded the car and got into the driver's seat. She looked across the car at Donny and could tell by his color that he had used up nearly all the stamina he had left.

"Listen, lean back, and try to relax. We're about twelve miles from the farm. Maybe you can get some rest on the drive home."

"Thank ye luv, foe everything." He smiled warily and leaned back. "Do ye ha` a cell phone store in this town?"

"A what?"

"I need ta be getting` a charger fer me cell phone. I'll ha` calls ta make when we get ta yer house. And me cell phone hasna been charged in days"

This guy isn't for real. She thought. "I have plenty of chargers of all kinds and shapes." she said. "We're not stopping for anything. I need to get you into bed."

"It's a bonnie offer, lass, and in a day or two, I may be able ta take ye up on it, but right at the moment, I do'na think I'm quite up ta the exercise." He gave a weak smile then sobered. "I will be needin` a charger fer me cell. The Bureau will be needin ta know where I am."

"You know perfectly well what I meant, and we're not stopping so you can buy a charger. I have a phone. You can use mine." She pulled out of the parking lot, turned left at the light and headed north to the farm.

They didn't speak during the drive to the cottage. Megan mulled over in her mind what little he had told her about himself and his job. Then figuring in the information she had received from the Troopers, she thought about Donny's reaction to the Tiffany question. Megan was fairly sure Donny, and the State Police were involved in the same kidnapping investigation. What she couldn't quite understand was Donny's reaction to the young Troopers card. *What was that about?* She wondered. *Was he some kind of relative? What are the odds of that?* She mused. Before she knew it she was home and parked. She turned the ignition off and glanced over to see that her houseguest/patient had fallen asleep. Megan looked him over. *He's a big man,* she thought, *how am I going to get him up the steps and into the cottage? It took two of us just to get him into the car.* "I think there's a dolly in the barn," she chuckled.

She sat for a few seconds watching him sleep. *He really is nice look-ing,* she decided. *Wonder why I didn't notice that before now? Nice face, straight nose, full lips, and a strong chin. Actually not bad looking all in all. Good strong build.* She smiled. *I know several women who would say he's a "hunk".* "How am I going to get you into the house on my own?" she whispered.

"Well, we can't just sit here." She sighed. She hated to wake him, but she could hardly pick him up and carry him in. "Donny," she said softly. He didn't stir. She put her hand on his shoulder. "Donny, wake up." No response. "Agent Mackay, you have to wake up now." She got out of the car and went around to the passenger door. When she opened it, Donny was still sleeping. "Donny please wake up." she rested her hand on his knee squeezing gently.

"A little higher luv." He turned his head toward her and opened his eyes. Even in the fading daylight, he could recognize the blush creeping into her cheeks.

She caught the twinkle in his deep green eyes, and smiled. "You really are an ornery bastard, you know? How long have you been awake? And why didn't you answer me the first time?"

"Ye're wrong, lass. I'm nay a bastard. Me parents were married before I was born. And I ne'er slept, luv. I was ta busy trying ta keep the bumpy road from jarin` me insides oot. Do ye no` ha` road crews in this part o` the world?" She didn't know what to respond to first: the fact that he hadn't slept at all, his response to her rather childish name calling, or defending PENNDOT. And nobody defends PENNDOT. "Well?" Donny continued "Shall we try ta get me inta yer home, lass?"

"I told you about calling me that," She began.

"Ye told me ta no be callin` ye *lassie*, and I didna, but there's no a reason I canna be callin` ye *lass*. Since that's what ye are. Habits ere hard ta break, Megan. Remember tha` I am a Scot, and we've been callin` our women 'lass' since the beginning o` time." He laughed, and then winced.

"Thanks for the history lesson, professor. Now, let's see if we can get you in the cottage... *laddie*." She mocked "Place your arm over my shoulders and try to slip out of the seat." She instructed.

It was slow going and tiring for Donny, but together they made it from the SUV and into the cottage. Max met them at the door.

"This is yer dog?" Donny was amazed at the size of the animal. Megan helped Donny to lower himself onto the sofa.

"Yes. Max, this is Donny. He's going to be with us for a few days. Donny, Max. Now why don't you two sit here and get acquainted while I see to the guestroom." The big dog seemed extremely interested in the man his owner had brought home with her.

Megan smiled and walked through the kitchen/dining room to the back bedroom.

Donny watched her walk out of his field of vision, leaving him staring nose to nose with the big dog. Max took a sitting position smack dab between Donny's feet. "Hello Max." Donny murmured as he wasn't really sure what to make of the dog. He was huge. Black and white spotted. "Ye look like an oversized Dalmatian." he said, but Max didn't move. His ears had never been cropped and oddly enough he had blue eyes. Donny had heard that Dalmatians who had blue eyes were sometimes blind or deaf. He couldn't remember which. But given that Max was watching him so intently, Donny gathered he wasn't blind. And noticing how Max's ears perked whenever Megan made a noise in the bedroom, Donny knew, the dog wasn't deaf either. He smiled at Max, but Max didn't smile back. "Is he friendly, lass?"

"Excuse me?" Megan called from the bedroom.

"Yer friend here. Does he bite?"

"Only on command." Was her only response.

Donny chuckled and carefully offered the back of his hand for the dog to sniff, and Max inched closer to the big Scot. Megan poked her head around the doorway to see how Max and Donny were interacting, and grinned when she saw the stare-down contest the two were having. Max was a wonderful judge of character, and she was interested in his reaction to the "secret agent man". It seemed to be going well, so she went back to putting clean sheets on the bed, and laying out towels from the linen closet. When she heard a groan from the other room, she made a beeline to the doorway and stopped in her tracks. There was Max sitting on the sofa with his front paws draped over Donny's lap and slathering kisses on his face.

"Well I'll be damned." She smiled.

"T'would would seem he likes me." Donny stated.

"Yes it would. You should be honored; Max doesn't usually take to anyone this fast."

"Did ye hear that, laddie, I'm special, but would ye mind gettin down? Yer shoulder is crushin` the hole in me side." His face was turning crimson with discomfort, and she could see beads of perspiration on his forehead.

"Oh, God! Max, get down! I didn't even think!" She rushed across the room. Max got off the sofa immediately, but with the same grace and agility as he used getting on in the first place. Donny grunted in pain and leaned his head on the back of the sofa waiting for the stabbing pain to subside. " Donny, I'm so sorry. Here, let me see if he did any damage." She sat next to him and gently raised his shirt to see the front bandage was bright red with fresh blood. She leaned him forward to look at the back bandage and found it to be the same. "Yeah, well, this isn't exactly an exemplary start. I'll need to change these. Sit still for a minute while I get fresh supplies. Ok?"

"Aye, lass, but can ye keep the animal away from me while yer gone?" He pleaded.

"Max stay off the sofa." She ordered. The dog hung his head and laid down at Donny's feet. "I think you have a new friend." She smiled on her way to the bathroom for the bandaging materials she needed. Returning to the living room area she knelt in front of Donny. "Max, get out of the way." She was all business now, as she helped him to scoot forward on the sofa, and placed a clean protective bed chuck under his uninjured side. She raised his shirt well above his wound and then pulled on a pair of latex gloves. Looking into Donny's eyes, she explained. "Ok I'm going to wet the gauze with a little warm water. Then I'll remove the bandage, and we'll see what we've got. I'm sorry, I can't pull the tape up fast cause I don't want to take a chance of disturbing the sutures, so the tape might pull a bit." She told him as she tilted the squeezable water bottle and squeezed until the liquid hit the gauze.

"Bloody hell Woomon!" Donny bellowed, and then he laughed. "Ye said warm. Do ye have a different definition of warm than we do then?"

"Of course," she smiled, briefly noticing the goosebumps raise up on the man's skin. "Just like you do about cold?" She peeled off the tape and the four-inch square gauze pads to reveal the wound. "That doesn't look bad at all. Just a little pressure damage. Sutures intact. You're fine."

She laid the old bandage on the edge of the chuck and picked up a pump bottle. "A little soap and water, and we're ready for fresh pads" She announced and when she noticed the goosebumps return, she looked into Donny's face. "This stuff I keep in the freezer." She smiled. "Now hold still so I can finish."

"Are ye sure ye're a doctor?" He winced as she laid the new pad on and taped around it.

"Quite sure. Now. Ok time for the back."

"Oh nay, lass I think ye've done enough."

"Did I hurt you?"

"Nay, ye dinna hurt me, but ye tried ta freeze me ta death." He grumbled.

"Yes. It's the best way to curtail bleeding. Frozen blood doesn't seep out as easily. Now try to lean forward a bit more and we'll finish this." Donny did as she asked, and she placed a thick pillow on his lap to support his weight. She rebandaged the exit wound following the same procedure and pretty much getting the same reaction from the patient.

"There, all done." She looked at her watch. "Time for your meds. You can sit back now, and relax a bit, and I'll get them for you." She gathered up the old bandages and her supplies and headed for the kitchen when the phone rang.

"Hello?...Hi Nathan!" She smiled. Donny watched her and wondered who Nathan was. She was apparently glad he called. And suddenly Donny wondered why this bothered him. Megan listened, continuing to smile, but then a frown began to form and then deepened.

Whoever this Nathan bloke is, Donny thought, *she doesna seem so happy ta hear from him anymore.* And Donny had the sudden urge to protect her from Nathan.

"That's wonderful." Megan said, but Donny noticed she didn't look like whatever it was, was so bloody wonderful. "Oh no that's no problem...Sure, I can do that. No problem. Yeah...Ok! I'll see you then. I love you too...Bye-bye." She hung up the phone and stared at it.

She loves Nathan? Donny thought.

"Great. Now what?"

"Is there a problem, luv?" Donny asked from the sofa.

"That was my brother, Nathan. He and his family are coming up this weekend. They weren't supposed to be here for another two weeks. What the hell am I going to do?" She looked at him.

"I do'na understand?" He was absent mindedly rubbing Max's head now resting on Donny's lap. "Do ye need me to find somewhere else ta stay so ye can ha` me bedroom fer yer brother?" He also felt relief that Nathan was a close relative.

She looked up from the floor "What? No. You! You're the problem! How do I explain you being here?" She took her hand off the phone, and retrieved his meds from the large envelope containing his discharge papers and the glass of water she had set down when the phone rang. Donny waited until she was sitting next to him before he spoke.

"Why can ye no` just tell him the truth?"

"What? That I found you at the back of my car with a bullet hole in your gut? And now you're going to stay with me while you recover? Oh yeah! *That* would go over real well. Here swallow these." She handed him the pills and the glass of water.

"Nay, I agree. That probably wouldna go over so well."

"Besides, I thought your identity was such a big state secret."

He was silent for a minute. "Why do ye no tell him the truth, but omit some o` the details?"

"Like what?" She leaned back resting her head on the back of the sofa and then turned to look at him. It suddenly occurred to her that he was just about the most attractive man she had met to date.

"Tell him I'm a friend and I needed a place ta stay while I recovered from surgery. Is he a doctor?"

"No. A film director. I guess that might work. But how do I introduce you? As Donovan Mackay, the spy or Sam Watson, the...What?"

"I'm no` a spy, luv." He smiled warmly. "And ye introduce me as Donny Mackay. Me occupation need ne're be mentioned."

"Well, whatever you are, we had better come up with some sort of occupation. Because you see, I'm the baby sister and my big brother will want to know all he can about you. So you'd better come up with something, and have answers to rattle off just as fast as Nathan shoots the questions."

"Tell him I'm a real estate agent from Skye, and I needed ta ha` surgery, and we thought it would be better ta ha` it here, so I could stay wi` ye while I recovered."

"Ok, Yeah. Right. That sounds plausible. Why would you come all the way from Scotland to have surgery in Honesdale, Pennsylvania? Who would do that?"

"Someone who knew what a great group o` physicians ye ha` here at Wayne Memorial?" He offered.

"I don't think so." Megan arched her eyebrow. "We have a good hospital for a small town, and it services the area quite well, but I don't think it's a facility you travel halfway around the world to utilize.

"And how come I know a real estate agent on Skye? I've never been to Scotland." She sighed. "Nope, I've got to come up with something more believable than that. And quickly. Can I ask you a question?"

"Aye, lass."

"Who is Steven Mackay to you?" she watched him stiffen. "Donny?"

"Nay someone ye can trust." His voice was hard and filled with malice.

"I take it you know him."

"Aye. I do." He said. Megan waited for him to say more but the room remained silent.

"Well, so who is he?"

"Me younger brother."

"Your brother?" She was shocked. She had considered the young trooper might be some distant relative, maybe, but a brother was definitely *not* what she expected. "You have a brother right here in town?!" *And I'm the one who's stuck with you in my house*, she thought. "You told me you had nobody here. And he's a cop no less..." Her voice trailed off when she saw his frown deepen.

"I dinna know he was in the area. Nor did` I ha` any idea he was involved wi` yer law enforcement."

"You don't seem very happy to know you have such a close family member nearby. You told me your family was close knit. And yet when you learn you have a brother right here, you act as if you hate the man. I don't understand."

"I do'na want ta talk aboot it." He leaned his head on the back of the sofa and closed his eyes, and Megan softened.

"Come on." She said. "We don't need to talk about this now. And you need to get into bed." She rose to her feet and leaned down offering her arm to help him up.

He turned his head and looked into her violet eyes. "Thank ye, luv, fer no pressin` the issue."

Megan slid her arm behind him when he leaned forward. "Yeah, well, it's been a long day for both of us. You especially." She helped support his weight as he stood and walked him slowly toward the bedroom. "I can't promise that I won't ask again, but I can accept that family dynamics are sometimes difficult to deal with." She eased him onto the bed. "There you go. Now lie back and I'll help get your legs up." When he was fully reclined, she drew the covers over him. "Now rest. Sleep is the best medicine." She chuckled. "Boy, every time I say that, I want to cringe. It sounds like somebody's aging Aunt Hilda would say, but it's true." She turned back toward him when she reached the doorway. "I'll leave a light on low in the kitchen if you need to go... to get up during the night. My room is just on the other side of the kitchen. If you need anything in the night, don't hesitate to call me." She smiled at him. "Good night Agent Mackay."

Megan had not realized how tired she was, until she walked into her bedroom and turned on the light by her bed. She pulled off her clothes and dropped them into the hamper, pulled on a nightshirt, turned down the bed, and slid between the crisp green sheets. She expected Max to be right in, but when he didn't come, she got out of bed and walked back to the living room. Max wasn't there either. Megan peeked into Donny's room and there on the floor next to the bed lay the big dog. He looked at her with questioning eyes and she smiled.

"It's ok buddy, you can stay there." She whispered and gave him a scruff behind his ears. When she settled back into her bed, sleep came very quickly.

Chapter Six

Megan woke the moment she felt tugging on her bed covers. She sat up and saw Max at her bedside.

"Max?" She yawned. The big dog backed up toward the door of her room and whimpered. "What do you want, lovie?" She pulled her robe from the foot of the bed and slipped it on as she followed Max out to the main room. Megan watched Max trot into the guestroom where Donny was sleeping. As she moved closer she could hear Donny writhing in his sleep and speaking in what sounded like a strange language. Being familiar with several foreign languages and not recognizing this one, she could only assume that it was Gaelic. Fearing that he might pull some sutures, she went in to wake him. "Donny?" she called from the doorway. Not knowing how he would react upon waking in a strange place she turned on the bedside lamp before approaching him completely. "Donny, wake up, you're having a nightmare." She soothed and sat on the edge of the bed resting her hand on his leg. Knowing it would never work since she had no idea how to speak Gaelic she tried to listen and see if he would say anything that she might understand. However, his movements were becoming more and more agitated. "Donny," she said louder, "wake up." When he still didn't wake, she stood and put her hands on his massive shoulders and gave him a shake. "Donny, you're dreaming. Wake up."

"Arabella!" he bellowed in the saddest voice Megan had ever heard. "NO!" he woke with a start and sat straight up in bed. His eye lashes were damp, and there were wet streaks down his cheeks. She grabbed a tissue from the box on the nightstand and wiped his face. His eyes were open and as he looked at her she watched as a myriad of emotions raced across his face, from pure childlike joy to complete confusion and finally unequivocal hopeless grief.

"Shh," she soothed, "It was only a dream."

"I couldna get there fast enough," he murmured. "I failed her and Marie. I failed them both. Can ye ever forgive me?" He pleaded to the void. He sank toward her and wrapped his arms around her holding her while his body trembled, and silent tears raced down his face and soaked into the front of her robe.

"Donny, shhhh. You're ok now." She had no idea what the dream was about, but she was beginning to think it was more memory than dream. *Dear God*, she thought, *what happened to those women?* She stroked his back and spoke soothing words of reassurance as she rocked back and forth, and Donny clung to her like a terrified child after a nightmare. She had done the same thing with her brother's children when they came to stay with her, but had no idea if this method of comfort would help a grown man. Finally, his trembling and the tears subsided. He straightened and took the tissues from her hand.

"Are you alright?" She looked into his jade eyes that were now blood-shot and swollen. And she saw anguish and grief that she only saw on the faces of family members who had been told there was no hope for a loved one.

"Megan?" He leaned back into the pillows "I'm sorra aboot tha`."

"Shh, don't be, are you ok?" She brushed his hair back from his forehead that was wet from perspiration.

"Aye, luv."

"Who are Arabella and Marie?" she asked and handed him dry tissues.

"Did I say their names?" He sat forward and winced at the pain at his side.

"Be careful," she warned with concern that made Donny smile, "Yes you did." She braced her arm behind his back while she positioned the pillows to make him more comfortable.

"What else did I say?"

"I have no idea; you were speaking in what I can only guess was Gaelic. Would you like some water?"

"Aye, I would. Thank ye." He watched as she left the room. He petted Max who was at the bedside looking at him with sad puppy eyes. When Megan returned she moved Max back, sat down on the side of the bed, and handed Donny the glass. He drank the entire glass in four gulps and handed it back to her. "Thank ye. "

"Are you sure you're ok?" She placed her hand over his. "Bad dream, or memory?"

"Memory." He looked down at her hand over his. Her fingers were slender and graceful.

"Do you want to talk about it?" When she saw his indecision she spoke again, "Maybe later, huh? Do you want to try and get back to sleep?"

"I do'na think there will be any more sleep fer me this night, luv." He blew out a deep breath and brought his gaze to hers. If there was any doubt about her caring or wanting to help him they were washed away when he looked into her eyes. They were full of compassion and concern for him. "Did I wake ye?"

"No. Max did. He must have noticed your..." she hesitated, "discomfort and came to wake me up."

"Smart dog," he smiled and tossed a sleepy grin at the animal, who was stationed at the foot of the bed. "Thank ye for bein` here when I woke."

"You're welcome. Um," she looked around the room and back to Donny who watched her intently. "Well," she smiled. "I am wide awake now and I imagine so are you. Can I get you anything?" Donny shook his head. "What would you like to do?"

"Talk." He answered.

"Ok. About what?" She had so many questions but bit her tongue and decided to leave it be. He could see she had questions racing around in her head and was grateful she chose this time to hold back the interrogation.

"Well now, this is a change in ye lass." He chuckled, "Ye who are always so full o` questions, and ye have none at the moment? How odd."

"Like you said before, I have been the one asking, and I thought it might be nice for you to have a turn tonight, or at least what's left of the night." She smiled.

"Are ye givin me leave ta ask wha` e'er I choose o` ye?" he arched his eyebrow and a devilish grin appeared on his handsome face.

"Within reason, sir." She smiled and started to move off the bed, when Donny's hand grasped hers.

"Where are ye goin?"

"To get a chair."

"Nay need fer tha`, here." He took a deep breath against the pain he was about to cause himself and moved himself farther to the center of the double bed. "Sit here." He patted the bed and smiled.

"Remember, Max is right here if you should try anything funny." She teased and scooted further onto the bed crossing her knees as she faced him.

"I canna try anything 'funny', lass. In case ye havena noticed, I am no movin so good." He straightened and smiled smugly, "But I do'na think Max will hurt me, as ye said earlier, I have a new friend in him."

"New friend or not, he will defend my honor." She challenged, in good humor.

"Are ye sure aboot tha, luv?"

"Positive. Now, what would you like to talk about?"

"Ye." He said quietly.

"Why am I not surprised?" She smiled, "What would you like to know?"

"When I asked ye why ye dinna have a man in yer life, ye dinna answer. Why?"

"I think men make women messy." She blurted.

"Pardon me?"

"Ok. Maybe that's the wrong word. Stupid?" She looked at the ceiling. "That's not the right word either. Gullible? Naive? To be honest I have no idea what the right word is. Pick one that covers the inability to see what's probably been right in front of their face for weeks, months...who knows how long. Do you think women are unable to see or are they so infatuated with what everyone calls 'love' that they don't want to see?" She looked away from his prying eyes and smoothed an imaginary wrinkle from the bedcovers.

"Have ye been hurt by luv, then lass?" he asked softly. Watching her body language told him to tread lightly on this subject.

"Um, I guess you can say that I was stupid, naive, and gullible." She looked up and smiled. Now it was her turn to blow out a deep breath. "It's pretty simple; and not exactly a new story. I was engaged to be married and the night before the wedding I found Tim, my *sterling* groom, in bed with my best friend. Who was also my maid of honor. Sort of a whole new meaning to the old saying that it's bad luck for the bride to see the groom before the wedding."

"How long ago was this?"

"Oh," Looking at her wrist as if her smart watch was still there instead of on the charger. "Five years ago."

"Has there been no one since then?"

"Oh, I've dated, but no one seriously." She shrugged. "I haven't missed anything. I don't sit at home alone with my cat and no outside activity. I know several men who I enjoy seeing on a social level. I go out to dinner occasionally; I go to parties. And every now and then when there's something I'm interested in, I go into the city to see plays. But I'm busy with my practice and haven't had the time nor the need to become involved in America's favorite pastime. I don't need to be in love or all the junk that goes with it."

"I dinna see your cat."

"I don't have a cat." She smiled. "That's my mother's thing. Cats. Lots of cats." She looked at the smile on his face. "Oh, you know what I mean. I'm not exactly the old maid aunt who sits at home every night waiting for my nieces and nephews to come to visit me because I don't have a life of my own. I have exactly the life I want. I'm active. I'm social.

And I'm busy. I like my life, and I'm happy." She looked directly into his eyes, daring him to contradict her.

"Everyone has *needs,* luv." He smiled as she crossed her arms and tugged her robe more tightly around her.

"Maybe a lot of people do, but I don't. Relationships are messy, restrictive and from what I've seen, unfulfilling, disappointing, and *grossly* overrated. And I've found that suppressing my *needs* isn't all that difficult. Besides, don't you realize this is the mechanical age?" She laughed out loud at her own outburst and could feel herself getting flushed.

"Why e're ye blushin` lass? Oh that's right ye do'na blush." He corrected himself as he chuckled. Then a realization hit him. "Wait, am I ta believe tha` ye havena been wi` a man since ye're betrothed?"

"Betrothed?" She laughed. "God, I thought only people in romance novels used that word. And period novels at that. Do all Scots talk that way?"

"I guess we do." Sensing her trying to change the subject, Donny felt compelled to keep the conversation on track for the present time. "So, ha` ye?"

"Have I what?" *I guess he isn't going to let it go,* she thought

"Been wi` a man since him, wha` was his name? Tim?"

"Not that it is any of your business, but no I haven't." She stated and waited for him to make some snide or smart comment.

"Huh. Well, is tha` nay somethin`."

"That's it? That's all you have to say?" She couldn't believe it.

"Wha` did ye want me ta say Megan? Ye are obviously a woomon who takes makin love ta heart and willna jump inta bed wi` the first man who crosses yer path. I think tha` is verra admirable. And verra wise in taday's society." He took in her expression and began to laugh. "Why do ye look so shocked?"

"I'm sorry. It's just that I've never heard a man say anything like that before. Hell, I'm not sure I've ever heard a *woman* say anything like that before. I'm just surprised, that's all."

"At wha`? Tha` a man like me would think tha` makin` luv is no just something` ta pass the time and shouldna be reserved fer two people who ha` strong feelins fer one another?"

"Oh, Donny please," She could see her comment had caused him to be defensive. "I didn't mean you personally. I meant men in general. Please don't be offended. It's just that," she sighed, "I've been on dates. I've had to fend off multiple offers to jump in the sack. It's practically the required end result of dinner and a movie."

"I know wha` ye mean, people do na seem ta treat it as a token o` luv anymore, merely as a..." he paused.

"A sport." She finished for him. Then deciding this had turned too much into a one way conversation, she said the first thing that came to her mind. "So have you ever been in love?" But as soon as the words were out, she realized it was a mistake.

"Aye. I ha` been." The boyish grin faded from his lips, and he dropped his eyes from her face to his hands.

"I'm sorry, Donny. We don't have to talk about it. Maybe you could get some sleep now."

"Nay. I havena talked aboot it in years mayhap it's time." He took a deep breath and began. "Arabella and I were a couple all through school. We ha` been best friends as wee ones chasin` over the village tagether. By the time we ha` finished wi` Secondary schooling, wha` you would call high school, we were betrothed. We both knew we were tae young ta marry then, and our parents all wanted us ta attend university. So we went ta university wi` the plan ta wed when we ha` our degrees. The summer before we went off ta university, Arabella's parents were in a car accident, and both killed. Arabella was granted guardianship o` her twelve-year-old sister Marie."

"Those are the two names you mentioned in your sleep." She said quietly.

"Aye. Arabella's family was no wealthy, but there was insurance money after the accident and Arabella ha` a small fund fer her own schoolin`. Me parents helped Arabella arrange fer their home ta be sold and wi' the money from the insurance and the sale o` the house there was enough money ta send Marie ta a private boardin` school fer girls in Inverness. Bella and I went off ta university in Edinburgh. It was a difficult first year fer Bella and Marie both as they ha` ne're been separated. And wi` the parents havin` passed. It was even more difficult fer them. Bella would take the train ta visit Marie durin` class breaks, but tha` first year only Marie went ta me parents home fer the winter holidays. Then the second year, we were all ta be together at me family home fer Christmas. When the day came fer Bella and I ta leave Edinburgh, I was goin ta be held up at school fer another day and Bella needed ta get on ta Inverness ta collect her sister."

Nineteen-year-old Donny picked up the phone in his dorm and called home.

"Steven?" Donny asked.

"Aye, Donny tha` ye?" Steven was Donny's younger brother and home from classes for Christmas break.

"Aye when did ye get home?"

"Aboot and hour ago, when are ye comin` home?"

"Well tha` s why I'm callin`, I'll be held up here fer another day. I need ta talk ta me professor aboot a paper and I willna be able ta pick up Arabella and Marie from the train tanight. Would ye mind gettin them fer me?"

"Sure, what time?" Steven yawned.

"Ten-thirty. Please do'na be late. I do'na want them standin` alone in the station tha` late at night."

"Nay problem. We're aboot ta ha` dinner. Then I will go and collect Bella and wee Marie."

"Thank ye Steven, tell our mam tha` I luv her and I will see ye all tamorrow night."

Donny spent the rest of the night working on his paper and waiting impatiently for morning to come.

The following morning Donny woke and took his paper to his history professor spending a good deal of the morning discussing it with him. It wasn't until three in the afternoon that Donny was able to get himself packed and on the road home to Skye to spend Christmas with his family and Arabella. He couldn't wait to see her. He asked her to marry him after they got out of Secondary school, but was not able to give her a ring. Donny had spent whatever time he had not studying or in classes working any job he could find in order to buy the small ruby ring that was tucked safely in his pocket for Arabella's finger.

The trip was long given the snow and it was dark by the time he arrived at the family home on the Isle of Skye. As he approached the house he saw the lights from the police cars. He pulled to a sliding stop at the front door and bolted from the car. He raced into the house to find the family and two policemen in the parlor. His mother was crying and the rest of the family seemed to be in a daze.

"What happened?" Donny demanded as he entered the room. His mother rose from her chair and went to him immediately, wrapping her arms around her tall son.

"Come and sit down, dahlin`.'" She said and moved with him to the sofa where they sat together. He looked around at all the faces and didn't see Arabella and Marie.

"Where e're Bella and Marie?" He looked to Steven who was sitting in a corner with his head in his hands sobbing. "Steven, where e're they?"

"I take it ye're Donovan, Miss Arabella MacLeod's fiancé?" one of the policemen asked.

"Aye, wha` is this aboot?" Donny felt icy fear begin to consume him. "Mam, where e're Bella and Marie?"

"Donny," Steven stood and moved toward his brother. His face red and streaked with tears. "I'm so sorry, it's all me fault. I ne'er should have lain down after dinner."

"Wha` is this aboot?" Donny bellowed to the room.

"We got a call aboot eleven-thirty last night," one of the officers began. "From Mr. Steven Mackay tha` he was at the train station where he found Miss Arabella MacLeod lying on the floor. At tha` time there was nay sign of Miss Marie Macleod."

Donny sank back into the cushions behind him and tried to breathe. Arabella on the floor of the station? Marie missing? He nearly leaped from the sofa. "Where is Bella now?" he glared at his brother. His mother took hold of his hand and tried to pull him back down onto the sofa, but he shook her off. Eleanor MacKay rose and placed her hands on Donny's shoulders and forced him to look into her face.

"She's dead, dahlin`. Therea's no easy way to tell you, baby. She's gone."

"Wha` happened?" he looked into his mother's sad eyes as his own began to well.

"I do'na think it would be wise te go o'er the details." Tommy Mackay, Donny's oldest brother, stepped forward.

"Nor I." Alex Mackay another brother stated.

"Well I do!" Donny slashed his hand across his face and turned to his younger brother, Steven. "I want ta know wha` happened, *brother*." Donny said through clenched teeth.

"From what we can gather," the officer began. "Miss Arabella was accosted and assaulted. Then suffered a fatal blow ta the back o` the head. We ha` searched and so far found nay sign o Miss Marie and we believe tha` she ha` been abducted." Donny stared at the police officer unable to speak for the moment.

"Ye said ye got the call at eleven-thirty, but their train came in at ten-thirty. Why was the call so late?" Donny had to force himself to stay on auto pilot. He couldn't think about what the officer had told him or he would go mad.

"Tis me fault Donny," Steven sobbed. "I fell asleep after dinner and when I woke, it was already eleven. I tried ta get there as fast as I could, but it was tae late. I found Arabella and called the police."

Donny stood and stared at his youngest brother and felt the hatred begin to rise. "I put me trust in ye. I put their welfare in yer hands. I told ye tha` ye needed ta be there when the train arrived and tha` I dinna want them ta be there alone at night." He stalked toward his brother. "I told ye!" Be bellowed and lunged at Steven.

Tommy and Alex got a hold of him before he reached his target.

"Ye e're dead ta me!" He screamed "Do ye hear me ye son-o-a-bitch? Dead! Let me go I willna touch him." He told Tommy and Alex. "I ne'er want ta see or hear from ye again. Do ye understand me?"

"Donovan," his mother pleaded as she stood, "he is yourah brotha."

"Nay anymore." Donny turned and left the house without another word.

"Three days later we ha` the funeral fer Arabella." Donny was silent for the first time in almost two hours.

Megan sat and listened to his story and the history between Donny, Arabella, Marie, and his youngest brother Steven. She waited for sometime before she spoke.

"Did they ever find Marie?" she asked.

"Nay, I hounded the police and was told that there was likely no way she would e'er be found. Since there was no letter or call fer ransom they concluded tha` she was taken so she could be used in prostitution or sold overseas as white slavery." He took a deep breath and continued. "I ne'er went back te school and instead I searched all o'r the British Isles fer some sign o` her. When I couldna find anythin I joined the service and was shipped abroad fer two years."

"What did you do in the service?"

"All kinds o` things, but the training and the job I had in the service gave me the skills ta do what I do now. After me time was up I came home and began ta search for Marie again ta nay avail. I went back ta university and studied criminal law. I started in the *business* as ye ha` called it and four years ago while I was under cover I found her by accident."

"You did?" she smiled.

"Aye, however," her smile instantly faded as he went on. "She was, as the police in Skye suspected, sold into prostitution. I saw her and at the time I was wi` the men o` the case I was workin, and was no able ta approach her. So later tha` night I went back ta her and she recognized me. I took her ta dinner and she told me what ha` happened ta her. I wanted her ta get oot, but by then she said it was ta late fer her. She ha` seen tae many things and done tae many things. She ha` been on drugs since she was fifteen and ha` many abortions. Her face was almost unrecognizable due ta the many beatings she ha` suffered. I told her tha` I would come back fer her the following night and get her the help she would need and send her back ta Skye ta live wi` me mam an da." He had a tear falling from his eye and Megan took his hand in hers for some comfort. "When I went back the next night I found her in the ally wi` a needle in her arm and no pulse. I took her ta hospital, but it was tae late. She was already gone and the doctors couldna do anything fer her. By this time, the case I was working on ha` closed. I called me mam and told her I was sendin` Marie home ta be buried next ta Arabella and their parents."

"Did you go home with her?" she asked quietly.

"Nay I went ta the director o` the agency I was working wi` at the time, and told him as much o` the story as he needed ta know and I asked if he could put me in the way o` cases tha` dealt wi` similar circumstances."

"And had he?"

"Aye, there was a group that was working oot o` Europe taking young girls and sellin` them ta other countries fer this verra reason. I've worked a couple o` similar cases. So, he knows I'm particularly qualified in this area o` crime. As a result, when activity o` the same nature come up, I usually get the assignment."

"Is that what you're doing here?"

"Ye know I canna answer tha` luv." His tone was almost apologetic.

"I don't think you have to," she raised her hand to his cheek and used her thumb to brush away the single tear. "I think I understand without you telling me. And you never did speak to Steven again?"

"Nay, after Arabella died he finished school and then came here ta the states. I am told he goes home ta visit wi` the family, but I have nay seen him since tha` night. Me mam willna give up her quest for peace between us, and I'm sorra I canna do as she wishes, but I said he was dead ta me and he is. I accept tha` I ne're should ha` trusted him ta do wha` I should ha' done meself, but I didna think asking him ta collect the girls from the train something he couldna accomplish wi` ease." He took her hand from his face and held it in his hands. Moving her fingers in between his and sighed.

"Donny I can't even begin to imagine what you have gone through in such a short time. Words cannot express how deeply sorry I am. I only wish there were something I could do for you." Her voice was soft and full of heart.

Donny tore his gaze from her hand and looked into her eyes. Eyes of violet that were misty from the horrific story of the girls and the pain he had endured. "Ye've done it lass, by takin me inta yer home, lookin after me, and givin me the comfort tha` I havna allowed anyone ta give me since the nightmare began. I do'na think I can e'er thank ye enough fer the kindness ye ha` shown me o'er the last days. And this night

ye've helped me by forcing me ta talk aboot it. I havna spoken o it wi`
anyone save my former agency director in all these years. Until now.
And I didna go inta such detail when I spoke ta him. Thank ye."

"There's no need for thanks, Donny. Talking usually helps heal. If it's
helped you to speak of your tragedy, I'm happy that I could be here to
listen." She smiled and looked out the window. The sun was coming
up over the pasture and the sky was brilliant with pinks and oranges.
Donny followed her eyes to the window and sighed. Bringing her gaze
back to him. "You ok?"

"Aye, luv. I do'na think I ha` e'er seen a better sunrise. It's almost
sayin` this is the beginning o` a new day and a fresh start fer a tired
broken soul."

"Your soul isn't broken Donny, it's just badly bruised. And maybe it's
time to mend it."

"I do'na know if I can do the mendin`." He answered quietly.

"Oh yes you can, and if you are willing to let me, I want to help."

"Thank you Megan." They both turned back to the sun rising over
the land and wondered what this new sunrise had in store for them
separately and together as well.

Chapter Seven

Donny and Megan watched the sunrise together until Donny finally drifted off to sleep. When Megan felt sure he was sleeping peacefully, she adjusted the covers over him and went to her own room and climbed into bed. Before closing her eyes to find sleep herself, Megan thought about Donny, Arabella, and Marie and the pain they all three endured. She wanted to cry for the two young women she had never known. Arabella's life had ended with such terror and pain, and poor Marie had to spend the rest of hers in torment, until she also met an untimely death. And as much as she wanted to cry for those two young women, her heart was nearly breaking for Donny. It was obvious he held himself partly to blame for what had happened that night at the train station. And of course, for not finding Marie in time to save her. He had said as much himself.

He felt responsible for their safety and had, in his eyes, shirked that responsibility by putting it on Steven's shoulders, who he also blamed, for what had happened to those two young girls. And then her thoughts turned to Steven. How old was he at the time? Sixteen? Seventeen?

What kind of guilt had he been carrying with him all these years? There had been four people involved in that tragedy. And apparently both men had been trying to make amends to society ever since. Donny as a secret agent for whatever agency he was with and Steven with the State Police right here in Pennsylvania. Four lives affected by the events of one night so long ago. Two had died and two left to carry with them the guilt they felt they deserved. Megan knew the real guilt belonged to the men who committed the crimes, but who probably would never pay for them.

After learning what she had last night, she could better understand his reasons for not being as forthcoming with her about his investigation. However, she was somewhat puzzled as to why he would agree to stay with her while he recovered. Somehow it seemed a little odd that he would risk his cover, then it struck her. If he was working on a kidnapping investigation, had he put her at risk?

"Why do I have the faith in this man that I seem to have?" she mused aloud. *Thank God the office is closed today,* she thought. "I'm afraid my questions aren't over yet, Agent Mackay." She said.

Donny had felt he had just closed his eyes when he was awakened by the sound of voices outside the building. He recognized Megan's voice but not the man he heard speaking. Years of training and instinct kicked in immediately and he tried to get up, and go to the window, but he was stiff and sore making his movements difficult.

"Bloody hell!" he muttered. "Fat lot o` help I am now." Then he heard laughter and relaxed a bit. *Must be someone she knows*, he thought. He struggled again to get to a sitting position, and then stopped to take deep breaths. "I'm gonna be real handy should the need er'er arise ta protect the lass or me self." Donny told Max who seemed to have set up shop next to Donny. The big dog rested his head on the side of the bed. "Guess tha` s wha` she has ye fer." he smiled at Max and ruffled his ears. "OK. Move oot o` the way, ye beast. Let's try this again."

He eased himself until he could look out the window to see Megan talking to an older man in his late fifties, very early sixties. Donny was able to hear the conversation only in bits and pieces. Apparently the man was a fisherman and had come to try his luck in the lass's lake. *Lake?* Donny thought, *I do'na remember a lake here, do I?* Donny sat for a moment trying to remember what he had seen and heard over the last few weeks, and what Megan had told him about her home. He had heard mention of a place called Butler's Pond, but he had never been there. Donny sat back and went through his mental rolodex trying to remember what he had been told and overheard. Normally his memory was impeccable. It had to be in his line of work, but currently, it was as if his brain was sifting through a massive cotton ball with no end in sight. Donny knew that this was a symptom of the trauma and the meds he was taking for pain. Some might enjoy the temporary reprieve of the working mind. But for Donny the sensation was likened to being in a prison with a straight jacket. In short, he hated it. *Aye,* he thought, *there was a somewhat private lake tha` was in between two camps around Butler's Pond. Now if I can only remember the name of the two camps.* His thoughts were interrupted by the sound of a car door closing and Megan coming back into the cottage.

She peeked into Donny's room and smiled when she saw him sitting up in the bed. "Good morning. How are you feeling this morning?"

"A wee bit stiff, but better, I think, lass. Thank ye. Do ye usually get callers this early?" He nodded his head toward the window

"Early?" She half laughed, "Donny, it's almost noon and he's late."

"Oh?"

"And I wouldn't exactly refer to him as a 'caller'. He comes here to fish, and we talk for a little while about this and that. Would you like something to eat?" She asked as she leaned against the door jam of the room.

"Fish? Ye have a lake here then?"

"A lake?" Megan looked confused for a moment then realized it had been nearly dark when she brought Donny home last evening. *Had it only been last evening?* she thought. "Oh, well, yeah. We have a small pond about sixty acres. It's private, basically. We share it with the two camps. There was a guy who lived at the other end of the lake, but when he left we bought up his property and the ones surrounding it. So in the summer it's us and the camps. The rest of the time it's just us. But there are a few guys that we let come to fish. Some of the older guys who have been coming for years. Some even for generations. They're nice guys and don't cause any trouble. Friends. Relatives. You know. Are you hungry?"

"Relatives? Ye say?" He asked. "Do ye have many relatives nearby?"

"Yep! The place is crawling with them!" she laughed.

"And ye all live here together on yer farm then?"

"No. This is the family homestead. The children grew up and married. Some married locals and some went to the city. But several already owned or bought adjoining land parcels. We actually have quite an enclave if you want to call it that. Or maybe even a Clan."

"Tell me." Donny urged.

"Well, my great, great, great grandparents settled here in the 1800's. They had children. The children grew up and had children and so on. My great great aunts bought land adjoining the homestead and those parcels have been passed down through generations just like the homestead has. Now don't ask me if my cousins are first, second or third, or how many times they're removed. I have no clue. I have enough trouble remembering how many 'greats' I have to count back. Now, would you like something to eat?"

"Aye thank ye, I would." Donny started to get out of bed and Megan rushed to help. Once she had him standing he smiled down at her. "Thank ye again."

"You're welcome." Letting go, Megan moved back toward the door.

"Isna it unusual for American families ta stay close like yer's has? I've worked a good bit in yer country, but I do'na think I've er're come across the same situation." Megan looked back at him. "Well, I mean, I admit I've ner're had the opportunity ta know many American families, but the general feeling is tha` ye're no a verra close knit people."

"Just goes to show you how wrong you can be about a country and its people." She stopped and looked directly at him. "Besides, we're Irish. We're very clannish. Much like the Scots." She grinned as she entered the kitchen.

He hung his head rather sheepishly. "I deserved that, luv. I didna mean ta offend ye."

Megan chuckled. "You didn't. And in a way, I think you're correct in your assumption. We're a big country and we tend to move around a lot. People do lose track of their relatives." She stood with the refrigerator door open. "I haven't met many Europeans, but I suppose it could have to do with the fact that we can move more than three thousand miles away from family and not have to be bothered with passports or changing citizenship." She returned her attention to the refrigerator shelves. "It's just lunchtime..." she glanced at her watch. "Oh! Wait a minute." Megan walked to the tv room that was the former sun porch and picked up the TV remote. "The news is on at noon. I missed it last night. I hope you don't mind." She flipped until she found the news in time for a special report.

"This just in," the anchor began. "Fifteen men and women were arrested in North Scranton early this morning on charges of kidnapping, the FBI announced moments ago. The arrests were made after a long running joint criminal investigation by the FBI and law enforcement agencies overseas. The surprise raid took place at the abandoned Shulter warehouse on Maintenance Street just after two a.m. this morning. The men and women arrested are being charged with kidnapping, and transporting minors across state lines, forced prostitution and shipping minor children overseas in connection to international slave trade and human trafficking. Along with the fifteen arrested, the FBI recovered twelve young girls ranging in age from ten to seventeen years old. Some of the girls recovered have been missing for as long as four months. Their names have been withheld out of respect for the children and their families. But the FBI stated that all the children have been identified and their families notified of their rescue. No other details of the investigation have been released by the FBI as of yet, but we will keep you posted as this story unfolds."

The anchor turned to his on-camera partner. "My heart goes out to the girls and their families..."

"Oh my God," Megan breathed and looked at Donny standing across the room in the bedroom doorway. "Did you hear that?"

"Aye luv, I did." He sighed, thank God they got ta them before it was ta late, he thought to himself.

"Donny?" Megan kept her eyes glued to Donny's face as his strained words replayed in her mind, *I'm beggin ye...lass's life...identity...secret..* "You know about this don't you?"

"Aye." Donny was about to explain when the phone rang.

"Yes?" Megan answered the phone and glanced at Donny. "Just a moment please." She turned to face Donny who was now at her side "There is a Director Duncan looking to speak to Donavon Mackay." She handed him the receiver and backed away.

"Aye, sir."

Megan went to the kitchen and started to prepare lunch for Donny and herself while he spoke to Director Duncan. Questions flew through her mind. *How did the FBI get her phone number? Well, I guess if anyone can, it's the FBI. But how did they know he was here? Simple, his cell phone. He called them from the hospital. Well,* she sighed. *At least they won't be asking me if I shot him!*

She heard him ask about an Agent Sheridan and a Tiffany. *Tiffany!* Her ears perked up; *That was the name of the little girl the troopers had told her about. Who was Sheridan?* She heard Donny tell the director that he would be staying there to recover from his wound then he wanted to take some time off. "I'll be needin some time," he said. He remained on the phone a few more minutes and then ended the call. Megan glanced at Donny's profile. She could see him clenching and unclenching his jaw.

"Sandwich?" She smiled and put the plates on the table, pulled out his chair and sat down in her own. Megan watched as he took his seat and stared at the food in front of him. "Listen I may not be the best cook in the world, but I doubt I can screw up a ham and cheese sandwich."

"Mmm?" he met her gaze, "Oh sorry luv, I had me mind elsewhere." He picked up the ham and cheese and bit into it.

"So, can you tell me about it now?" She asked casually.

"Aye. I knew aboot the raid reported on the news program. And the girls tha` were taken. Everyone was arrested and the girls are back home wi` their families."

When he said nothing more Megan knew she was going to have to probe for the answers she wanted. "Was Tiffany one of the girls taken?"

"Aye, and one of the last."

"Who is Sheridan?"

"She was the agent workin undercover wi` me."

"Is the case closed?"

"Nay quite yet, Agent Sheridan is missing."

Megan stood and went to the bathroom and retrieved Donny's medications, and handed them to him. "So does this mean that you no longer have to remain incognito?"

"If ye're asken can I tell the world who I am, then the answer is nay."

"Why?"

"Because this wasna me first assignment and it willna be me last. Me identity needs ta be guarded."

"So you are never able to tell anyone who you really are, or what you do, for the rest of your life?" *This was becoming more and more difficult,* she thought.

"Ta be honest, I ha` ne'er been around anyone long enough ta let them know anythin aboot me. Like I said, me own family dinna know what I did until I was forced ta involve them and even then there are only a few o` them who know the truth."

"So the story about the real estate agent is still a go for my brother and his wife when they come for the weekend?" *I really need to come up with a better story, that one is ridiculous.* She told herself.

"Aye."

"Have you ever thought about quitting?" she asked quietly.

"Nay I ne'er did, but I ha` ta admit tha` since I was wi` Ian and Madison in Philadelphia a while back, that idea has crept inta me mind from time ta time. And since this last case I think I might think on it a little more." He answered faintly.

"This one was difficult for you, wasn't it?" Even before he spoke, Megan knew the answer. After what he had told her about Arabella and Marie, she knew that this was personal. "Don't answer that. Listen, I think it might be a good idea, seeing that the case is mostly closed, that you call your family in Scotland, and let them know what has happened to you."

"Well now, there ye go again, switchin` the conversation." He chuckled "But nay, I willna do that."

"Why not?"

"Because if I rang me family every time I was hurt," he stopped, *nay I canna lie ta her*, he reminded himself. "Like I said nay all me family know wha` I do. And the ones who do would only worry. Wha's the good o` that. Nay, I willna ring them. At least no` for tha` reason."

"How many times have you been hurt on the job, Donny?"

"Nay many, a few bruises here and there. No` much more." Which was essentially the truth.

"And how many times have you been shot?"

"Ne'er."

"Not a good feeling is it?"

"Nay." He sighed.

"Well," she wiped her mouth and laid her napkin back in her lap. "I realize; I don't know you very well, but I think you should get out of the business, and count your blessings that you have only suffered one bullet wound, and a few bruises. Next time you could end up dead." She smiled smugly. *There, chew on that for a while*, she thought.

"Ye sound like Madison." He smiled back at her

"I don't know her at all, and I like her already." She chuckled. And when he looked at her, their eyes locked, and she realized that her statement inferred that one day she would know Madison. For reasons she couldn't explain, the idea filled her with joy and nerves. She broke the connection first and cleared her throat. "Now finish your sandwich and we'll see about a small walk or better yet a ride down to the lake in the golf cart."

"I had an idea tha` I might go back ta the bed and rest a while."

"Nope. You've had a good sleep and it's time for some fresh air. Besides," she added, "A little exercise is good for you. Get the blood flowing and good circulation is best for healing."

"I willna be gettin oot o` this then?"

"Nay." She smiled and bit into her ham and cheese once more. Then another thought popped into her head. "So you actually are a secret agent with the FBI."

"I've worked with several agencies o're the years."

"Yeah, like who?" She set her elbow on the table and rested her chin on her fist looking directly at him.

Donny looked at her then down at the array of medications she had set on the table. "Is one o` these fer pain?"

"Yes."

"I do'na like them. They make me fuzzy minded, and sleepy."

"That's Ok. They also help you to heal faster." She said and he looked at her with a smirk. "It's true! The pain meds relax your body allowing it to direct all your internal energy to the healing process. Without the pain meds your body tenses due to pain and can't heal nearly as quick-ly." She glanced over at him and found him staring at her. "What?"

"That sounded a wee bit rehearsed, lass. Would ye by chance own stock in the companies?"

Megan laughed. "No, I don't own stock. That was my Great Aunt Monie's line. I'm not surprised it sounds rehearsed. I've certainly heard her say it often enough. Aunt Monie was a nurse. A damned good one. And when Aunt Monie speaks, you don't argue. You believe. And she's right about the pain meds. Which is probably one of the reasons she was a damned good nurse." she looked down at the pills he was pushing around on the tabletop. "So take them." *He's not going to answer my question*, she realized. *At least not yet.*

"So how did your director know to call you here on the landline?" She asked to clear the silence.

"He's the FBI Director of Opps, he knows everything." Donny smiled.

They finished eating while trading stories about her work and his family in Scotland. As he spoke Megan became enthralled with the old-world sound of his voice, his accent, and the stories he told of his childhood. When they had eaten their fill, Megan cleared the table while Donny went to the bedroom to slide his feet into the Crocs. She helped him outside to the golf cart, and when he was ready, she got behind the wheel. Knowing that he would be sensitive about a bumpy ride, she realized she had to take it very slowly.

"It would probably be better for you to walk, but even if you made it as far as the lake, you probably wouldn't be able to make it back. The golf cart is better this time out." She said

As Donny sat down on the seat he noticed the massive white house up the rise on the other side of the lake road. He stared at the big house.

Why in bloody hell was she livin in tha` small biscuit box when she had tha` magnificent structure, he wondered to himself, or so he thought.

"Because I like the cottage." She said when she noticed his apparent fascination with the house. He turned to look at her, and she explained. "It's obvious that you wonder why with that big house I live in this little one. It's only me and Max. I don't need all that space. This way it's vacant whenever anyone wants to come and stay. They don't have to deal with my schedule or me if they don't want to. I don't have to be responsible for their meals or groceries or making up beds or washing sheets after they leave. They can come and go as they please, and there is plenty of room up there if they have kids or bring guests with them. Besides the cottage is where my family stayed when we were up here as kids. And my mother never really cared for the big house. She always preferred the cottage once my Dad finally got her down here to stay in it one summer. After that, she fell in love with the cozy little building."

Donny understood her reasoning, but he wasn't sure he could resist living in the old house. He looked at the grounds surrounding it. The big pine tree in the front yard and two gigantic silver maples in the backyard. They looked to be over a hundred years old. He smiled when he saw that there was a tire swing dangling from the branch of one of the massive Silver Maples.

Megan pulled the cart onto the red shale road that separated the big house from the cottage, and headed down toward the lake. Midway to the lake was a gate of sorts standing open and over the gate was a big sign with Megan's family name inscribed on it. He had also seen the name on the road sign coming in the night before, and on the barn when the car lights shone on it, just before Megan pulled up beside the cottage.

"Are ye afraid tha` people willna know who the place belongs to, lass?" he chuckled.

"Oh no. The signs have been there for as long as I can remember. There's really no reason to remove them. And anyway when I have to tell someone how to get here. I just tell them to go past the camp and they can't miss it. Our name is written on every flat surface available." She smiled.

Donny laughed with her and then let his gaze turn further down the road to the lake. Megan slowed the cart to a crawl and steered it between two large painted rocks. Then down the slope close to the shoreline and stopped. There was a cool gentle breeze blowing in off the water.

God almighty, Donny thought to himself, *this is breath takin*. He was greeted with the scent of fresh mountain air that carried the smell of newly cut grass, the unpolluted woods, and the surprising fresh clean water. Donny never realized the water had a scent until it was pleasantly carried to him. The breeze danced over the water and in tandem with the sun the lake sparkled like millions of diamonds happily twinkling away.

"Tis truly a beautiful place, Megan." He said quietly. The dock leading from the shoreline was long, wide, and carpeted.

"This is our swim area. No boats or wave runners or fishing allowed in this area. That dock further down is for boats and to fish from if you don't want to get in a boat." There was a rather eclectic assortment of director chairs, lounge chairs, and picnic tables scattered about the shore.

"Would you like to get out of the cart and sit on the shore for a while?" she offered, and they each chose chairs facing the water, but Donny didn't sit down right away.

"Ye picnic doon here then?" he questioned. "I noticed the tables there."

"Yep. We eat and cook down here, and usually on an afternoon like this the shore is full of relatives, kids. and grandkids. Don't know where everyone is today." She looked around. "Place looks kind of deserted and forlorn, doesn't it?"

"Yer tables are magenta and scarlet." He said. "Why? Are ye afraid people willna see them?" Donny asked, gesturing to the picnic tables..

"My mother is a member of the Red Hat Society, and every few years, she hosts a pot-luck lunch on the shore. Since this was her year to host the potluck we painted the tables for that, and they're not magenta and scarlet. They're plain old purple and red." She smiled as Donny walked over and looked at one of the tables.

"*Floozies?*" He read the name on the top of the table, and looked down at her.

"Yeah." Megan smiled. "Mother's chapter is the *Fireball Floozies*. They are a great bunch of gals, and they have a grand time together."

Donny chuckled to himself. *Floozies*, he thought, *I think me mam would like her mam.* "What are those two buildings down there?" He pointed to the tree line where a large, weathered wood shack stood up a little from the lake and next to it a much smaller white one.

"The white one is the spring house and the grey one is the vat. That's where we used to get our water during summer and winter. We put in a well several years ago. So, now the vat is only used for the garden hoses in the summer months. The water in there is ice cold. When we have parties down here we put the beer and anything else that we need kept just below freezing in the vat." She looked back at him and smiled. "Maybe when you're a little stronger, we can walk back to see them."

She smiled up at him. His green eyes were like deep pools. *Yummy,* she thought.

"Aye, lass. I donna think I am up fer tha` kind o` walkin yet." He tore his gaze from hers and scanned the area clearing his throat. "Ye've got a lot o` trees on the place." He said and cleared his throat again.

"There used to be a lot more, but they were never really looked after, and we lost a lot of them." She turned and took in the view. "Now we have a man who comes every spring to make sure that the limbs are sound and to trim the ones that need trimming."

"Sound thinkin. And those wee ones?"

Megan laughed. "My brothers and I wanted to bring back some trees so every few years we plant seedlings in hopes that they'll grow big and strong." She chuckled, "Most of them die off in the winter, but we keep trying."

"Ye cook doon here often?"

Megan followed his gaze to the two stone fire pits. "Yeah, this one," moving to the smaller of the two that consisted of a huge rock embedded in the ground with smaller field stones placed in a connecting circle in the center of the big rock, "is the oldest, and the one I use when I cook down here. My oldest brother did that when he was a kid. He has to rearrange the stones about every year."

"And this one?" Donny pointed to another equally large rock that had high walls of cinder block held firm with concrete mortar.

"That one was put up years later by some of the cousins. It works very well too, especially when we have big gatherings down here, like family reunions, but..."

"Ye prefer tha` one." Donny finished

"Aye." She mocked in fun and they both laughed and continued to stand staring at each other.

"Another field." Donny waved his arm to the left, but didn't take his eyes off her.

"Yes... Used to be one of the apple orchards." She said and was finally able to tear her eyes from his. "There aren't many fruit bearing trees left anymore. Apples used to be one of my great grandfather's cash crops. When my father was a kid they had a saddle horse named Rainy Day. But according to the stories she was a real knot head, and they used to have to chase her out of the apple orchard all the time."

"How many fields are there here?"

"Let me think," Mentally counting, "eight, not including the orchard."

"How large is this place, luv?" Donny asked slowly.

"Um, about three hundred-sixty-eight acres." She laughed at Donny's shocked and surprised expression.

"Our family home doesna sit on tha` much land, and tis the  home o` the Laird and Clan Chief."

"Laird and Clan Chief?" She ushered Donny to one of the lounging chairs to sit.

"Head of Clan Mackay." He explained as he gladly took the offered seat.

"Does your father hold that distinction?" Megan had always been interested in Scotland.

"Aye he did, but me father died four years ago."

"Oh, I'm so sorry."

"Ye didna know. Besides, we do'na use those terms anymore. But if we did me Mam wouldna."

"No?"

"Nay now the head of the family, the patriarch or matriarch holds that responsibility." He smiled thinking of his mam. *Oh how she would hate being called the Matriarch*, he thought, *ta her tha` meant she was old, and mama is far from old.*

"What are you thinking about?" she asked when she saw the smile play across his lips.

"Me mam."

"*Mam?* I thought only deep southerners called their mothers Mam."

"She doesna like it. But tha`s what we call her. Behind her back, mostly. She's an American, or used ta be."

"Really?" Megan was surprised although she didn't know why she should be.

"Aye. From Charlston, North Carolina. She still has a wee bit of a quaint accent. It gets thicker when she's nervous or hoppin` angry." He chuckled.

"I see." She smiled. "*She* has an accent."

"Aye."

"And it's *quaint.*"

"Aye."

They sat in silence watching the campers in the water across the lake. Some in row boats others in sail boats. There was a wave runner that Megan was sure was carrying one of the counselors. She glanced over to Donny who was watching too, as well as looking at what the scenery had to offer. The wind had died momentarily making the water still if not for the people in the water. The trees that lined the water's edge around the sixty-five-acre lake reflected off the water like a mirror, until the wave runner disturbed the image. Then he smiled as the waves made the lily pads dance on top of the water.

Megan watched the lilies too. She loved sitting down here on the shore. It was as if the water, wind, and lilies were all playing in a magical ballet. Everything was as it should be, moving in graceful unison for no other reason than to please whoever happened to be there to witness it.

The peaceful solitude was interrupted suddenly by a young man of about twenty-five. Tall and built very well, in Donny's opinion. He had brown hair and even features.

"Megan, I have to go to town to get some feed for Dolly and Steve. Do you need anything while I'm there?"

"Oh, hi Jack." Megan smiled at the young man. "I didn't hear you coming. We were watching the ballet." Joe's forehead furrowed and he looked at Megan like she had finally overworked herself and lost her sense of reason. "Never mind." She grinned. "No. Thanks though. I don't need a thing." She glanced at Donny and saw him speculating, and decided that it would be a good idea to introduce them. "Jack, this is Donny. He'll be staying with me for a little while to recover from surgery. Donny, this is Jack, he lives in the little cabin back in the top corner of the field above the house. He takes care of Dolly and Steve for me."

"Nice to meet you man." Jack smiled and held out his hand to shake Donny's.

"Same here," Donny smiled and took Jack's hand. "Who are Dolly and Steve?" he asked Megan.

"My horses. Since I have to be at the office all day Jack here was kind enough to move into the little cabin up there, and take care of them for me."

"Yeah it's a sweet deal. I get to be around the horses, and I get room and board. Can't beat that." Jack smiled. "Well I have to be getting on. It was nice to meet you, Donny. See you later, Megan." He started to walk away and stopped to turn back to Megan. "By the way, you better go in there and see your boy. He's getting pretty lonely. Only had me to look over the last few days."

"Thanks Jack," she chuckled. "I'll go and see him later this afternoon. And I might even take him out for a ride later." She waved as the young man walked away and looked back to Donny who was now staring at her. "What?"

"Steve?" Donny chuckled. "Ye named yer horse Steve?"

"Yeah, Steve. It's a pretty name." Her eyes twinkled with mirth.

" Mmm. I thought ye said there wasna anyone else livin on the farm?"

"Oh, well Jack hasn't been here very long, and I'm not the only one living on the farm. My parents built their retirement house in the corner of the Rye lot."

"How long ha` ye had Dolly and Steve?"

"A little over two years now. I got them from a rescue center in Texas."

"Ye rescued them, then?"

"Yeah, but the owner wasn't taking care of them or any of the enormity of other animals he had. Dolly and Steve were only a year old when I got them. They're both really sweet. But Steve and I took to each other right away. I'm the only one who rides him, generally, and whenever I take out Dolly he pouts for a while."

"I would assume tha` it's hard ta ride them both equally wi` only ye here."

"Well sometimes Jack and I will take them out and other times I have company. And my mother likes to ride Dolly when she is here." She looked up at the blue sky and the fluffy clouds rolling by in the breeze.

"Wha` kind o` company?" *Girlfriends,* he silently hoped.

"Friends from work, neighbors, and people I know from town."

"Would ye mind a personal question?"

"Nope."

"Do ye e'er take men on moon light rides though the fields?" he smiled devilishly, and his jade eyes twinkled.

"Oh, sure all the time. Sometimes we stay out all night and commune with nature for hours on end." She smiled. "Did that answer your question?"

"Tha` s sarcasm. Is it no?" He chuckled and she laughed along with him.

"Would you like to meet them?" she asked as she stood and stretched her back.

"The moonlight riders or the horses?"

"I keep all moonlight riders chained in the attic until I want them again." She declared and smiled. "Come on, I'll help you up."

"Aye, lass. I would enjoy seein yer horses, but I do'na think I'm much interested in meetin` the men ye've sequestered in yer attic. And I do'na think I am up fer a long  moonlit ride ta commune wi` nature just yet, although tis an interesting idea."

"Can't handle it, huh?" she teased.

"Wicked." Was all he said as he eased into the cart and braced for the ride to the barn.

Chapter Eight

When they reached the end of the lake road Megan stopped the golf cart and turned to Donny. "It's going to be a bit bumpy going across, so brace yourself." She eased the cart up over the storm ridge at the edge, then up onto the main loose red shale road. After the slow crossing, Megan pulled into the barnyard. She looked at Donny and chuckled. "You can open your eyes now."

"Jesus Mary and Joseph!" Donny breathed. "I ask ye again. Are ye sure ye're a doctor and no` a torture expert?"

"Yes," Megan chuckled. "I'm a doctor, but I'm not a roadmaster. I am sorry though. Are you alright?"

"I wish ye dinna keep askin me tha` ." He looked up at the weathered wood barn in front of them. "Are they in there then?"

"No, that's the horse barn. I have the horses in the old hay barn." She nodded to the left and following her gaze, Donny saw the massive gray weathered building built into the slight hill in the middle of the barnyard.

"Nice barn." He said. "Exactly why," he motioned to the weathered wood structure sitting closer to the road, "if tha` s the horse barn, do ye keep the horses in the hay barn?"

Megan chuckled. "Well, it has been a long time since we've had any livestock here. My Dad had a horse when he was young, but even Rainy Day was boarded in the winter. After my great grandfather died, my great uncle ran the dairy for a while, but eventually all the cattle and livestock were sold. Nobody was really interested in farming. My grandfather had a job in the city and my great uncle married and he and his family moved to Kansas. There was really nobody to farm the land anymore. My grandfather would be here weekends in the summer or for the holidays. After he retired, he spent the summers here and my mother looked after him. The horse barn became basically a storage barn. If I had wanted to put the horses in that barn it would have taken me months just to clear out all of the tools, tractor equipment, boats, golf carts, snowmobiles..."

"I ken get the picture." Donny laughed. "So, the hay barn became home ta yer horses."

"Yeah, pretty much. It used to be the cow barn."

"Are ye sure ye know which building is which?" he asked.

Megan laughed. "Here, I'll show you. Can you do a little walking?"

"When I canna keep up, I'll let ye know."

She drove across the barnyard and stopped the cart on the grade at a small doorway. They got off the cart and she led him into the interior of the barn cut into the side of the hill.

"This is where the milking was done. See those long troughs in the floor? Those are the 'drops'. They would bring the cows in from the pasture and line them up at those posts. Head-in parking so to speak, and the troughs were at the rear of the cows so that if the cows had to..." She waved her hands toward the evenly cut ditches in the concrete floor. "eliminate... While they were being milked..."

"Aye, I get the picture." Donny held up his hand, indicating that she needn't go further with her explanation.

"My grandfather said he hated to clean out the drops when he was a kid."

"I canna say I blame him."

They walked the length of the long room and then came to a short set of steps. She turned questioningly to Donny.

"I'm fine." He said and they climbed the few steps which brought them into the main part of the large structure.

"And this is where the hay was kept." She said, holding her arms out wide. This area had three levels. To the right was an old wooden ladder going up to the loft where Donny could see bales of straw stacked neatly a few feet from the edge of the drop-off to the main floor. In the center of the main area was a massive mound of loose hay. A thick hemp rope hung from the ceiling over the mound and draped up into another loft opposite containing loose hay and a few feet lower than the loft containing the straw bales. She indicated the rope. "We used to swing down from the loft on that, and land in the hay-mound when I was a kid. My mother hated that. She was always afraid we'd break our necks."

"I bet ye were good at it." Donny grinned at her.

"What-da-ya mean 'good?' I was a great hay-mound jumper." She laughed. "And a lot more graceful at it than my brothers." She turned to her left and waved at the two horses standing in their stalls under the loose hay loft. "This is Dolly and Steve."

"Who is who?" Donny asked. *I canna believe the lass named her horse Steve.*

"This one is Dolly." Megan indicated a sleek black and white mare, with a white wide stripe going down her forehead and white feathers around her lower legs covering her hooves. She was roughly fourteen hands tall with a muscular build. Her mane and tail were long, thick flowing locks of black and white like her coat. Dolly whinnied as Megan moved closer to rub her snout. "According to the vet she is an Irish Cob, or a Gypsy Vanner. They are basically the same thing. These guys are kinda like the mountain lion or puma. Same animal, but known all over the country by different labels. When I got them my mother fell for her right away. She was smaller then, and her mane and tail were still short, so she looked like a dairy cow." She looked back at Donny. "Mom loves dairy cows, so she named her and declared that Dolly was hers."

"She's a verra pretty filly." Donny rubbed her snout. "So, this one must be Steve." Donny glanced over at the midnight black stallion in the next stall. Steve is seventeen and a half hands tall with a very muscular build, but still graceful and almost regal in stature. His coat was glistening black with feathers on his lower legs like Dolly, only his were black. His mane and tail, like Dolly's, were also long thick flowing locks. "I ne're had much need fer horses, but I can say tha` this one looks ta be a magnificent beast." Donny moved to get a better look at the black horse. "He's black from nose to tail, ye might have named him Ghost fer he'd ne're be seen after dark."

"Yeah," Megan cooed as she walked to Steve. "This is my baby boy. How you doing big fella?"

Big fella is right, Donny thought, he looked massive next to Dolly. "What kind o` horse is he?"

"Not really sure, but he looks like he might be a Friesian. The vet took blood to be sure."

"A what?" Donny cocked his eyebrow.

"Did you ever see the movie Zorro with Antonio Banderas, Anthony Hopkins, and Catharine Zeta-Jones?"

"Aye."

"Do you remember the horse that Zorro rode in the movie?"

"Aye."

"Well, that was a Friesian named Ariaan. Now granted that particular horse was chosen because he wasn't very big. If they had used a bigger Friesian Banderas would have been dwarfed on the screen." She shrugged her shoulders. "Anyway, after some research I think that's what Steve is. Or some sort of mix. Beautiful isn't he?"

"Aye, he is. Ye're a wee thing yerself, Megan. How do ye get astride o` him? He's a massive beast."

"Easy when he's saddled. Whenever I ride him bareback I need to use a stool." She smiled.

"Ye said hay barn, so I assume tha` the horse stalls were built in later years."

"Yeah, my brothers and I built them after I decided to have some horses here with me. When I contacted the rescue center in Texas, they came to make sure that what we had here was correct for the two of them. However, when they got here, they told me that the stalls were too small. Dolly's needed to be a little bigger. All we really had to do was move the wall over about six feet. The height was fine. However, Steve's had to be rebuilt. It was too small and too short. So, we raised the ceiling above his stall and expanded it by ten feet."

"And how does Dolly feel aboot being second best wi` ye?" he asked as Dolly nuzzled his neck demanding attention.

"Oh, don't let her fool you." She chuckled "She gets lots of attention. She loves men as you can tell, and when my nieces and nephews come to visit she is the one they all go to. And when my mother comes down to ride with me, she takes Dolly. She is gentler than Steve and has a better temperament."

"Steve's nay a gentle soul?" he laughed as Dolly nipped at Donny's sleeve when he tried to back away.

"He is, but he's a wild ride and I love it. Where Dolly might want to walk he wants to run. When Dolly wants to canter Steve wants to race. He's fast and powerful. However, when she wants to or needs to, Dolly can run like the wind."

"How does Max get along wi` them?"

"Steve finds him a nuisance, and I think he's a little jealous of my puppy. But Dolly likes him. When we let them out in the pasture to roam, Max will run and hang around with her."

"Ha` ye ever thought o` gettin more?"

"I might someday, my Dad likes to ride sometimes, so I might for that reason. But I think two is more than enough for now. Besides, if I had more, then, I would need to hire more help, and I don't need a whole lot of people mucking around the place." She smiled but when she glanced at Donny, she noticed he was starting to droop a little. "How about we get you into the house, and off your feet and—"

"Ye said yer mother comes ta ride wi` ye." Donny was ignoring her concern. He liked it when they were out of the house and talking about the land. He was getting tired of being a patient. "And she and yer father live here on the farm close by?"

"Yes, remember, I said they built a new house at the corner of the Rye lot." Megan's face fell. "Oh shit." She sighed.

"Wha`?"

"I not only need to explain you to my brother, but my mother and father as well. And If Nathan told me he was coming, he would no doubt have told my parents."

"Which means they will be here as well." Donny smiled.

"This isn't funny," she glared, "I don't like lying to my brother and I hate, I repeat HATE, doing it to my mother and father."

"Ok lass, let me ask ye." He began, "How will yer family feel aboot ye housin` a man wi` a gunshot wound? A bloke ye dinna know from Adam, who as best as ye can tell works wi` shady characters?" The question brought a frown to Megan's face and Donny instantly regretted; he'd asked the question *Ye silly ass,* he thought. *How di ye supposed her family will feel aboot it?* He turned the question on himself.

"I could omit the not knowing you part, and tell them the rest." Before he could protest she put up her hand and went on. "Donny you said yourself the case was closed and—"

"Megan—"

"No, Donny please, listen. I didn't know you. I took you to the hospital and offered you a place to stay and recover with little or no questions asked." Donny raised his eyebrows, but said nothing. "All I am asking is that I don't have to lie to my family about it."

"Aye, ye've been verra generous. I dinna know of many who would ha` done the same. So how will ye get around the no knowin` me before-hand?" Donny could already see he was losing the battle.

"My family doesn't know everyone I'm acquainted with, but if I can think of a way to avoid the question from the beginning, I would rather, as opposed to an outright lie."

"And if ye canna?" Donny was getting tired.

"I won't lie." She stood straight and gave him a look that said, *go ahead, try and make me back down.*

"God ye're a stubborn lass." Donny smiled.

"Yes I am. Come on. Let's go back. You're tired. You're starting to fold in half." She gave Steve and Dolly both a peck on their noses and ushered Donny back to the golf cart.

They made the short ride back to the cottage in silence. Although she knew he would never admit it, Donny was tired and more than likely in some pain. Once back inside Donny sat on the sofa while Megan got his medication and some water.

"Here take this I need to take Max out. Will you be alright here by yourself for a little bit?" she asked.

"Aye lass I will. I think I'm gonna lie doon fer a while." Donny yawned.

"Do you want some help getting to bed?"

"Nay luv, I can make it on me own. Go wi` Max." He smiled.

"Ok, Come on, Baby." She called to her dog.

Donny smiled as he watched Max trot after her. He sat on the sofa for a few minutes knowing it was going to hurt like the very devil to get up. He could hear Megan's laugh as she romped with the big dog in the back yard. With effort he rose and shuffled to the bedroom. *The lass wasna wrong when she said I was startin` ta fold in half*, he thought as he slowly made his way to the side of the bed. He sat on the edge of the mattress and eased himself back onto the pillows. Raising his legs onto the bed was the hardest part. "Bloody, drug addicted bastard." He mumbled. He blew out his breath and closed his eyes trying to relax against the pillows. Behind his lids, Megan's image breezed into his head and a smile played across his lips as he mentally ticked off the things he was learning about her. *She's a pretty lass.* He thought. *Pretty stubborn! Strong, but carin` and willin` ta help. I was right about that. She has a great love fer her family and this land. She also isna afraid or* *apprehensive aboot standin up fer herself.* He liked that, and so would his family. *Strange,* he thought, *no since Arabella ha` I a thought aboot what me family would think o` a woman.* Finally, his thoughts became fuzzy, and he drifted into sleep.

Max and Megan stayed outside for about an hour. When they came back into the cottage. Max wasted no time resuming his post on the floor beside Donny's bed. Megan looked in and saw Donny was sleeping soundly and decided to check her email and poke around on the internet for a while.

An hour later, Megan was nearly finished with the computer. She had received an email from Jess asking what was happening with her houseguest/patient. Staring at the message for several minutes, not sure how to respond, she finally chose not to respond at all until she talked to the patient himself. What *could* she say? She had been considering hers and Donny's situation in reference to her family while she was outside with Max and thought she had a solution. But of course, couldn't use her idea until she had discussed it with Donny. He wouldn't like it. She knew that already, but it made perfect sense, and it was a lot closer to the truth than that hair brained real estate story he had come up with, which was total fiction. She looked at the clock and realized it was time for dinner. When she walked into the main room she glanced into Donny's room and saw he was propped up on pillows, and that Max was now *on* the bed enjoying Donny's attention.

"Why didn't you tell me you were awake?" She smiled as she walked into the room.

"I could hear ye peckin` away at the computer, and decided ta occupy meself wi` Max here." He ruffled the dog's ears and smiled. "We're bondin`."

"How ya feeling?" She smiled.

"Better. Refreshed."

"Good. Hungry?" She was fidgeting and Donny wondered why.

"Aye. Are ye alright Megan?"

"I'm ok." She loved the way her name sounded coming from his lips. "What would you like for dinner?"

"Megan." He nudged the dog off the bed, eased himself out of bed and closed the distance between them, never taking his eyes off hers. He knew something was wrong; he wasn't sure how he knew, but he did. "Ye've got something on yer mind. What is it?"

"Nothing." She smiled

"Ok," *I'll wait*, he thought. "How aboot breakfast?"

"Really?" she smiled, "I thought my family was the only people who liked to have breakfast for dinner. Sounds good." She turned and went to the kitchen to pull eggs from the fridge. Donny settled himself in the rattan chair across from the dining table and watched Megan move about in the small galley kitchen. "Bacon or sausage?" she asked.

"Sausage." There was a tension about her that hadn't been there earlier in the day. He wanted to get her talking but wasn't sure how to go about it. "So, tell me aboot yer ex. Were ye wi` him long?" It was the first thing that popped into his head. *Stupid arse,* he cursed himself. *In the brain, oot the mouth. Bloody damned pills!*

"Uh," she stammered. She dropped the sausage in the pan, drizzled some water in and covered the pan with a glass lid. "That was blunt."

"Sorry. Was tha` tae personal then?"

"No. Yes. Not really I guess. Just caught me off guard that's all. We were together for three years." She cleared her throat. "Have you been with anyone since Arabella?"

"Equally personal, luv." He laughed.

"My turn." Even though her back was to him, Donny knew she was smiling.

"Touche, and the answer is nay. No seriously anyway."

"You have not had a woman in your life since you were nineteen?" she turned to face him.

"I didna say I hadna had them in me life. They just ne'er stay long."

"Do you ever think about settling down and having a family of your own?"

"Like I said, after Bella died, it wasna somethin` I thought aboot much. But in recent months... Aye. I admit, I ha` thought aboot it."

"Do you like kids?" By now the sausage was sizzling, and she was cracking eggs in a bowl. "What do you like in your eggs?"

"Cheese." *This is a strange conversation*, Donny thought. "Why do ye ask?"

"So, I can make them the way you like them."

"Nay. No the eggs lass." He chuckled. "Why the question aboot kids?"

"Just trying to get to know you. So do you?"

"Do I what?"

"Like kids?" she laughed.

"Ah, well I havena been around' them enough ta know the answer. Do ye?"

"If I didn't, I wouldn't have put in a day care center above the office." She smiled over at him. "Yes. I like children. My brothers have children and I'm crazy about them."

Megan finished preparing the meal, filled two plates, and placed them on the table. "Do you want to sit at the table, or would you rather stay where you are?" she looked at him and their eyes locked. Neither of them spoke for several seconds.

"Nay. I'll sit at the table wi` ye." He rose and moved to the dining table, and they ate in silence for a few minutes.

"Are ye workin` tomorrow?"

"Yeah, I'll come back here when we close for lunch. Will you be alright here alone?"

"Och sure. Do'na worry aboot me, lass."

"I need to tell you something." She fairly flushed the statement out of her mouth. And concern was evident in her expression.

"Aye?"

"Well," she blew out her breath in a whoosh, "after I left you at the hospital that first morning, I came back to the office, and ...confided in a colleague." She confessed. "A friend really. About what had happened." When he raised his eyebrow she went on. "I didn't tell her you were FBI. I went with the Sam Watson story."

"I have a feelin` there's a *'but'* commin`."

"Maybe. She sent me an email, and wants to know what has happened with you. I had told her that I agreed to have you stay with me, so, naturally, she's concerned..."

"And ye want ta know what ta tell her?" he sighed. "Is this what was pullin` at ye before?"

"In a way."

"Tell her the truth."

"The whole truth?"

"And nothin` but the truth." He smiled, "Since ye've already told her aboot finding me behind yer automobile, I assume wi` a gunshot wound." e looked at her and she nodded. "Well, then she's already aware tha` ye didna know me, so go ahead and bring her inta the loop."

"You wouldn't mind?"

"Nay luv, I wouldna." Donny put down his fork and leaned forward locking eyes with her and resting his hand on top of hers. "She's a physician, aye?" Again Megan nodded. "Well then, she knows how ta keep private information private. Listen luv, I know this hasna been easy for ye, I ha` put ye in a difficult position." He returned his attention back to his plate and continued. "As long as yer family is goin ta know the truth, ye might as well be honest wi` yer friend and colleague. The case *has been* closed, but as far as the public is concerned Sam Watson is a criminal. I canna use the alias any longer. I ha` ta caution ye though, she needs ta understand; she canna let anyone know tha` Sam and I are one and the same."

Megan sighed with relief and let out a nervous laugh. "Good, because while I was out with Max I was thinking about my parents, and came up with a story quite different from the real estate thing. However, I was reluctant to suggest it to you."

Donny grinned. And rested his chin in the palm of his hand looking at her. "And wha` was tha, lass?"

"There's no need to even discuss it now."

"Mayhap there isna, but ye may as well tell me and I will tell ye wha`s wrong wi` it. And it will give me an insight inta yer imagination. Think o` it as entertainin` yer houseguest."

"Well, it was simple really and basically the truth. You were mistakenly shot by an out of season hunter, while visiting your brother the State Trooper. He works all day; the hospital was short on beds...and I...agreed..." her voice trailed into silence as she observed the changes in Donny's expression.

His grin faded quickly at the mention of his brother and a dark cloud covered his face. He straightened himself in the chair as Megan stared at him. "No," was all he said.

Megan picked up her glass of juice and sipped from it. "Yeah, I didn't think you'd like it." Now there was an unspoken tension between them that hadn't been there before. "I'll make sure Jess understands, and my family as well. Thank you, Donny."

They finished with dinner in comparative silence. What little conversation there was, was stiff and forced. When they had finished eating, Donny offered to do the dishes. She thanked him but suggested he rest on the sofa instead. He wanted to be angry with her for suggesting the use of his brother to explain why she had agreed to house a total stranger, but he couldn't. The story she had dreamed up might do just that. As she said, the facts were essentially the truth, if you discount the fictitious errant hunter. His brother's work schedule gave her a plausible explanation for his being in her house, and being the visiting brother of a State Trooper, gave him a measure of respectability, which apparently would appease her family. *All in all*, he thought, *it wasna a bad story. I've no reason ta be angry wi` the lass.* And suddenly he was ashamed of his silence and attitude through the remainder of the meal. *Bloody pig-headed oaf!* he thought. She was finishing up the dishes when he appeared at her side. He took her wet sudsy hand in his.

"I'm sorra aboot me behavior, lass," he said. She looked down at her hand in his and then raised her eyes to his face. "I've put ye in an untenable position and added restrictions ta what ye can tell yer family and friends. Then I've acted like, in the American vernacular, a jerk. And... I'm sorra."

Wow! Megan thought. "You don't need to apologize to me, Donny." She withdrew her hand from his and rinsed it under the running water then reached for a towel. "I understand your need for secrecy concerning your undercover work." She turned to him again and looked up into his eyes. "I'm the one who should apologize to you really. I shouldn't have tried to include your brother in my reasoning." She smiled sheep-ishly. "It just seemed like an easy way to explain to everyone why you're staying with me, without...explaining why you're staying with me." She grinned then and so did he. And at that moment, he realized he *liked* her. *Really* liked her. She was funny, loyal, responsible, and sexy as hell. "*Bloody hell.*"

"Excuse me?" she frowned.

"Wha?" he said, still holding her eyes with his. "Oh, nothin. Ye may as well tell yer family tha` I work with the FBI. The case here is mostly closed and done wi` anyway. Do ye accept me apology, luv?"

"Of course." She smiled and it struck Donny; how odd it was going to feel without her when she went to work the next day. He turned and went back to the sofa. *Does she take the big dog to work with her?*

"Hey, do you want me to leave Max here with you while I'm at the office?" Megan sang out over the sound of running water. Donny was stunned, it was as though she were reading his mind.

"Funny ye should ask, I was just wonderin if ye were planning` ta take the beast wi` ye or no." He smiled. *Unnerving*, he thought.

"Very often I do, but I can leave him here if you'd like me to. It would mean you'd have to take him out. A couple times during the day." She turned off the water and moved to the stove to wipe it clean with a disposable tissue she pulled from a plastic tube-like container. Then rinsed her hands again and dried them before applying lotion from a pump bottle on the counter. *She moves with grace and efficiency*, he thought, as she came toward him. "Do you think you'll be up to that?"

"Does he need ta have a leash on him?"

"Nah, you can just open the door and let him out. He'll do what he needs to do and then come back in." She sat in her deep overstuffed chair next to the big window and pulled her feet under her.

"What time do ye think yer brother and his family will arrive?" *She looks so cute in tha` position*, he mused. *Cute?* That was the second time that word had popped into his head in the last half hour. It was not a word normally in his vocabulary.

"Don't know, they're flying. Why?"

"Would they no find it strange fer Max be here alone?"

"Oh." *Not nearly as strange as finding a man in my house*, she thought. "No. They know he doesn't come with me every day." *And they'll find out soon enough that Max wasn't here alone*, she thought.

"Then I wouldna mind havin` him here wi` me. He's a fine bonnie companion." He looked around the room and saw all sorts of DVD's. "Would ye like ta watch a movie?"

"Sure, anything in particular?" she asked as she stood and walked over to one of the many shelves holding her DVD's

"Nothin` tae funny." He smiled, pressing a hand lightly to his side and Megan laughed.

She found a movie that they both agreed on and popped it in. When the film was over, Megan looked over and found Donny fast asleep. She picked up the remote and turned off the player and the TV, then leaned down to wake Donny. When he opened his eyes she once again was taken aback at what a deep jade color they were. *Fantastic eyes,* she thought.

"Let's get you into bed." She whispered. "Max get down." Max groaned as he lifted his head from Donny's lap and lumbered off the sofa.

When Donny was standing upright, she went ahead to turn down his covers. Donny yawned and followed to sit on the edge of the bed.

"Donny?"

"Aye." He yawned again.

"I'll need to check your dressings." She said almost apologetically.

"Wha?" Now he was awake.

"I'm sorry," she smiled, "but I do have to check the dressings."

"Now?" he moaned.

"Yeah. It'll only take a minute. I should have done it before the movie." She sat down next to him on the bed and lifted his shirt. "I have to change these."

"The devil ye do!" He growled.

Megan chuckled on her way to retrieve the replacement bandages. After some grunting, the bandages were changed and Donny was settled beneath the covers, wondering if he would ever get back to sleep.

"Wha` time do ye leave in the morn?" he asked before she got to the door.

"Seven. You get some sleep, and I'll see you at lunch."

They said their goodnights and Megan went to her room. She wasn't aware until then how tired she was. Even though he really didn't require a lot of care, being responsible for another human being in her home wasn't what she was accustomed to. She checked her alarm, and climbed into bed pulling the comforter over her. She had to admit, she had enjoyed his company. *He's got a wicked sense of humor*, she thought. *And he's definitely easy to look at,* she smiled. Before sleep found her she acknowledged that it had really been a very pleasant day.

Chapter Nine

The following morning Megan woke with her alarm clock. After she was dressed she took Max out for a short walk, and made sure his food and water dishes were full. With a quick look in on Donny she grabbed her keys and headed out to her SUV. As she started to reach for her cell phone, she realized she had left her purse in the cottage. She was halfway to the door when she was met by Donny and her purse.

"Good morning." She smiled.

"Ye forgot somethin`." Donny said as he handed over her purse.

"Yes, thank you. Did I wake you up?"

"Nay lass. I was awake when yer alarm went off, but I dinna want ta open me eyes."

"I know that feeling," she chuckled. "You should go back to bed and try to sleep some more."

"Do ye realize I ha` had more sleep in the last few days than I ha` in the last ten years?" He complained.

"Are you telling me that you're bored?" *Typical reaction*, she mused.

"Nay no` yet, just restless. I do'na know how ta sit still fer any length o` time."

"Yeah? Well, sorry to hear that, however," she sighed, "you're going to have to suffer along through your recovery period, just laying around, doing absolutely nothing for a little while. I feel so sorry for you." She whined.

"Tis is sarcasm, aye?" he smiled.

"You got it. Now I have to go to work, and you need to go back to bed." She patted his arm and smiled. "See you at lunch, Donny old *lad*." And with that she turned on her heel, climbed into her Wagoneer and drove away up the road.

Donny smiled as he reentered the cottage. When he closed and locked the inner door he turned and surveyed the empty house, save the dog, and sighed.

"Wha` the hell am I supposed ta do now?" he asked the big dog now sitting at attention at Donny's feet. "I do'na know how ta sit and do absolutely nothin`. Wha` do ye do all day here by yerself? But then most o` the time, she says, ye get ta go wi` her." While he stood wondering what to do with himself, the phone rang, and he wondered if he should answer it. "Och wha` the hell." He walked to the phone, lifted the receiver, and listened.

"Donny?" Megan asked.

"Aye, do ye miss me already lass?"

"Ha ha. Listen I'm here at the office and it occurred to me that you should have the number here in case you need to speak to me."

"Thank ye luv, let me get a pen and paper." Donny wrote as she spouted off the office phone number. "By the way do ye want me ta be answerin` the phone should it ring?"

"Um," she thought for a moment. "No, I don't think that would be a good idea. Just let the voicemail get it and I'll check the messages when I get home. Oh wait! Will any of your people be calling?"

"I do'na believe so, but if they did they would use me cell first. It's a good thing yer charger fit, or the blasted thing would be dead now." He chuckled.

"Well, we'll have to get you one of your own soon. Listen, I need to get to work, I'll call you later in the morning to see how you're getting along."

"If ye do'na want me ta answer the phone luv, how do ye propose that ye ask me anything?"

"Oh yeah," she laughed. "Give me your cell number and I'll call that." Once he gave her the number she needed they said their goodbyes and hung up.

Megan sat in her office for a moment before going to the front reception area for her first cup of coffee. Liz was, as always, the first to arrive and gave Megan her schedule for the day.

"I have a lady I know coming in to interview for my job while I'm out on leave. Her name is Hannah Brown. I know that you didn't initially want to hire someone we all knew, but she has worked in this field for a long time and just retired." Liz explained as she settled into her chair.

"If she's just retired, why in the world would she want to come and work here?" Megan wondered.

"Jimmy and I were at her house last night for dinner, and I told her how we have been having trouble getting someone to fill in for me. So she said that if it were only temporary; she would be more than happy to come in and meet with you." She explained.

"What time?" Megan smiled as she looked over the concise scheduling of her docket. *I will never stop being impressed by this girl*, she thought to herself.

"At lunch while the office is closed. I thought that after we meet with her we could both go to the corners for a bite to eat."

"Lunch?" Megan stopped looking at her files and glanced down at Liz who was going through the overnight faxes and jotting down voicemail messages for the staff. "Lunch today?'

"Yes, why is something wrong?" Liz looked up from her multitasking. "Did you have plans for lunch?"

"Not really, I was planning on going home today." Not knowing whether she was ready to announce to the world that she had a houseguest, she decided not to elaborate.

"Oh, to let Max out? I noticed he didn't come with you today." Liz asked as she made notes to the other doctors.

"And other things." Megan answered soberly. She watched as Liz listened to the voicemail, jotted down notes to Megan's colleagues and set up each doc's docket for the day. *The girl was remarkable. How were they going to survive without her? Well I can't miss the interview*, she thought, *especially if Liz thinks this woman will do well. I'll have to call Donny and let him know I can't go home at lunch. Funny*, she thought, *I was actually looking forward to seeing him and having lunch together.*

"Hello girls." Jess sang out as she walked through the front door. "I smell coffee. Good I need it."

"Rough night, Jess?" Megan chuckled as she moved to clear the path to the coffee pot.

"You wouldn't believe it," she sighed. "The baby kept Nancy and I up just about all night." Regardless of how hot the liquid was Jess downed the whole cup and poured another.

"I will never understand why you didn't take a small leave when you guys brought Christina home from the agency." Megan challenged in good nature.

"Because Nancy wants to be home with her, and she wants me out of the way." She laughed, "I guess she wants me to take on the role of obligatory *father* figure. At the office, bringing in the bucks, but out of her hair." Shaking her head and chuckling. "Did you get my email Meggie?"

"Yeah I got it, but I didn't have time to answer." Megan looked back to Liz, "My first patient isn't until nine, so I'll be in my office working if you need me."

"Ok, with only you and Jess here today do you want me to allow last minute appointments?" Liz responded.

"As long as we have the time to see them, then let them come." Megan smiled and went down the hall to her office.

Megan barely had her tush in the chair behind her desk before the door to her office creaked open and Jess popped her head in. "How about answering it now?" She smiled as she crossed the room and sat in the chair across from the desk.

"Answer what?" Of course, she knew what Jess wanted, but Megan wasn't as ready as she thought she would be to reveal Donny's true identity. However, she also realized she had to tell Jess what was what, before her friend told the world that Megan was housing Sam Watson. As Donny had said the case was basically closed, but you never know if the bad guys have contacts on the outside.

"My email, of course! What the hell do you think? Did you end up bringing this Sam guy back to your house to heal?"

"Yes I did. I picked him up at Memorial the other night." She held up her hand to hold off the oncoming argument from her friend. "Listen there is something I have to tell you. Did you by any chance hear on the news about the arrest in Scranton of fifteen men and women in connection with the kidnapping of twelve young girls?"

"Yeah, as a matter of fact. Yesterday. Frightening, isn't it? White slavery! UGH!" she shivered. "Why?" Jess shot out of her chair. "Megan you're not harboring one of those guys are you?"

"Not exactly, no. And keep your voice down. Please sit and let me explain." Megan waited until Jess was seated and began. "First thing I need to tell you is that Sam Watson is the man I took to the hospital."

"And then took him home with you?" Jess grumbled.

"The very same." Megan ignored her friend's obvious disapproval and went on. "His real name is Donovan Mackay, and he was working with the FBI undercover on that case. Somehow, I still don't know how, he was shot and ended up at my place. The rest you know."

"I can't believe it." Jess breathed.

"Jess there's more." She leaned forward on her desk. "This is extremely important; did you tell anyone about Sam Watson?"

"No, why?"

"Not Nancy?"

"No, I said you had an early emergency and didn't get to the office until later, but the baby was fussy, and Nance was frazzled, and we never got any further into your emergency than that."

"Good, because Donny is an undercover agent with... somebody who occasionally works for the FBI and if it got out that Donovan Mackay and Sam Watson were the same person, it could be... well..." Megan didn't want Jess to worry more than she already was, but she needed Jess to understand the danger should the two names become synonymous with each other. "It could be dangerous." She explained.

"I don't understand." Jess leaned back in her chair.

"There's no real way of knowing whether the people who were arrested have contacts still in the area, and if they do and the bad guys learn Donny was working with the FBI as Sam Watson then the bad guys could come after him."

"Megan, do you realize; that means those slime bags would come after anyone connected with him? That means you! What were you thinking?" Jess was even more concerned now than she was an hour ago.

"I understand that, but," she took a breath, "the case has been closed. It apparently was a huge operation both in this country and in Europe. They arrested everyone involved in the states and the ones overseas. I don't really think I'm in any real danger. But I don't want you to let anyone know that Donny and Sam are the same person. Ok?"

"When did you know all this and why didn't you tell me this before?" Jess demanded.

"Because I didn't have all the facts before, and because as far as I knew the case wasn't closed yet, and..." she hesitated. "And because Donny entrusted me to keep the secret." She finished.

"He entrusted you, a total stranger, to keep *his* secret?" Jess bellowed.

"Jess, keep your voice down!" Megan snapped. "You have made your opinion clear. Now, I need your word not to say anything about Sam Watson's identity. Believe me I'm fine. And perfectly safe. Hell, I have an FBI agent staying in my house; you can't get much safer than that." She reiterated.

"Safe! Someone shot him! How the hell is he safe?" Jess threw up her hands. "Ok, ok. I won't say anything." She took a deep breath and conceded. "And I suppose you're right. He's a fed so you probably can't get much safer than that, although I might point out once again, that the guy managed to get himself shot to shit!" At Megan's glare, Jess relented. "Ok, I'm just worried about you honey."

"I know," she sighed.

"Have you told Emma and Patrick about this yet?"

"No, but it won't be long now." Megan groaned.

"How's that?"

"Nathan and his family are arriving today, and you know that when the children make an appearance, the grandparents are Johnny on the spot."

"Holy shit!" Jess chuckled, "Nathan and his family too, huh? What are you gonna tell them?" Oh, how she wished she could be a fly on the wall for *that* explanation.

"The truth. I can't say he's Sam Watson for the reasons I've explained to you. So the truth is what I'm going to tell them." She winced as she thought of her mother's reaction to her choices.

"And this is ok with the agent... what? Mackay?"

"Yes. We talked about it last evening."

"Is he good looking?" Jess wondered.

"Why? Are you thinking of switching sides?" Megan laughed.

"Not on your life." She smiled, "So, is he?"

"Good looking?" Megan smiled as she thought of Donny, "Oh yeah. Very."

"Then Emma might not be as angry as you think."

"Why do you say that?" Megan narrowed her eyes at her friend.

"He's single, I take it?"

"Yeah?" She was now suspicious.

"Well, he's gainfully employed, single, good-looking, and where is he from?" she smiled.

"Scotland." Megan informed her.

"Oooooohooooo! Scotland!" Jess grinned like the Cheshire cat. "Then he'll also have a devilishly seductive accent. Emma might find him a real catch." Jess wiggled her eyebrows as she watched her friend's cheeks become pink. Jess looked at her watch "I'd better go, my first patient should be arriving any minute." She rose from her seat chuckling as she sailed out of the private office.

Megan was left glaring at the closed door while wondering exactly what her family's reaction to Donny would be. Especially her mother. "I'll find out soon enough." She grimaced as she picked up her phone to inform Donny of the change in lunch plans.

"Tha` s ta bad." Donny sighed.

"I'm sorry about it, but I really need to take this meeting. I have to find a qualified person to fill in for Liz before she goes into labor." She explained. Megan was surprised at how actually disappointed she was that she wasn't going home for lunch. After spending the day with Donny, she found him to be a warm, gentle person. Stubborn, but friendly with a seductive sense of humor. Yeah, she was sorry she would miss having lunch with him.

"Do'na concern yerself, lass. Ye have responsibilities. And I understand tha` ." He was silent for a moment. "When does the office close fer the night?"

"We're open until seven tonight." She frowned, "Will you be alright there alone until then?"

"Och sure," he said. "Do'na worry aboot me, lass. I can find things ta keep meself occupied." He rolled his eyes at the ceiling wondering what the hell he was going to do for twelve hours to keep from being bored stiff.

"You sure?" She chuckled, "I can practically hear you cringing and rolling your eyes skyward."

"I'll be fine." He assured her. Although he was disappointed she wouldn't be with him for a short while in the middle of the day. He knew she had a practice to run and responsibilities to take care of.

"If I have any time during the day I'll try to make it home and check on you." *This is bizarre,* she thought. *Do I want to see him because he's a patient, or just because?* She wondered.

"Are ye worried aboot me luv?" He smiled, before she could answer, Donny heard a woman tell Megan that her patient had arrived. "Ye go ta work lass, I'll be fine."

"Ok, I'll see you later." She replaced the receiver and collected her thoughts before walking to the exam room to greet her patient.

She always dreaded these kinds of appointments. Telling a mother and daughter that the mother was suffering early-stage dementia was never easy. Thankfully, Megan knew the mother and daughter both had a good idea of what was coming. The daughter had noticed that some things with her mother were off and asked for a mini mental test. The results of the mini test proved to Megan that the mother should have the full battery of testing done and those results were in line with the suggestions from the neuropsychiatrist .

"Good morning ladies." She smiled as she walked into the exam room. "Why don't we go to my office where we'll be more comfortable, and have a chat?" The three went to Megan's office and took their seats. "Ok, how are you Mrs. Blandings?" Megan smiled. Patty Cromwell's mother was in her early seventies; however, you would think the two women were sisters rather than mother and daughter. Mrs. Blandings didn't look much older than her daughter.

"Fine, I guess." She smiled. "Just want to know what's going on with my silly brain." She chuckled.

"And how are you doing Patty?" addressing the daughter. She was in her early fifties, tall, slender, and very striking.

"Ok I guess." She knew of course that there was something wrong with her mother and given the results of the mini test she also figured it was some sort of dementia.

"Well let's go over everything, alright?" Megan smiled, and spoke directly to Edith Blandings. "As we all have already suspected, the test results show that you are in early stages of what we call simple dementia." Megan always made sure that she addressed and spoke to the patient unless they were not able to understand. "Now since this was caught very early, and with the new meds we have now, and the Mediterranean diet, along with exercise, I think you should do very well."

"Will she go back to being..." Patty trailed off.

"Probably not, but she's still in the early stages. With diet exercise and the right meds there's a possibility of some cognitive improvement, but we won't count on it." Megan knew she wanted to know if her mother would go back to being normal. This was a common reaction; one Megan was used to. "What we need to do, now," she turned her eyes back to Edith. "is concentrate on keeping you at the cognitive level you are now for as long as we can." She addresses both ladies. "I'm sorry. This disease will progress. However, with medications, diet, and regular exercise we can slow the progress and give you and the family more time to make decisions about the future." She opened her desk drawer, pulled out some papers and gave them to Edith. "This is the Mediterranean Diet. I'd like you to change some of your eating habits and this diet is recommended to patients in your situation. It was designed originally for heart patients, but as we have learned what is good for the heart is good for the brain. It should be recommended for everybody." She groused, "But it is especially important for you. I'll send a fax to our best physical therapy unit, and they will set you up with appointments with them."

"Is this Alzheimer's?" Mrs. Blandings asked quietly as she took the papers from Megan.

"There are many forms of dementia. Alzheimer's is only one of them. And there is no definitive way to know, at this point, if Alzheimer's is what you've developed. There is what we call a PET scan which I can order, but that is up to you. Some insurances won't cover it and they are very expensive."

"Will I have to move into a nursing home?"

"I don't think that's necessary at this stage." Megan smiled reassuringly. "The assisted living facility where you're living now will be more than suitable for you at the present time."

"What about when this progresses?" her daughter interjected.

"You should know that this disease affects every patient differently. There are some common symptoms, but basically the disease affects everyone in different ways. And at different speeds of progression. We've caught this very early and I think, with the meds we have now it can be managed." She looked at Mrs. Blandings. "You may never have to leave your current assisted living. Eventually, you might need to advance to their secure memory unit, but I have other patients in the same unit and it's a very comfortable, attractive extension of the same facility and the staff is excellent." Megan wanted to give them hope, but always knew she needed to be upfront and honest with her patients. "You should understand that this disease will progress. What we need to do is select the medications that will slow the progression as much as possible so that you can maintain your current level of stability for as *long* as possible. Stick to the diet I have just given you and get lots of exercise. Take walks. Make use of the exercise room at your facility. The therapist will make sure you don't start out so fast that you keel over with exhaustion the first day." She smiled at Edith. "I have a patient who was diagnosed five years ago and is doing wonderfully. But I also have patients who have not been so lucky. I can also tell you I had a patient who was diagnosed over ten years ago, and she followed all the rules of treatment religiously. She lived to be ninety-five and remained in her assisted living apartment until she passed. She was one remarkable lady and I have the same confidence in your ability to do as well. And I can give you one little piece of advice. Stress can be one of your biggest issues. When talking to people, and you can't come up with answers to questions immediately, don't try to fake it or hide what your issues are. Simply say that you've been diagnosed with a form of dementia, and they'll have to forgive you if you're not as quick with memory. It will save you frustration and the feeling of trying to hide what your issues are. Most people will understand, and the few who don't, you don't need anyway. Those who care about you will understand. And they are the ones who are important to you." She looked at the two women across her desk and went on. "Why don't we go over the meds and work from there. Please know that I am here should you ever need anything."

"Will you still be my doctor?" Mrs. Blandings asked.

"Of course," Megan smiled. "You don't think I would ever let you go, do you?" she laughed. Mrs. Blandings was one of the first patients that came in when Megan opened the practice. She was an incredibly sweet woman and a formidable gossip. "Besides, where would I get all my news if you left me?" All three women laughed, and Megan was pleased that she was able to put them somewhat at ease.

She went over the meds with them and answered all the questions they had. There were some she didn't know the answers to and told them that she would do the research and call them before the end of the day. When the consultation was over she led them both out to the reception area.

"Liz, would you please schedule Mrs. Blandings for an appointment next month?"

"Thank you very much." Mrs. Blandings smiled as she took Megan's hand in hers.

"Don't you worry, and if you have any questions please feel free to call me. And if I don't hear from you before, I'll see you in a month." She pecked the older woman on the cheek, handed her the appointment card and opened the front door for them to exit. She stood watching as they got into their car and waved. *This disease fucking sucks* she thought as she ground her teeth, *I think I'd rather cut my heart out with a spoon.*

Megan walked past the front desk and took the next chart from her box and walked to the appropriate exam room. After a few hours, the office had cleared of patients, and it was time to break for lunch.

"Liz, I'll be in my office. You can bring Mrs. Brown back when she arrives."

Megan was seated behind her desk checking her phone messages when she heard Liz greet who she assumed was Hannah Brown. Megan put her phone down and met Hannah and Liz at her office doorway.

"Megan, this is Hannah Brown, the woman I was telling you about." Liz smiled

"Nice to meet you, Mrs. Brown." Megan held out her hand.

"Nice to meet you as well and please call me Hannah. I think formality is highly overrated." She smiled and grasped Megan's outstretched hand firmly.

"Wonderful, and I'm Megan." Megan laughed, "Would you like to sit down?" she motioned to the chairs opposite her desk.

"Oh yes, but I know this is your lunch break, so if you prefer, we can sit out in the reception area. I don't want to keep you too long."

"No, it is fine here, and we won't be disturbed if someone pops in the door. Sometimes 'out to lunch' doesn't always mean a lot." Megan chuckled.

The ladies sat and talked for about thirty minutes regarding the job and responsibilities that went with it. Liz blushed several times when Megan reported on her abilities and how smoothly she kept the office running. Hannah gave Megan her resume and explained that she had retired, but was finding the adjustment a bit difficult to deal with.

"I have worked all my life and I just don't know what to do with all this free time. So when I had this little lady and her hubby over for dinner last night, she was telling me about the issues you have been having getting help." She leaned forward and whispered, "It's so hard to find good help these days." she chuckled, "I thought that maybe I could be of some use to you."

"Well, I have to admit, I was concerned about how we'd get along while Liz was away, but I think you would be perfect, and I might add, that you will fit right in with our group." Megan smiled and extended her hand. "When can you start?"

"As soon as you need me honey."

Hannah agreed to start the following morning. Liz would train her in the ways of the office and introduce her to the doctors with whom she would be working, and Hannah would get acquainted with the rest of the staff before Liz's OB doctor took her out of work. When they were finished Megan invited Hannah to join her and Liz for lunch at the corners, but Hannah had another engagement.

As Megan and Liz walked across the road to the café, she noticed a State Trooper car parked in front of the building, and her thoughts turned to Donny.

Chapter Ten

Megan and Liz walked into the Rileyville Café and sat at the round table in the back corner by the window. The small country diner had at one time been the Rileyville general store back in the 1900's and then all but abandoned for several years. About twenty years ago someone decided the little village needed a local eatery and the Rileyville Café was born. It had been run over the years by several people. Now it was run by a husband-and-wife team and had become a family business.

It was small but quaint and did a booming business. The exterior walls were lined with windows and each window was large enough to support two tables. There was a long counter with stools that took up the center of the room, and when Megan came in alone or with her mother she often sat there. Once she and Liz were seated, Megan took the opportunity to scan the room for the troopers who belonged to the car out front. When she was unable to find the uniformed Troopers she turned her attention to the menus brought by the waitress.

"Root beer for you, doc?" Michelle asked.

"Yes, thank you."

"And what would you like, Liz?"

"I think I'll have water, thanks Michelle." Liz smiled and went back to the menu.

"I'll bring your drinks right out. Do you need a few more minutes to decide what to eat?"

"Megan probably doesn't but I do." Liz smiled up at Michelle who nodded and headed toward the soda machine behind the counter.

Megan was scanning the menu when she was startled by a male voice.

"Doctor Dunnegan?" he asked drawing Megan's attention up to him

"Yes?" she didn't immediately recognize him, but his smile was familiar. "Trooper Mackay?" Megan asked, stunned.

"That's right." He grinned.

"I'm sorry I didn't recognize you." She smiled.

The handsome young man indicated his snug stonewashed jeans and tee shirt "No uniform. Am I disturbing you ladies?"

"Not at all." Liz flashed her brightest smile. "Would you like to join us?"

"Are you sure?" he asked looking directly at Megan, but Liz overrode anything Megan might have said if given the opportunity to speak.

"Of course Trooper MacKay, have a seat." Liz answered brightly. *Handsome* she thought. *Tall, maybe about six feet two, give or take. Soft dark brown hair cut short, striking blue eyes with divinely even features,* she evaluated the trooper. *He and our doctor would look very well together* Liz decided.

"Thank you," he said as he pulled out a chair. "I'm Steven." He said and reached out to offer his hand.

"And my name is Liz." She shook his hand, "Now tell me how you ever come to meet Megan here?" *This is a man who should hook up with her,* she thought. *Talk about a dream boat. If I wasn't happily married and about to pop myself...* Her thoughts trailed off as she listened to what Steven was saying.

"My partner and I came to her office to ask a few questions about a case we were working on." He looked directly at Megan now. "The case is closed by the way, Dr. Dunnegan." He smiled.

"I don't think I've ever seen you in here before, are you new in the neighborhood?"

Steven struggled to drag his eyes from Megan's to answer Liz. "No I've been here for a couple of years, but I don't usually eat out."

Oh yeah, he likes her, Liz mused. "Lucky us that you decided to today." She smiled brightly and glanced at Megan for confirmation and found her friend studying the "dream boat". *This is promising,* Liz giggled inwardly. "Megan, you ok?"

"Huh?" Megan snapped to attention "Oh, yeah, fine." *I don't know what to do,* she thought. Normally she would smile and might even flirt a little with him. *Lord knows he's attractive, but he was also Donny's brother. Estranged brother at that.* "I'm sorry I was thinking about something. Did you say you have lived in Rileyville for a couple of years now?" she asked Steven.

"Yes, I'm a little north up the road from here in a log cabin." He explained. He had remembered that she was good looking, but his memory did not do her justice. "Do you live around here as well?"

"I live on Dunnegan road between Rose Lake and Rosemont camps."

"Wait, you don't mean the big farm?"

"The very same, why?" she asked.

"I know where you are. I have often thought about stopping to ask if I can fish in the lake there, but you have signs posted for private property." *Maybe I can stop now for other reasons,* he thought, *never hurts to get to know your neighbors.*

"Yeah. Generally only family fish in the lake. I have a few non-family members come to fish. Guys who knew my grandfather and have fished there all their lives or were brought to fish as kids." She was rambling and she knew it, but couldn't stop herself. "They're all nice guys. One is an EMT. He and his father come occasionally." She trailed off. "The father is or was a baker by profession and often brings me pies, cookies, or other things he bakes. They are always delicious." *Now I'm nervous and rambling.* She chided herself.

"Isn't one of your guys a retired trooper?" Liz asked.

"Really? Maybe I know him. Wha`s his name?" Steven offered.

"Michael and Jack Stephens." Megan smiled, "Jack is retired now, but he and his father come here about once a week."

"Is Michael the EMT then?" *My God! She is breath taken',* he thought.

"No, Gary is the EMT. He brings his Dad to fish, but Jack and Michael are a different pair. Do you know Jack Stephens?" *Well, he hasn't lost the accent completely,* Megan noted to herself.

"Let me think, tall fellow, nicely built, always wears a ball cap. Is that him?"

"Well, tall anyway, I guess he's built well, I never really noticed. Jack's Dad knew my grandfather and he used to bring Jack to fish when he was a kid. My mother always said it was a good idea to keep on friendly terms with the local authorities. Besides, these are men who have been coming to our place to fish for years. They're all nice guys and we enjoy seeing them. They're old family friends now."

"Do you have any non-retired officers fishing there now?" Steven was entranced by her.

"As a matter of fact I don't." She smiled.

"Trooper Mackay," Liz shot in. "Do you like to fish?"

"Yes I do, but I don't get to do it very often."

"Why not? Does your wife keep you off the water?" *Please say you're not married*, Liz moaned inwardly.

"No. I'm not married," Steven smiled, his eyes on Megan. And then his smile widened into a full-fledged grin as Megan blushed slightly when they both realized simultaneously what Liz was doing. Megan snapped her menu shut and briefly glared at Liz. "I don't get to fish because my work hours are long and varied. Besides, when I do get time off, the last place I want to be is on an overpopulated, polluted lake, like some of the public ones we have here."

"Megan's lake is neither overpopulated nor polluted." Liz grinned. "Megan, you should invite Trooper Mackay to fish."

"Steven, please." He interjected "And I wouldn't think of invading your privacy, Dr. Dunnegan." Hoping to stop Liz from openly putting Megan on the spot.

"Well, I see we have added one to your table." Michelle noted when she set the soda and water on the table. She smiled at Steven. "Would you like something to drink?"

"Coffee, please." He answered.

"With pleasure, are you all ready to orders?" Michelle took their order and headed for the kitchen leaving the trio to their own devices.

The three of them sat and exchanged small talk until their lunches were brought out. As they ate, Liz and Steven did most of the talking. On Liz's part it was more of an interrogation. Asking about his family, about which Megan noticed, he seemed slightly uncomfortable answering. However, she learned that he had been with the troopers for about four years and was very happy in his work. Other than that she had tuned out most of what was said. Her mind kept going back to Donny and the background he had given her about himself and Steven. *Should I tell Donny that we met and had lunch?* She wondered. Did the man who she barely knew have the right to inadvertently dictate who she should be friendly with? *Steven was just a kid when Arabella was killed, and Marie taken.* Megan mulled everything over and over again in her mind until she had a headache. She finally decided to let it go for the time being and just enjoy eating lunch.

As she was about to rejoin the conversation her cell began to vibrate.

"Excuse me," she looked at the number and realized it was the cottage. "Hello?"

"I'm sorry ta be botherin` ye luv," Donny's magnificent brogue flowed over the line, "but I think ye might want ta find a wee moment ta come back ta yer home?"

"Why? Is there a problem?" Alarm ringing in her voice. "Are you alright?"

"Och, I'm fine luv, but there is lady here that isna dooin so well."

"Who?"

"Yer mother dropped by and was given a wee shock ta find me here."

"Oh, for the love of God." Megan groaned, propped her elbow on the table and dropped her forehead into her free hand. "How long has she been there?" She looked up from her hands long enough to see that Liz and Steven were no longer in conversation but had directed their attention to her.

"No` long, but ye might want ta come back and speak wi` her. How much time have ye got left on yer lunch?"

"Enough, I hope. I'll be right there." She picked up her purse and dropped her phone inside as she started to rise from the table. "I'm sorry. I have to go home, there's a problem with...the dog." She managed to get out.

"Max?" Liz asked, "Is he ok?"

"Um, yeah I think so, but I need to...I have to go home and check on ...things." Megan gathered her purse and withdrew her keys.

"Do you want me to drive you home?" Steven asked concerned.

"WHAT? NO!" Megan snapped nervously. *Cool it,* she thought "Sorry," she forced a laugh. "No. Thanks, though. My car is right across the road. You could make sure Liz gets back to the office though. We don't want anything to happen to our newest mama!" she smiled.

"Sure."

"Megan," Liz piped up. "Who called?"

"What? Oh, my mother is at the cottage. Don't worry I'll be back before the lunch break is over." *I hope*, she thought. And without further delay, or explanation, she was out the door and dashing across the road to her Wagoneer in the office parking lot.

As she drove the mile home she rehearsed in her mind what she was going to say to her mother. As she pulled up to the cottage she almost laughed, because she had no idea *what* to say. Megan squared her shoulders, took a deep breath, and made her way to the front door.

Megan stepped inside to find Donny sitting on the sofa with Max curled up next to him. However, upon quick inspection she found no trace of her mother Emma.

"Where is she?" she asked Donny.

"On the deck." He smiled, "She's quite a little chimney isn't she?"

"Huh?" she asked puzzled "Oh you mean she smokes a lot. Not really. Only when she's worried. Or," she said under her breath, "on the warpath." Megan looked but still couldn't see her mother and decided that she was on the side portion of the deck. "Did you say anything to her?"

"Like what luv?"

"Like your name and what you're doing here?" she half hissed.

"Oh!" he smiled. "No."

"NO? Why the hell not?"

"She's yer mother. I dinna know anything aboot her. Fer all I knew she could have a knife or a gun in her purse."

"Oh, for the love of God! She's my mother, not a serial killer! And she's probably not carrying a purse."

"Aye, and I'm a strange man in her daughter's house. I do'na know aboot ye luv, but I do'na want ta be shot, stabbed, or bludgeoned wi` a handbag." He chuckled.

"Oh, what's the big deal?" she was exasperated. "It's not like you've never been shot before."

"Cute, luv." A smirk formed over his gorgeous face.

"Oh, be quiet." And with that Megan made the long walk out to her mother on the side deck. She spotted her mother sitting at the bistro set she and Megan had found at the weekly auction. "Hi Mom." Her mother looked up. Emma Dunnegan was in her mid-sixties with silver hair that she had recently cut short and styled. Emma was five one or as she was in the habit of saying, "five one and a quarter inch". She was petite and slender. She had hazel eyes and skin like her father's, which always tanned to a nice golden brown in the summer and nearly always had color in the winter. Megan was always jealous since she was given her own father's skin and was always pale and most always burned unless she slathered herself in tanning lotion and or sunscreen. Emma was a very attractive woman, as her mother had been. Megan and her mother had always been close. They had been lucky even in Megan's teen years to have a good relationship, and rarely kept secrets from each other.

"Megan," Emma was obviously trying to remain calm. She was never very good at hiding her frustration. "I would like to talk to you. Please, sit down." She waited for Megan to sit, and she went on. "Nathan called this morning to say they were coming east. So I came down to see that the "big house" was in good shape for them. When I got down here, I noticed you were at the office which I expected. What I didn't expect was the dog out in the yard and a man I have never seen before was with him. Naturally I came down to introduce myself in hopes of learning who he was, and I find out *he's living in the cottage with you.* Would you care to explain?"

"He's not *living* with me, Mom."

"Well, he's not dead, and neither are you. That says *living* to me. I'm open minded, Meggie, but I think if you were going to invite a man into your house, you'd at least let your Dad and I meet him first."

Good grief, Megan thought, *she's not angry as much as she is hurt!* "Mother," Megan took a deep breath. "He's not living with me. His name is Donavon Mackay. He is a Federal Agent who was injured in the line of duty and he's staying with me while he recovers." After she had finished her rather rushed explanation, Megan realized that she not only blurted out the truth, but without even pausing for a breath. *So much for subterfuge,* she thought.

"I see, and how long have you known him?" When Megan didn't answer right away Emma went on. "Megan, you and I have always been so close. My memory may be rusty, but to my knowledge, you've never kept anything from me. Now I learn that you have been seeing a Federal Agent for God knows how long, *and* not only have your Dad and I never met him, but he is now living with you." As Emma spoke, her tone became increasingly sad and strained. "Why didn't you tell me any of this?" She stood and walked to the railing of the deck looking out to the marsh garden that Megan's father Patrick created years ago.

"Mom, listen to me." Megan followed her mother in hopes of putting her mind at ease. Although she knew there was no way Emma's mind would be easy once she knew the whole story. "You don't understand."

"Oh, I understand perfectly!" Emma half whispered. "You've been upset with me ever since David because I didn't care for him much. That's why you didn't want to tell me about the new man in your life."

Megan chuckled. "'Didn't care much for him'? Mother, you loathed the man, and everyone for miles around knew it!" She held up her hand when Emma started to speak. "But that's alright. You had every right to dislike David. He was a liar, a cheat, and a fraud! If you hadn't disliked him so intensely I might be married to the bastard and miserable right now. And Donny isn't the 'new man' in my life."

"No, you'd be divorced." Emma stated. "I know you think I interfere in your life, but that man was a sleaze from the get-go."

Megan put a comforting arm around her mother's shoulders "No I don't think you interfere, and I didn't come home to rehash David. Now would you like to hear about the man inside and my current situation?"

"Fine." Emma crossed her arms and turned to face her daughter.

"'Fine' or 'Ok Fine'? Because I know the difference." When Emma simply raised her eyebrow, Megan continued. "Thank you. Now calm down and listen carefully. It's really very simple, and not at all what you're thinking." Unbeknownst to either woman, Donny was inside watching mother and daughter hashing it out, so to speak. He fully understood Emma's point of view. He could picture his own mother in the same situation concerning his sisters, but wanted desperately to help Megan explain why he was there. However, he knew from his own mother and sisters, *never* to interfere in an argument unless absolutely necessary. And since the fur wasn't exactly flying yet, he figured it would be better to remain inside and out of the line of fire. It may be the twenty-first century, but he didn't think mothers as a general rule cared much what the century was where their daughters were concerned.

Megan took a deep breath. "The other day I was washing dishes...no wait, that will only confuse the issue. Um... You see it happened this way..." unable to soften the blow Megan decided to just let her mother have it, right between the eyes. "His name is Donavon Mackay or Donny. He was working with the FBI, and he was injured. So, he's staying with me while he heals."

"You said that, but I don't remember you ever telling me that you knew an FBI man." Emma was still stone faced. "Funny, FBI and Honesdale just don't seem to go together, somehow."

Megan chuckled nervously again "No, they don't actually seem exactly synonymous, do they?" smiling at Emma, she went on. "Oh! Yes! Well, that's because I didn't. I met Donny a few days ago when he stumbled out of the woods with a bullet hole in his gut." There it was, both barrels right between the eyes.

"I'm no` sure tha` was the best way ta break the news, lass." Donny mumbled under his breath from inside the cottage.

The expression on Emma's face was not exactly what Megan had hoped for but pretty much what she had expected. "Are you telling me that you had never met this man before? A complete stranger wanders down the road with a bullet hole and you take him in? Are you nuts? I never thought of you as a total lunatic." Emma screeched.

"No. I didn't take him in right away, I took him to the hospital first."

"Don't be a smart ass, Meggie. This is serious."

"Then don't call me names or question my sanity or my judgment. Look, you're right. I didn't know him from Adam, but he was injured and laying on the ground behind my car. What was I supposed to do? Let him lie there and bleed to death? I'm a physician! I called 911 and the squad came and took him to Memorial. Over the last several days, I've gotten to know him and he's a very nice, upstanding, honorable man. He works for the FBI for Christ sake! How bad can he be?"

"Do you know what the qualifications are for being an FBI person? Because I don't. He could be some crazed power-hungry maniac! You read about that stuff in the papers all the time. Some nut case who is only in law enforcement for the power it gives him along with the right to carry a gun, and then goes home and beats the shit out of his wife and kids!" Emma sat heavily back down in her chair and took a deep breath. "What does he do with the FBI?"

"Mother." Megan sighed, taking the chair across the little table from her mother.

"Alright." Emma took a breath. "Were his injuries serious?"

"No, the bullet passed through clean without hitting any vital organs, but his blood loss was vast and that is serious."

"Well if you took him to the hospital, why isn't he still there?"

"It's summer, mother. The camps are in session. The summer people are here and the hospital is crowded. They needed the bed space. He was in good enough shape to leave the hospital, but not good enough to be on his own until he is fully recovered. He has dressings that need changing on a regular basis, and he can't do that on his own. Sam Otis asked if I would agree to house him until he was capable of taking care of himself. I agreed. Now, he's a nice man. He doesn't seem like a crazed lunatic and he's a federal agent. If we can't trust the federal government, who can we trust?"

Emma looked at Megan with raised eyebrows. Megan laughed out loud.

"I don't think he's running for office, mother."

"Your grandfather was a physician and he never brought patients home from the hospital to recover."

"Mom!" Megan blew out.

"Alright, alright. What's done is done, I suppose." Then she lowered her voice to a barely audible whisper. "I don't think he's from around here. Did you notice he has an accent?"

"Yeah." Megan chuckled. "I noticed; how could I miss it?"

"What does he do for the FBI? And why is he doing it here?"

Damn, Megan thought, ask anything but that. "Um, well that's complicated. I can't really tell you that."

"Why the hell not?" Emma asked, her eyes wide. "You said he isn't running for office."

"I think I can answer tha` Mrs. Dunnegan." Donny answered from the doorway of the deck. "Ye see I was workin undercover so ta speak, and even though the case is closed, the la... I mean Megan is still no able ta make my association wi` the case public knowledge." He hoped that would be enough to get Megan out of trouble. He was wrong.

Emma glared at the tall, handsome young man who came out onto the deck and entered the conversation. *I wondered just how long you'd hang around in the house and let her do all the explaining,* Emma grumbled silently, as she looked up at him.

"*I* am not the public, young man, *I'm* Megan's mother. Sit, please." Donny pulled a wrought iron rocker close to the two women and sat down. "If I understand you correctly, you expect me to let it go at that?" Emma feigned shock and stared at Donny, a million things running through her mind at once. Megan was right actually. She could hardly let the man lie behind her car and die of blood loss and an FBI agent was better and more respectable than some vagrant bum. And in all honesty, Emma supposed having federal credentials were fairly reliable her point of view. But she saw no reason to let the guy off the hook too easily. Besides, she was now in the position, as the irate mother, to get a good deal more information than she had received so far. Especially if this rather nice-looking young fellow wanted to remain in his current situation. *And he better come up with some more answers or I'll call the goddamned Troopers and have his ass hauled right out of here,* she thought doggedly.

"Yes." Donny and Megan both said in unison.

"You both expect me to sit quietly by while my daughter, my unmarried, unprotected daughter, takes a total stranger into her home to live, however temporarily? *Who* suffered a gunshot wound and turned out to be some kind of gun-toting federal agent? An agent who was apparently involved in some kind of business where he had an occasion to get shot during his acquaintance with non-federal agents? Who apparently carry their own guns and are not opposed to shooting other people with them?"

"Yes." Again was the joint reply.

"Are you married, Mr. Mackay?"

"Nay, Mrs. Dunnegan."

"Does your mother know what you do for a living?"

"Not precisely."

"Well," Emma huffed. "I shouldn't wonder!"

"Mom listen," Megan leaned across the small bistro table and took Emma's hand. "I know this is upsetting to you, and difficult to understand and I'm sorry it has to be this way. But you really must accept that this is complicated. I wish I could tell you everything. You know I hate keeping things from you, but in this instance I must keep Donny's work secret." She ran her fingers through her glossy auburn hair. "Hell, even I don't know everything. Please try to be patient until I can answer all your questions. For now, I can tell you that the case he was working on is closed, and the suspects have been caught. However, Donny was working undercover, and he can't run the risk of said fringe bad guys finding out what he was doing or who he was pretending to be."

Donny looked at her with a stunned expression. *I canna believe she said that,* he thought.

"FRINGE bad guys?" Emma repeated softly and with some fear.

"Mrs. Dunnegan, 'fringe bad guys' as Megan so eloquently phrased it, if there are any, wouldna be lookin` for Donovan Mackay. So please do'na be concerned. And if it will make ye feel any better, I'm in constant contact wi` the bureau. If there is any trouble in the near future, I'll know aboot it and can act accordingly."

"He is perfectly safe." Megan smiled.

"I'm not worried about *him* being safe! I'm worried about *you!*" Emma fretted.

"Well you don't need to be. I'm fine and—"

"Do you have any idea what kind of people he might have after him?" Emma questioned.

"Donny is right. No one is looking for *Donavon Mackay*. Please trust my judgment." She smiled at her mother reassuringly. "I'm telling you that everything is fine."

Emma sighed and looked at her daughter and back to the man in question. "There's nothing I can do to talk you out of this, is there?"

"Nope." Megan answered.

"Ok, but you are going to be the one who explains this to your father and brothers." Emma smiled.

"Fine, I'm not afraid of them."

"Did you say you were not married, Mr. Mackay?"

"Nay ma'am, I'm nay married." Donny replied, his eyes starting to sparkle.

Nice eyes, Emma thought, *gainfully employed and single. Federal government, good pension if she can get him to retire and get rid of the gun. Even I know the FBI requires a college education.*

She stood and offered Donny her hand which he shook gladly. "I'm going home. I'm tired. You've caused me to argue with my only daughter, young man. I don't like to argue with Meggie. It always makes me dog tired. I rarely win anymore anyway." She looked skyward and sighed. "I don't know why I bother." He winked at the older woman and she gave him a half smile. Emma turned to Megan for the expected hug, walked off the deck, got into her little red golf cart, and drove away.

Chapter Eleven

Megan watched as her mother drove away in the red golf cart with the purple fringed top. She took a deep breath and blew it out in a whoosh. She turned toward Donny, still seated at the bistro table.

"Well, I think that went well." She sighed. "At least she wasn't doing the 'ok fine' thing so much."

"Are ye alright lass?" he was too concerned about her to try curbing his normal use of the word *'lass'*.

"Yeah, I'm fine." She all but chuckled. "I guess. I just hate keeping things from her. We've always been so close and shared everything with each other. It's tough to not continue to do that. However, I know I can't be completely forthcoming with details concerning your work. With her or the rest of the family." She leaned back against the deck railing facing Donny.

"I am sorra aboot this luv, I wish ye dinna have ta remain silent." His expression was sympathetic for several seconds and then split into a wide grin. "But ye didna exactly keep me identity a complete secret, ye know. Ye told her I was wi` the FBI, ye told her me correct name and ye told her I ha` been here workin on a case. It's no` as if ye're keeping her completely in the dark then, is it?"

Megan chuckled. "Well, I was going over this in my mind most of last night and then on the way here this afternoon, it occurred to me, if you were an attorney, it would be ok for her to *know* you were an attorney, but I certainly wouldn't fill her in on the details of your clients. Just like I'm a physician, but I don't tell her the intimate details of my patients' medical problems. That's privileged. So basically, what's the difference between you and an attorney or a doctor?"

Donny looked at her with close to awe. Then smiled. "Ye're a verra clever lass. Do ye know tha`? However, I'm no` so sure I care fer bein` compared to a lawyer. I and me associates risk our lives ta capture the crooks and the lawyer's wheel and deal ta set them free."

"Hmm. That's an interesting description of the entire legal profession." She granted as she looked squarely into his eyes. "As it happens, I have several family members who are attorneys. My cousin is a judge in town."

Donny took in her expression and body language and burst out laughing. "Good glory!" he said. "I've put me foot in it this time!"

Megan laughed too, "Maybe just a *wee* bit." She mocked. "Don't worry about it." But she was relieved that he wasn't upset with her for revealing as much about him to her mother as she had.

"Have ye eaten yet?" he asked. "I was aboot ta fix a sandwich when yer mother came ta call." He was actually hoping to keep her with him a little longer. He found he enjoyed talking with her.

"I was about to eat when you called."

"I'm sorra fer spoilin` yer lunch."

"You didn't, and besides it wasn't your fault. Well, not really." Smiling and looking at her phone at the text form Liz coming though.

"Looks like I have a little extra time." Slipping her phone back in her pocket. "The office still has a little bit of lunch left and now my patient is going to be about twenty minutes late." They stood staring at each other with such intensity, Megan felt she was going to start blushing. "Why don't I make us both something? It won't take me a minute." She smiled and shoved away from the railing.

"Sounds good." Donny smiled, stood, and followed her into the cottage. He was not accustomed to being taken care of and tried to no avail to get Megan to let him help her with the lunch. While she made sandwiches Donny asked how her day had been going before his phone call.

"Good. Busy. Liz and I met with Hannah today about filling in while Liz is out with the baby. Thankfully, she has agreed to take the job and it seems as though she'll fit in with our group very well." Megan placed the plates of sandwiches on the kitchen table and they both sat down to have their lunch. "The whole interview took less than thirty minutes. Then Liz and I walked over to the corners for lunch." Megan decided it was better not to mention that she and Liz were not the only ones at the table. Unfortunately, Donny was able to see instantly that she was leaving something out.

"What happened?" he asked.

"Huh?"

"At the corners? What happened?"

"I don't understand?"

"Well, yer face changed when ye mentioned the Café." He informed her. "Tha` tells me tha` either ye do'na like the place or there is something tha` ye're leavin oot."

"No, I love that place." *Damn*, she thought, *he pays too close attention.*

"So ye left somethin` oot then?" He watched her eyes. They were beautiful deep violet pools. Very expressive and very revealing. *I could get lost in there*, he thought, *they show her every emotion.* And suddenly he could feel alarm creeping over him. *Did someone approach her?* "Megan did someone come up ta ye in the café?" *Maybe they didn't get them all*, he thought.

"Um," she was about to lie, then she saw the immediate concern on his face and in his eyes. *Oh hell*, she thought, *just tell him and be done with it.* "Yes, someone came up to Liz and I. But it's not what you think. He was very nice."

"He?" jealousy was an unfamiliar emotion to the Scot, and he couldn't readily identify the feeling in his stomach. *Huh, tha`s odd*, he mused. "Who is this 'he'?"

"I don't think you're going to like what I'm about to tell you."

"Why?"

"And I'm not into tantrums or anger, so I'm going to ask you now to stay calm."

Donny relaxed and grinned. This was becoming somewhat of an amusing game.

"Ye donna really know me well enough ta accuse me of throwin` tantrums, lass. I'm a verra even tempered man and I do'na have tantrums." He chuckled in mock defense and his green eyes sparked with mirth. "If ye're goin ta tell me yer ex-boyo is comin between us, I can take it." He slapped his hand against his heart and flashed a confident smile. "I have confidence in me ability ta keep yer heart me own!"

Soften the blow, or right between the eyes? She wondered. "While Liz and I were there, Steven came over and joined us." *Right between the eyes.*

"Mackay?" his voice was strained and quiet.

"Yes." She whispered. "Listen, I know how you feel about him, and I can respect that. But you can't..."

Donny raised his palm and silenced her while he sat quietly. She could see him trying to control his feelings. The room was silent for several minutes. He looked up and she could almost read the emotions fly across his face. "I suppose tis possible tha` we'd both end up in the same place sooner or later, but why here and why now? Does he live here in Honesdale?" Without waiting for her to respond, he continued. "Megan, I have no right ta be tellin ye who ye can and canna speak wi', luv. As much as I wish ye wouldna, it is yer decision who ye deal wi', but ye ha` ta know he's nothing but trouble. He's irresponsible and he cares for nay but himself and his wants and desires." His voice was hard, but he spoke softly, but even to Megan she could see that his eyes were cold and filled with hatred. "Does he know I'm here?" again he didn't wait for her to answer. "Wait! How do we really know this Steven Mackay is me brother? This man could be any Steven Mackay. Tis no such an uncommon name even in this country." His voice and his face held so much hope for mistaken identity. She almost felt guilty for having to crush that hope.

I think I'd like to go back to bed and start this day over again, she thought. *First my mother and now this and tonight there will be Nathan.*

"This is the same Trooper who came to the office shortly after you were shot. The one who came asking questions about missing girls. He came with his partner. I showed you his card and you ripped it to shreds. Remember? He's your younger brother, Donny. He looks like you and although his accent isn't as strong, he's got one. It's just uncanny, really," she half mumbled to herself, "to meet two brothers from Scotland, estranged brothers to boot, in Honesdale." She glanced at his face as his expression saddened. "But as far as I know, he has no idea that you're here unless the FBI informed the local state police of whatever operatives they had in the area working the case."

"Ye didna say anything?" he sighed tiredly.

"Of course not!" She said, insulted, then straightened in her chair. "Listen, what goes on between you and your brother is your business, not mine. I'm not involved. And I certainly wouldn't—"

"Hold it," Donny put his hands up to stave her obvious anger. "It was a knee jerk reaction. I know ye wouldna tell anyone I was here wi` ye. I'm sorra, I dinna mean ta offend ye, lass," he looked into her eyes and then his clouded again. "Wait a minute. Was he asking ye questions about the kidnappings? Ye said he was asking questions about the missing girls when he came ta yer office. Is he still askin questions? Does he nay know the case is closed?"

"He's a trooper, Donny. He's a state trooper." She said softly as she leaned forward across the table and placed her hand on top of his. "We don't have a local police force out here in the townships. The state troopers are our local police force. There are several in the area. They frequent the local eateries. And no, he wasn't asking questions about the kidnapping. I assume he was at the corners for lunch, and we happened to be there, and since we had met previously, he stopped by the table to say hello."

"Good God." Donny blew out his breath and scrubbed his eyes with his hands. "What kind of kids do yer authorities scrape the barrel for ta work for them?"

"He's not a seventeen-year-old kid anymore, Donny. He's a grown man now."

"Aye." He sighed "So how did ye like him?" *Please say ye didna, he* hoped.

"We don't have to talk about it."

"I was just wonderin." He tried to sound casual. "So…" He hedged.

"He was nice. Polite. Personable. And he doesn't live in Honesdale. Actually," she took a deep breath and continued, "he lives out here in Rileyville. Right up the road as a matter of fact, in the log house just over the hill." Now she almost cringed. "Across the road and sort of nestled in between some of my relatives."

"Good God… a neighbor." He groaned.

Megan looked away and scanned the kitchen. "Yeah, so it would seem."

"Ye're hiding again." He smiled. She was so easy to read.

"No, not really…Well, Liz was trying to hook us up." Between the eyes again.

"Ah, and how di tha` go?" he was annoyed, and the feeling was instant, but he struggled successfully to keep the emotion from showing as he observed the pink rise to her cheeks with embarrassment. It was a wonderful addition to her already lovely face.

"Not well," she smiled. "He seems like a very nice man, but I don't know about him, and I'm just *not* interested." She didn't know why she felt the need to tell him that.

"How was she tryin ta set ye up?" If the conversation had to do with anybody other than his brother and Megan he would be enjoying it immensely. She exhibited instantaneous embarrassment when talking about herself. And he suddenly enjoyed her blush and lack of composure.

"Apparently he likes to fish, and I have a lake, so Liz invited him to fish in my lake on his days off."

"Is she in a habit of inviting` men here for ye then?"

"She is happily married and thinks I should be as well. She doesn't mean any harm. But I've learned that happily married people think their lives are so wonderful that they want everybody else to get married and share the wealth of such unions."

"She wants ye ta marry me brother?"

"Not necessarily. She wants me to marry every single man we meet. Not collectively though, I hope." She chuckled uneasily.

"So will he be makin` an appearance here ta fish?" he asked.

"I doubt it. I didn't encourage the invitation. And as he's a trooper, I doubt he'll presume to trespass on private property uninvited." Megan began to fidget with her napkin. She didn't know why, but she was feeling uncomfortable with the conversation. Donny once again sensing her need to change the subject did so.

"So, luv, when do ye think I can take a swim wi` ye in this lake of yers? I ha` a fondness fer swimming` wi` a pretty lass." He grinned, hoping that if he changed the subject, he would succeed in easing her obvious tension.

"Well," Megan laughed. "I think you should wait until your sutures come out, at least." She chuckled as she picked up the lunch plates and took them to the sink. She was about to wash them when Donny's hands were on hers.

Her reaction to his touch was not subtle. His hands were warm, smooth and she felt as if an electric currant had run through her. Enormous butterflies began to flit around in her stomach. She looked up into his eyes and was taken aback at the warmth and gentleness that came from them.

Donny smiled and wondered if she could feel the electricity fly as he could. "Ye made the lunch luv," his voice was as smooth as velvet as he spoke. Megan hoped her knees would not buckle. "Why do'na ye let me do the dishes?" Unable to answer she simply nodded her head and backed out of the way.

She walked to her bedroom and stood in front of the mirror over her dresser staring at her reflection. *What the hell is wrong with me?* She wondered. *Stop it! You're acting like a horny schoolgirl!* She ordered herself. She dragged a brush through her hair, took a deep breath and glared at herself. "Get a grip." She muttered.

"What was tha?" Donny asked from the doorway of her room and chuckled as she jumped slightly.

"I didn't know you were there." She smiled.

"Tha` was obvious." He chuckled. "Do ye need ta start back ta the office now?" Once again he was hoping that she would say no but knew that she had patients to see. He had to admit to himself though, that she was a fascinating woman, *and* he was enjoying her company more than he had anyone else's in a very long time.

"Um," she looked down at her watch and unhappily noticed that she did indeed have to head back. "Yeah, I do." She said quietly. "Will you be ok?"

"Unless ye know of any more family members tha` might be droppin` by this afternoon?" He smiled

"Spare me." She rolled her eyes at the ceiling. "The office closes at seven so I will be home shortly after that." She headed toward the door and Donny moved out of the way. The two of them walked out to her car. As she slid behind the wheel she suddenly remembered her brother and his family's impending arrival that evening. "Oh crap!" She grabbed the steering wheel and dropped her head on the backs of her hands, and groaned.

"What is it, luv?" Donny was alarmed.

"I forgot. Nathan and his family." She told him as she raised her head and looked toward the big white Victorian sitting across the yard and up on the knoll.

"Yer brother?" Donny understood and chuckled.

"It's not funny." She glared at him.

"Oh," he sobered and struggled to maintain a somber expression. "Sorra, luv." He cleared his throat. "What do ye want me ta do?"

"Do?"

"Aye. Do ye know when they are ta arrive? And do ye wish me ta close the blinds and turn out the lights?" The sobriety vanished, and he laughed out loud. He would like to put her at ease, but he realized there was no way he could accomplish that, so he opted for humor.

She glared at him and then she laughed too. "You are a great deal of trouble Mr. Perdicaris! The plane gets in at eight-thirty. So, they'll be here no later than nine-thirty. They'll probably want to put the kids to bed and then I have no doubt that Nathan and Angie will either come down here to visit with me, or go up to see Mom and dad."

"If they go ta visit wi` yer parents first, do ye think yer mother will inform them tha` ye ha` an unsavory house guest?"

"I don't know. If she's going to tell them, she's already been on the phone with them and done it. And if she has, I'll probably get a phone call at the office before long. And I'll have to go through all the gory details of our introduction all over again, which I'll have to do anyway, I suppose."

"I am a great deal of trouble for ye, aren't I, luv?"

Megan looked up at Donny and tried very hard to glare but failed. "AYE!" she said. "But, I canna worry about it now." She mimicked, "Or I'll be late getting back to the office. I'll call you later to check in on you. In the meantime rest and try not to move around too much." Slipping back into her doctor persona.

"Yes ma'am." Donny said, slipping into a perfect American accent. "I hope the rest o` yer day is good." He winked and closed her car door.

"Thanks." *Anything will be an improvement,* she thought, but smiled at him and drove off up the road toward her office.

Megan made it back to the office with ten minutes of her extra time to spare. She wasn't surprised to find Liz still checking messages from the lunch hours. She was surprised however to find Steven Mackay sitting in the chair next to her.

"Well, hello." She smiled at Steven and raised her eyebrows at Liz, who winked in response.

"Everything alright with Max?" Liz asked as she hung up the phone.

"Yes he's fine. So how was the rest of your lunch?" *And why the hell is he here?* She wanted to demand.

"Good, we came back and Steven didn't want to leave me here alone."

"That was very thoughtful of you." She told Steven as he walked out from behind the reception counter to stand in front of Megan. She could definitely see the family resemblance between Donny and this tall handsome man, and he is, she admitted to herself, *incredibly handsome.* There was no denying that, and she once again realized that she was a little surprised that he held no interest for her at all. *Odd,* she thought, *God, I hope I'm not turning into a female eunuch!* she thought. "I'm sorry I had to leave so abruptly." She smiled at him.

"Don't worry about it. Something came up and you had to leave, I understand that. Besides, Liz and I had a very enjoyable lunch. She's going to introduce me to Jimmy." He smiled warmly.

"I'll bet you did," Megan looked back at Liz and smiled. "Liz is always fun to be around. And you'll like Jimmy. He's a nice guy" She looked down at her watch. "Unfortunately, it is time to reopen the office and I think I heard a car outside."

"Of course. It was nice to see you again, and I hope to see you again soon." He smiled and turned to Liz. "It was wonderful to meet you Liz."

"Same here. Come around again. Megan and I usually eat lunch at the Café. On your days off you should come by and eat with us." She smiled and winked at Steven. Steven felt a little embarrassed for Megan who had to be more than aware of what Liz was trying to do.

"Well, we'll see." He waved and left the office.

Megan turned back to Liz and glared at her. However, she was not able to give out the piece of her mind she would have liked to at the moment, because patients were trooping through the door.

The rest of the day went by quickly. Megan loved it. She was busy and never had time to think about what was waiting for her at home. She had a small break between patients and called Donny to see how he was doing. The conversation was brief as her next patient arrived. She told Donny that she would not be late and that she would bring home dinner from the "Corners."

When the last patient had left, Megan locked the front door and went across the road to pick up sandwiches for dinner. She chose a burger for Donny and a BLT wrap for herself. While she was waiting for her order to be ready Liz and her husband came in for dinner.

"Hey guys." Megan smiled as they walked by.

"I thought you were leaving right after me." Liz commented.

"I had to close the office down, then pick up some dinner. I'm waiting for it now." Then Megan remembered that she wanted to talk to Liz about her not-so-subtle maneuvering with Steven Mackay. "Hey, Liz. Do you have a minute? I'd like to talk to you if you have time."

"Sure." Liz settled herself on a counter stool while her husband Jimmy chose a table for them and sat down. "What's up?"

"Well, I wanted to speak with you briefly about Steven Mackay." Megan started.

"Isn't he a dream boat?" Liz gushed. "I mean, wow! And just think, *single*."

"Yes. He seems very nice, and he is attractive. And I know what you're trying to do here, and I'd like for you to stop doing it." Megan smiled at Liz and rested her hand on Liz's back. She loved this kind-hearted young girl like a little sister. But she really hated it when Liz tried to do the unsolicited fix-up thing.

"I don't understand you." Liz was exasperated. "How do you ever expect to meet a man if you don't date, and you won't allow your friends to fix you up?"

"Look, I know your heart is in the right place, and I do appreciate your concern for me, but I have to tell you; I am *not* interested in Steven."

"What?" Liz's mouth dropped open. "Are you blind? How can you not want a piece of that?"

"Oh Liz," Megan let her head hang slightly then looked back over at her friend and laughed out loud. "No. I'm not blind, and I have eyes. I can see that he is good looking—"

"Good looking?" Liz cut her off. Then she lowered her voice and looked around to make sure she hadn't spoken loud enough to draw attention "Good looking doesn't cover it, Meggie. That man is absolutely drop-dead gorgeous!"

"Liz, wipe your chin, before Jimmy notices that you're drooling." Megan smiled even wider. "And besides, I have seen better." She smirked thinking of Donny and was somewhat surprised when her mind immediately offered up a picture of her house guest until she remembered the other brother who was a film star. *So I guess it's alright where my mind went.* she thought. *"drop-dead gorgeous" must run in the family.* Steven was nice looking, and Megan decided right then that if *I hadn't become so involved with Donny professionally and been inadvertently tangled up in his web of secrecy, I would more than likely have been interested in seeing Steven on a personal level,* she mused. *After all, I'm not exactly totally immune to good looking men.* Just then Michelle appeared from the kitchen with Megan's order.

"Thanks Michelle." Megan smiled and paid the bill.

"*Two* dinners?" Liz asked suspiciously.

"I have company." Not wanting to get involved in further explanations, she gently squeezed Liz's hand, and smiled at her friend. "So how about you relax your quest to get me hooked up and married, please. Ok?"

"Ok, fine." She had adopted Emma's term and loved to use it on Meggie.

"Nice. You hang out with my mother entirely too much!" She chuckled and waved to Jimmy at the back of the diner and left the building heading for her car. She drove with the windows down and the radio blaring. Her favorite tune from The High Kings, Irish Pub Song, came on and she was singing along when she pulled into her parking spot on the side of the cottage.

She entered the building to find it empty. She checked Donny's room and it was also empty. She went out to the deck to find Max stretched out sound asleep and Donny sitting at the bistro table, clicking away on her laptop computer.

"Hi there, whatcha` doing?" Megan asked, she smiled as Max's ears perked and scrambled to his feet to greet his person.

"I hope ye do'na mind me taken yer laptop oot o` yer room." Donny smiled.

"Of course not. Got bored, huh?" She chuckled and looked over his shoulder to see what he was doing. "What are you doing anyway?"

"Checkin` me email." He closed the screen down a little so she could not read what was showing.

"Oh, sorry, I didn't mean to pry." She straightened up and put the dinners on the table.

"Ye're no prying luv," he explained. "It's just that I have several email addresses and this particular one needs to be kept confidential." He was closing down the machine as he explained.

"Oh, you mean it's sleuth stuff?" Megan asked as she took the dinners out of the plastic bag and set them on the table.

"Nay, lass. I'm no` a 'sleuth'. I work with the FBI on occasion, but there are several other agencies all over the world tha` I work with as well. I was responding to a request for help." He took the burger from the container.

"You can't work now." She said in her firmest physician voice.

"I know tha` luv, I was turning them down." He looked at the contents of her container. "What is tha?"

"A BLT wrap." She smiled. "Oh I love these things. As a matter of fact if it weren't for my mother I think I could eat these three times a day!" She chuckled.

"Yer mother doesn't like yer BLT wrap?"

"Oh! No. She loves them too. Actually she got me started on them, but she had a cholesterol issue a few years back and now she's a cholesterol Nazi. Which is ok really because I'm the salt Nazi. So we play well together."

She decided not to return the conversation to his career of sleuth for now. She'd had a long day and knew she was in for a long night with Nathan and Angie coming. "Listen I was thinking, after we finish dinner if you're up for it, maybe we could walk down to the lake or a ride in the golf cart through the fields."

"Sure, other than takin Max oot, I havena been oot o` the house all day." He smiled "it would be nice ta stretch the legs." He was silent for a minute. "How was the rest o` yer day?"

"Busy." She sighed. "But I love it that way. When I have patients back-to-back it makes the day go by quickly and I have a real feeling of accomplishment by the time I get home in the evening."

As she spoke of her day Donny watched her eyes sparkle with delight. "Ye really luv yer work." It wasn't a question, but an observation.

"Yes I do. But you don't love yours?" Once again it was an observation rather than a question.

"Nay always, but there are times, when a case has been closed, the bad guys are behind bars and justice has been served tha` is extremely rewardin."

"But you think about getting out." Not a question. When he just looked at her she shrugged. "What? You said so yourself, the thought was creeping in more and more since Philly and now this." Gesturing to his side. "It doesn't seem that far fetched that you've been giving, *now*, some serious thought to quitting."

"Are ye ready for tha` ride?" Donny asked. He was uncomfortable with how perspective she was. "Me family would prefer tha` I do somethin` else, I admit. But this is what I do and I'm good at what I do."

"Oh. Ok. Well, let me throw this stuff away." She jumped up and scarfed up the food containers, put them back into the plastic bag and took them inside to the waste can. She put Max back in the house before she and Donny made their way down the steps to the golf cart for their ride.

Chapter Twelve

The pair piled into the golf cart, with Megan behind the wheel, she headed toward the road and up to the fields. At the top of the hill, she turned into the entrance of the first field. "This is the Rye lot," she said. Megan named each field as they rode through the bar-ways dividing one from another. It was haying season so there were several large round bales littering the landscape. Megan loved seeing hay bales scattered over the large expanses of grass. In her mind, the fields looked rather naked without hay bales here and there. She felt the bales made the place look complete.

"I can remember when we took care of the fields ourselves," she said. Then she chuckled. "My Dad would say I was speaking French." She smiled at the mention of her fathers phrase. "*I didn't mow anything but the yard. But Dad and my brothers and sometimes my cousins cut the hay every year, but they never baled anything.*" She told him as she settled the cart at the top corner of the Rye lot. She had turned the cart around facing the direction from which they had come. They sat overlooking the Rye lot, the field above the house and on down to the lake. It was a picture-perfect view.

"Why is tha`?" Donny asked.

"A number of reasons really," she looked at the scenery on front of her. "lack of equipment for one. The fields have to be mowed every year to keep them from becoming woods, but we don't have the baling equipment for the big rolled bales and no place to store that many of the old rectangle bales. Nor did we have the manpower to mow and bale and then collect and store them. We didn't live here year-round. My mother was here during the summers and we kids were here with her until one by one we had to get jobs to support a car and insurance. Then after high school we went away to college. That of course cut down on the manpower we did have. My dad, his younger brothers and the cousins usually got the fields cut but it would take all summer as they had to depend on rain free weekends to do it. They all worked full time and weekends were all they had up here. So, the added project of baling was really not an issue. We weren't set up for all of that though. People who really farm, have someone hired full-time to repair the machinery when it breaks." She laughed, "And it always breaks. Sickle bar knives snap and gotta be replaced. The knives have to be continually sharpened. Not everybody greases before they get on the tractor. Tires go flat. It's a constant shift from one repair to another which makes getting the job done on weekends in the summer a long ordeal. Now and then there would be someone who wanted the hay and agreed to mow the fields if he could have the hay. That worked out fairly well for a few years, but it was a hit or miss thing. Eventually we struck a bargain with a guy down the road. He would mow and bale. He got the hay. We got our fields cut and we were able to keep enough bales to store in the barn for my horses."

"Is he still doin` the job then?"

"No, we've got three hundred-sixty eight acres here and adding that to his land got to be too much for him. I found a group who agreed to mow, bale, and sell the hay." She smiled, "Just another way for the place to pay for itself."

"Well I have ta admit, ye've got a nice spot here. And did ye no tell me it's been in yer family for many years?"

"Yes. My dad's family came from Ireland in 1861 and settled in Bethany. In 1883, my great great grandfather bought this farm." Megan smirked just a little when she turned from the view to look at Donny. "Of course I realize that by European standards, that's not such an impressive timeline."

Donny tore his eyes from the view and looked into Megan's. "Aye, lass. That's the right of it, but ye're a young country. Ye've got time yet." They sat in the golf cart gazing at each other for several minutes before Megan broke contact and looked toward the lake. Donny smiled and looked around him. "Ye know, and I'm no` sure why, but this place reminds me a little o` Ian's place in Scotland."

"Really?" Megan beamed, "I have always wanted to go to Scotland."

"Why?" he half grumbled.

"Why do you ask like that? Don't you like your homeland?"

"Aye I do, I just do'na understand why everyone else has ta make it theirs."

"I think you're going to have to explain that. Because it sounds to me like you don't want anyone to visit or move there permanently. What? Do you want Scotland all to yourself?"

"Nay it's no like tha`. Let me see if I can explain. Ye see, I know the place. All the wonders and the hell of liven there and I love it, but when people come from other countries they want to make changes.

They go on about how beautiful it is, but it's not like 'home', and they want all the same things they have in their own countries. Big houses clustered together on tiny plots o` land and neatly paved roads tha` take up more land. They basically near destroy the beauty o` the place they thought was so great when they arrived. They want ta string wire and cable so they can ha` television and digital internet service. They do'na want ta drive five miles ta the grocer so they insist on shopping malls wi` superstores. They come into the shops in Lusta, laughin` and scratchin` and want special treatment because they are tourists. They've got money ta spend and act like the shop owners should be grateful fer the business. And most o` the time, they're rude. I've always wondered why they do'na stay home in the first place."

"Donovan Mackay! You don't like tourists!" She slapped the steering wheel of the golf cart and roared with laughter.

"I ne're said I dinna like tourists. Tourists are welcome but after they've seen their imagined paradise and bought their trinkets ta take back wi` them, they should take themselves back ta their own country."

Megan pulled a tissue from her pocket and wiped at her eyes but couldn't seem to curtail her laughter.

"Wha's so bloody funny?"

"You are! Oh my mother really would like you. Ever since my mother started living here from mid-May to mid-October, she has thought of herself as a local and from then on, she began to hate the 'tourists' who would come in the summers. And now that she lives here full time she's even worse." She continued to chuckle.

"And what aboot ye, lass. Do ye love the tourists?"

"I like the relative peace of fall and winter when the population shrinks, but I don't mind the summer people. It's progress and it makes life interesting. Besides, nothing ever stays the same. And, even the added summer folks don't make this area as wild and difficult to live in as the city with drive-by shootings and drug trafficking." Then she sighed and looked out over the rye lot. "Of course your white slave trade case kind of put us into the mainstream, I guess."

"Aye." To keep the case from putting a damper on their excursion, Donny looked around and indicated the break in the stone fence.

"Where does tha` lead?" Pointing to the little path that went through the stone wall and into the next field.

"Oh that goes to the Back Lot." She sighed. "Mom and Dad were going to put their retirement house there, but they couldn't see the lake. So they put it here in the Rye Lot."

"Their house is up here?" Donny indicated the house further back.

"Yeah. When Dad retired, they sold the house in Jersey and built a house up here. They keep a condo in Jersey for the couple of roughest winter months so they can get to Mother's eye doctors easier if they need to. In the beginning, Mom wasn't sure she could stay up here all winter, and deal with the snow and ice for months on end. But she actually does pretty well. However, she does need to see her eye doctors on a regular basis and being down there for the hardest weather months makes that easier. They have a gorgeous view up there. They can see the lake and the pasture. It's really spectacular in the fall and winter." She considered driving on up past the house but decided it could wait for another day, maybe when her parents were out for the day, and she could be sure her mother didn't highjack them.

"Why don't we head down to the lake now?" She turned the key and brought the cart to life, turned, and headed out of the field to the narrow dirt road. However, to Donny's surprise she didn't turn onto the road but crossed it to the field that flanked the other side. "This is the field above the house." She told him.

"Aye, and the other name fer it should be bumpy field." He cringed as she went over yet another bump.

"Oh God." Megan pulled the cart to a soft halt. "Donny I'm so sorry, I forgot how bumpy this field is. Are you alright?"

"Aye luv, but can ye find a better way doon?" He held his side and tried not to show her how much he really did hurt.

"Of course." She turned the cart around and moved very slowly back toward the road. She drove to the lake road and stopped.

"Why are ye stopping`?"

"You're hurting and I think it would be better if we ended your tour here and went back inside."

"Nay, I have been cooped up tae long as it is. I'm fine, luv."

"No, you're not, look at you. You can't even sit up straight."

"Sure I can." And to prove his point, regardless how painful it was, he sat up good and straight and smiled at her.

"I don't know who you think you're fooling. Your face is beet red! You've had enough."

"If ye want I'll take another one o` those bloody pain pills."

"I'm not going to sit here and argue with you about this. You've had enough for one afternoon. You're here to heal, not relapse."

"Listen luv, I'm no in the habit o` beggin—"

"Now Meggie, is that any way to treat an injured member of law enforcement?" came a male voice from the side lawn of the big house.

"Nathan?" Megan hopped out of the cart and raced up the incline to her oldest brother who scooped her up in a huge bear hug and whirled her around in a circle.

"Hi ya, kid." Nathan was tall and well built. He towered over her as did her other brother Morgan. Nathan had movie star looks, thick wavy brown hair highlighted with the family red. He had his mother's hazel eyes that at the moment were green with mirth.

"What are you doing here so early? I thought your plane didn't get in until eight-thirty."

"The airline overbooked our flight and called to ask if we were interested in an earlier one. So here we are." He placed her on her feet and smiled down at his little sister. "Angie is upstairs with the kids getting unpacked and we heard the cart, so I decided to get out of her way and come to see you..." He looked past his sister to the man he figured was Donovan Mackay sitting in the golf cart. "Both."

"Oh, Nathan this is—"

"Donovan Mackay, FBI, shot in the side and staying with you while he recovers. You met him the day you found him." He pulled his sunglasses down his nose and peered over the top of them at his sister and grinned. "Mom called."

"Mmmm. Big surprise." She said under her breath. She looked at Donny and then back at her brother. "Is that why you suddenly got an earlier flight?" she asked suspiciously.

"I told you the flight was overbooked, and they offered us an earlier one. Mom called after we landed." He smiled and walked down to Donny who was still seated in the cart. However, as Nathan made his approach Donny made a move to rise to his feet. "Oh, lord no." Nathan said as he closed the distance between them. "Stay seated or my sister will have your head on a spike. Hi," he reached out to clasp hands with Donny. "I'm Nathan, or Nate, Meggie's oldest brother."

"Nice ta meet ye Nate, Donny." He focused on Megan's brother who was eying him closely. Nathan couldn't get past the feeling that his sister's patient looked familiar in some way.

"Ha` we met before then?" Donny felt the need to ask given the look on Nathan's face as he looked Donny over.

"Nope, don't think so. But now you mention it, you look very similar to an actor I met with a few days ago."

"Are ye an actor?" *Maybe I've seen him in a photo wi` Ian,* Donny thought.

"No, Nathan is a director. Although there are many who would love to get him in front of the camera." Megan laughed as she dug her elbow into Nathan's side. "Who was the actor you met with?"

"Nice guy. Talented as hell! Fairly new to American cinema. Gonna be big though. Ian Mackay." Nathan looked at Donny for another few seconds, then it hit him, and he pointed to Donny and laughed. "Mackay! Related?"

"Aye." Donny grinned. "He's me younger brother."

"No kidding? Son-of-a-bitch! I'll be damned! Small world, huh?" Nathan laughed and turned to Megan. "You know who Ian Mackay is, don't you? You've seen his stuff. We're going to work together when he's finished up the picture he's working on now. He's—" at the sound of a crash from inside the big house Nathan cringed. "Uh-oh. I think I had better go make sure the kids are still breathing. Nice to meet you, Donny Mackay. The family and I will be down later to see ya, Meggie." Nathan turned and started back up the hill. "Oh, and by the way, Mom also called Morgan."

"Another big surprise." Megan grumped under her breath. But before Nathan took any further steps toward the house, he stopped and took hold of Megan's hand, drawing her aside.

"Say, honey. You didn't shoot him did ya?"

The answer he received was a frustrated glare and he laughed as he headed up the incline to the house

"By the way, Morgan told Mom he and his crew will be here tomorrow" He flashed her a wide grin as he reached the side porch and disappeared into the house.

"Morgan?" Donny asked as she climbed back into the cart and turned the key.

"My other brother. How are you feeling?"

"I feel fine luv, and I still do'na want tae go inside yet."

"Alright," she sighed. "But we're only going down there for a little while." She frowned and drove the golf cart down the red shale road to the lake.

They stayed on the shore for about half an hour sitting quietly, enjoying the breeze off the water. When Donny looked back to the cottage he noticed Nathan and his family and there appeared to be two other people with him.

"I believe ye are ta have company at the cottage, luv."

"Yeah. Looks like it's time for the family talk." She muttered as she turned the key to the cart and started back up the lake road to the cottage. "There are times when being an orphan wouldn't seem so bad." She pulled up to the back of the cottage and parked. Her family was up on the deck waiting for her and Donny to join them.

"Hi there. Donny, you know my mother and Nathan."

"Nice ta meet ye again, Mrs. Dunnegan." Donny smiled. "Nathan."

"This is my wife Angie, and these two hooligans are Mitch, and Sara."

"Nice ta meet ye." He smiled at Angie and looked down to her two children. "And how old ere ye?"

"I'm six and she's three." Mitch spoke up and pointed toward his sister.

"And this is my father, Patrick." Megan held her breath.

"Nice ta meet ye as well sir." Donny extended his arm and offered his hand to her father, who readily took the hand in a shake.

"So you're FBI, huh?"

"Of sorts. I was workin wi` them on a case." Donny moved so he could lean against the railing of the deck.

"Why don't you sit down, and I'll get your meds." Megan slipped into physician mode and turned toward the cottage door. Donny found the persona changes amusing and smiled at her. His smile grew larger when he saw that she had pink rising to her cheeks. *She's lovely when she blushes,* he thought.

"I'm fine luv, I have been sittin all day and do'na mind stretchin` me legs a wee bit."

"You talk funny." Mitch spoke up again.

"Mitch!" Angie whispered harshly. "That wasn't a very nice thing to say. Apologize right now."

"I'm sorry." Mitch bowed his head and looked sheepishly at the floor.

"Do'na worra yerself aboot it, lad," Donny chuckled. "I suppose I *would* sound funny ta ye. The same way ye sound funny ta me."

"I sound funny to you?" Mitch looked up at Donny with wide round eyes and an open mouth.

"Aye ye do. Now wha` ha` ye ta say aboot tha`?"

"Cool!" the little boy breathed. "Mom, I sound funny." Mitch clapped his hands, grabbed his sister Sara's hand, and headed down the steps of the deck to play in the yard.

"That was very sweet of you Mr. Mackay." Angie smiled "You couldn't have given him a better treat. However, he should never have made the comment."

"Donny," he smiled "and please do'na worry aboot it. Kids will say wha` e'er pops inta their minds and in a lot o` ways tis verra funny. I wasna in the least bit offended."

"Thank you." Angie turned her attention to Megan as she returned to the deck with a glass of water and medications. "So Meggie have you heard that Morgan and Sue will be joining our little party tomorrow?" She grinned, her eyes twinkling.

"Yes Angie, I was made aware of it. What I want to know is why?" This question she aimed at her family as a whole. Then zeroed in on her brother.

"What?" Nathan smiled. "Ok, so he called me after Mom talked to him and said that you had a visitor and that he was coming to have a look-see."

"Oh for heaven's sake. Look, I am a grown woman, and if I want to let a man stay here while he recovers it's my business."

"Meggie," her father came to stand by her side, draping his arm over her shoulders. "We are all aware you're a grown woman, and have your own life. But you can't be angry with your mother and brothers for wanting to look after you a little."

"And what about you?" She looked into her father's face.

"Oh, I mind my own business. I never say a word." He smiled and kissed her forehead. "So how long will you be under the weather Donny?"

"Fer a while, or at least tha` s wha` the lass here tells me."

The rest of the evening was spent with Nathan and Patrick talking to Donny about his work. Although Donny couldn't give much information on the subject, he was able to put them at ease. While Donny was being interrogated by the two men, Megan had questions fired at her by her mother and sister in-law.

Before long the kids grew restless, and Angie announced it was time to take them to the house and put them to bed.

"Come on kids." She called them to cries of 'awe, Mom!' and she walked down the deck stairs toward the big house.

Patrick and Emma had promised to drop in on one of the cousins "over the hill" and agreed it was time to go. Megan walked them off the deck. She watched her mother and father climb into the red and purple golf cart and head up the hill.

"He seems nice enough to me Meggie." Nathan told her as they stood together by the lake road. "But you never answered my question earlier."

"What's that?"

"Well, you didn't shoot him did you?" Nathan smiled and side stepped a punch directed at his shoulder.

"Oh Nathan, leave her alone for god's sake!" Angie admonished with a laugh.

"Goodnight Nathan." Megan said and turned back into the cottage.

Donny was sitting on the sofa with Max next to him. "Yer family is verra nice, luv. I notice yer brother calls ye '*Meggie*'?"

"Oh, well my mother was... *is* a big fan of the novel and mini-series "*Thornbirds*". The main character in the book was Megan Cleary, her family called her Meggie. She named me after her and I inherited the nickname as well."

"Ah, Meggie, I like it." Their eyes locked and she began to fidget under his gaze, and he found her to be even lovelier for it. "Ye seem ta be a wee bit tense luv."

"Do I?" She tugged at her shirt tail. Why was he looking at her that way? She wondered. "Um, how's your pain?"

"Always the doctor aren't ye? I feel fine... Meggie."

She could feel the color rise in her face. "I think I'll take my shower."

"Ok." He answered never taking his eyes from her face. She turned and headed to her room to collect clean clothing and her hair towel.

Once she was in the shower stall with warm water running over her, she ran the last few days through her mind. *Few days,* she thought.

"Seems like it's been much longer." She mumbled to herself. It *had* only been a few days and she was feeling like she had known Donny for months. How the hell could she be attracted to him after such a short time? The thought slammed into her like a wall. *Attracted to him?* "I'm not." She told herself. "I'm just housing him until he's healed and can go his merry way. That's all." She lathered up her hair and thought about her family.

She was annoyed at them for coming here and intruding in her life. Then she scolded herself for her attitude. *Why should I be annoyed?* she wondered. *They care about me.* She had allowed a total stranger to live at her home while recovering from a bullet wound. If it were one of her friends or a family member doing what she was doing, wouldn't she be as concerned as her family was? Wouldn't she feel the need to check up on the situation just as her family had done? *Yes,* she decided she would. So why was she so annoyed? *Because they are intruding on time you would have with Donny alone?* The little voice in her head sang. "Oh, for God sakes! Don't be ridiculous!" She stuck her head under the shower spray to rinse out the shampoo. "They just think I can't handle this on my own, that's all, and that's why I'm annoyed. Nothing more." She grabbed the luffa, squirted on some body wash, and began to scrub her arms. As she continued to rub the luffa over her body, she wondered if Donny would be able to swim by the end of next week. That would give his sutures close to two weeks to heal. She should get him some swim trunks. "I wonder what he'd look like in swim trunks?" The mental thought turned up her internal temperature. "Oh hell!" she muttered and turned the dial on her shower from hot to cold.

As Donny sat on the sofa he wondered if she knew she talked out loud to herself and if he should bring it to her attention. He looked down at Max.

"Better no," he told the big dog. "She may no` be so happy ta think I was eavesdropping on her private time. But it's a verra small house." He was getting some very odd feelings himself. He knew women found him attractive. He'd learned that way back when he was in school. And it had worked for him until he and Arabella became a real couple. After Arabella, he didn't much care what anybody thought of how he looked or what he did or where he went as long as Arabella loved him. But this was the first time in years that he was genuinely thrilled that a woman found him attractive. The realization shook him. She was interested in him as a man, not just a patient. And that knowledge set him back because he was pleased. She was strong in her own right, but there was a tender caring side to her as well. He could see that with her family, no matter if she were put out with them due to their over protectiveness. "So she wonders wha` I look like in swim trunks huh?" he chuckled and rubbed the dog's head. "I ha` been wonderin what she looks like a bathin` suit." Max looked up at Donny and gave a soft "ruff!" "Nothin` fer ye ta be worried aboot, bucko. Me intentions are honorable," he laughed. *Good god*, he thought. *Me intentions are honorable.* He leaned his head on the back of the sofa and let his mind wander. *I'm in no position ta have dishonorable intentions.* He heard the bathroom door open and looked up. There she was in a yellow tank top and matching shorts with a towel piled on her head. The smell of the body wash she used seeped into the room and engulfed Donny's senses. *God help me,* he sighed to himself.

"Have you had a shower yet?" Megan asked as she walked toward him.

"Nay yet. I wasn't sure about getting the bandages wet and there was no one here ta redo them if they got ruined."

"That was a wise choice. Why don't you take your shower now, and I'll put fresh bandages on when you're done. Try not to let the water spray hit the wounds directly. They can get a little damp, but I don't want them sopping." She told him as she walked into her room. His eyes followed her as she took off the towel and began to rub her hair with it. *I think I'll be needin a cold shower now though.* He thought. Just then the phone rang.

"Hello?" Megan answered the phone in her bedroom. "Liz, what's wrong?...Oh no...I'm so sorry." Donny listened to Megan for a while and decided to go and turn down his bed and take his shower.

An hour later Megan joined him on the deck where he had seated himself to look at the stars. She handed him a plate with a sandwich on it, and placed fresh bandages on the table. Before sitting with him she walked the perimeter of the deck lighting the torches to ward off the onslaught of mosquitoes.

"What might this be, lass?"

"A very poor excuse for a snack. An American favorite. Peanut butter and jelly." Her voice was clipped. "But it's the best I can do for the moment."

He lifted the sandwich to his mouth and took a bite. "I've had this before. I liked it." He looked at her again and recognized the agitation from her body language. "I still like it. Verra tasty."

"Everythin` ok?" He asked once she was done lighting the torches and seated in the chair next to him.

"No, not really. That was Liz on the phone, her husband just left her. The bastard! She is nine months pregnant with his child and he decides he can't live a lie anymore and needs to be who he really is. So he and Michael are going away together and live in Hawaii."

"Michael?" Donny asked, trying not to crack a smile.

"And get this," she went on, not realizing Donny had said anything. "He told her that she didn't need to worry about anything, that he would "pay", *pay,* "for their child". She can have the house. But until he and Michael are settled in the house they've *already bought, in Hawaii,* he wouldn't be able to be here for her. He's apparently already had divorce papers drafted and they will be ready for her to sign in a week. That... that... *fucking bastard!* If I ever get my hands on him I swear to *God* he will *never* be able to father another child again. And now she is left to raise their child alone and has to live with the fact that her husband not only left her, but left her for another man! Which I know isn't the biggest issue in the grand scheme of things, but, ARRGGG."

"What will she do?"

"She doesn't know yet, she is in shock, this was out of the blue for her. She had no idea that there were any problems, let alone that he was gay. Neither did any of us for that matter. They always seemed so happy and in love." By this time she had left her seat next to him and was standing with her back to him at the railing of the deck again.

"Well mayhap they were, he might have loved her, but it wasna enough. He couldna lie ta her or ta himself anymore."

"Are you defending *him*?" She whirled around to him outraged.

"Nay lass I'm no defendin` him." He raised his hands in peace. "I'm lookin` at this as an outsider." He stood and walked to her. "I do'na know either of these people and can look at the situation wi` a clear unemotional head. I'm lookin` at both sides. Wha` he did was wrong, but how wrong would it be if he stayed and allowed the lie ta continue fer years and years. As much as she is hurtin` now, she would be in much more pain if he had stayed longer." He placed his hands on her upper arms and looked deep into her eyes. She was indeed a caring and loving person. To feel just as betrayed and angry for her friends as she would if she were in Liz's place, was more proof for him of what a good person she was.

"She is so hurt, mortified, and scared right now." Megan was so angry and upset she had to fight the sting of tears behind her eyes. Unfortunately, one tear slid down her cheek.

"Ye feel for her," he gently wiped the tear from her cheek with his thumb. She brought her fantastic eyes to meet his and he was unable to help himself. He lowered his head and touched his lips to hers ever so slightly. He brought his head back up. "I'm sorry I did tha` ."

"I'm not." Megan's voice was so soft, he was barely able to hear it. However, Donny could hear it loud and clear. He brought his lips back to hers in a fury of passion. She met his need with her own. He was strong and his lips were deliciously soft. He had both hands on either side of her face and backed her up against the railing as he deepened the kiss even more. She tasted like rainwater and spring. He heard a tiny murmur creep up her throat. She wanted nothing more than to touch him. Her hands were on his hips and began to move up his sides and torso. She forgot about the injury and moved her hand right over the wound.

"Ah!" He drew in a startled breath and broke away from her, placing one hand on the railing to brace himself and the other to his sutures.

"Oh God, I'm so sorry! I...I was so wrapped up in...I mean...I...I forgot." She looked at his crimson face and down at his hand protecting his wound. "I didn't mean to hurt you, I'm sorry, do you want me to look at it?"

"Nay, it will be fine luv, forgive me but, please do'na touch me." He smiled some so she knew he wasn't angry.

"Why don't we get you into bed."

"As much as I would wish ta take ye ta me bed, luv, I do'na think I am up fer the task."

Now it was her turn to turn crimson. *Fine way for a doctor to treat her patient,* she thought. *I forgot? Good God!*

"Come on, *laddie* , once your laying down in bed I'll put on fresh bandages."

She walked him to the bedroom and helped him lie down on the bed. She removed the damp bandages and examined the wound. Satisfied that he was in fact fine, she applied fresh bandages, pulled the sheet up over him and said goodnight without mentioning what had happened between them. She entered her bedroom, turned on the light and took the throw pillows from the bed. She knew sleep would evade her tonight. Between Donny's kiss and Liz's situation, she didn't know who to be more upset with, herself or Liz's bastard husband! "You don't live to be nearly thirty years old and not know you're gay!" She muttered. "Why would you marry a girl and allow her to become pregnant and then decide you can no longer live a lie? The son-of-a-bitch should have realized that a long time ago." She slid under the sheet and drew it up to her chin. "And your behavior isn't much better Megan Dunnegan. Doctor of Medicine! Pawing a patient! GOD! Even if he did paw you first." She smiled and closed her eyes.

Chapter Thirteen

Megan settled herself in her bed and then noticed through the windows that she had forgotten to extinguish the torches on the deck. She rose and went onto the deck but stood for several minutes reliving Donny's kiss. It had been unexpected to say the least. But definitely not unappreciated. *It was really a damn hot kiss, and had the promise of so much more.* She mused. She walked around the deck rail slowly capping off each torch and then stood for a few moments longer breathing deeply of the sweet night air. It had been a difficult evening for her with her family descending on the cottage, and grilling both her and Donny the way they had, with their questions, suspicions, and concerns. She understood their motives, but she didn't have to like them. And then Liz's phone call. She was so angry with Jimmy for what he'd done. She was also worried about Liz and the stress this desertion would cause her. *What if this pushes her into premature labor? Didn't think about that did you, you bastard?* Megan had suggested to Liz, this evening, that Liz take a few days off to rest and regroup, but Liz refused. She said she needed to train Hannah Brown to take over her job and Hannah was coming in the morning for her first day on the job. Liz insisted she had to be there.

"Oh Liz, we can all pitch in for a few days and let her know what she needs to do ourselves." Megan had told her, although she didn't know how in the hell she would be able to arrange that. There were other staff members at the front desk that could help, but the fact was; nobody really knew how to do all the things that Liz did. Or how she was able to accomplish it all in the time she did. Liz was a dream to have and they all knew it. Megan also knew that the entire staff would rally behind Liz because they all cared for her very much. They would give her all the support and help they could. This was going to be a tough time for Liz on several levels and she knew she could count on the people at the office to help. Thank God for the daycare center upstairs because Megan already knew keeping Liz at home for six weeks after the baby was born was not going to be successful.

She thought about calling Jess and letting her know what had happened, but a glance at the clock told her it was too late to call. Jess and Nancy had their own new baby in the house and sleep for them, as well as the baby, was top priority. With time alone together running a close second. "I'll tell her in the morning" she sighed, returned to her room, and slid between the covers again.

Megan tried to push her heartache for Liz out of her mind. She knew she had to get to sleep herself or she'd be no good to her patients tomorrow. *Think about something nice,* she told herself and immediately Donny's image on the deck this evening popped into her mind, her eyes flew open, and she snickered. "Yeah, well that ain't gonna do it, sister." She whispered. *Thank God tomorrow is Friday,* she thought. Even though the office was open on Saturday and until noon on Sunday, it was Megan's practice, and she did have the option of not going in, although she rarely took advantage of that option. She had learned it was a good time to get paperwork done, pay bills, and make phone calls she never seemed to have time for throughout the week. She would read up on new medications that the reps were always peddling. Actually, she generally accomplished a great deal when she was in the office on weekends, and she rarely accepted appointments for Saturdays but was almost always there if needed. But this weekend, with her brothers and their families here for their visit/interrogations, it might be better for her to stay home. And she admitted she could use two days off, although she wasn't holding out a lot of hope for peace and tranquility as long as the question-and-answer sessions were still in full swing. By the same token, it wasn't really fair to leave Donny here alone to face the family with explanations and reasons. *Stop thinking about him*, she told herself. *Go to sleep!*

While Donny lay in his own bed fighting the demons of wakefulness, he could hear Megan's restlessness and assumed she was having as much trouble finding peaceful sleep as he was. His mind wandered as it had several times in the last half-hour to the kiss they shared on the deck this evening. And he imagined what might have happened if her arm had not slid around over his bandages. *Well this is no` the way ta find sleep!* He thought. They hadn't spoken about the kiss afterwards and it was hanging over him. He wanted to talk about it. It changed things. *Aye, we should talk aboot it,* he thought. Then reality hit. No! He didn't want to talk about it! He wanted to kiss her again. And again! *Let's be honest here laddie,* he told himself. He was attracted to her and she to him he knew. *Aye let's be honest. Ye want ta go ta her now and finish what ye started on the deck.* But how could he, he wondered. His hesitation had as much to do with Megan herself as it did with his still painful injury. *She's no` a woomon who leaps inta bed wi` someone* *she barely knows,* he realized. "Hell, she put her arms around me, and I nearly dove off the deck" he muttered. "Wha` the hell kind o` lover does tha` make o` me?" He groused. Added to that she really didn't know him. Nobody did, but he wanted her to get to know him and feel safe with him, he decided. *So mayhap it's best ta take it slow.* He thought. It had been a very long time since he had wanted to let a woman know him. He hadn't let any woman into his life for years. Maybe he was healing in more ways than one.

After his inner discussion with himself he tried to find sleep, but the more he tossed and turned looking for a comfortable position, the more his side began to hurt. Right now pain seared through him. Where did she keep his pain meds, he wondered.

"Bloody hell." He whispered as he gingerly sat up and swung his leg over the side of the bed. "I think I'm in need o` some drugs." He whispered to Max who stood at attention by the side of the bed watching with interest as Donny struggled to rise on his own from the bed. "Are ye gaurdin` me or the lass, ye beast?" He asked as he ruffled the big dog's ears. He took a deep breath and stood.

Megan closed her eyes and told herself she would be asleep in ninety seconds. This method had always worked for her father, but she had never been very successful with it. Her Dad would say, "You just make your mind a complete blank". How this was accomplished, she had no clue. So she lay in the bed mentally telling each section of her body to relax, first her neck, then her fingers and then her arms. She was beginning to feel the effects of her own mantra when she jolted back to reality by the sound of crashing pill bottles bouncing on the hard surface floor. She shot to a sitting position and turned on the lamp by the side of her bed. Throwing back the covers she raced to the door and rounding the corner, she skidded to a stop. There in the semi darkness of the bathroom, stood Donny. His arms hanging at his sides, his face to the ceiling, his eyes shut and brown plastic pill bottles littering the floor around his feet.

"Donny? Are you alright?" She asked as she made her way to the bathroom and flipped on the light.

"Please dinna keep askin me that, luv." He dropped his head and looked at her. "Did I wake ye?" he asked even though he knew the answer.

She couldn't help it. The sight of him was so pathetic, she wanted to laugh but was able to curtail it to a chuckle. "No, I was awake." She scooped up the pill bottles and placed them back on the turntable shelf on top of the enclosed hot water tank.

"What are you doing out of bed?" She asked.

Donny just looked at her.

"Well, you said not to ask if you were alright. I'm doing my best to ad-lib." But she couldn't hold in her laughter any longer and it burst from her in what Donny thought was the sweetest sound he'd ever heard. And he had to smile too. As he figured, his middle-of-the-night-drug-raid must have created quite a picture.

"Me side was hurtin` a bit and I wanted ta take some o` those blasted pills ta dull the pain."

"Oh, well here." She opened the bottle and handed him a Percocet, then went back to the kitchen. "I should have left these on your nightstand," She mumbled almost to herself as she filled the glass with water before handing it to him. "so you wouldn't have to get out of bed in the middle of the night and look for them. I'm sorry that was thoughtless of me."

"Ye do'na sound so verra sorry, lass." he grumped as he tossed back the pill and drank the water. But when he handed her the empty glass, he was grinning.

"Well, I am." She smiled and placed the glass in the kitchen sink.

"Where do ye usually keep *yer* meds, luv?" he asked as they moved into the kitchen.

"On top of the hot water tank on the merry-go-round tray... in the bathroom."

"Then it was nay thoughtless, just habit. And do'na worra aboot it. I said me self tha` I dinna want ta take the damn things in the first place because they make me sleepy."

"Then why are you taking one now?" she smiled

"Because I canna sleep and me side hurts." He moved closer to her and captured her eyes with his. "Though, I canna imagine why." and his eyes began to sparkle in amusement when her cheeks went pink.

"I said I was sorry about that." She kept her eyes downcast.

"Are ye sure it wasna yer way ta put an end ta me kissin` ye?" he continued to move closer to her and she backed up a step, but he kept closing the distance between them.

"No! I wasn't trying to...you know," her voice was a bit unsteady. "I should have a regular medicine cabinet, but the merry-go-round on top of the hot water tank has been the system for so many years it never occurred to me to change it."

"In yer bathroom." He confirmed her new topic while smiling into her eyes, as he continued to move closer.

"Exactly! Actually I did make some changes in the bathroom. You see," as she stepped back again. "When mother and Dad used the cottage during the summers she had him remove the bathroom sink. And replace it with a small pantry."

"He removed the sink?" Donny smiled.

"Yes, she said it was an old sink with separate faucets and she never used it, so she had him take it out and build a pantry..." Donny brushed his fingers through her hair.

"She dinna like the old sink?"

Megan closed her eyes for seconds when his hand brushed the back of her neck. "No...two faucets are so awkward."

"Aye. They are?" Donny stepped closer, and Megan moved back.

"Yes." Donny was so close now that their lips were only inches apart. *This is not good,* she thought. *Stay in control.*

"I asked her why she just didn't have him build a pantry for her where I have mine now..."

"And wha` did she say?"

"What?" Megan could feel Donny's breath on her lips. His eyes were focused in the same area, and she was having a difficult time breathing.

"Wha` did she say when ye ask her aboot the pantry location?"

"Oh, she said if she put a pantry there, she wouldn't have a place to put her summer..." Donny brushed his lips against hers and the teasing touch lit a fire she could no longer deny. His hand engulfed the back of her neck as he pulled her into the kiss. She brought her palms up to his chest and rested them there while he deepened the kiss. It was several minutes before he broke contact, and several more seconds before she opened her eyes.

"Stemware."

"Meggie?" he sighed before lowering his mouth to hers again. When he ended the kiss, he whispered against her lips. "Do ye mind if I call ye Meggie?"

"Of course not. You..." she looked up and saw the smile on his fantastic lips.

"Would ye mind if we try this again?"

"I think we should get you back in bed before that pill takes hold." Donny could tell she wanted to avoid his question; however he had no intention of letting her.

"I will be in bed soon enough, luv. First I'd like ye ta answer the question at hand."

"And what question is that?" she once again had her eyes cast down to avoid looking at him. She needed to keep her head and she knew she wouldn't be able to if she had to gaze into his jade eyes.

"Megan," he crooked his finger under her chin and drew her eyes to meet his. "Do ye want me ta stop kissin` ye?" he asked quietly and in complete earnest.

"You really need—"

"Answer me." He whispered.

"No, I don't." She placed her hands on his powerful chest. "But Donny—"

"Shh." He lowered his lips to hers. "May I?" He whispered against her mouth.

"Please."

He drew back some. "Please kiss me or please do'na?"

"I'm in no mood to argue with you." She slid her hand up his chest to his shoulders. "Please kiss me, Donavan Mackay."

He had intended to kiss her slowly, however when their lips met, a fire was released in him causing him to take her mouth with lust. Her hands moved up across his shoulders and she wrapped her arms around his neck to draw him closer to her. To match her, he clamped her body to his with his arms. In doing so, his side began to burn but he ignored it. She felt wonderful in his arms close to him. It was as if she was made to fit him in body, and by God in spirit as well. Her scent was intoxicating, and her mouth was wondrous. The more he felt for her the more he deepened the kiss between them. He wanted more of her, he wanted all of her.

She accepted that she couldn't resist him. Didn't want to resist him. Never in her life had she met a man who affected her the way he did. The draw to him was powerful. He was strong, handsome, sexy as hell, and a damn good kisser. His body was so hard and sensual next to hers and she wanted nothing more than to feel more of him. His hands were roaming her back and she felt at the same time exhilarated and weak in the knees. She could feel her legs turning to jello and butterflies in her belly running rampant. He was taking her breath away with his need and passion for her. He heard the small moan escape her throat and deepened the kiss even more.

Donny turned and backed her up against the kitchen sink. He had never wanted anyone as much as he wanted her at this moment. He broke away from her mouth, trailing his lips down to her neck and shoulders. His hands moved from her back up to the sides of her breasts. Megan gasped with pleasure as he cupped her breast and her growing desire turned into need. As his lips roamed down her throat she leaned her head back to give him more access loving the feel of his lips, hands, and body pressed to hers.

He pulled his hands from her breasts to reach for the hem of her tank top and began to caress the bare skin underneath the fabric. The realization of what she wanted to come next dragged her out from under the spell Donny had created for them both. She placed her hands on his chest and gave a slight push. Donny stopped immediately.

"Megan? Did I do somethin' wrong? I'm sorra, I dinna..." Her whole body was flush with heat and when she opened her violet eyes, they were deep midnight blue with want and need. He rested one hand behind her on the sink and raised the other to the side of her face.

She pressed her fingertips to his mouth to stop his words. "Dear god, no, you didn't do anything wrong. In fact," she smiled and slid her hand to the side of his face. His eyes were trying to focus, and she could see he was caught between concern and near animal lust. She wanted to reassure him, but she also knew she had to slow this down. "You were doing everything right." She took a deep breath, and he could hear the smile in her voice. "That's the problem."

"I do'na understand luv, maybe the pills are startin` ta take effect." He chuckled and touched his forehead to hers.

"You have no idea how hard it is for me to say this, but I must."

"Ye dinna want this ta happen?" He whispered.

"Oh, yes I do!" she nearly laughed as she tried to control her breathing. "But we both know where this would lead, Donny, and it can't. Not now." She brought her hand down and rested her palm on his chest. "*You* can't do this now. You've had a serious injury, tremendous blood loss, surgery, and your sutures are too new. That bullet went clear through your body. In one side and out the other. If you pull sutures now, you're in big trouble. Under those circumstances, the next step in this type of exercise could and undoubtedly would be very unhealthy for you. In fact," she laughed, "It could be disastrous."

"So, yer putting` on the brakes fer m*e own good* benefit?" he smiled. "Remind me nay ta thank ye later when I'm in the shower with the cold water sloshin` over me body."

"I'm sorry." She sighed and rested her head on his chest. "You have no *idea* how sorry I am." She groaned.

"No` as sorra as I am, luv." He closed his eyes and forcibly willed his body to back down while he kissed the top of her head. He accepted that she was right and felt he should tell her so. "As much I hate ta admit it luv, but I think ye're right."

"Really?" she looked up at him "Are you sure?" she was almost pleading, and it made him laugh.

"Aye, I'm sure." He traced his fingers down the side of her cheek.

"Damn it." She whined and then laughed.

"Ye do know tha` we have changed things between us tonight." He said quietly.

"Yes I do. How do you feel about that? Then there are also ethical issues I have to consider if I haven't already blown them out of the water." She raised her hand to the side of his face and traced the small scar on his left cheek. Her touch was feather light and it seemed to arouse him more than the kiss, but it was not so much sexual as emotional. She had touched his heart like it hadn't been touched before and Donny was struck by it.

How *did* he feel about that? Was this something he wanted, could he handle it? The answer to both questions surprised Donny. The answer was yes, it was what he wanted. She was what he wanted, needed and more than anything must have. Megan saw what he was feeling and the realization in his eyes before he spoke. And it warmed her heart more than anything he was going to say.

"Aye. I want this, I want you, heart, and soul, luv." He leaned down and kissed her. When he began to sway Megan knew the pain killers were kicking in and she needed to get him down before he fell down.

"Donny, you have to get to bed. Come on." She led him into the bedroom and helped him sit on the edge of the bed. "Are you alright?" she asked when he grunted.

Despite his discomfort and the wooziness caused by the medications he rolled his eyes to the ceiling. "Will ye ne're stop askin me that? Aye, luv, I'm fine. Will ye sit beside me fer a moment?" Megan sat next to him and felt his forehead. He had a fine sheen of perspiration forming on his forehead and she was concerned, as post-surgical infection was a major issue.

"I realize the repetition of the question is irritating, but it's important. You feel a little warm to me. Wait here." She got up from the bed and left the room. Moments later she came back with a thermometer. "Open your mouth, I want to take your temperature." As she instructed Donny obeyed. She waited until the digital device pinged and then looked at the read-out. He had a temp of 100.4 "You are running a low-grade fever. It could be due to standing for so long. I need you to lay down and be still." She helped to lie back into the bed and covered him with the sheet and comforter. "I'm going to get some water; I'll be right back." As she turned to leave Donny grasped her hand.

"If I'm running a fever, lass, I doubt it is due to the standin." He grinned at her."

"I'll be right back." She chuckled. When she returned Megan handed Donny the glass of water. He followed the unspoken instructions and handed the glass back to her.

"I've also brought your pain meds. They're right here on the night-stand in case you need them when you wake in the morning."

"Will ye sit a while?" Donny scooted more to the center of the mat-tress and indicated the extra space on the bed he had created. Megan looked at him steadily for a few seconds to gauge if this was a safe exercise and then sat on the edge of the bed.

"Wha` did ye mean, before, aboot 'ethical issues'?"

Megan sighed and looked at him. "It's highly unethical for a doctor to enter into any type of emotional or physical relationship with a patient, Donovan."

"Wha` patient? Me?" he sounded shocked to the core.

"YES! You! Of course you." She laughed out loud. "You're the patient. I'm the doctor. That's how it works."

"Aye. Mayhap. But I'm no *yer* patient, luv. I'm Dr. Ottis's patient." He looked up at her with a satisfied grin on his face.

"UH, well technically I suppose that's correct, but he released you into my care, and—"

"Nay, lass, he released me into yer care as a house guest, no` a patient" he maintained. His grin growing wider and becoming more smug. "The fact tha` ye're a physician is a convenience, I grant ye, but tis merely a convenience o` me presence in yer home wi` ye." She looked back at him with what really amounted to awe.

"It appears you've given this more than a second's thought."

"Aye. I ha', luv. I've been mullin` it in me mind since last night. Ye're an upstandin` member of the community and what do ye American's call it? 'A straight arrow'. It occurred ta me the question o` ethics might pop up in yer mind sooner than later." He took her hand and brought it to his lips. "I wanted ta be ready. So ye can dismiss yer concerns from yer mind. Our relationship is social, no professional."

She gazed at his face and nearly lost herself in his smile. "Do we have a relationship?" she asked finally, and he chuckled.

"I'm tryin` awfully hard here." He said. "Can I ask ye a favor luv?"

"Anything." She smiled.

"Would ye place those lips ta mine again mayhap ta seal our nonprofessional standing?"

"I could offer that as a reason for your spiked fever. Way too much excitement." She ran her hand over his forehead and down his cheek. "I know better."

"So is tha` a nay then?" he smiled.

Megan leaned over and placed a small kiss on his cheek. "I think it would be better to keep the excitement down to a minimum."

"Would ye come ta bed then?"

"Donovan Mackay! You're an incorrigible flirt," she laughed out loud.

"Nay, Megan, I just feel better when ye're near me." He smiled.

"I will most definitely not come to bed with you! But if you like, I can loan you one of my stuffies if you think that will help." She chuckled.

"I'm thinkin` the only thing tha` will help me now is a cold shower." He sighed and gently traced her jaw line with his fingers. The gesture was so intimate that Megan closed her eyes and leaned into the feeling. "Promise me somethin`."

"What's that?"

"Tha` in the morn ye willna regret what has happened here tonight and change yer mind aboot wha` I think we are goin ta become."

Megan leaned down and kissed him. At first it was soft and slow, then she deepened it. Donny ran his hands up the sides of her face into her hair. With his hand on the back of her head he pulled her even closer.

"I will never regret what happened tonight." She murmured on his lips. "And I don't think I have the strength to change my mind about what you and I might become."

"If I ha` me way darlin, the word *might* willna be a factor." He kissed her again.

"You're making it very difficult for me to be the responsible party here, you know." She sighed, her mouth so close to his.

"I know." He chuckled devilishly.

"Oh! You're good!" She laughed, giving him a quick peck on the lips, and then abruptly stood up and out of his reach. "But I'm better, and have more self-control." She smiled brightly and placed her hands on her hips. "Now, go to sleep and I'll see you in the morning. If you're awake I'll fix you breakfast before I leave for the office."

"Ye're the devil lass, ye know tha` do ye no?"

"*Aye*, goodnight and sleep well." She chirped as she sailed out the door.

"Nay bloody likely." He grumbled. Although he smiled as he heard her laugh on the way to her own bed.

Megan slept later than usual so the question of a big breakfast together was a non-issue. She made coffee and set out milk and a box of cold cereal while Donny took a shower. Whether it was hot or cold, she had no clue. She retrieved a Nutri-Grain bar herself and was just pouring a cup of coffee when there was a knock at the front door. She glanced out the window and saw a State Trooper cruiser parked in the lake road. She walked over to the door and couldn't believe her eyes.

"Oh shit." She groaned inwardly. She glanced back toward the bathroom door to listen for water still running in the shower. "Now what the hell do I do?" she muttered as she pasted a smile on her face. *Answer the door dummy*, she thought as she reached for the knob and pulled open the door. "Trooper Mackay, what can I do for you?"

"You can call me Steven." He smiled.

"Well not while you're in uniform." She smiled and then opened the door and stepped outside. She held the door open for Max, who had spied Mitch and Sara in the backyard of the big house. Max raced through the door, bounded off the stone porch. He made a beeline for the children only stopping momentarily at the lilac bushes and willow tree. Megan and Steven watched the big dog on his way up the slight grade to the backyard and the two children. "How can I help you?"

"We got calls from both camps this morning about a fair amount of vandalism, in their infirmaries during the night. A couple of staff car alarms went off during the night too, but you know, nobody pays much attention to car alarms around here. And since you're sitting smack in between both camps, I thought I'd stop and ask if you saw or heard anything unusual last night or if you had any disturbances around here in the wee hours."

"You're kidding?" Her earlier dilemma of having Donny's estranged brother on her front porch, right out of her mind. "No, I didn't see or hear anything out of the ordinary." She said. "It seems odd that there would be break ins and vandalism while camp is in session. I mean, it seems to be an awful risk, what with so many people wandering around all the time. Even at night, we have an almost constant procession of councilors walking up and down the road."

"Yeah, well, if it was kids, they generally don't think about precautions and getting caught. If they're planning illegal activities, they're only interested in the product desired." He turned at the sound of children laughing and smiled. "Cute."

"Thank you, my niece and nephew. My oldest brother and his family came into town yesterday. They're staying up at the big house. Did you say that the infirmaries are what were broken into at both camps?"

"Yeah, the odd thing is that in most cases of break-ins to medical facilities the perp is looking for drugs. Most medical offices have a lot of sample packs from drug reps...well, you know that." He and Megan exchanged smiles. "But in both cases here, what was taken were things like bandaging materials, syringes of course, few bottles of antibiotic, and a set of crutches from Rosemont. "

"That was it? I know that some of the kids from this camp down here especially have to have some powerful medications. I don't really know exactly what the infirmaries keep on hand in the way of pain meds. Not much I would imagine, but I know that some of the special needs kids take some pretty strong behavior modification meds."

"Well if the perp or perps were looking for serious drugs, they apparently weren't looking in the right places. Or just assumed all medications were kept in the same place. All scripted medications other than antibiotics were accounted for this morning. You haven't gotten any bad news from your office this morning, I assume."

"No, and if the office had been broken into, I would have heard by now and so would your barracks. But I appreciate you stopping by...Steven. I won't keep you any longer since you're in the middle of an investigation."

"Hey sis." Nathan was walking down from the back yard. "Are you in trouble with the law again? You didn't shoot anybody else did you?" he laughed.

"Very funny, Nathan." She wanted to smack him. With a ball bat. She had been hoping to end the conversation and encourage Steven to be on his way before Donny knew he was there. "There were some break ins at the camps last night. Trooper Mackay is investigating."

"No kidding?" Nathan stepped closer to the porch and offered his hand to the Trooper. "Nathan Dunnegan."

"Nice to meet you." Steven stretched his hand out to accept Nathan's. "Steven Mackay. You didn't happen to hear anything unusual during the night last night, did you Mr. Dunnegan?"

"Nope. Not a thing. Other than those two hooligans jumping on the beds and giggling in the next room. Heard my wife yell at them a few times. But other than that, nothing. So what happened?" Steven relayed the facts to Nathan as he had to Megan and while he spoke,

Nathan took in Steven's build and facial features and narrowed his eyes. "Mackay, huh? You know you remind me of…"

"Nathan, Trooper Mackay is in the middle of an investigation here. I don't think we should keep…"

"Dad! Sara won't get off the swing and it's my turn!" Mitch yelled from the tire swing in the backyard of the big house. Nathan waved at the boy. "Duty calls, It was nice to meet you, Trooper Mackay. Hope you catch the bad guys." As he turned to return to his own back yard he noticed Donny standing by the big window next to the front door and raised his hand in greeting. "Morning, Donny. How you feeling? Gotta go." And with that he turned and trotted back to where the kids were squabbling.

Yeah, that's right! Stir things up and then scram, you schmuck! Megan thought.

Megan turned toward the window to see Donny standing in a pair of black sweatpants, with his T-shirt hanging suspended in both hands. His hair was wet from the shower, and it was obvious he had been in the process of putting on his shirt when he saw Steven on the porch with Megan. She saw the look of shock mingled with pure hatred on his face as his eyes locked with Steven's.

"I've been better, Nathan. Thanks for askin." Donny answered but Nathan had already gone.

Chapter Fourteen

"Donny?" Steven whispered, "Is that you?" Steven looked at the brother that he had not seen in eighteen years. He was older and it showed in his build and in his face. And by the look on his face it did not appear that Donny's feelings toward the younger brother had changed over the years. "Are you hurt?" he asked when he noticed the obvious and numerous sutures on Donny's side. When Donny did not respond Steven turned his attention back to Megan. "I didn't know you knew Donny."

"Well there's really no reason why you would know." She said nervously. She had no idea what to do, and Donny wasn't helping. The phone rang and broke the silence. "Excuse me." She stepped back in the door and answered the phone. "Hello?...Oh hell no, I'm fine. I'm sorry, I should have called...something came up here at the house. I'll be there right away. No, no. We're all fine. It's nothing like that. I'll be there in a few minutes. I'm leaving now." She hung up the phone and faced Donny.

"Donny," she waited until he drew his eyes from his brother and looked at her, he was still holding his shirt in his hands. "That was the office," she said slowly. Megan moved toward him and looked at his sutures. "You don't seem to be seeping. I think we'll leave the bandaging off today. If you do notice any seepage, call me right away, and I'll come home and apply a dressing." She picked up her purse and keys on the way to the door. Steven was still on the front porch. "Ok guys," she began. "That was Liz on the phone. I'm already late for the office." She hesitated looking first at Steven on the porch and then at Donny standing perfectly still by the window. Neither had said another word. "Steven, you're more than welcome in my home if you'd like to stay and talk with your brother. Donny," she turned to him, and he glared back at her. "Remember, you're injured. Too much physical activity would reopen your wound." *He's so angry and I think part of that anger is for me,* she thought. She walked to stand in front of him, and resting both of her hands on his broad bare shoulders, she raised on her tiptoes and kissed his cheek. "Be nice. And if you can't manage that," she gently kissed him on the lips, "Please, for the love of God, don't wreck my house, or yourself. You're healing well so far, and if you screw that up now, you'll be back in Memorial hospital faster than you can say...*one single word! And that's no joke.*" she looked fiercely into his eyes. "You may not survive ER surgery. And anything we might have hoped for last night might never happen." *How's that for a serviceable threat?* she thought.

Donny raised an eyebrow at her parting request and couldn't conceal the trace of humor that appeared on his face. "Aye, luv." He murmured.

"Thank you." She grinned. "Remember, your pain meds are on your nightstand and the antibiotics are in the bathroom..."

"Aye, on the hot water tank, I remember." And he actually smiled at her responding blush.

"There's milk in the fridge and cereal in the pantry. I'll try to come back for lunch if I can, but I might need to stay with Liz ."

"I understand." He said, "*Everythin`* ye're sayin` ."

"Ok. I have to go." She went out the door Steven held open for her. "I thank you for letting me know about the break-ins at the camps, like I said as far as I know nothing here was taken or messed with. If I find anything I will be sure to let you know. It was nice to see you again and I hope to see more of you in the future." She smiled and glanced back at Donny to see him stiffen at her last remark. "Gotta go." She patted Steven on the shoulder as she walked past him, waved to Nathan and the kids up in the backyard of the house, got in her car and drove away.

Steven looked back at his brother. "I would like to come in and talk wi` you."

"We have nothin` ta say ta each other, *brother.*" Donny growled.

"Yes we do, *brother*. You wouldn't listen to me before and it's been nearly twenty years."

"I know how long tis been!" Donny walked to the inner door and grasped it. "I didna want ta talk ta ye then and I do'na want ta talk wi` ye now." And with that he slammed the door so hard that several of the glass panes shattered. Donny looked at the glass on the floor, "Shite." He muttered remembering Megan admonishment about not wrecking her house. He turned his back on the mess and Steven and walked out of his brother's view.

Up at the tire swing Nathan's head shot toward the sound of the slamming door and breaking glass. He saw Trooper Mackay standing on the front porch with his head hanging down and shaking from side to side.

"Kids, wait here, and *behave*." He looked down at Mitch who was the instigator. "Do you understand?" Mitch shook his head yes and went back to watch his giggling sister on the swing.

Nathan started down toward the cottage but stopped at the lake road as Trooper Mackay was making his way toward Nathan. "Hey what was that all about?" Nathan asked when Steven was close enough.

"A family discussion that didn't go well." Steven answered grimly.

"Family. You two *are* related? I thought there was a hell of a resemblance." He laughed.

"Aye, Donny is my brother."

"Ah, well, I heard glass break."

"Yeah three panels if you can give me the measurements I'll pick up some new ones in town and bring them back out."

"Why should you get them? Donny slammed the door." Nathan stated.

"I know," Steven looked back at the cottage. "but in a roundabout way it was my fault I guess. Besides, I don't want Megan to have to come home to a broken door."

Nathan laughed. "Do you know how many of those panes we broke when we were kids living here for the summer with Mom? I'm an expert glass replacer. Don't worry about it. I'll have Angie watch the kids and then Donny and I can go into town and get what we need. We'll have the door in tip top shape before my sister comes back." He smiled. "By the way, I met your brother Ian a few weeks ago in New York. We're going to do a picture together."

"Really?"

"Yep! Nice guy, I liked him. I like Donny too. Looks like he might have a small temper, but seems like a good guy all around." He laughed.

Steven offered again to pay for the glass, but Nathan refused and said that Donny broke it, and he would pay to fix it. "Thanks. I appreciate it." Steven shook hands with Nathan and headed to his cruiser.

"Good to meet the family!" Nathan chuckled as Steven drove away. Then Nathan turned back to the big house to let Angela know that he and Donny were going to town. She needed to watch the kids. By the time Nathan made it to the cottage Donny was already cleaning up the broken glass.

"Hi there." Nathan smiled at Donny through the big window. "I thought maybe you'd like a ride to town for some replacement materials."

"Thank ye." Donny said rather sheepishly as he slowly stood up. He had pulled his shirt on and slid his feet into the pair of crocs Megan had purchased for him. "Before she left, she asked me nay ta wreck her house. I guess I failed in tha` respect." As he walked to the kitchen to throw the shards away, Nathan inspected the damage. He retrieved a measuring tape from Megan's tool drawer, and began to measure the openings for the three panes. "Ok, I assume you have money?" Nathan asked when he was finished.

"Aye, I'll get me wallet and cell phone." He grabbed what he needed from the bedroom and joined Nathan on the front porch. "I think I should probably explain some o` this ta ye."

"I'm willing to listen. Hey, can you make it up the hill or would you like me to bring the car down here?"

Donny looked at the grassy knoll he would need to climb to get to Nathan's car and decided it was the price he'd have to pay for breaking the door, and told Nathan he would walk to the car where it was parked. They climbed into the white Lincoln Navigator that Nathan had rented at the airport and started up the road to town. Donny waited until they were out on the main road before he began his explanation.

"So let me see if I understand this straight." Nathan said. "You two had a falling out eighteen years ago. You haven't spoken since because he did you a grave injustice. This morning is the first time you've laid eyes on him in all these years. He wanted to talk about it, and you didn't. As a result we're on our way to town for new glass. Have I got it about right?" He looked over and Donny nodded his head. "Well without knowing the particulars of the injustice, as an outsider looking in," Nathan paused, "eighteen years is a hell of a long time to be holding a grudge."

Megan cornered Jess in the back hall of the offices and told her she needed a few minutes with her when they both had some time. But it was two hours before there was enough of a break in the patient load for the two of them to close themselves in Megan's private office.

Jess stood at the edge of Megan's desk peeling a banana. "Ok, chickie, what's up with the private conference in the middle of the morning? And what the hell is going on with Liz? The 'baby-blues have hit her a bit early haven't they? Or is she unhappy because she has to be away from this place for six weeks? I realize this is the greatest place on the planet to work, but I think she's taking her maternity leave a bit too seriously. She looks like she's been crying for days." She laughed.

"She hasn't been crying all night because she has to be away from the greatest job on the planet. She's been crying because Jimmy walked out on her last night."

"He left her?" Jess was astonished. "You must be kidding; Jimmy is crazy about her. They're going to have a baby." Jess sank into the chair opposite Megan's desk.

"Yeah, well he left her alright and do you want to know why?" Megan waited while Jess nodded her head. "He told her he can no longer live a lie. He's gay, he's out of the closet and he and Michael are leaving for Hawaii where they will live in a house they've already purchased."

"WHAT!" Jess shouted as she jumped from her chair.

"SHH, do you want the whole office of patients to hear you." Megan scolded, "Sit down."

"That bastard! What about this baby he was so anxious to have?" She was so steamed, she nearly choked on her banana. "Christ, I helped him find the right doctors to help him get her pregnant. He came to Nancy and I to ask about adoption if there was no way he and Liz could conceive."

"Apparently he thought having a child of his own would make it easier to live a straight life. And now he knows it's not enough." Megan was so angry. She took a deep breath to compose herself and continued.

"He told her that she could always count on him to support the child financially, once he and Michael get settled, but basically until then, she's on her own financially and emotionally."

"That son-of-a-bitch!" Jess breathed. "Just like that, huh? No warning? No prior discussion? No nothing."

"Jess, he's already seen an attorney. He's going to file for divorce this week and she'll have the papers in hand by the end of the week, he says."

"Do you still have those cigarettes in your desk?"

"Yes, why?"

"Give me one, I'm gonna need one later. Give me two. One for now and one for later." Jess took the offered Salems and slid them in her pocket. "When did you hear this"

"She called me last night."

"How is she handling it?"

"Well last night she was a mess of course. In shock to be honest. I mean she never saw this coming. Hell, neither did anybody else."

"What the hell is she doing here today then?"

"I tried to talk her into taking a few days, but she wouldn't hear of it. She said Hannah was coming today, and she needed to be here to start training her as soon as possible. She said she would not allow her personal problem to interfere in the workplace." Megan rolled her eyes and smiled in a loving way.

"Well you have to admire her work ethic." Jess commented sarcastically. "She may look like shit, but she certainly is behaving like normal. She's out there busy as all hell and being helpful to everybody with a smile pasted to her face." She was amazed. "If Nancy had come and told me she was secretly straight, I'd be a basket case for weeks." Then she smirked. "I'm a doctor, though; I *could* have her committed to a psych ward."

"Yeah, well Liz isn't a doc, and she can't have Jimmy committed anywhere." Megan saw a small smile creep over Jess's face. "Why are you smiling?"

"No, but I bet she could get a couple of those good old boys to castrate him in a New York minute."

"I'm so angry with him!" Megan looked out the window. "You don't live to be in your mid-thirties and not know you're gay! How could he marry her knowing he wasn't straight?"

Jess took a swig of water from her water bottle. "Meggie, it happens all the time. Some guys are in denial for years, women too. It's a miserable life for them. They either don't really believe their feelings and emotions, or they don't want to admit to them, and let's be honest, society isn't exactly chomping at the bit to welcome us with open arms. The thing that pisses me off is that he used Liz. He told her over and over how he loved her, asked her to marry him and begged for a family. Now she's going to be alone with the new baby, so basically he's used the child to try to convince himself he's straight. It never works and when it happens they leave heartbreak and destruction in their wake. And you can put part of the blame on society and part of the blame on those poor schmucks who can't or won't accept who they are. I'm sure he does love her but not the way a straight man loves a woman.

"Ok, so now," Jess pressed her hand to Megan's shoulder "How can we help her?" she asked soberly.

"I don't know, I honestly don't know. She'll need a birthing coach first off since prince charming is going to fly the coop in a week."

"We can handle that." Jess smiled

"I guess we just be there for her when she needs us and back off when she needs to be alone."

Jess chuckled and picked her banana off of Megan's desk where she practically dropped it when she sat in the chair. "Uh, does Jimmy's mother know about this yet?"

"I don't know. But I imagine if Jimmy has broken the big news to Liz and is planning to leave this week, he'll have to have dropped the bomb on Eleanor." Megan guessed.

"Bomb is an understatement! How will she ever face her bridge club?" Jess chuckled. "I'd love to be a fly on the wall when he breaks that news. You know, she tried to black-ball this practice when she heard I was gay."

"Poor Eleanor. First he marries Liz and now this. It'll be the 'final nail' in her coffin." Megan sighed dramatically.

"Hell, she's got so many nails in that coffin already, she could sell it now for scrap metal! That woman is as healthy as the proverbial horse, and she can't stand it!" Jess dropped her banana peel into the wastebasket.

"Hey, take that outside. I don't want my office smelling like ripe bananas." Megan laughed.

"Oh, right. Sorry, kiddo." Jess laughed as she retrieved the peel. "So, what's the first move? Do we haul Liz in here and talk to her or wait till she comes to one of us?"

"I'll mention the birthing coach to her first later this afternoon and find out when the next class is. She should also probably talk to Roina her OB and let her in on the situation. This is going to be a stressful time for her and she's so far along now, I think Roina should be aware of the potential and keep a close eye on symptoms."

"We'll keep an eye on her too." Jess said.

Megan sighed. "Yes, it never rains but what it pours as the saying goes. One thing after another, etcetera. I hope my house will still be standing when I get home."

"What?" Jess looked at her queerly. "You've lost me."

"You're lost? How do you think I feel?" Jess continued to gaze questioningly at Megan. "Well you know I've got Donny staying with me."

"Oh yeah, "secret agent-man' secret agent-man,'" Jess sang.

Without fully divulging a confidence Megan told Jess briefly about Steven and Donny being brothers and a more than eighteen-year unhappy separation between them. She said, "Donny is pretty adamant about continuing the separation."

"Damn what a story." Jess said. "And Donny didn't know you even knew his brother."

"Yes well I told Donny I had talked to a trooper named Steven Mackay and he confirmed that our trooper was possibly his brother. And I also told him I had seen Steven again at the corners the other day. Actually he took it rather well, considering. However, I had an unexpected visitor this morning."

"Let me guess, Steven." When Megan nodded Jess snickered "What did he want?"

Megan told her about the camp break-ins and that Steven was making a house call as part of the investigation.

"Did Steven know that you are not only acquainted with his brother, but that secret agent-man is living in your house?" Jess moved to sit down on the ledge of the window.

"Would you stop calling him that?" She chuckled. "And no, I didn't mention to Steven that I knew his brother or that he is a *guest* in my home. There was never any reason to relay personal information to Steven and I've only met him a couple of times. I barely know him."

Jess chuckled "You didn't know Donny at all and he's living with you!"

"He's a *guest* in my home recovering from an injury."

"Yeah. Ok." Jess smirked. "And when Steven showed up this morning, Donny saw him?"

"Oh better than that, thanks to my brother. Steven and Donny saw each other. Steven was obviously shocked, and Donny looked like he wanted to commit homicide. Jesse, I didn't know what to do."

"So, what did you do?" Jess all but laughed out loud. She was getting enormous satisfaction out of the new complications in what she felt was Megan's normally boring life.

"I left." Megan stated.

"You...you left?" Jess stammered. "Without staying for the second act?"

"Liz called. It was late and I was late getting over here. So, I left." Megan flopped herself into her chair behind the desk.

"Just like that? You just...*left*?"

"I thanked Steven for letting me know about the camps, told him I hoped to see him again, gave Donny a kiss, asked him to be nice and not to destroy my house!" Megan grimaced after completing her statement. She hadn't intended to mention the kiss, even if it was only a peck on the cheek.

"I can't believe you just walked away...wait a minute, you did what to Donny?" Jess began grinning like an idiot while Megan turned bright red. "You little *hussy, you!*" Jess clapped her hands together and began to giggle. "Why Dr. Dunnegan, have you stepped over the lines and slept with your patient?" the giggle was quickly turning into full-blown laughter.

"No! I haven't slept with him!" Megan sighed, *not yet anyway.* "For God sakes, Jess. What do you take me for? And he's not technically my patient. He's Sam Otis's patient." *So there,* she thought. "But we have shared some..." she didn't know how to explain it.

"Some hot make out time?" Jess leered at her, wiggling her eyebrows.

"Yes, and I might remind you again that he's Sam's patient. Not mine!"

"So, how was it?" Jess smiled. When Megan flushed Jess smiled even bigger. "That good huh?"

"You have no idea." Now it was Megan's turn to laugh.

"Are you going to sleep with him?"

"*That,* friend of mine, is none of your business." Megan chuckled.

"That would be a 'yes.' So has he met the family?"

"Most of them. Nathan and his group came in yesterday and Morgan and Sue are coming in sometime today. Mom met him yesterday. She came to the cottage when she saw Max outside and thought I was home. Dad met him last night."

"What did Emma think of him?"

"I don't really know, she was hurt when she thought he was a boyfriend that I hadn't told her about. Then when she found out the facts she was even more upset that I would take him in. But before she left, yesterday afternoon, I swear I saw her wink at him. I took Donny on a ride up to the Rye Lot when I got home to give him a little fresh air. While we were up there, Nathan and Angela arrived, and Mom must have had him on the phone as soon as he walked in the door. I swear she has that house wired for sound! Later they all descended on the cottage for meet and greet. I would have felt sorry for Donny if I hadn't been so busy being sorry for myself." There was a knock on her office door and Hannah popped her head in.

"Sorry to interrupt, ladies," she smiled at Jess and Megan. But Dr. Andrews, your next patient is here, and Dr. Dunnegan, Mrs. Atwater called to say she would be a little late. But in the meantime, there is a 'walk-in' here, and he needs to see a doctor, if you wouldn't mind."

"Hannah, please call me Jess." She smiled and started toward the door.

"Have the gentlemen fill out the forms and show him into exam room three. When Mrs. Atwater gets here let me know." Megan smiled.

"You got it!" Hannah smiled and backed out of the office, shutting the door behind her.

Megan took a few deep breaths to get herself back into doctor mode. She took a swig of water from her bottle, smoothed out her white coat and headed up the hall to exam room three. In the bin hanging on the outside of the door was the new chart. Before going in she scanned the chart to get the particulars of the man's visit and then entered the room.

"Good morning, Mr. Smith. You didn't give us your first name on your chart, may I have it so we can get it into the computer?" She looked up from the chart and smiled at the man sitting on the exam table. He was thin, appeared well built. He looked like he'd been through the wringer. He was wearing jeans that were obviously way too big and a plaid shirt that fit the same way. A pair of crutches rested against the wall. His brown hair was wet with sweat and his face was pale. This man was sick, and according to his chart, had a serious gash on his knee.

"Harry." Gavin answered. He was embarrassed by his appearance. He was used to dressing with a lot more style. He had to. He needed to be professional and always dressed in what he referred to as "class". If he wanted to lure the girls with modeling and acting jobs he needed to look the part of the talent agent. But his own clothing had been torn and covered in blood stains from his run through the woods several days ago. What he was currently wearing he'd stolen from a clothesline the night before. He realized during the night that what he'd pilfered from the camps' infirmaries wasn't going to be enough to get his knee healed and knew he needed to see a real doctor. But he sure as shit wasn't about to give anyone his real name. While eating breakfast in the local diner that morning he listened to the buzz about the kidnapping ring and the arrests of those involved. Even though he managed to escape the feds the night of the raid, he knew it was only a matter of time before Jason handed over Gavin's name to the feds. If the slimy shit hadn't already. Gavin was relieved that he had plenty of cash on him in moderately small bills. He didn't need to worry about not paying a bill and risk being caught. But as much as it pained him, Gavin wasn't comfortable going back to the cabin in the woods to retrieve his belongings.

"Ok Harry, let me have a look at the gash on your knee. Can you pull up your pant leg so I can have a look?" She washed her hands, then looked at the wound. "How did this happen?"

"It was stupid really. I was running after my dog in the woods and tripped over a fallen tree limb and fell on a rock." He told her. He had dreamed up the story while waiting for the doctor to come in. It seemed plausible enough.

"I see. How long ago did this happen?" Megan asked as she examined the injury.

"Couple of days." He said.

"Well, You should have had this seen to right away. This needed sutures. And it's badly infected." She rested his leg on the exam table and rose, turning to the cabinets over the sink. "It's too late for sutures, but I can steri-strip it which will help, but it's going to scar." She collected the materials she needed to dress the wound and pulled on rubber gloves before turning back to the patient. "I'll have to clean out the wound first." She glanced up at him and smiled. "I apologize ahead of time because I know this is going to be rather painful." She said before pouring betadine onto his knee. She wasn't kidding. The brown liquid antiseptic burned like fire as it dripped onto the chuck pad she had placed under his knee on the exam table. She blotted and pressed the gash forcing fresh blood to ooze from the wound. Then she dabbed at the gash and pressed more antiseptic into it with gauze. When the torture seemed to finally come to an end, she blotted with fresh gauze to dry the area and then stretched his leg out straight. "Steri-strips aren't as good as sutures of course, but they will help to keep the wound closed if you're careful. Try to keep your leg as straight as possible." She smiled up at him again. "You'll have to walk with a limp for a while, but the less you bend your knee, the better." She placed the narrow strips of adhesive over the gash and applied clean gauze and tape for the dressing. "Are you allergic to any medications? Especially antibiotic medications? Penicillin?"

"No." He said. "I don't think so."

"Ok. I'm going to give you an antibiotic injection and a script for oral antibiotics to clear up the infection. Make sure you take *all* the pills." She rose from her stool and pulled off the rubber gloves dropping them into the trash, washed her hands and pulled a paper towel from the dispenser. "I'd like to see you again in a week to check the wound. Keep your knee dry as much as possible and change the dressing every day. Twice if it becomes soiled or wet. The nurse will give you some extra steri-strips. You can get a type of steri-strip at the drug stores, but they don't work as well as these." She walked to the door and turned looking back at him. "Wait here and the nurse will be right in with your injection. You can pick up your script at the front desk"

She hesitated at the door as he spoke. "Uh, I'm just sort of passing through." He said.

"Oh, well, if you're still here in a week, stop back in and I'll check your knee. If not, have your own physician check it when you get home." And with that she smiled and went out of the exam room.

"If I'm still here in a week, lady, I'd rather check you out." He leered at the door she closed behind her.

Gavin waited in the room for the nurse and when she had given him the antibiotic injection he slid off the table and she handed him the crutches. When Gavin reached the front desk, Megan was standing at the counter. She had written the prescription and handed it to him. Then like she did with most of her patients she walked him to the front door and held it open for him to pass through. While she was holding the door open for Gavin, a car drove by, and she waved at Donny and Nathan sitting in the front seat. When Megan waved at the white Navigator, Gavin looked up in time to see the occupants..

"What the hell?" he murmured to himself.

"Excuse me?" Megan turned her attention back to her patient. "Did you say something?" Nathan and Donny were up the road and out of sight by now. So Gavin stepped out of the office.

"No, sorry for the language, doctor. Guess I'm not so good yet at working these sticks." He indicated the crutches. "That your husband?" He asked as nicely as he could muster. *Gotcha ` you bastard,* he thought.

"No, my brother and a friend." She smiled as she reached in her pocket for her ringing cell phone. "Excuse me. Hi Donny, I see you and Nathan are taking a trip out. Where are you headed?" She was headed back inside when Gavin stopped her.

"Dr. Dunnegan," he waited while she turned around to face him. "I think my plans might change some. I'll call and make an appointment to come and see you in a week."

"Good. I will see you then Mr. Smith, and be sure to keep that knee as immobile as possible." She smiled and went back inside.

"I'll have to find myself a place to crash for a while." Gavin muttered to himself and went across the street to the diner. "Maybe some of these yokels know of a place that rents rooms". He had to make plans, and he needed to do some research on Sam Watson and find out exactly how to eliminate him. Gavin hated Sam more now than he ever did. For he now knew that it was *Sam, or Donny or Nathan, or whatever the hell his name is,* was the traitor. He was the man sent in to bring down Gavin and cost him more money than God. *He* was the cop. As Gavin set off in search of a room he thought about the night he found out good old Sam was a mole.

Gavin and Jason were seated on the bench in the wagon watching the FBI round everyone up.

"How the hell could this happen?" Gavin roared. "No one but us knew about the change in plans." He turned to Jason who was slouched even more than he was before. "YOU! You're one of them!" he shoved Jason off the bench onto the floor of the wagon and began to kick the stuffing out of him.

"NO! NO!" Jason pleaded trying to stave off the blows, but his hands were cuffed behind his back and defense was impossible. "It wasn't me; I swear it wasn't me!"

"If not you then WHO!?" Gavin roared.

"Sam! It has to be Sam!" Jason yelled. Gavin stopped his assault.

"Sam? You told that bastard about the change?"

"He has money on this too, I didn't think it was right to cut him out." Jason panted.

Gavin was quiet for a moment while he thought. "He's a cop." He whispered finally. "I'm gonna kill him."

"How? In case you haven't noticed we've been arrested by the FBI in Scranton, and he is in the hospital back in Honesdale."

Gavin, being double-jointed managed to get his arms positioned so his handcuffs were in front of him, as opposed to the back. "Open your mouth." He ordered Jason. Gavin reached in, grabbed a hold of the studded tongue ring, and yanked it free.

Gavin used the stud from Jason's tongue ring to unlock his hand-cuffs while Jason laid on the floor of the wagon writhing in pain and bleeding profusely. *At last*, Gavin thought, as the cuffs clattered to the floor, and he was free of them. But now he had another problem, how to get out of the wagon. There were no handles on the inside. He peered through the grated back windows and saw some agents were strug-gling to bring some more people to the wagon. This was his chance, he thought. He moved to the side and waited for the doors to swing open. As they did Gavin stole his golden opportunity and slipped out while the feds were loading several other prisoners inside. He ran into the darkness as far as he could and as fast as he could. At some point he tripped and fell down a ravine. As he fell his knee had hit several sharp rocks.

"But now I have the healing touch of the good doctor." Gavin said as he settled himself on the double bed. He looked around the room he had rented in the John Riley house that was recommended by someone at the diner across the street. "Not my taste, but given the circumstances I guess that's a good thing." He closed his eyes and drifted off to sleep as he planned his revenge.

Chapter Fifteen

Megan and Jess were trying to convince Liz to call and change her OB appointment, when there was a knock at Megan's office door.

"Come in." Megan called and then gaped as Steven opened the door and popped his head in. "What are you doing here? I mean of course you're more than welcome, but…" She smiled sheepishly. "How can I help you?"

"I was just over at the corners checking to see if everything was alright over there. Just doing my rounds." He grinned "And I thought I'd stop in to see if you ladies were closing down for lunch." He smiled brightly at the three ladies and his eyes rested on Liz. "It's nice to see you again Liz."

"It's nice to see you too, Steven. Megan and Jess are going to lunch, but I have to go to the doctor." She smiled.

"Doctor?" pushed the door open wider and stepped into the office. He looked at Megan in question.

"I'm not an OB/GYN." She explained. "She has an appointment to see her baby doctor."

"But she insists on driving herself and she shouldn't be driving a car, unless she wants that kid to be born with a head shaped like a steering wheel," Jess piped up. Steven looked at the woman who spoke and realized he had never met her. Jess eyed the young handsome trooper and then turned her attention back to Liz. "You can barely fit behind the wheel and still reach the pedals. It's not safe for you or the baby." She turned back to Steven and smiled. *So this is the estranged brother.* She thought. *Well Donny must be one hell of a looker for Megan to not give this one a chance. I may not go for men,* she mused to herself, *but even I can tell this guy is a hunk.* "Hi. We haven't met," she extended her hand. "I'm Jess, Megan's associate. You must be Steven Mackay, State Trooper."

"Yes, ma'am I am, and it's nice to meet you." Steven smiled and grasped her hand in a shake.

"I don't know what else to do. I have to get to the appointment and that's that." Liz said for what she hoped was the last time.

"I told you that I would take you later this afternoon. I have a break in my patient load at two. I can take you over and drop you and my cousin can drive you back to the office when she comes out to the lake to swim at 3:30 p.m. I checked with her, and she said she'd be happy to do it." Megan told her gently. "I'm sure Roina would work with us to change your appointment time under the circumstances."

"Look." Liz sighed. "My circumstances may have changed, but I'm not going to impose on you guys or your *relatives*," she looked at Megan, "because of it. I can handle these situations on my own."

"Listen, Liz—" Megan began in a stern voice.

"Excuse me." Steven smiled at the heat this discussion seemed to take on. "I don't mean to jump into a conversation that does not concern me," he grinned at Liz, "but, if you need a ride to your appointment, I would be happy to take you. I'm on my way into town anyway."

"Really?" All three women said in unison.

"Sure. I'm happy to serve." He chuckled as he placed his hand over his heart. "That is, of course, if you don't mind riding in the cruiser."

"Thank you! If you're sure it's alright." Liz actually blushed. "I've never ridden in a cruiser before. It might be exciting!" She laughed. "Are you sure you wouldn't mind? I mean, what about your lunch?"

"Oh, I can eat anytime. And if you'd like, after the doctor's appointment, we can stop on the way back here and have lunch together."

Megan and Jess watched the exchange between Liz and Steven and they both had the same thought. *Oh, is that perfect or what?* As if they picked up on each other's thoughts, they looked at each other and winked.

"I think that would be lovely. Thank you." Liz smiled and looked back at Megan and Jess. "I'll see you guys in two hours."

Jess and Megan watched through the window as Steven helped Liz into the cruiser and drove away in what appeared to be animated conversation with his grateful passenger.

"I realize this is going to sound completely inappropriate considering the newness of her situation," Jess hedged.

"But Liz and Steven would be a really nice-looking couple." Megan finished.

"Yeah. That's why we get along so well, Meggie. A lot of the time, you think just like me." Jess smiled. "Come on, let's go to lunch."

While Megan and Jess were eating lunch Nathan and Donny were hard at work replacing the three panels of glass in the front door of the cottage.

"Now if I were you, when Megan gets home, I wouldn't say anything about the door unless she expressly notices the new glass." Nathan advised.

"Do ye want me ta lie ta yer sister then?" Donny choked.

"No. Now, I didn't suggest you lie to her. I only said if I was in your shoes, I'd not mention the glass unless she notices. Then of course I guess you should tell her the truth. But only if she asks."

"Nay matter how ye phrase it, it's a lie o` omission. I canna lie ta the lass." Donny sighed as he put the third and final piece of glass in its place.

"What was it she said to you before she left you alone with your brother?"

"Ta behave, and no ta wreck her house."

"And what did you do?"

"I wrecked her house."

"Do you see my point?" Nathan smiled.

"Aye, and I will go along wi` it fer now." Donny sighed.

"Good, now let's get this finished before Angie comes down and wants to know what's going on."

"Are ye planning` ta lie ta yer wife then?"

"Have you ever been married, Donovan?"

"Nay, I've ne're been wed."

"Well, I've been married to Angie for a long time, and I've learned over the years that simple two sentence explanations over minor situations can turn into a two-hour discussion if you don't develop some form of discretion."

Donny finished with the glass and Nathan was about to ask him if he'd care to come up to the house for some lunch when Donny's cell phone rang.

"Go ahead." Nathan indicated the cell. "And when you're done, if you feel up for the climb, come up to the house for a bite of lunch." Nathan smiled and went out the door.

Donny picked up his cell noticing the number and a chill went down his spine. "What's goin on Ted?" Donny asked the head of the FBI.

"I'm afraid we have some bad news Mackay. After we got everyone over to Scranton PD one of the agents noticed there was blood all over the wagon floor and found Jason Masters in the back bleeding. After we took care of his tongue he told us that Gavin Mathews pulled out his tongue stud and escaped. Long story short Gavin knows you're a cop and knows where you are."

"He knows I'm here with Megan?" Donny's heart stopped.

"As far as Jason knows you're still in the hospital, so my guess is that will be the first place Gavin will go, but we've removed Sam Watson's medical records from Wayne Memorial. We've spoken to the head of the hospital and explained that as of this moment there was never a patient by the name of Sam Watson treated at that hospital. All future visits you may need are to be granted, however nothing will be documented."

"I bet tha` raised a lot o` eyebrows."

"It did. It's not easy to do battle with hospital bureaucracy. They have their own list of good guys and bad guys, and I can tell you for future reference, we're not on the best list. Mackay you have no idea how much trouble you caused by getting yourself shot, going to the hospital, and being admitted as Sam Watson."

"It wasna like I planned it, *Teddy*. How aboot I promise if I e'er get shot again, I'll phone ye first, and ask ye where ta go before I bleed ta death." Donny said dryly.

"You do that. Now, what about this doctor woman?" Ted asked and Donny could hear him flipping through papers.

"Wha` aboot her?"

"Does this woman know who you are?"

"Megan Dunnegan." Donny stated.

"What?"

"Tha` s her name. Remember it. Dinna refer ta her again as *'that doctor woman'*, or *'this woman'.*"

"I'll do that." Ted said, noticing the edge to Donny's voice. *Interesting,* he thought.

"See tha` ye do." Donny warned. "And aye she knows who I am and wha` I was doin here. Most o` it anyway."

"Well, that's an unnecessary risk I would have advised you not to take, Mackay." Ted was astounded. Donny never told anyone who he really was. Never.

"Tis no` a risk ta me." He explained warmly. "However now tha` I know Gavin escaped and knows aboot me, it may be a risk ta her."

"How do you figure? We have removed your records from the hospital and instructed everyone who was involved in your case not to discuss any part of it to anyone unless it was the FBI."

"Did ye tell them no` ta talk aboot her as well?"

"Not specifically. But it was implied." Even to Ted's ears he sounded doubtful.

"Besides, people will talk whether they want them ta or no`." Now Donny was worried. He could be putting Meggie and her family in danger.

"We'll let the state police know to be on the lookout and I'll send a few agents out there to snoop around and try to flush him out. Don't worry Donny, Gavin will get nowhere near you."

"I'm nay worried aboot me Ted." Donny replied. "Do ye have any more good news fer me?"

"We found Shelia back at the shack." Referring to Donny's partner Sheridan.

"How was she?"

"Dead. She had been shot twice in the heart at close range. Can you think of any reason she would have been killed?"

"Nay unless Gavin knew tha` she was a plant and instructed Jason ta kill her before they went fer the drop."

"Yeah but you told us that Mathews lit out the night he shot you. Jason was the one who moved up the timetable. This means Mathews would never have had the chance to give the order to kill her."

"Aye, but we ha` no idea what happened after Jason left me at hospital. He could ha` gone back ta the cabin and Mathews could ha` already been there and either killed Shelia himself or had Jason do it."

"Ok I'll give you that. We'll keep looking for him. Mackay, why won't you accept my offers for a permanent job with the FBI?"

"Ye can barely afford me now." Donny chuckled. "Ted," his voice turned serious. "The agents ye send oot here, can ye have them look around here at the farm and Megan's doctor's office until I can do it meself. I do'na want anything ta happen ta Megan or her family because o` me."

"Mackay, is this compassion I am hearing from you?" Ted smiled "What does this doctor look like?"

"Ted." Donny warned.

"Ok. Ok, yes, until you are up and around I will have some agents there. I assume you don't want them to be seen."

"Ye assume correctly. I do'na want ta cause worry fer Megan and her family. Like ye said Gavin is probably no` even in the area, but I want ta be on the safe side. Do ye ha` a composite drawing of Mathews oot yet?"

"Yes. Jason has been with the crime artist most of the morning." Ted wound up the phone call. "Ok Mackay, if we get any word I'll be in touch. You do the same for me."

"Aye. Bye Ted, and remember I do'na want the agents seen. I do'na want Megan and her family spooked."

Donny put his cell on the table and sat for a moment to mull over the conversation with Ted. Donny felt instinctively that the best thing for him to do was leave. If Gavin was in the area then Donny was putting Megan and her family at risk by staying. However, if Gavin *was* in the area and knew that Donny was with Megan, Gavin might use Megan to get to Donny. In which case, Megan was safer if Donny stayed close to protect her. *If he knows I'm wi' her*, he thought. *WI' her*. The two words kept running through his brain as well as the question of whether she was safer with him there or as far away as he could get.

The idea of leaving her actually caused him physical pain. He didn't want to leave. Not now, when he had finally found her. Donny sat there on the daybed going back and forth trying to decide which was the best plan. It was the first time in years he had been in this kind of dilemma. It was the first time in years he had felt anything like this for a woman. He had to do what was best and safest for Megan and her family. If it turned out that she needed protection from Gavin, he couldn't do it if he weren't here, by the same token if he weren't here, maybe she wouldn't need protection. Back and forth his mind went for over an hour until he gave himself a headache. In the end and for now he decided; he would stay put. At least for a while until he and the authorities could be fairly sure Gavin had left the area for whatever parts unknown he could find. He tried putting himself in Gavin's shoes.

"I wouldna hang around once arrests were made. They'd ha` ta be lookin` for accomplices. Jason would ha` given Gavin's name and description ta the feds. They'd be lookin` fer him. Aye, I'd be gone by now." Donny said aloud. And let out his breath. "I hope ta hell, I know wha` I'm doin`!" he said to Max who was lying at his feet. His stomach began to growl, and he remembered Nathan's invitation to have lunch with he and his family at the big house. He had never been up there, he was hungry, and he liked Nathan and his family, so he pulled a hat from the front door closet and shoved it down hard on his head. "In the way o` a disguise." He explained to Max, and headed to the big house for lunch.

Megan and Jess returned from lunch and were in full swing seeing patients when Liz called to say her appointment ran longer than expected, and would it be alright if she went ahead and had lunch before returning to the office. Megan told her, "Of course it's alright. Hannah's doing wonderfully. I'm sure that she can handle anything that comes up until Steven brings you back from lunch."

"They're having lunch." Megan chuckled to Jess when they passed in the back hall, and Jess laughed as she entered the exam room to see her next patient. Liz came back an hour later looking vibrant in Megan and Jess's opinion. Steven walked her into the office and wanted to know if Megan had a few minutes to spare for him. She explained that she had a full schedule of patients until five, but she could see him then. "Are you sick?" she asked.

"No ma'am." He said.

Ma'am? Megan mouthed and glared at him.

"No. I'm no sick, Doctor Dunnegan" he laughed sheepishly. He'd heard from the other troopers who spoke to her at the hospital and remember his own brief introduction with her when he and Hallet came by that she disliked the term "Ma'am". He thanked her and told her he would be back.

Around five Megan walked her patient to the door and saw Steven talking to Liz as she walked by. When she came back in she stopped at the desk.

"What time is my next one?" She asked Liz.

"Not until five-thirty."

"Well, it seems I have a break, do you still need to see me Steven?" She smiled.

"Yes, please. If you can take the time. I'll talk to you later, Liz." He smiled and followed Megan to her office. "I know you have three doctors, but the few times I've been here there only seems to be two." He took the seat across from Megan's desk.

"Sara works the weekends and one day during the week."

"I would think you'd have to have a very large practice to support three doctors, but you never seem to have a backed up waiting room." He rarely had the need to see a physician but when he did he had to wait for sometimes an hour before he got called in.

"It would be if we didn't have Liz. I don't know how she does it, but she arranges the appointments in such a way that we never have someone sitting out there for more than a few minutes." She explained. "So what's up, do you need a physician, Trooper Mackay?" she teased.

"Well, I'm thinking of changing doctors." He chuckled. "I was wondering if you could ease my mind about something."

"Things didn't go well with Donny, I take it." She assumed that was what he wanted to talk about.

"Huh?" realizing where her mind had taken her he understood. "Oh, no this isn't about my brother."

"Oh, well then I'm afraid I don't..."

"It's about Liz." He clarified

"Oh, I see." she smiled, propped her elbows on the desk and rested her chin on her fists.

"Well I..." he hesitated and looked down at his own large hands. "I'm not sure how to put my question without seeming to push my nose in where it doesna belong." He looked up at Megan again. "I was under the impression she was married." He waited while Megan nodded her head. "Well I...I was just wondering why he wasn't wi` her today for her appointment. It *is* so apparent that she shouldn't be driving anymore, and she told me that Hannah had driven her to work, and I...well, I was wondering why her husband hadn't. I also found it strange that she never mentioned him at all today and had made such an effort to suggest that I meet him a few days ago. I wanted to ask her, but I didn't know how to broach the subject."

"Ah, well," she straightened and leaned back in her chair.

"I'm sorry. I didn't mean to put you in an awkward position."

"No it's not that, well not entirely. I can tell you that Jimmy is not in the picture right now. Actually, she's quite on her own. However, I think Liz should be the one to tell you any more details. If the two of you become friends, she will."

"How close does Hannah live to Liz?" Steven asked after a few silent moments

"Not real close. Actually, Liz lives up near St. Josephs Parish, why?"

"Well I was wondering if you think she would mind if I offered to bring her to work in the mornings. I don't know if I could always be here to take her home though."

"You could certainly ask her." Megan smiled "Now, may I ask *you* a question?"

"Sure."

"You like her don't you?"

Now it was Steven's turn to sit up straight in his chair. "She's pregnant!"

"Well," She chuckled, "Trooper Mackay, how do you think she got that way? Besides, so was your mother, many times I might add, and I don't think your father minded!" Megan shot back.

Steven held up both hands to stave off an attack. "Wait! Wait! That didn't come out right." He hesitated again. This was obviously a little difficult for him to explain and Megan got the distinct impression that he didn't spend a lot of his time explaining anything to anyone. *You're more like Donny than your brother would like to think,* she mused to herself.

"Yes." he breathed. "I like her, and I like talking to her. But if you are asking what my intentions are, I have no idea." He chuckled. "Where is her husband? Away serving his country?"

"Fair enough. I think you should get whatever answers you need from Liz. If she would agree to you bringing her to work in the mornings, we can always find a ride home for her. Either Jess or I could take her."

"Does she have any family?"

"No, she was an only child. Her mother died three years ago and her father five years before that. As far as I know neither parents had any siblings, and her grandparents are also dead."

"Wow, she really is all alone."

"Well, not completely alone, she has us. And soon she'll have the baby."

"Yes, I can see that. She's very lucky in that aspect." *She doesn't need a guard dog,* he thought, *she's got you.*

Megan smiled and glanced at her watch. "I hate to have to cut you off, but I have a patient due. Liz really gets on us if we leave a patient to wait." She stood as Steven did.

"I understand. I'll ask Liz about driving her, and see what she says." He smiled and they both left her office.

Chapter Sixteen

Megan finished out her day and was pleased to hear via the office grapevine that Steven would be stopping by to drive Liz home from work that evening. She also learned that Liz had accepted his offer to pick her up in the mornings. "Well, he lives just down the road from me, really, so it's not that much of an inconvenience for him. At least that's what he said." Liz justified when she came in with the last of Megan's messages. "He's awfully nice. Don't you think so, Megan?"

"Yes, he is, and I think he is beginning to form a friendly attachment for you, Liz."

"For me?" Liz choked.

"Yes, you. I think he would be a very good friend for you to have, living out here alone like you do now. Especially with the baby coming. He's a nice guy and seems like he would make a very supportive friend to have in your corner." Megan looked Liz square in the eyes. "What? You think a man and woman can't be good friends?"

"Of course I don't think that. You know me better than that. But I'm..."

"Married?" Guilt assailed her as soon as the word came out of her mouth. "I'm sorry, sweetie. I didn't mean to put it exactly like that."

"No no, it's ok. Technically I'm not married anymore." She sat down in the chair in front of Megan's desk. "I can't really fault Jimmy for what he's done."

"Liz," Megan spoke gently, "are you ready to talk about it?" Megan sat down in her own chair behind the desk. "I'll listen if you want to talk."

"I know you're angry with Jimmy, Meg."

"Well, I..."

"No, that's ok too. I'm angry with him as well in some ways, but not for being gay. He can't help who he is. He didn't just wake up one morning and say, "Hey I've decided I don't like girls anymore." He's been denying himself for his whole life because of how homosexuals are viewed in society. It must have been agony for him. It's a very difficult road for them. What I'm angry about is that he didn't come out of the closet before we were married. Before I got pregnant. So much time down the tubes in his life when he could have been happy with someone else. And me too for that matter. I'm hurt, because in a way I feel I've been used. I wish he could have been honest with himself and with me."

"And with his mother?" Megan raised her eyebrows. And Liz smiled ruefully.

"Yeah, well, I can understand why he wasn't honest with her."

"Have you heard from her since he made his announcement?"

"No. Not a word."

Bitch! Megan thought to herself. "Have you talked about this with Jess?"

"No. I will. I'm sure she can help me to understand better why he did what he did."

"And what about the baby?"

"Oh, Well, it'll be difficult to raise a child on my own, but my expenses are small. My rents pretty low and I have a good job. And although it would have been easier had Jimmy come out before I got pregnant, I'm not sorry about the baby. You weren't worried about that were you? Because I'm not sorry about this baby at all!" Liz smiled and pressed her hand to her belly. "Jimmy was all the family I had after mama died, but now, with this baby, I've got family. My own flesh and blood family." She looked up at Megan and tears gathered in her eyes. "I love this baby, Meg. And he'll love me, and I'll take good care of him."

"How in hell did you get to be so damned smart?" Megan rose from her chair and came around the desk to take Liz in her arms giving her a gentle hug. "Him or her. I know you will, Liz. You'll make a great mama for this little guy. And don't worry ever, about not having a family. You've got me and Jess and of course my folks love you. And as for grandmothers, my Mom is the consummate professional grandma. She won't allow you to leave her out. You've got a big family, kiddo. Make use of us." Megan released Liz and turned back toward her desk to grab her purse. "And I think Steven would very much like to be your friend."

"I think so too. He's been very nice. But won't it be a little awkward for him?"

"Awkward? Why?"

"Well, I'm pregnant."

Megan looked to the ceiling and rolled her eyes. "God deliver me from the both of you!"

Just then Jess strolled into Megan's office. "Are you ready to get out of here, Meggie? Oh, and your ride is here, little mama."

"Oh!" Mildly embarrassed, Liz pulled a crumpled tissue from her pocket and dabbed at her eyes. "Thanks, Jesse. I better go. See you tomorrow!" she called as she sailed through the door and out of the building.

"Did I interrupt something?" Jess asked as she watched Liz disappear.

"No. You heard of course that Steven is going to chauffeur Liz for a while in the mornings and evenings when he can?"

"Yes. I did. You talked to him today didn't you? I heard he came in and asked to see you. I assumed he wasn't sick and in need of a physician." Jess grinned and wiggled her eyebrows. "Big young strapping hunk like that."

"For God's sake, Jess." Megan laughed.

"Hey, I'm gay not blind!" she laughed. "So? Does he like her?" Jess smiled. "He does, doesn't he?"

"So it would seem," Megan chuckled. "but I think he's a little uncertain how to proceed because of her *husband* and the baby. I think he wants to just be her friend for now and see what happens." They continued to talk as they locked up the office and headed to the parking lot.

"Did you tell him Jimmy was no longer in the picture?"

"More or less, but it's Liz's information to tell when she feels comfortable enough with Steven to tell him."

"Did you ask how it went with Donny?"

"I didn't really get the chance. I thought at first; that was what he wanted to talk about but like I told you it wasn't. Then I had to cut him off since I had a patient." She climbed into her Wagoneer, closed the door, and put her window down.

"Morgan and Sue are coming in today, aren't they?"

"Yes ma'am they sure are. And with any luck the cell phones have been busy all day and I won't have to explain Donny's situation and mine all over again."

Jesse raised an invisible cigar to her lips and wiggled her eyebrows again "Just what exactly is your situation?"

"You're insatiable and twisted!"

"Yeah. I know. " Jess grinned. "But I'm lovable. So, when do the sutures come out?"

"It's been five days. I'll get in touch with Sam Ottis tomorrow and find out when he wants to see Donny. He's Sam's patient, remember? It's his call." She looked at Jess more closely. "Why do you ask?"

"Well... the sooner they come out the sooner you two can..." The invisible cigar returned as well as the wiggling eyebrows.

"Oh for the love of God! Get your head out of your ass or better yet out of the gutter!" She chuckled, "Go home and annoy your wife and baby!

"Ok! Have a good weekend and I'll see you Monday Meggie." Jess smiled "Oh and by the way," she slowed her retreat and leaned back toward the car window. "Don't let the family intrude too much on your private time with secret agent man this weekend." She winked and backed away from Megan's playful slap to her shoulder.

"Goodnight, Jess." Chuckling as she drove away.

Megan wondered on the short drive home, what she would find when she arrived. She was excited and looking forward to having her whole family around her, but she really did hope the whole question and answer thing was over. She passed through the camp, rolled down the hill and pulled into her spot next to the cottage. Up in the front yard of the big house, was parked yet another white Lincoln Navigator. *This is beginning to look like a Ford convention,* she thought to herself.

Deciding to change into shorts and a tank top before facing the latest arrivals, she went inside expecting to find Donny napping. But as she entered the little house she found it empty. *But not destroyed*, she smiled to herself remembering her admonition when she left the house that morning. Not Even Max was there. Feeling slightly deserted, she went into her bedroom and stripped off her hot work clothes and replaced them with the cooler alternative. Given the heat of the day she pulled her hair on top of her head and secured it with a clip. With her feet slipped into flip-flops, Megan grabbed her sunglasses and headed up the grassy knoll to the big house. Stopping as she heard laughing from the lake. Standing on the little red shale road she saw that her family had congregated on the shore. Since Donny would most certainly be there as well, she went back into the cottage, grabbed the keys to the golf cart and headed down to join the party.

"Auntie Meggie!" A little redheaded girl yelled and ran toward Megan as she pulled the cart to halt at the rocks that lined the parking area for the lake.

"Hello Bridget." Megan laughed as her four-year-old niece ran into her arms. "How are you, honey?"

"Mommy and Daddy brought me and Joey here to swim!" she giggled as Megan twirled her around.

"They did?"

"You go in with me." Bridget ordered.

"Well, not right now, sweetie, I don't have my suit on." She placed her niece back on her feet and walked to the others. Morgan was the first to rise from his chair and meet Megan and his daughter. He, like their oldest brother, towered over her. He was very handsome with his dark brown almost black hair and striking blue eyes. He used to have a full beard, however much to Megan's dismay, he had turned it into a goatee.

Except for the red hair, his daughter was his mirror image, had the same vibrant blue eyes, and was already very tall for her age. She also had the same button nose and a smile to melt hearts.

"Hi Meggie," he said as he engulfed her in a bear hug. "It's good to see you. How was work?" He asked as he released her.

"It's good to see you too, and work was good. Lots of patients. Very busy. You know about that." She smiled. Morgan was a highly respected plastic surgeon in Beverly Hills. He had some very high-profile patients and had several articles written about him and the practice he owned. "I assume you came here to have a look at my house guest like everyone else."

"Well I could lie and say no, but I won't. It's only right that I have a look at the guy who's living with my little sister." He smiled and held up his palm before Megan had a chance to argue the inference. "I gotta say though, after spending a couple of hours with him, he seems like a honorable character. Mom won't admit it yet, but I think she is very taken with him." He raised one eyebrow. "However, I do have one question."

"Do I even want to ask?"

"You didn't shoot him did you, Megan?" he asked very seriously.

"No but I might shoot the next person who asks me that!" She said through clenched teeth.

Morgan laughed and draped his arm around Megan as she took Bridget's hand and the three headed toward the rest of the family. Megan gave Morgan's wife, Sue, a hug and peered down to have a look at four-month-old Joey who was enjoying his bottle. If Bridget was the image of her father, then Joey was the image of his mother.

"Look at that red hair!" Megan chuckled as she peered down at Joey.

"Yeah. The Irish will come out, won't it?" her father laughed.

"Yes, but he's got that German stubborn streak of mine." Joey's mother grinned while she set the bottle on the picnic table and brought Joey up to her shoulder and began gently rubbing his back coaxing a bubble to be released. Sue was a pretty girl, about the same height as Megan. She had short wavy blond hair, and green eyes.

After saying hello to all her family, Megan noticed Donny walking back toward shore on the dock, while Max remained sitting in the water at the edge of the lake keeping watch on the children. Megan met Donny in the middle of the dock. He was wearing a pair of black swim trunks and no shirt. He looked like a Greek god. Bronzed from the sun, very broad in the shoulders, massive upper arms, and chest. *Whoa!* Megan thought and had to remember to breathe.

"Hi," she smiled when she finally reached him. "How are you feeling?"

"Good luv."

"Where did you get the trunks?" She didn't dare look down.

"When Nathan and I were in town we stopped at yer Wal-Mart, and I picked them up there. How do ye like them?" He smiled remembering the night he overheard her wondering what he'd look like in swim trunks. *I hope I dinna disappoint ye, lass,* he thought.

"I think they look fine." She swallowed so the drool wouldn't show.

"Just fine?" He arched an eyebrow. "According ta Angie and Sue I'm lookin damned sexy." He chuckled and watched pink rise in Megan's cheeks.

"Well, then I guess you passed..." then something hit her. "Donny you haven't been in the water have you?"

"Nay lass, I wanted ta, but Morgan said I wasna allowed until these blasted things come out." He indicated his sutures and then took both of Megan's hands in his and held them out away from her sides. He looked her up and down and took a deep breath. "Can I tell ye tha` ye look good enough ta eat, luv." He leaned over and breathed in by her ear placing a kiss on her neck.

"Hey! There are children present here, you guys. Let's try to keep this a G rated picnic." Nathan laughed from the shore. Megan, who had momentarily forgotten about her family, blushed all over but was willing to fight back.

"What? No skinny dipping with cocktails, Nathan?" she called.

"SKINNY DIPPING! SKINNY DIPPING!" sang the kids in the water.

"Can we go skinny dipping, Dad?" yelled Mitch.

"Sure!" Nathan called back "Just watch out for the fish." He muttered.

Donny listened to the banter while Megan grinned back at her brothers.

"Do ye do tha` here then, luv?"

"What?"

"I'm assuming` the term 'skinny dippin` is a universal one, meanin` the same in all English speakin` countries."

Megan looked at Donny and the thought crossed her mind that she wasn't really prepared for all of this. "What?...Oh! Yeah, it means what you think it means."

"Aye, and do ye do tha` here in yer lake?" he slid his hand up her arms and they now rested on her shoulders.

"Sure! Exhibitionism runs rampant on Butler's Pond. Although personally, I only expose myself at night after dark and rarely in mixed groups." She nearly shivered as she turned toward the shore.

"Thank you, Nathan." She called out to her brother. "Morgan is right about the swimming." She turned back to Donny. "I'll call the hospital in the morning and make an appointment for you to see Dr. Ottis. He'll decide about how soon the sutures can be removed. But it's been five days. It shouldn't be much longer." She backed away slightly and tugged on her shirttail. Donny had been around her long enough to know that this was what she did when she was uncomfortable.

"Shall we join the others, luv?" He smiled.

"Auntie Meggie, you come in the water?" Bridget laughed as Mitch splashed water at her.

"Not today, sweetie. Maybe tomorrow." Megan and Donny were back on solid ground and taking seats with the rest of the family.

"Tomorrow?" Emma questioned. "Aren't you going to the office tomorrow?" She knew that as the practice owner, Megan didn't have to go in on weekends, but usually did.

"No. I thought with the whole family here, I would stay home this weekend."

"Ah yes, the family!" Emma smiled and looked at Donny.

"Have you all had dinner?" Megan, catching the undertone of her mother's comment, decided to change the subject.

"No." Morgan answered. "We decided to wait till you got here, then cook on the shore. Sue and I went to town and got burgers, dogs, beer, and salty chips! Hey! Hide the chips! The salt Nazi is here!" he yelled.

"Funny, Morgan." Megan glared at him. "Sounds good, I'll start the fire." Megan smiled as she began to get out of her chair.

"No, you won't!" Nathan shot out of his chair. "The last time you started the fire, you nearly burnt the place down." He chuckled.

"I was twelve!" Megan defended herself. "And I only did what you told me to do. How the hell was I supposed to know I didn't need to pour the whole jar of kerosene on the wood?"

"Growing up here you should have." Morgan added laughing at the memory and his sister's scowl.

"You never should have done that, you two." Emma scolded. At the time, she was furious with both boys, but now had to smile at the banter between her grown children. "She could have been seriously injured, and likely burned the place to the ground."

"Oh Mom, that would never have happened." Nathan told her as he was placing the wood in the barbecue pit. "We had a bucket of water standing by."

"Would someone mind fillin` me in on the joke?" Donny laughed in anticipation.

"When I was twelve I asked Mom and Dad if I could start the fire for the family reunion." Megan explained. "I was allowed, but only under the supervision of my idiot brothers. I had never done it before, but I had seen them do it, so I knew the basics. However those jerks decided that it was the perfect opportunity to get me in trouble and have some fun in the process. We filled a glass jar with kerosene, and I knew that you were only supposed to use a small amount, but they told me it would catch faster and burn better if I poured on the whole jar and lit it. It's not funny." She glared at her brothers who were laughing over by the fire.

"Yes it is." Nathan croaked, "You should have seen the look on her face!" And he began to roar with laughter as did Morgan. To Megan's dismay her father had begun to chuckle along with them.

"Dad!" Megan was astounded.

"I'm sorry Meggie, but looking back on it, it was funny."

"What happened?" Donny pressed.

"Well I poured the jar on the wood and lit the damn thing. It all but blew up in my face."

"It did blow up in your face," Morgan laughed. "And she didn't have any bangs or eyebrows for the rest of the summer. It was hilarious."

"It was not. And as I recall, you guys got in a lot of trouble for it." But by now Megan was finding it hard to keep a straight face. "Mom wanted to pull some hair forward to give me bangs, but she had to wait until my forehead stopped hurting."

"Were ye burned then?" Donny asked with a concerned smile.

"No, not really, but the fire scorched me a little. By the end of the night I was fine. Since then I have never lived it down and I was never again allowed to start the fire when the jerk twins are around."

"It wasn't the least bit funny, as I recall." Emma spoke up again. "And now that you both have children of your own, I'd hoped that you'd grown up." she smiled at all of her grown kids. "However, I can see that once again, I was wrong."

"Ma has a very low threshold when it comes to the safety of her youngins." Morgan spoke to the group behind a raised hand.

"Yes, I do! And don't call me Ma." She laughed.

Donny enjoyed the laughter and hijinks between Megan and her brothers and was reminded of his own brothers and the tricks they played on each other and their younger sisters. The memories brought a smile to his lips.

"Meggie," Sue stood and walked to her. "If you'll take Joey, I'll run up and get the food. Morgan, behave!"

"Sure, give me my nephew." She held her arms open to accept the cooing baby. "Take the cart."

"Thanks, the keys in it?" When Megan nodded, Sue called out as she got behind the wheel. "Is there anything you need, as long as I'm going up, Mr. Mackay?"

"Nay thank ye, and please call me Donny." He smiled.

"Will do. Angie, do you want to give me a hand?" She called over her shoulder as she put the cart in reverse.

"Sure, back in a jiffy." As the two women sped down the lake road Megan could hear laughing and smiled. She was so blessed to have a family where all parties loved each other and got along so well together.

"Ye look right wi` a babe in yer arms." Donny told her quietly.

"Do I?" Megan smiled "Thank you. You have no idea how right I feel." She chuckled as Joey gurgled and cooed.

Emma, who had been watching her daughter and Donny interact with each other, had recognized their mutual attraction. She had watched Donny all day with her sons, daughters-in-laws, and her grandchildren. He seemed to be kind, and considerate, great with the children and was able to join in on the banter that the boys enjoyed so much. He fit in. She smiled at the thought. He laughed with the family and stood guard on the dock when the kids began to move toward the water. She also noticed that at ten minutes to six he began checking his watch constantly and looking up the lake road on a regular basis until Megan finally pulled up in the cart. She then heard his sigh and saw the gleam of a man newly in love when she finally arrived on the shore. That's when Emma Dunnegan decided; that even though she did not know the particulars of the case he had been working on, or how he had gotten hurt, or for that matter, what he really did in law enforcement. So far, he seemed to be a good match for her only daughter. She smiled as Megan and Donny both laughed with Joey.

"Do you like children Donny?" she asked after a moment.

"Well I hav'na been around many, but Aye. I do." Donny looked at Emma. "Me oldest brother Tommy and his wife Sara are expecting their first child now and I couldna be happier for them." *So are Ian and Madison*, Donny thought with a smile. However, he decided to keep that to himself. *I should call Ian and see how the lass is fairin`*, he thought. He figured it was safe to call and congratulate her and Ian on the baby. They were back in Scotland now and preparing for the wedding. *I need ta get a date and time so I can be there fer it.* he thought. *Damn, I hope I can be there fer it.* he frowned.

"Why are you frowning?" Emma asked, breaking Donny's thought and bringing him back to the present.

"Huh? Oh, sorra I was thinkin aboot me younger brother and his lass. They had a time o' it getting together."

"How many brothers do you have Donny?" Nathan asked as he took Joey from Megan.

"Hey." She protested.

"My turn."

"I have five brothers and two sisters." Donny said as he smiled at Megan and her brother.

"Counting you, that's...your mother had *eight* children?" Emma gaped.

"Aye." Donny smiled remembering Maddy with the same expression on her face.

"God love her." Emma breathed.

"God love who?" Sue and Angie asked in unison when they returned carrying food and handing it to Morgan and Patrick.

"Donny's mother had eight kids." Megan put in. She too was amazed at the number. "What number are you Donny?"

"I was the fourth boy." Donny was not used to answering questions about himself. And as a rule he avoided it like the plague. But he noticed the longer he was with Megan and her family the more at ease he was, and the questions didn't seem to bother him as much.

"Eight isn't so astounding. My great great-great-grandfather had eleven children." Patrick said as he reached for baby Joey.

"Yes. The Irish will out, as you put it so perfectly, dear." Emma said as she transferred Joey to her lap. "However, I don't think Patrick was the one who gave birth."

"Nah, he was probably 'down the pub hoisting a few with the lads', eh, pop?" Nathan laughed.

"Well at least it's pretty safe to say he was allowed 'down the pub' eleven times!" laughed Patrick. "Are any of your siblings married, Donny?"

"Aye, Tommy me oldest and Alex are both married. And..." He was about to say that Ian and Madison were not far from the alter themselves but thought better of it. Ian was such a private person and Donny knew he would not like the marriage announced by anyone other than himself. "Me younger sister was wed two years ago."

"Are you close to your family?" Patrick sat down in the chair next to Donny with a red plastic cup holding what Megan assumed was his favored Irish.

"Aye, fer the most part we are a close-knit family. But me work keeps me away from them most o` the time." He accepted the cup Megan handed him, and raised an eyebrow at her when noticed it was water.

"You're on painkillers and antibiotics. No booze." She informed him and took a sip from her own cup.

"What are ye drinkin` then?"

"Irish." She smiled.

"Wicked woomon!" He grinned.

"Does all of your family live in Scotland?" Morgan asked as he handed a bottle of Smithwick's to his brother.

"Fer the most part they do. Ian travels a great deal." He began to shift under the questions. Megan sensing his comfort level had been reached and swiftly changed the subject.

"How are the burgers coming?" she looked back at Donny and saw gratitude in his eyes.

"Some are done." Angie said. "Grab your plates. Let's eat. Kids, out of the water, time to eat."

Donny watched as the children stampeded from the water grabbing towels on their way to the food tables. He stood and joined the family around the fire to collect his burger then moved to the picnic table where a makeshift buffet of side dishes and condiments had been set up by Sue and Angie. He overheard Emma asking Megan to ride with her in the morning. Donny could only assume, but he figured she wanted to get Megan alone to grill her with questions concerning the two of them. He smiled because he too wanted to get Megan alone. *Very* alone.

As the sun began to set the kids were getting sleepy and the air was turning slightly chilly. Nathan opted to take the kids up to bed and then come back down. However, since the children could not be left alone Sue told the group she would go up and stay with them. She was beginning to have a problem with her allergies and would not be able to stay outdoors anyway. Since the rest of the family had been smarter than Megan, and brought warm clothes to pull on over shorts and t-shirts, she needed to head up to the cottage to change. Donny decided to go with her to do the same and take his nightly meds.

"Do you guys want a ride?" Megan asked Nathan and Sue.

"No, there's no room in the cart for all of us." Nathan told her. "Besides, the walk up will tire out the kids even more." He smiled.

"Ok see you in a bit. Night kids! Sleep tight! I hope you feel better in the morning Sue."

"I will. I always have an issue the first day I'm here. Goodnight, see you in the morning."

"Max! Come!" Megan yelled to the big lumbering dog who climbed into the flatbed box on the back of the cart.

"That's handy." Donny laughed as he ruffled the big dog's ears.

"You have no idea. We used to have to haul water from the lake just to flush when there was a storm. We always lost power."

"Ye donna now?"

"Well, we will lose power, but since I live here full time I have installed a generator for both the big house and the cottage. So I don't really have an issue anymore."

Once at the cottage Megan went immediately to the bathroom retrieving Donny's meds and handed them to him with a glass of water.

"More water." He grimaced which made Megan laugh.

"Yes, more water. Drink it. It's good for you." She said as she went to her bedroom to put on jeans and looked for her oversized brewery hoodie to put on over her tank top. She picked out a hoodie from her closet and threw it on the bed while she got out her sneakers.

Donny finished the blasted water. "Ye do know don ye tha` I was born in a country where the best Scotch whiskey in the world is made." He said, and instead of heading into his room to change he went to Megan's room. She was rooting through her drawers when Donny walked in.

"Meggie." He said which brought her attention from her drawer to him. He closed the distance between them and took her mouth with urgency. She was surprised; however it didn't last long. As she ran her hands up his bare chest, he wrapped his arms around her body, drawing her closer to him. With her body pressed up against his, his kiss became a seduction. Her arms reached up to circle his neck. When the fiery kiss grew hotter, Donny tightened his hold on her. While clenching the back of her top in his hands Megan raked her fingers through his hair. She heard him groan and knew that like herself, he wanted more. But knew that they couldn't go any further, no matter how much she wanted this to continue. Donny broke from her mouth and chuckled as she whimpered at the lost connection.

"I have been wantin ta do tha` ever since ye stepped off tha` cart." He breathed in her ear. "Have ye any idea what ye're doin` ta me, lass." He kissed her neck, "I canna remember when I wanted a woman as much as I want ye."

"I wish I could tell you to take me." Megan breathed.

"I wish ye could tea." He groaned against her shoulder. He was still holding her tight as though by clutching her to him, he might be able to control the situation and himself.

"I'd like to get my hands on whoever put that hole in your side." She whispered.

"But if no` fer tha` we wouldna er'er met, luv." He chuckled and leaned back to look at her eyes.

"Oh yeah." She chuckled and laid her head on his chest.

"And I'm beginning` ta think, ne're ta ha` met ye, luv, would ha` been a verra sad thing."

"Yes. It would have been a very sad thing." She raised on her tiptoes and pressed her lips gently to his, but he accepted the invitation and heated the embrace with fire of his own.

When they separated again, both were breathing heavily. Megan had the sensation that if he weren't holding her up, she'd end in a puddle on the floor. She dropped her head and rested it on his bare chest. "I need to take a shower. A *cold* one."

"Now how would that look ta yer family if ye went back doon there wi` wet hair?" He chuckled.

"Not good." She lifted her head from his chest and looked into his eyes that were now a deep emerald. "Oh god this is so unfair." She smiled and kissed his lips ever so slightly.

"Do'na start somethin` tha` we canna finish, luv. Have some mercy." He traced her jaw line with his fingers.

"Hey, you started this, you know." She laughed.

"Aye. I know and I think twould be a good idea ta end it as well." He kissed the top of her head and backed away. "I will go and put some clothes on, and we should head back before the gossip starts."

"Are you sure you wouldn't rather finish this?" She smiled.

"Ye really are the divil." He laughed.

"So you keep telling me. And if you're trying to avoid gossip, it's too late. It's already started." She called to him as he walked to his room to change. "Yeah, for god sakes put on some clothes." She whispered. She pulled her socks from the drawer and sat on the bed to put them on, *Megan Dunnegan, get a grip on yourself!* She thought, just as she heard Donny grunt.

"Are you alright?" She called to him.

"Dinna I ask ye ta stop askin me tha`?" He pulled off his trunks and grabbed a pair of boxers.

"I know you did, but I can't help it." She walked to the main room just as Donny pulled up his black lounging pants.

She waited while he put on a shirt, socks, and crocs. "Are you ready to go back down?"

"I will go anywhere ye want me ta, lass." He grinned at her.

"Now who's the devil? Here." She handed him his jacket.

Chapter Seventeen

The weekend went by with laughter, banter, and inquiries from Megan's family to her and Donny. Megan had called the hospital on Saturday to ask Dr. Ottis about Donny's sutures. Donny wasn't too pleased to hear that he had to wait two weeks to see the doctor. Trials of understaffing and not enough appointments. But to his dismay he was told it was the only way the sutures could come out. However, Megan was told that if she felt the sutures were ready to be removed before the appointment, as a doctor herself she could remove them. Megan and Emma did take their ride together, and the conversation was what Donny had thought it would be, but Megan had assured him that all was well. During the day Donny spent time with The Dunnegan Clan on the shore. The more time he spent with Megan and the family the stronger he was getting. And he had to admit that he missed his family more than what was normal for him. At night when everyone went to their respective beds for the night, Donny and Megan were alone. They both loved this time of day, but after nearly two weeks, it was becoming harder and harder to keep their hands off each other. They shared the role of responsible adults, but not at the same time of course.

On Monday morning while Megan was getting dressed to head in to work she realized her feelings for Donny were more than just physical, they were very emotional.

"You knew that already you idiot," she murmured to herself in the mirror. "And the sad thing is that you're just admitting it to yourself now. Hell, even your own mother said it before you did." As she finished putting her hair up she heard movement in the other room and went to the kitchen to investigate. "Morning." She smiled at Donny who was getting two mugs down from the top of the stove.

"Mornin`. How did ye sleep?"

"Fine. What are you doing?" She looked at the table and saw two places had been set.

"First, ye should know I canna cook, that is Ian's talent. So, this is the best tha` I can do." He picked up two bowls filled with cereal and the milk and placed them on the table. "I know ye prefer coffee, but I canna find anything` but the flavored stuff, so I settled fer tea." He poured the hot water into the mugs with the tea bags and carried them over as well.

"You made me breakfast?" she whispered.

"Well, tis no like what ye make, but aye." He paused while she looked at the table and wondered what to say next. "Ye have cooked fer me every day since I have been here, I thought it would be—" He was stopped by her lips on his. The intimacy was brief, but long enough for Donny to lose his train of thought.

"Thank you." She smiled.

"It's just cereal and hot water luv."

"No, it's more than that. And I love it." She kissed his cheek and backed away.

They both sat and poured milk on the Raisin Nut Bran and began to eat.

"I was thinking of heading into town after work to get food for Max, is there anything you need or would like?" Megan asked as she dunked her tea bag up and down.

"I'll ne're get used ta yer American idea of tea," he said as he watched Megan continued dunking the tea bag in the mug of hot water.

"What?" she asked and looked up at Donny eyeing her tea bag exercise. "Oh!" she smiled. "Yeah well, we Americans don't make the issue of tea that you Europeans do. My mother used to make iced tea with the loose stuff. It seemed to take forever for all the leaves to sink to the bottom of the pot, but I admit, the result was delicious."

"Ye could use some more cereal."

"Huh? Oh. Really? That was a brand-new box. It's empty already?"

"Nay it's full enough. But I prefer a different brand."

"Oh yeah? Ok sure, what would you like?" She took another bite.

"Fruit Loops." He stated and Megan choked.

"*Fruit Loops*?" she cleared her throat.

"Aye." He looked at her queerly. "Wha`s wrong wi` tha?"

"Aren't you a little old for those?" She smiled.

"Nay." He smiled back. "Breakfast o` champions."

"My nieces and nephews who are all under the age of seven don't even eat those anymore." She chuckled. "Besides, it's full of sugar and not really good for you."

"And?"

"I don't think it's a good idea, you should be eating healthy things while you recover." She patted his arm like his mother would have done when he was a child.

"Ye mean I have ta eat *grown up* stuff?" he mockingly pouted.

"Sorry, but yes."

"Ye're a cruel, strict lass." He bowed his head and pushed his spoon around in his bowl.

"Oh, good god." She laughed. "Fine, I'll get you the damned stuff."

"Thank ye luv." He smiled. They finished with breakfast and did up the dishes.

Donny walked Megan to her car, kissed her whole heartedly and waved as she drove away. He was feeling much better and had more of his strength back, so he decided to take Max for a walk. He wasn't sure Megan would care for his choice in going for a walk and didn't know if her brothers would rat him out. Donny went back into the cottage, grabbed a ball cap, the dog and went out the door and up the road. About halfway up he realized he forgot his cell phone.

"Bloody hell." He sighed and looked down at Max. "I don't suppose yer're smart enough to fetch it fer me?"

"Whoof" was the dogs reply.

"Dinna think so."

Reluctantly Donny and Max turned around and made their way back to retrieve the cell phone. Finally with phone, water and dog in hand, Donny was able to set out on his walk.

"This is better than ridin` around in tha` cart o` hers." He told Max who was watching the wild turkeys in the field. "Ye can see everythin` slowly and smoothly, and ye can come along tae." He wanted to walk in the fields but since he didn't have sneakers or boots he stuck to the road. He walked past what Megan called the yuppie ducks all the way to the horse farm. Donny and Max stood and watched the horses for a while until the horses began their usual after breakfast elimination tasks, then turned back the way they had come.

As they made it past the tunnel of trees, as the kids called it, Donny noticed Nathan and Morgan's families walking down to the lake with towels in hands.

"A bit early fer tha, is it no?" He took a look at his watch and realized it was noon. "Well I guess it was a longer walk than I thought. Would ye like ta join the kids in the water?" Donny noticed Max was getting antsy. The dog barked and streaked across the field above the house and lake to join the kids. He stood and watched as the dog reached the group. Nathan looked up to see him standing at the top of the hill and waved. Donny decided to have something to eat before he went to the lake to join the others.

While he ate he could hear the kids in the water and he longed to get in with them. Hell he was having the stitches removed in less than a week anyway. What could it hurt? He was ready to don his suit when he remembered Morgan was a doctor and would most definitely rat him out to his sister. Donny decided to call Megan and confess his intentions beforehand.

Megan's day so far had been nonstop, and as always she loved it that way. However, when she was taking a much-needed break in her office to reboot before the next wave of appointments, there was a swift knock on her office door.

"Come in." She swiveled in her chair to see Steven poke his head in. "Well, hi there."

"Not disturbin` you, am I?" he asked before stepping in.

"Course not. Come on in." She smiled. "What can I do for you?"

"Well," he settled in the chair across her desk. "I have a few things I would like to ask you about, if you have the time."

"I can give you about," she looked at her docket and saw her next patient wasn't for another thirty minutes. "half an hour. What's on your mind?"

"Ok, first is about Liz. As you know her divorce papers were signed last week and all that remains is the court date to finalize everything."

"Yes, but she has to wait the ninety days for the court date." Megan still got angry when she thought about that poor girl going through all this and about to give birth at any moment. *Bastard Jimmy,* she thought, *you should be shot.* And here she was talking to a man who went around carrying a gun on his hip. *I wonder if he would take offence if I asked him to hunt Jimmy down and take care of him for her?*

"Where did you go?" Steven asked

"Hmm?" she looked back at him and smiled. "Oh, I'm sorry, I had just had a thought about asking you to hunt Jimmy down and shooting him for me." She chuckled at his expression. "Don't worry I wouldn't really ask you for that. Go ahead."

"Well, not that I wouldn't enjoy the task, but I was wondering how you think Liz would feel if I asked her out to dinner?"

"I don't understand." Of course she understood perfectly. She just wanted to hear him say it out loud. "You two go out all the time. You drive her anywhere she needs to go, why should this be any different?"

"Well, I was thinking along the lines of asking her out on a date." His heart was pounding when he looked back to Megan's smiling face. "You knew that already?"

"Yeah. Now listen, I think it might be too soon to bring it up." She watched his face fall. "But I could be wrong. Tell you what, I have a novel idea on how to handle the situation. It is simply brilliant."

"What?"

"Well you walk out to her," she leaned forward as if to tell a great secret.

"Yeah?" He mirrored her stance.

"Lean down to her."

"Yeah?"

"And ask." She laughed at his expression. "I'm sorry Steven, but that's all you need to do. If she is ready she'll say yes, if not..." She held her hands out palms up.

"That was mean." He chuckled. "But I get your point."

"Good, now what was the other thing?"

"Donny." In one word she lost her smile and all the delight in her eyes and what replaced it was sadness.

"Oh, Steven." She looked down at her desk. "Please don't."

"I know I am putting you in an awkward position." He interrupted.

"You have no idea how awkward. Listen, I can't get in the middle of this. If you want to patch things up with him you're going to have to do it on your own."

"How can I when he won't even talk to me?" he countered. "Do you realize the other day was the first time I have seen him in eighteen years?"

"Yes, I know." She said quietly. "I don't know what to tell you. Except that I can't get in the middle." She looked at her hands. "However much I would like to."

"Did he tell you what happened?"

"Yes he did. I am sorry about Arabella and Marie. I can only imagine what it has done to you...both."

"Thank you, can I ask you something?"

"Sure." Her answer was guarded, and Steven knew it.

"How long have you known Donny?"

"Uh," how should she answer this? *The truth idiot!* "About as long as I have known you." When he looked bewildered she went on. "I met him the same day as a matter of fact."

"But isn't he staying with you?"

"Yes, for a while. And before you ask," she paused. And thought about all the questions Steven may be about to ask concerning she and Donny. Donny and his job, how Donny got injured. She thought about how she could answer, what she could answer truthfully, what she should and should not answer and what she didn't want to answer. It was so complicated. She huffed out a breath. *I got nothing,* she thought. She leaned back in her chair and stared at the ceiling. They sat in silence for seconds, each with their own thoughts.

"I think you need to talk to your brother." Megan finally said. She lifted her head and saw the question and doubt in Steven's face. "I don't know." She threw up her hands and stood. Looking around for something to do. Megan opened her desk drawer, saw her Salem Lights, and wished she could have one. "Let's take a short walk." She took her pack and thanks to her very large floor to ceiling double hung windows all they had to do was step through them. And just like that she was legally allowed to smoke.

"I didn't know you smoked?" Steven said as he took the offered cigarette.

"Only on occasion." *And lately the occasions seem to have increased,* she thought. "How is your investigation going with the camp infirmaries?"

"Not well." He looked at her and began to catch on, "I think I might need to head back out there and have another look around."

"Oh, that's too bad. Well, stop by and let me know if there is anything I can do to help." She stabbed out the remainder of her cigarette. "That's all the time I have, my next patient will be in soon. I'm sorry I couldn't be of any help with your problems." She said as they retraced their steps through the double hung window back into her office.

"That's ok." He smiled as he closed the window and walked to the door of her office. "It's nice to talk anyway." He smiled and reached for the handle. Before leaving her office he turned back to her. "Megan?"

"Yeah?"

"Thank you. You may not think so, but you really were a big help."

"Sure, don't mention it." She smiled "Oh, Steven?" He looked back at her, "I mean it, don't mention it." He smiled, winked, and walked out just as Hannah came back to let Megan know her next patient was waiting for her. "Thanks Hannah. How are you making out there?" She asked as she pulled on her lab coat.

"Just fine. Liz was right, this is a really nice group you have here."

"Thank you." She smiled.

For the rest of the morning Megan was too busy to think about her talk with Steven. When it was time to close down for lunch She noticed that Steven, now back in civilian clothes, was picking up Liz. Megan smiled as he helped her into his car and waved her hand as they drove off in the direction of his house.

"Well, well." Jess said as she came out the door. "Now what do you think they're up to?" She wiggled her eyebrows.

"My guess would not be what you are implying, gutter brain." Megan chuckled as she locked the office. "You going to the corners for lunch?"

"Nope, home. Nancy is fixing me lunch then maybe afterwards…" She wiggled her eyebrows and laughed as she sauntered to her car.

"Jessica, you should have been a man." Megan chuckled.

"You're just jealous that I might get lucky over lunch, and you won't." She waved as she drove away.

"Well you might be right." Megan mumbled on her way to her car.

She pulled into her spot in time to see her family and Donny coming up from the lake. They were all laughing and having a good time, and all of them were wet. Including Donny. She closed her car door with a little more force than necessary and stalked over to the group.

"Oh, you're gonna get it pal." Nathan said to Donny as he pointed over to her. "Good luck. Well kids, how about some lunch?" The kids all ran toward the big house and cheered.

"Thanks so much, Nathan old boyo." He moved to Megan and met her halfway. "Hi luv, home for lunch?"

"Yes and I see you went for a swim?" she had her hands on her hip and scowled at him. He didn't say anything but only smiled. "Oh Donny, you know you weren't supposed to go in the water yet."

"Ye're magnificent lookin` when yer angry, luv." He rested his hands on her shoulders. "I didna swim." She only raised an eyebrow. "Honest. I was playen` wi ` the kids and they splashed me."

"You are pretty damn wet for just a little splash of water." She accused.

"I only went in up ta me hips. The kids did the rest." He held up his hand and crossed his heart with his other. Megan looked up at the kitchen of the big house and saw her brothers watching and laughing.

"You should be ashamed of yourself." She smiled, "Blaming kids so you won't get into trouble." She shook her head and chuckled, "Come on let's have lunch. I suppose Morgan said you could go for a swim?" She asked as they entered the cottage.

"Oh, he did more than tha`." He said as she walked to the kitchen and waited until she was rinsing the soap off her hands. "He took the stitches oot."

"He did WHAT!?" she bellowed as she spun around to face him. "Donny You have an appointment at the hospital for that."

"No` anymore." He stepped away from the door and moved toward her at a slow and deliberate pace. "I ha` been feelin' fine," he said conversationally. "Takin less an less o` those bloody pills and when I woke this morn wi` no pain I asked Morgan ta look at them. He said the spots were *perfectly* healed, there was no tenderness around the area, and they could come oot." By this time he was in front of her. He rested his hands on either side of her face and gazed into her eyes and watched as she began to understand the motives of his advance on her person. She watched as his jade eyes became deeper and darker.

"Donny, I—" her whisper was cut short as he brought his lips to hers and touched ever so slightly.

"Aye?" He asked as he trailed feather light kisses along her jawbone and down her neck. She laid her hands on his bare chest and slid them up to his shoulders. Megan shivered when he moved those fantastic lips back to hers, only this time instead of connecting, he hovered. *This is not a good idea.* She thought. *He lost so much blood; he has had little to no real exercise since he came home from the hospital. God look at his eyes, I can't say no to those eyes. I really should,* she continued to herself, *this is reckless and irresponsible.* "Did ye say somethin` luv?" *The hell with it,* she finally decided.

"Kiss me." She breathed, and he crushed his lips to hers as if to devour the very breath in her body with his force. His lips were unyielding, hot, and passionate. There was a carnal feel to his need for her and she was both excited and slightly scared by the nature of his strength. Her heart was pounding in her ears. Butterflies flew in her belly and her body turned molten. Breath became ragged in her need for air, but she didn't dare break from him. She couldn't bear to end this near savage seduction. As her heat and need for him grew, she dug her fingers into the flesh of his shoulders before splaying her hands up to his hair and grabbing hold as he pressed into her. She felt as if she were molded to fit him and only him.

He wanted more of her, wanted to feel her, touch her, and God help him taste more of her. A fire had been released in him he didn't know he had. His hands moved over her back, down to her backside, up her sides to her breasts. As he cupped the sides of her breasts a throaty moan was released. He lost whatever shaky control he had and spun her around with her back against the refrigerator before he broke from her mouth. He untucked her blouse from the waistband of her skirt in one fluid motion, took a hold of the bottom and pulled it over her head. Finally, he was able to feast his eyes on her breasts that were showcased in dark blue lace. Unable to hold back, he hoisted up her skirt pulled down her lacy panties, and thrusted his fingers in. She cried out, as he drove her to her cresting point she held onto his shoulders.

"Donny," she moaned, "Please," She begged. "God please, now."

"No yet luv." He watched her fantastic face as he drove her higher and higher. He wanted to see her break. When she did, she collapsed against him breathing heavy, her skin glistening with sweat. Donny then began to ravage her lips, while moving her to his bedroom. Finally, with them at his destination, he lowered her to the bed and continued his assault on her neck and finally her breasts. When he could no longer hold back he pulled off his swim trunks and plunged into her. He swallowed her gasp with his mouth. She felt magnificent around him, warm, wet, and right. Her hands roaming his back, feeling the muscles ripple with every movement. He drove into her harder and faster than he had intended but he couldn't stop. He heard her cry out, felt her hold on to him tighter. Felt her orgasm as he buried his face into the crook of her neck and continued to ravage her. "Meggie," he whispered as he felt her crest again. He called out her name yet again and emptied himself into her.

They stayed where they were, holding each other as they panted. Megan began to melt further into the mattress.

"Oh nay ye do'na." Donny whispered as he took her mouth again with a hot and passionate kiss. "I am nay doon wi` ye yet." He told her as he began to slowly roam his hands over her body. "I'm sorra I was so rough," he spoke softly into her neck. "Ye didna deserve tha. I got carried away wi` me need fer ye." He was determined to take her slowly this time. And with the gentleness she deserved. "I should ha` done better fer ye." He confessed when he raised his head and looked apologetically into her eyes.

Megan smiled as she moved her fingers to his face. "Oh, now, I think you did just fine." She kissed his lips.

Chapter Eighteen

"Donny, I don't think I can do that again." Megan was breathless as Donny's hands ran over her already highly sensitive skin, while trailing kisses down her throat and removing her clothing. What was left of it at any rate.

"Hmm, why no` luv?" Her skin was pure luxury and silk. He nipped at her shoulder as his hands came to her breast.

"Because...oh god that's nice." She whispered. "I don't think my body can take the abuse." He froze instantly.

"Did I hurt ye?" His eyes and face were full of concern. "I'm sorra luv, I didna mean ta..."

"Donny," She placed her hands on either side of his face and smiled. "You didn't hurt me. You." She kissed him lightly on his lips. "You took me by surprise, but you didn't hurt me."

"I should ha` had better control o` meself." He rested his forehead on hers and sighed. "I should ha` slowed doon. I'm sorra Megan."

"Look at me." She said with more force than she intended. "If you had gone any slower I might have killed you for it. Now knock this crap off."

"Yes ma'am." He slipped into his American accent and smiled.

"God you're a nut." She chuckled "Are you ok?" He arched his eyebrow at her in question. "I meant your side, is your side alright?"

"Aye luv, I'm fine." But as he said it, he was beginning to feel light-headed, and Megan saw some color leave his cheeks.

"Oh no you're not." Knowing that he had overexerted himself, with her help. She scolded herself internally. She scrambled out from under him and had Donny lay back down. "You overworked your body and now look as if you're going to pass out. I'm going to get you some water."

Donny watched as she left the room and heard her in the linen closet and then the water kicked on in the kitchen. When she came back to him she sat on the edge of the bed and handed him the glass.

"I ne're get anything ta drink around here but water." He grinned.

"Here, sip this." She told him. "I should have known better." She said to herself more than to him. She ran the cool washcloth over his face as he looked at her. "Even though you have been moving around you have not built back near the stamina you had before you were shot. By pushing your body the way we just did, you overdid it and drained yourself." She sighed. "I should have known better."

"Why, luv?" He closed his eyes as she ran the cool cloth over his forehead and down his face. Her touch was the best kind of medicine.

"For all the reasons I just said. Your mind was ready, but your body sure as hell wasn't ready for this kind of exertion. This was reckless, irresponsible, and insane, of me." Donny opened his eyes to gaze at her while she was on her tirade. His eyes were full of longing and passion, and the look sent heat right to her loins. "And god help me, I want to do it all over again." She groaned. When he reached for her she pulled away. "But we won't. However much I want to, I intend to think with my head and not my...other parts." She smiled when he chuckled. "How do you feel now?"

"Tired and," he paused, "hungry." He wiggled his eyebrows.

"Donny," she warned warmly.

"For food, luv." He smiled.

"Oh you silly scot." She leaned down and kissed his lips lightly.

"Donna start what ye willna finish." He warned before taking the kiss to a whole new level. "How much longer is yer lunch break?"

"More than enough time to clean up and eat." She pulled away. "Which is what we should both do." Megan stood up and backed away from the bed. "Can you get up on your own or do you need help?" She asked while looking down at him still on the bed in all his naked glory. *Need to keep control, need to keep control.* She chanted in her head. *You could grate cheese on his... well god everything.* She shook her head. "Focus!" She said aloud.

"Megan," Donny warned as he stood and moved toward her as she was backing further away. "I got meself a little lightheaded, wi` yer help I might remind ye, I am nay a damned cripple." And to prove his point he grabbed her upper arms pulled her to him and crushed his mouth to hers. Megan placed her hands on his bare chest, taking the movement as an invitation. Donny released her arms and wrapped his around her waist drawing her even closer to him. As his blood began to boil, the kiss deepened. This time the moan that broke was his own. He wanted her, but knew he couldn't take again for all the reasons she had said. But as she said, his mind, his body, and his stamina were not on the same wave link. Donny indulged himself a small time longer in the abyss that was her luscious mouth before breaking away.

"Wow." Megan panted as she leaned her head against the wall of his bedroom that until now she had not realized she had been backed into.

"Ok, point taken." She smiled at his low chuckle. "I think we need to move."

"Ye need ta give me a moment ta… calm meself." He dropped his head to her shoulder and groaned.

"I really don't think my staying put is going to help you any." She tried to move only to have his hold tighten. "Donny you need to let me go." At her words there was a tightening around his heart.

"I donna ever want ta let ye go, lass." *What is happening ta me? Get a grip laddie buck.* He kissed her neck. "However I can see yer point, fer the moment." He dropped his left arm so Megan could move away. "If ye donna mind I would like ta take a shower."

"Sure, and while you're doing that, I'll make some lunch." She went to the fridge and sucked in her breath as Donny stepped behind her and wrapped his arms around her middle.

"Would ye like tae join me in the shower, Meggie?" He growled as he nuzzled her neck.

"Now who's the devil?" She chuckled and leaned her head back to rest on his shoulder. "Go take your shower so I can take mine before I need to go back to the office."

"Ye might be wantin ta put some clothes on lassie," he ran his hands down her legs making her shiver. "runnin` around in nay but yer skin will likely put ideas in a man's head."

"Are you trying to make this difficult for me?"

"Aye, is it working?"

"Mumm," she turned, brushed her lips on his neck and sighed. "Nope." She answered matter of fact, straightened, and opened the fridge. "Now go and take your shower."

Donny chuckled as he headed into the bathroom and closed the door. Megan didn't draw a clear breath until she heard the water running. Then she opened the freezer door and stuck her head in to cool off.

"Heaven help me when he reaches full strength." She closed the freezer and pulled out meat, cheese, and other things to prepare the sandwiches and placed everything on the stove. Before making lunch she pulled on the panties and blouse Donny had removed. Once she made lunch Megan went to her bedroom and got new under things. As she rounded the corner she was greeted to the site of Donny emerging from the bathroom with nothing but a towel wrapped low on his narrow hips. His hair and body still glistened from spray. *Holy Shit! He looks like sex on a stick* she thought.

"There is plenty of hot water left, luv." He smiled as he kissed her on the cheek.

"I won't be needing it." She muttered as she sailed into the bathroom.

Donny went to his room, put on a pair of shorts, straightened the bed, and picked up Megan's skirt off the floor. As he pulled on a shirt he froze. What if now that he no longer had the stitches and in need of medical attention, Megan wanted him to leave. He knew it was a rotten thought to pass through his mind, but he couldn't help it. There it was, and the damnedable thing was, the idea of him leaving, of her not wanting him to stay, brought him pain that was too real to ignore. He sat on the foot of the bed and thought about the pain and where it was coming from. He wanted to stay, he wanted to stay with *her*. It wasn't because of the protection that she may or may not need from the possible threat of Gavin. He wanted to see her smile, hear her laugh. He wanted to share a bed with her and have her reach for him in the middle of the night and first thing in the morning. He wanted to walk with her, swim with her, share her family with him. Christ, he realized he wanted to share *his* family with her. It was then he realized where his pain and fear were coming from. His heart. Could he possibly be... no, Donny thought. *I willna go there, nay this soon.* He put his head in his hands. *I have no idea what ta do now.* This was how Megan found him.

"Donny, what's wrong?" She rushed and knelt in front of him. "Are you ok? I know you hate when I ask you that, but are you?" When he said nothing she pulled his hands from his face and forced him to look at her. "Well?"

"Ye forgot yer skirt." He couldn't think of anything else to say. He couldn't tell her what was running though his mind until he was sure of what it meant first. He needed more time.

"Huh?" She looked and saw her skirt draped over his lap. "Oh, thanks. But why?" she gestured to him.

"Oh I whacked me head on the dresser when I bent over to pick it up off the floor." He answered quickly. When she cracked a smile he went on. "Aye, ta answer yer other question, I'm fine, lass."

"I'm sorry about your head." She stood taking the skirt from him and kissed him on the forehead. "Do you want to eat? I only have twenty minutes before I have to be back at the office."

"Aye." He stood and traced his finger lightly along her jawbone. "Shall we?" he waited while she finished pulling on her skirt and tucking in the blouse she was wearing. "What ha` ye under those garments now?"

"Nothing for you to see at the present time." She smiled, "Let's eat." Megan took his hand and led him to the table to eat the sandwiches she had made.

They spent the remaining time eating and gazing at each other both unsure of what would happen when she came home that night.

Megan was in full swing with appointments back-to-back. She had a few minutes in between patients and decided to use the time to go and have a look at the daycare center and see if there was anything they needed. When she stepped to the top of the stairs the kids saw her and wanted to know where Max was.

"Oh, he's at home." She told the little girl who asked.

"Why?" the children asked in unison.

"I have my family in, and they have children of their own who love Max as much as you guys do, and they wanted to spend some time with him. But I'm sure he misses you guys as much as you do him."

"Will you bring him back some day?" a little boy wanted to know.

"Of course I will, don't you worry." She assured them.

Happy with the response the kids ran away to play hide and seek with each other. Megan made the rounds upstairs and found all was well and came back in time to see her next patient.

By the end of the day Megan and Jess were all that was left in the office. Megan told Hannah she could go home, and she would close up the office for the night.

"Thanks, see you tomorrow." Hannah waved at the two women and left the office.

"So, how was your lunch?" Jess asked as Megan locked the door and moved to the back of the office to begin shutting down the place for the night.

"Fine, why do you ask?"

"Oh I don't know, you looked bright eyed when you got back." Jess smiled her cat ate the canary smile.

"Jess ,why don't you ask what you want to know."

"I don't think I have to. I can see that answer all over your face. You got lucky at lunch didn't you?" Jess followed behind Megan as she turned out the lights in the exam rooms, then moved toward the front.

"Not that it is any of your business, but yes I did."

"I knew it!" Jess raised her fist in the air and jerked it down toward her waist. "How was he?"

"Jess!" Megan laughed. "I don't ask you how Nancy is in the sack for god's sake."

"That's just because you have more restraint than I do. I'll be happy to tell you, at length, if you really want to know." She wiggled her eyebrows.

"No! I don't want to know. It's not my business anymore than my sex life is yours!"

"Come on Meggie, spill it." Jess stepped in her path so she could not get away. "How was he?"

"Earth shattering." Megan sighed.

"In a good way or..."

"Oh you have no idea how good." Megan smiled and blushed at the same time. "Jess I can't remember ever having that much...." She waved her hands in front of her. "I can't even come up with the right words to describe it. It was intense and almost frightening. And..."

"Better than ol' pickle ass David what's-his-name?"

Megan wiped the dreamy expression from her face. "'Pickle ass?"

"Yeah, 'pickle ass'." Jess leaned closer to her friend "And you can't wait to go home and jump him again."

"No I can't. But I can't."

"Why not?" Jess almost whined.

"Because he just got his stitches out today. And he really doesn't have his strength back yet, thank god."

"Wait, how did he get them out if you have been here all day, and why thank God, he is not at full strength?"

"Morgan took them out for him this morning after I left for work, and if what happened today at lunch is what he's like at half strength, god help me when he is fully recovered. I don't think I'd be able to walk for a week."

"Morgan took them out huh? Handy. So how does the family like Studley-do-right?"

"So far fine."

"So how long is he staying?"

"What?" Megan stopped in mid motion turning out the last light. "What do you mean?"

"Well, sweetie, if he doesn't have the stitches anymore and in no need of medical attention, how much longer will he be staying?"

"Oh god." Megan felt as if all the air had been leached from her body all at once. "I never thought about that. I never thought about what would happen when he was all-better." She placed her hand over her heart to stop it from coming through her chest cavity.

"Meggie?" Jess put her hands on Megan's shoulders. "Are you alright?" When she didn't answer Jess continued. "You don't want him to go, do you?" Megan slowly shook her head. "Then I think it's time you and your secret agent man have a talk, heart to heart."

"Maybe, but I think it might be a little early for *the* talk. Don't you?"

"Not from what I just saw." Jess mumbled as they made their way out of the office and toward their cars. "Think about it, ok? See you in the morning."

"Yeah, bye Jess."

Chapter Nineteen

On the very short drive home Megan became more churned up over her newfound feelings toward Donny. She still had no idea what to do about it by the time she pulled into her spot next the cottage.

"Well, just go in and see how the lay of the land is." She told herself.

As she made her way into the cottage she found Max passed out on the floor and Donny on his cell phone. She patted the dog and waved at Donny as she made her way to the bedroom to change out of her work clothes and into her more comfortable digs. Megan finished putting on her shorts and re-combing her hair when Donny appeared in her doorway.

"Hi." She smiled.

"Hi yerself." He answered. He wanted to gather her up in his arms and dive into that succulent mouth, but he stayed where he was. After his phone call from Ted Duncan of the FBI he knew he needed to apprise Megan of the new situation. "I need ta talk ta ye, Meggie." He had no idea how much dread he had managed to put in her with those words.

"Oh god," she moved to sit on the edge of her bed. "You're leaving." Her color drained from her face.

"No." Donny wasn't prepared for her immediate reaction to his words, but he had to admit he was pleased to see the distress that the possibility of his departure put on her. He moved to sit with her on the bed and took her hands in his. "Nay luv, I'm no leavin, No` until ye want me oot."

"But?" She knew there was more to come and wanted to know what it was.

"I was just on the phone with Ted Duncan."

"That's the guy from the FBI that called you before, right?" She interrupted. "The Director of Operations?"

"Aye, well the director of *me* operations anyway. There have been some developments that I need ye ta aware o'."

"Ok." Megan said slowly. "Well before you drop what I think will be an atomic bomb on my evening, why don't you give me a kiss hello."

Donny leaned in a smidgen then stopped. "Nope. As ye Americans are so fond o` sayin`. If I start wi` kissin` ye I willna be able ta stop and this is important."

"Well damn! If you're going to be all adult and responsible," she huffed her breath and stood. "I guess there is no need to have this conversation in the bedroom. Let's go to the kitchen table and you can tell me what you need to say while I get dinner started." Still having his hands in hers she gently tugged, and he followed her out to the other room.

"Ok, let her rip." Megan said as pulled plates from the cabinet and reached into a drawer to retrieve flatware.

"As ye know from the news report, the raid in Scranton busted those involved in the human traffickin`, and recoverin` all the missin` girls."

"Yeah."

"Well there was a man who was put in custody and in all the confusion, somehow, he managed tae escape said custody."

"How?" Megan interrupted,

"I'm no` sure ye need ta hear all the gory details." Donny remembered Ted's description on Jason's condition when they found him in the back of the wagon. "The man who escaped is dangerous and bat shit drug-crazy ta boot. His name is Gavin and they ha` been on the look oot fer him but ha` no been able ta find him yet."

"You knew this before right?" She set the plates and silver on the tabletop and sat down in her chair.

"Aye." He knew what her next question was going to be and wished he had a way to make her not ask.

"So why are you telling me this now, what's changed?" She was beginning to get butterflies in her stomach.

"Because up until now there was no reason ta think there was any danger. But Ted has been hearin` some reports that Gavin might ha` been sighted in the area."

"You mean here? In Rileyville?"

"Possibly." He took her hand in his and squeezed gently. "They're no sure the reports are viable, so the FBI has given a description and most recent photo ta local law enforcement."

"Donny," Megan just had a horrible thought. "Is this the guy who shot you?"

"Aye, luv, he is."

"How did the FBI know when to raid the docks?"

"I told them the timetable had been moved, why?"

"How did you know that it had been moved? You were in the hospital?"

"When I was in hospital Jason, another in the crew, heard about a man who was shot. Since I had no` come back ta the shack, he figured it was me and came ta hospital fer a look. Tha`s when he told me aboot the new timetable. After he left ta go meet back wi` Gavin, I called Ted and told him aboot the drop-off time change."

"And this Jason was arrested with the rest of the kidnappers?" she asked.

"Aye, but up until now Jason was tae badly injured ta tell the FBI what had happened in the wagon wi` Gavin."

"Too badly injured? What happened to him?"

"Once again I donna think the gory details o` Gavin's escape is necessary ta rehash. The important thing is Jason is now able ta talk and in his interview he told them tha` he had met wi` Sam Watson in hospital and told him aboot the drop off change. Also tha` he had given Gavin the same information while they were both in the wagon, just before Gavin managed to escape." He wanted to wait and see if Megan would come to the same conclusion that he and the rest of the FBI team had come to. Gavin was now aware of the fact tha` Sam Watson was the one who had tipped off the FBI and thus making the raid possible. He watched Megan's reactions to the information he had givin her and could almost see the wheels turning in her head.

"So this Gavin guy, he could know that Sam Watson was a mole, or plant, or whatever you call it?"

"Tha` is wha` we think." He watched as she took a deep breath. "Are ye ok, lass?"

"Well, I don't know." She stood up and walked to the TV room area and gazed out the lake view windows. "Is there any way to know if he knows your true identity?"

"We're nay sure." He stayed where he was seated at the table. "There's no real way fer him ta know me real name, but ye're right. He knows I was workin fer the Feds." *Give the lass some room ta sort it oot laddie,* he thought. "But ta be on the safe side I ha` asked Ted ta post some agents around the area and be on the look oot fer him should Gavin make an appearance."

"Agents?" she stammered and turned back to face Donny. "The FBI is trolling around my land?" Megan's voice hitched an octave higher than normal. Slightly alarmed by her new state of nerves, Donny rose and came to her and took her hands in his.

"It's only a precaution, but if ye would feel better I can ha` the agents and meself leave ye be."

"Leave me be?" She whispered. "You said you weren't going to leave."

"Aye luv, and I willna if ye donna want me ta go." he took her stricken face in his hands. "Boot ye ha` ta be aware tha` if Gavin knows aboot me and is after gettin revenge, stayin` here would be puttin` ye and yers in danger."

"Ok," she settled herself and gently gripped his wrists drawing his hands from her face. "But if you're right and he knows about you. That you've been here with me and you're not here when and if he comes looking, wouldn't I be in more danger of being used as bait for you to come back?"

"Ye ha` a quick mind Meggie." He sighed. "I donna want ye in the line o` fire should it come ta tha`." He lowered his forehead to hers and closed his eyes. "I want ye safe." He whispered. Megan ran her hands up his chest and cupped his handsome face in her hands.

"I will be safe as long as you are here." She kissed his lips softly. "I think I understand the risks of you staying and I have to wonder if the risks would be much higher if you left. Added to that," she kissed him once again with more promise, "I don't want you to leave. I want you here with me. And not just for the added protection should I need it. I want you here with me because I like what is happening between us and I don't want it to end."

"Meggie." Donny breathed and captured her mouth with his. He snaked his arms around her pulling her tightly against his body. She responded to the new hold by running her hands up the back of his head, gathering his hair in her hands and deepening the kiss. Megan's blood was boiling, and she could almost hear her heart pounding in her ears. As Donny's hands slid down her back and cupped her bottom there was a gurgle in her abdomen that was most definitely not a moan. Megan couldn't hold back the giggle.

"Are ye hungry, luv?" Donny chuckled as he looked down at the giggling woman in his arms.

"I guess I am." She looked up at him and couldn't hold back her laugh. "I guess we should eat."

"I thought I was aboot ta." He lowered his mouth to her neck and began to trail hot kisses.

"Oh god," Megan moaned, forgetting her hunger for food. That is until her body protested once more.

"Food now." Donny chuckled. "Dessert later."

"Food can wait." Megan almost sobbed.

"Fer what I have in store fer ye luv," he traced her jaw line with his fingertips. "Ye're gonna need the fuel." He stepped away from her and drank in the sight before him. "Why donna we see if yer family would like ta join us for dinner." He smiled.

"WHAT?"

"Yer family, up at the big house, why donna we see if they want ta join us fer dinner?"

"Oh no, I heard what you said. I just can't believe you said it."

"Why not? I like them." He sobered his features in mock surprise. "Do ye no?"

"I like them fine," she protested, "but I was thinking a quick sandwich and then..." How was she supposed to finish that statement she wondered? *A quick sandwich then off to bed to have hot sweaty sex?* Even in her own thoughts that sounded trampy. *Especially after what had happened at lunch,* she thought. *For god's sake get a grip!*

"Then what Megan?" he asked quietly.

"Oh never mind." She said. "Sure, let's ask and see if they want to go to the Red School House for dinner. I'll call my parents and you can go and ask up at the big house." Megan grumbled as she picked up the phone. Her fingers paused on the numbers when Donny wrapped his arms around her from behind.

"Donna worry, luv," he said softly in her ear. "It's all aboot delayed gratification." He kissed her neck and sailed out the door.

"Delayed gratification my ass," she punched the numbers to her parents house. "You just want to watch me squirm all night in front of the family."

"What was that dear?" Patrick chuckled on the other end.

"Dad!" *Oh shit.* "Oh nothing, I was wondering if you and Mom want to come to dinner with Donny and me. He is up at the house asking Nate and Morgan now if they want to come. So what do you think?" She rushed out.

"Uhuh. Where are you planning on going?"

"The Red School House."

"You bet! Your mother and I were just there, but sure why not."

"You were?"

"Yeah. She dragged me to dinner with some of her ladies and their husbands, with little to no complaint from me."

"Yeah, right."

"Close enough." She could almost see him smiling on the other end of the line. "We'll be down at the farm in a few. I guess it was a good thing this was one of your early closing days at the office huh?"

"Yeah, good thing. How are you going to get Mom here 'in a few'?"

"Blackmail is a wonderful thing."

"Bye dad." She laughed as she hung up the phone.

Megan looked out the window and saw Donny outside with Nate and Morgan in deep conversation and wondered what they were talking about, then decided it didn't matter. She looked down at her clothes and decided she'd better change out of her "grunge" clothes and put on something a little more appropriate for dinner out.

She heard the door to the cottage open as she pulled on dark blue denim capris. Donny came into her bedroom and saw she had changed her clothes. She was wearing capri pants that showed the gorgeous shape of her legs and a little white deep V T-shirt that hugged her upper body like a glove.

"Hi." He said as he walked to her. "This is a wee bit low cut donna ye think?" He traced his index finger over the edge of the deep V of her shirt.

"Delayed gratification." She smiled and stepped back from him as she slid her feet into flip-flops. "Mom and Dad will be here in a few minutes. How about the rest of the family?"

"Yer brothers said yes. But Sue's allergies are acting up and she wants to stay home. She has volunteered ta stay home wi` the kids while we head out to dinner."

"I bet Morgan wouldn't hear of that, so I guess he won't be joining us either?"

"Yer're right luv. So he and his bonny lass will be here watching the kids while the rest head oot."

Megan walked Max up to the house and handed him over to Morgan and Sue for the evening. Normally she would have just left him in the cottage but, since there were people still here and she knew the kids would love it, she figured Max could camp at the big house for a while.

The family piled into one of the Navigator SUVS and drove away from the farm, unaware that they were being watched from the shadow of the trees across the road.

Chapter Twenty

On the way home from dinner Donny's cell phone buzzed alerting him to a text message from Ted.

THERE WAS A PROWLER SPOTTED AT THE FARM. LOCALS HAVE BEEN CALLED.

"Megan," Donny whispered.

"Huh?"

He handed her his cell phone and she read the text from Ted.

"Oh God." She shot her gaze from the phone shaking in her hand to Donny. "Sue, Morgan, and the kids." She whispered with frightened urgency.

"What are you two chatting about back there?" Nate asked from the driver's seat. "I know you two wanted the way back seating but please no necking. My mother is back there with you." He chuckled as he passed through the trees, and the farm broke into view. "What the hell?" he said. In the front yard of the big house sat two State Troopers' cruisers and one on the lake road, blue lights flashing. Nate pulled the

SUV to a halt in front of the house and jumped out. "What happened?" He demanded.

The rest of the vehicle occupants followed suit. Megan was walking to the first trooper when she heard her name from another direction. As she turned she saw Steven walking up the hill from the cottage.

"Steven, what are you doing here?"

"I was at home when I heard the call from the barracks on my scanner. I called in and told them I would head over and meet up with the on-duty Troopers." He looked from Megan to Donny who was standing behind her. "Hello, Donny." He said, but the only answer he got was a slight movement of Donny's head.

"What happened?" Megan asked, not caring about the drama between the brothers at the moment.

"Your sister in-law called because there was someone prowling around. Apparently the dog was barking and growling at the doors and windows so Morgan... your brother, correct?"

"Yes."

"I guess he knew it wasn't Max's normal behavior, so he flipped off all the lights inside and turned everything on outside. That's when he saw a man dart away from the cottage and make a run for the woods by the camp."

"What has been done ta find him?" Donny demanded.

"We are doing what we can, but let's be honest here. The camps are in session. It very well could have been that a counselor was out for a stroll." Steven answered.

"Is tha` how ye do yer police investigatin`?" Donny growled. "By making assumptions and lettin` it go at tha`?"

"No it's not, but I don't have a lot to go on here." Steven's stance got straighter. "Unless you have something to add, there is nothing else we can do at this point."

"Are ye implyin' —" Donny had moved around Megan and was inches from Steven.

"Oh knock it off both of you!" Megan pushed in between the brothers placing her hands on their chests and applying pressure. "I don't give a flying rat's ass about your differences at the moment. So back off." She looked from one man to the other. "I mean it Donny, back off." She waited until both men took a step back. "Thank you. Now," she turned to Steven. "I am assuming that one of your guys will go to the camps and see if they are missing any employees or campers and take it from there?"

"Yes," Steven moved his eyes from Donny and focused on Megan. "As a matter of fact I have already been to Rose Lake Camp and as far as they know all of their employees are accounted for and so are the campers. Trooper Hallet is on his way to Rosemont Camp to make the same inquiries."

"Thank you." Megan rubbed her hands over her face. "It wouldn't be the first time we have had someone from the camps run around on the place. However, it would be the first time the police were called because of it."

"What are ye thinkin, luv?" Donny asked, drawing her gaze to him.

"I don't know really." She shook her head. Something seemed off. She couldn't figure it out, but something wasn't adding up. The text! "Donny you knew about this before we got here. Ted texted to tell you about the prowler. Why would he do that unless...?" she froze and remembered the conversation she and Donny had before going to dinner. *Gavin!* She thought.

Before Donny had a chance to answer, his cell rang. Looking down at the caller ID, Donny answered.

"Ted...I think ye ha` better...Ye're sure..." Donny looked over at Steven "Aye... he's me brother...No...Aye, I think tha` would be a good idea. Aye, I ha` told her...well, I donna bloody well care what ye think aboot it. It's done." And with that he ended the call, took a deep breath, and replaced the cell back in his pocket.

"Well that was illuminating." Steven mumbled.

"Steven." Megan warned and looked back to Donny. "Would you care to fill us in?"

"No` now, luv." When she started to protest he held up his hand to stop her. "Tae many ears around, lass." He glanced up at the house where the rest of the family were talking to the other troopers.

"Donny," Steven stepped forward a bit but was halted by the glare shot at him from his brother. "Listen, you may hate me for the rest of our lives, and if I have to, I'll live with that, but if you have any information that might help sort this out you need to let us know."

"There are some who would agree wi` ye, but no` now, and no` here."

"Fine." Megan interjected through gritted teeth. "I am going up to speak with the family and the remaining police. Then the three of us are going to sit down in the cottage, have some coffee and a conversation." Without another word Megan left the men standing on the lake road and trudged up the hill to the crowd milling around in the front yard of the house.

A half hour later the troopers had gone back to the barracks, Emma and Patrick had gone home with plans to come back in the morning to see their sons and families off. Megan collected Max and made her way down to the cottage to wrangle the dueling brothers and get some answers from Donny.

When she walked in the door she could smell that the coffee was already brewing and the men were at opposite sides of the cottage, not speaking. *If tension could be used as a protection shield,* Megan mused. *The tension in this small building emanating from those two could withstand a nuclear explosion,* she thought.

"Well, isn't this cozy." She said to Max. He looked from one man to the other, huffed a breath and lay down in the middle of the floor. He apparently didn't want to take sides either. "Well played Max old boy," Megan bent down and ruffled the dog's ears while his tail thumped on the floor. "Well played indeed."

Megan walked to her room, kicked off her flip flops and debated on changing her clothes. She sighed and decided it was better to get this going sooner rather than later. She went to the kitchen and poured herself a cup of coffee.

"Ok, who wants coffee?" Steven smiled and Megan poured him a mug and handed it to him. "Donny?" When all he did was incline his head she poured him one as well. The three of them stood in their respective spots sipping from the mugs in their hands not saying a word.

"This is *real* productive." She muttered and looked over at Steven and willed him to start talking.

"Donny, how did you get shot?" He asked suddenly.

"What?" Megan stammered. "Why would you ask that?"

"Call it a hunch." He said to her before turning his attention back to his brother. "Donny?"

"Ye're the state trooper. Shouldna ye already know the answer?" Donny's voice was quiet and resigned.

"What's going on?" Megan asked as the two men stared at each other.

"Megan do ye remember when ye took me ta hospital and I had ta talk ta the troopers aboot how I got shot?" he waited until she nodded her head. "And do ye remember wha` I told them?"

"Yes, you said you told them the truth." Then it dawned on her and she looked at Steven "Oh."

"How long ha` ye known wha` I was doin here?" Donny asked Steven now that he was sure Megan had caught up to his way of thinking.

"I dinna, until this moment. All I knew, was it was a deep undercover case, and we were told not to pursue it any further. I may be a trooper but since I was not the one who went to the hospital on the call there was no reason to give me any more information than that."

Steven took a deep breath and took a long draw of his coffee.

"So, I take it that you are involved with the kidnapping case and that is why you were shot?"

"Donny," Megan sensing Donny's reluctance to answer his brother, crossed to him and placed her hand on Donny's arm. "I really think it would be better to put away old grudges, no matter how deep and painful they are. I think it would be a good idea if we were all in the know and on the same page for the moment."

"Aye, luv," Donny ran his fingers down her cheek. He knew she was right. "Ye'er right." He looked at Steven. "What do ye need ta know?" It was the first time Donny had addressed his brother without hostility.

"How did you know there was a prowler before you drove up?" Steven moved to the table and took a seat.

Donny gave Steven the rundown of all the events leading up to arriving back at the farm. During the course of the conversation Donny and Megan both had taken seats at the table. By the time Donny was finished it was after ten at night and the coffee pot had been refilled twice. Megan wasn't sure she was ever going to get to sleep with all the caffeine running through her system.

"This Ted Duncan, is your boss with the FBI?" Steven had asked.

"On this case at least. I donna strictly work fer the FBI. I am what ye would call a free agent."

"Ok, I'm not sure what that means." Steven looked from Donny to Megan. "I also don't think I need to know what that means. I'm guessing your guys think the prowler was this Gavin guy, the one who escaped?"

"They donna know fer sure. This is a big place ta look after and as much as I hate ta admit it, ye might be right aboot it being a camper or employee from one o` the two camps."

"Huh." Steven smiled and looked, Megan and winked "Progress."

"Donna push it." Donny warned.

"Oh can it!" Megan ordered, causing Donny to raise his eyebrow at her. "So what is the next step?" She asked them both.

"There really isn't anything we can do at the moment." Steven answered. "Nobody got a look at the guy so there is nothing to go on. I would recommend that you keep an eye out and lock your doors when you're not in the house." He told her. "Do you have any weapons on you Donny?"

"Nay yet, but," he slid his gaze to Megan.

"What?" she asked.

"When you told me I could stay wi` ye were ye tellin the truth aboot havin a gun?"

"Yes I was. Why? Are you planning on me needing to defend myself against you?" she snickered.

"Nay darlin. What ha` ye got?"

"Well, let me think." She looked to the ceiling for a few seconds before ticking off what she had. "For long guns, I have a 6.5 Swedish Mauser with a scope, a 30-30 Winchester, a 12-gauge pump shotgun and a 22-bolt action. For handguns, I have three Glocks. A 22, 9mm and a 45. I also have my father's old 1911 Army Colt. That is my personal favorite. I hounded him for years until he finally broke down and gave it to me." She crossed her arms and leaned back against her chair. It was tough not to snicker at the surprised if not dumbfounded looks on both men. "And before you ask, yes, I know how to use them, and I am a pretty good shot."

Steven bent his head and rubbed his hand over his eyes. *Holy shit, she's got nearly an entire arsenal.* he thought, then clearing his throat. "That ought to do it."

Donny just looked at her in amazement. "Damn, luv are ye preparing fer the Zombie apocalypse!"

"No," Megan chuckled, "but northern Wayne County is gun and hunting country. I think Steven will agree that there isn't a local household within twenty miles that doesn't have at least one deer rifle, a shotgun and a 22 rifle for plunking. Most will also have at least one handgun. While most folks, men, and women, don't regularly carry guns, most have carrier permits. My father taught my brothers and I how to shoot as soon as we were big enough to hold a 22 rifle. We learned to shoot right off that side porch up at the big house. We started by kneeling and resting the rifle on the railing. We shot at a target he put on that old crab apple tree right over there. As we got better, he would take baling twine and hang tin cans from the limb of the tree. That poor old tree probably has more lead than wood in it. It still amazes me; with all the lead it hasn't been hit by lightning by now."

"So, who's better?" Donny wondered.

"Who's better what?" Megan asked.

"Ye said tha` yer Dad taught ye and yer brothers ta shoot. So, who's a better shot?"

"Oh, while they would probably dispute it, but I am a better shot with the Mauser. With a handgun, not so much. Anything over twenty yards and I might as well be throwing rocks."

Donny chuckled quietly and smiled lovingly at her and spoke, "Forgive me fer askin, luv, but are any o` yer weapons registered?"

Steven opened his mouth, but Megan held up her hand and looked at Donny. "In the state of Pennsylvania it is not necessary to register firearms. In fact, there isn't even a place in the state to register them if I had to, which I don't. In addition, it's against state law for a police officer to keep a personal record of people who have firearms. And if your next question is 'Do you have a permit to carry?' the answer is yes, Donny, I do. Although I do not carry...so far. And now, why do you ask if I really have a gun, that is?"

"Where do ye keep this armory ye have, luv?" he smiled at her. *She's her own army,* he chuckled to himself.

"The rifles are under your bed, but the 12 gage is hung over the door in your room, the shells for them are on the top shelf of your closet. The 45's in a lock box in the bottom drawer of my nightstand and the ammo is in the top drawer of the same nightstand. The other handguns are in their own boxes as well as the ammo in my closet. And I say again, *why?*"

"Well I can ha` Ted send me a weapon," Donny began.

"But if Gavin is indeed watching the place, wouldn't he notice an FBI brigade unloading weapons?" Steven wondered

"Aye, which is why I was thinkin of usin` Megan's if it came ta tha."

"Oh for the love of God." Megan lowered her head to the table.

"Are ye alright, darlin?"

"Do you remember how much you hated it when I kept asking you that?" She said while her head was still resting on the table. "Please stop asking me." She picked up her head. "Ok, here is what we know. This Gavin guy is on the move and may or may not know who you really are and where you're staying." She waited for Donny or Steven to answer.

"Aye." Donny answered.

"There was somebody here on the property tonight, but it was most likely nothing. You want to take precautions to insure the safety of all present by way of either having guns brought in or using mine should it be necessary."

"Aye."

"Fine, use mine." She stood and took her mug to the sink, washed it, and placed it in the drain rack. "Do you have a photo of this guy yet?" she asked Steven.

"Not on me, but I'm sure there is back at the barracks. If you want I can bring it to you so you can have a look at the guy." Following her example he washed his mug.

"Sounds good to me. Now, this has been a long night and I have an even longer day tomorrow what with my family leaving and work. Steven, you are more than welcome to stay and catch up with your brother, but as for me, I've had enough and I'm going to bed." She leaned down to Donny and kissed him gently on the lips and as she walked past Steven she gave him a quick peck on the cheek. "Thank you for coming out here tonight." And with that she made her way to the bedroom, changed into her tank and pj bottoms and slid between the sheets.

"That's twice she has left us alone in this place." Steven said.

"Hopefully there willna be any need fer repairs this time." Donny chuckled as he took his mug to the sink along with the remains of the coffeepot and washed them both.

"Donny, I know we have our issues and a past full of hurt and blame to work through," he waited until his brother was finished and facing him. "But I would really like to get to know you again and see if we can... I don't know." He sighed

"Come ta common ground?" Donny finished the question. "I know our Mam would like us ta. As would the rest o` the family." Donny sighed and looked toward the pass-through window into Megan's room. He knew she would also like for the two of them to work out the past. "Why donna we see if we can get through this now wi` oot killing one another and afterwards..." Donny shrugged his shoulders.

"See what we see." Steven supplied. He knew it was a lot to ask of his brother, but he took a risk and held out his hand. He held his breath as Donny studied it for a few seconds and released air from his lungs with satisfaction as his brother clasped his hand and shook. *Baby steps.* Steven thought. *This is more than we have had in eighteen years. I'll take it.* With that the men said their goodnights and Donny walked his younger brother to the door.

After the doors were locked and the light turned out, Donny put on his pjs and sat on the edge of his bed.

"Wha` do ye think Max?" He asked the large dog staring at him from the doorway. "Do ye think she would bash me bloody head if I went ta her?" Max whimpered and pawed at the floor. "Is that an invitation ta go ta the lass's room?" Max tilted his head. "I promise I ha` the best o` intentions." And with that Donny turned out his light and quietly walked to Megan's room. As he entered he saw she was sound asleep and on her side. Donny walked to the other side of the bed and carefully slipped in without disturbing her.

Megan stirred from her mock sleep as he nuzzled up to her back drawing her to him.

"Did I wake ye, luv?" he whispered.

"You don't move quite as stealthy as you think you do." She smiled. "But Donny if you're after—"

"Nay Darlin," he kissed her neck. "It's been a long and stressful night and ye need yer sleep. I just wanted ta join ye in yer bed for a night a rest."

"Oh, you have no idea how good that sounds." She said sleepily as she turned to face him. He kissed her tenderly then he maneuvered to his back while she rested her head on his shoulder. "How did it go with your brother?"

"Shh, in the morn, luv. Go ta sleep now and follow wherever yer sweet dreams lead ye." He stroked her back and listened as her breathing slowed with sleep. He closed his eyes and tried to match his breathing to hers. Soon both man and woman were fast asleep, and little did they know that their dreams were both of the same tenor, each other.

Chapter Twenty-One

In the days that followed the departure of Megan's brothers and their families, the homestead seemed very quiet, empty and a little sad. Megan was used to this. She always felt a little lonely after family and friends had been on the farm for any length of time, then suddenly they were gone, and she was alone. However, this time, even though she was sad to see her brothers and their families leave, she knew it was safer to have them gone and out of any danger that might occur. Besides, this time she wasn't alone, Donny was there with her, and she was thrilled.

She and Donny, without planning to, developed a routine. They ate breakfast together every morning before Megan went to work, and she was coming home more often to share lunch with him. She was also spending more time preparing dinner at home as opposed to eating out or bringing something in from outside in Styrofoam containers. In the past she actually spent more time in the office than she did at home, but she was beginning to truly enjoy her time away from the office. Her staff had noticed the difference and couldn't have been happier for her.

Although so far none of them had met the reason for the change, they were already predisposed to approve.

Donny was getting better physically by the day. His strength was returning, and his stamina and energy level was higher. He spent more and more time walking the farm with Max. He and Megan swam on her days off and often in the evening when she came home from the office. They took the horses out for rides through the fields and the woods. Although he had not ridden her giant black Steve, she was right about Dolly. She might have been smaller than her counterpart, but she had more than enough grit to keep up.

One evening in particular when Donny was feeling daring he gave Dolly the go ahead to let loose and learned what she was made of. She was fast and agile and all in all gave a wonderfully thrilling ride. Megan wasn't too pleased with the escapades of the horse and her rider at first, but began to see no harm in the fun. Not willing to be out done, she and Steve overtook the two in a matter of minutes. Donny admired her seat on the black beast. The two moved like one and it looked as though they read each other's thoughts. He had heard of what people called "Horse Whispers." Those that could connect with the horse on some level, but up until then he never really believed they existed. To watch Megan and her giant black beast zig and zag through the trees and leap over rock walls was enough to take his breath away. Although he had a good seat on a horse as well, even he knew he would never be able to keep up with the likes of Megan and her steed. He was thankful there was a full moon that night and not a cloud in sight because his first impression of Steve was right. He was so black it was difficult to track where he and his rider were when the dark of night took over the light of day.

Finally the two riders came to what Megan had referred to as the middle lot and rested the horses.

"Shall we get down and have a look around?" Donny asked.

"Better not." Megan looked at her surroundings. "It's late. Do you hear the coyotes?"

"Aye, I did hear them."

"I don't know about you, but I would rather be on the horse should the vicious bastards come to investigate." She laughed as she watched Donny scan the area for the wild dogs.

"Do ye think we should head back then, luv?"

"What's the matter?" She maneuvered Steve up next to Dolly. "Are you nervous?"

"If it's all the same ta ye luv, I would rather not be attacked on or off a horse." He leaned over to kiss her, and her black beast snorted in disapproval. "By either dog," glancing at Steve, "or horse." He chuckled. "Protective isn't he?"

"What can I say, he wants to guard his woman's honor." She cooed as she patted Steve's neck. "Come on, let's go back and let them get some rest." They rode back to the barn in a slow walk.

Upon entering the cottage Max bounded around letting them know he needed to go out. Donny took him outside, while Megan freshened his water bowl and checked for any messages. With both jobs done, it was still too early for bed, so Megan began to look for a movie to watch. Donny stood watching her when he and the dog returned from outside. Although they had shared her bed since the night of the prowler, they had not made love. Both of them seemed to have come to the same unspoken realization that they each needed more time before taking that step again. Emotionally for both parties and in Donny's case earlier, physically. He was somewhat ashamed of himself over their first and last lovemaking. He didn't think he had actually manhandled her, but she was special, a treasure and should be treated as such, and he felt he had been just a bit too aggressive with her. He knew he wanted to be near her, *och*, he thought, *tis more important ta be near her, to hold her and ha` her next ta me and know she's safe from harm, but...right at this moment, oh HELL!*

As Megan stood at the DVD shelves Donny slowly came from behind her and wrapped his arms around her torso. Not saying a word to her he began to trail feather light kisses from her ear to the top of her shoulder. Sensing his intentions, Megan turned in his embrace, ran her hands up his fantastically well-defined chest and laced her fingers at the base of his neck.

"What are you after Mr. Mackay?" she asked while gazing into the deep jade pool eyes.

"Ye," he lowered his lips to hers and tasted ever so briefly, testing the waters as it were. "Ha` ye any objections?" he asked as he laid a trail of kisses down the side of throat. He could feel her pulse quicken.

"None so..." her words were stolen as Donny captured her mouth with his. Gently at first then as she gave more of herself he deepened their joining to her delight. Her mouth was heaven, and her body was that of a goddess. With his arms still circling her he drew her tighter to his body. She was much smaller than he, but he loved that she seemed to have been molded to fit perfectly to him. In one quick motion he gathered her up in his arms and carried her to the bedroom.

Megan gasped in surprise at the movement and a giggle escaped from her lips causing Donny to smile in return.

"How romantic." She said against his lips.

"I can be when the mood strikes." He told her as he placed her on the bed. Before joining her there Donny turned to close the glass French door to her room and released the white curtain over the glass much to Max's dismay. "Sorra laddie, but I want her all ta meself." He said as the dog gave a groan before retreating back to the other room. Donny faced the woman sitting on the bed and was overcome with these new feelings. He had been so empty of emotion for so long, that these recurring feelings he was experiencing with Megan all seemed so new to him. Was he nervous? He wasn't sure, he couldn't remember ever being in the past. He wanted her more than he had dreamed possible after so many years. But he was afraid he wouldn't be able to steady himself to go as slow and as gently as he wanted to. Needed to.

Megan, reading the hesitation in his features, slid off the bed, crossed the room to stand only a breath away from him. Not taking her eyes from his she took the hem of his shirt in her hands and began to slide the fabric up, all the while keeping her hands on his body. Once his skin was bare from the waist up, Megan ever so softly ran her fingertips down from his shoulders, over his chest, down his abdomen finally to rest on the newly formed scar that was left by a madman. She gently placed a kiss on the site causing the muscles in his upper body to quiver. Donny cupped her face in his hands and watched as her violet eyes became deeper with want and need.

"Meggie" he whispered as he drew her in for the slow passionate kiss. Following her lead he took the hem of her shirt and pulled it up over head. His breath hitched when she traced the top of his jeans with her fingers and his heart raced when she began to undo the button and lower his zipper. Taking her hands in his, he halted her intention. He brought their enclosed hands to his chest and rested his forehead on hers. "I need ta take this slow, luv." He whispered.

"Are you afraid I'll hurt you?" she smiled as she kissed his cheek.

"Nay," he drew back so he could see her eyes, "I'm afraid I'll hurt ye."

"Oh Donny," she took her hands from his and placed them on either side of his face. "You didn't hurt me last time. I do believe there were two of us involved and we both rushed." She looked into his eyes grow-ing darker by the second and took his mouth with heat. "Please, make love to me." She moaned against his mouth causing him to groan as though he might devour her.

Neither one would remember who did what, but soon they were both free of clothing and moving toward the bed. Donny picked her up and placed her down on the sage green sheets only to join her in one fluid motion. This was not the same man who had taken her before. This man was slow and tender. Covering her body in scorching kisses and leaving hot finger trails over her. They touched each other everywhere and left no part of their bodies untended. Moans and hot breath per-meated the air all the while never leaving each other wanting. When he finally entered her, the cry of pleasure she released was only matched by his own. Not taking their eyes off each other, Donny began to move in a slow and sweetly torturing pace. Their hands clasped together, and they began to move as one. Each bringing the other higher and higher to the breaking point. Finally reaching her peak, Megan cried out in ecstasy, arching her back, exposing her throat, and pressing her head into the pillows. Donny placed his hands on either side of her shoulders raising himself above her. He drove himself deeper into her. Needing to hold onto his strength, Megan placed her hands on his sweat slicked back and drew her legs more tightly around his hips.

"Oh, god." She gasped and he drove her again. "Donny..." she cried out as she crested yet again. Unable to hold back any longer, Donny thrust into her twice, calling out her name as he emptied himself then collapsed on top of her.

The two lay panting, hearts racing and unable to move. Finally lifting his head from the crook of her neck Donny placed a tender kiss on her lips. He shifted slightly so his body was no longer crushing hers. Megan gazed into his eyes and couldn't remember ever being made love to so thoroughly and deliciously as he had just done. She would have said as much if he hadn't taken her lips again.

"Thank ye, luv." He whispered against her lips.

"You're most welcome. But in the words of one Donavon Mackay." She rolled over so she was now on top of him. "I'm no` done wi` ye yet." They both chuckled as she took his mouth. They made love twice more that night before they finally had to admit exhaustion and sleep.

Chapter Twenty-Two

The next morning Megan woke to the sound of soft barking and whining. Unwillingly she opened her eyes to find Donny still asleep. He lay on his back, with his one arm around her and the other lay over his chest holding her hand. The light from the rising sun filtered in through curtains covering the windows facing the pasture. She chastised herself mentally for not remembering to close the blinds on those windows before going to sleep. *Oh well,* she smiled, *I had other things on my mind at the time.* She watched as that soft filtered light played with the features of her sleeping companion. His hair swayed slightly in the morning breeze and his long lashes fanned over his cheeks. His face looked at peace while his body, her gaze followed down his frame. *Wow!* Was all she could come up with. She wanted nothing more than to nuzzle in closer, but Max's protests were becoming louder and more demanding. *Oh why didn't I ever put in a doggie door for him?* she grumbled internally. *Because it would have been as big as half a door!* She smiled and began to ease herself off the bed when Donny's grasp on her tightened.

"Where do ye think yer goin'?" he asked as if he were still asleep.

"Max needs to go out." She looked at the clock on her dresser, "And I have to get ready for work."

"No` yet." In a swift move he rolled over trapping her underneath him, seizing her mouth with his.

Max ended up having to wait another half-hour before Donny and Megan emerged from the bedroom. Because Megan needed to get ready for work and was now running behind thanks to Donny and his extremely enjoyable delay tactics, he agreed to be on Max patrol while she showered. Since Max had gone to work with her the last three days she agreed to let Donny have him for the day. Both man and dog were happy with the arrangement.

Megan's workday was light as far as her patient load went, but she had mounds of paperwork and phone calls to make up the difference. As she was finishing up her notes in one of her patients files her phone rang.

"This is Dr. Dunnegan."

"Hello Meggie." Emma's voice rang over the line.

"Hi Mom," Megan smiled. "What can I do for you?"

"Well I was thinking your father and I could come down to the cottage and have an impromptu cook out on the deck."

"Sure, I think I even have some steaks in the freezer." Megan was already writing herself a note to call Donny and ask him to take them out to thaw.

"Is this one of your late nights? I can never keep track of your office hours."

"Yes mother, we are open late tonight, but Jess and Sara are staying. I'll be home by four."

"Oh goody. Your Dad and I will be there by five. How about if I make up some potato salad and bring the wine?"

"Sounds good to me."

They said their goodbyes then Megan called Donny to let him know the plan for dinner. After hanging up she dove back into her paperwork and never looked up until Hannah came to tell her next patient was there.

For the remainder of the day she saw two unscheduled patients and her last was a recheck for a bashed knee.

Megan stopped outside the exam room and took a look at Harry Smith's chart to reacquaint herself with his injury before going in. Satisfied she entered the exam room.

"Good afternoon, Mr. Smith, and how is the knee feeling?" Megan smiled as she went to the sink to wash her hands before having a look at the knee in question.

"Much better, thank you." Gavin smiled at the pretty doctor.

"Good, let's have a look shall we?" Megan sat on her wheeled stool, folded up the baggy pant leg and carefully removed the bandages. She was pleased with the way the knee had healed up and decided that there was no longer a need to keep it bandaged. "Let's keep the bandages off for now and let the air get to it. How has the mobility been?"

"Surprisingly very good." *Good thing too,* Gavin thought, *otherwise I might not have been able to get away the night I came looking about your farm.*

"Good. But don't push it too much." She warned with a smile. "I would still like you to keep this leg as straight as possible. It's doing very well but not fully healed yet. We don't want to take a chance of pulling it open. There is still some slight swelling. I think maybe you might cut back some on your activities."

"Well I can't lie; I have been walking around quite a bit and scoping the area you might say." *Like at your place you stupid bitch.*

"Oh did your dog get away from you again?" She chuckled remembering his explanation about the gash in the first place.

"Huh?" *Oh shit, that's right I told her I was chasing a dog.* "Oh, yeah I really need to find a better way to keep that animal contained. What's your secret?"

"For what?" Megan asked as she rose to rewash her hands.

"For your dog?"

Megan stilled her hands under the running water. A cold feeling was starting to sneak up the back of her neck. "How did you know I had a dog?" She kept her voice calm and in the same conversationally tone.

"I saw it." He watched as she tried to hide the slight stiffening of her back and shoulders. "One day when I was passing by the office." He added, "Giant thing jumping out of your car." He didn't want to spook her too soon, but he was getting a thrill at her nerves. He liked to make women nervous at first then later make them scream. *Soon doc,* he adjusted his position as his cock grew harder at the thought. *Soon I will make you scream for me.* "I was impressed, he wasn't even on a leash."

"Oh well he was very well trained." Megan suddenly wanted him to leave. He was making her very uncomfortable. She dried her hands and made a note in his chart.

"Does he come to work with you often?" *There are her nerves again.* He smiled as her writing stopped short for a second, he was growing more and more aroused.

"Well," *he needs to go,* she thought as she straightened, closed his chart and turned toward the patient. "If there is nothing else I think you are good to go." She smiled. It wasn't the first time a patient had made her uneasy, but this guy was starting to cross into skin crawling territory. She wasn't really sure why; his conversation wasn't out of line. Lots of people had asked her about Max and commented about him coming to the office with her. "Let me walk you out." She went to the door, opened it, and waited for him to walk out. Megan walked him to the front door of the building. "Have a good rest of the day Mr. Smith."

When she shut the door behind him and faced Hannah, Megan exhaled and relaxed her shoulders. She rounded the reception desk as one of the nurses took the last patient in the waiting area to an exam room to see Jess.

"Here you go, Hannah." She handed her Mr. Smith's chart as she went to fill a mug with coffee.

"Will he be back for another check?" Hannah asked as she took the chart to be filed.

"Oh I don't think so." Megan answered thoughtfully.

"But?"

"How did you know there was a 'but' coming?" Megan chuckled as she took a sip of her coffee.

"Call it intuition."

"Oh I don't know," Megan sighed. "He just weirded me out a little, that's all. Silly really." She rolled her shoulders and neck.

"No it's not." Hannah told her. "It's better to err on the side of caution, I always say." She took her seat behind the reception desk then swiveled her chair to face Megan. "If the guy makes you uncomfortable then if he comes back let one of the other doctors see him. Or refer him to another practice." She nodded her head in agreement of her own statement. "What did he say to make you nervous anyway?"

"Nothing really, he just asked about Max and what not. I don't know." Megan threw her free hand in the air and sighed. "It was just a feeling. Oh well. What time is it?"

"A quarter to four." Hannah smiled, "Just about time for you to go home to your young man."

"Hannah." Megan laughed

"Oh we all know you've got someone special at home. And everyone thinks it's great." She leaned forward in her chair a little. "But don't you think it's about time we all had a look at him?" she wiggled her brows and her eyes twinkled with merriment. "Oh, have you spoken to Liz today?"

"Not yet. I'll call her before I leave. She glanced at her watch. "Well, maybe not now, she's probably napping. She usually does in the afternoon. I'll try to call her later this evening. At least she's not on the phone with you on an hourly basis anymore checking on everybody." Chuckling as she walked back to her office she remembered how difficult it had been to convince Liz it was time to give up the ghost and go on maternity leave.

Megan closed down her computer and put away the files she had been working on all day. She stood at her desk and realized she had completed the task in under five minutes and wasn't sure what to do with herself.

"Oh hell it's only ten minutes early." She collected her bag, turned out the lights and made her way to the front of the building. "Good night Hannah, see you in the morning." She waved as she left.

"Have fun tonight dear." Hannah chuckled as she watched the young doctor leave.

As Megan parked her Wagoneer she saw her mother's golf cart in the front yard. Going into the little house and directly to the back deck she was greeted by Donny and her parents.

"You're here already." She said to her mother as she gave Emma and Patrick pecks on the cheeks. She spied the cheese, crackers, and vegetable trays. "Oh thank god, I'm starving."

"I wouldn't wonder," Emma scolded her daughter. "You worked through your lunch."

"Guilty." She turned her gaze to Donny who came to stand beside her. "Hi."

"Evenin, luv." He placed a chaste kiss upon her lips. Both Donny and Megan glanced back at her parents in time to see Emma's raised eyebrows.

"Well, I'll change and get the steaks ready for the grill. Where are they?"

"In the microwave darlin."

"Good, thank you. Mom, is the potato salad in the fridge?" She patted Donny's arm as she went back inside fully aware her mother was on her heels.

Megan went into her bedroom and pulled the curtains over the French doors before changing out of the work clothes and into some jeggings and a t-shirt. Afterwards she went into the kitchen where her mother was removing a large salad bowl and fresh vegetables from the refrigerator.

"I've had this zucchini marinating all afternoon. I thought we could do them on the grill with the meat." She said.

"Good idea." Megan said as she took the steaks out of the microwave and patted them dry. Knowing the meat needed to be salted so they would tenderize, Megan took the grinder with sea salt and gave the meat a few good solid turns of the grinder. While they sat, she took the spices out of the cabinet, and butter out of the fridge. After setting them on a tray with the meat, Megan turned and faced her mother.

"Do you want to ask me questions, or would you rather have a narrative?"

"I'm not sure either one is really necessary, Meggie." She pulled a chair out from the table and sat to watch her daughter move in the kitchen. Emma was no dummy. As she liked to say, she didn't come with the milkman. She was a smart woman. When her daughter first established Donovan MacKay in the cottage Emma was not at all thrilled with the arrangement. Over the next day or so, it was obvious to Emma that the boy did in fact need to be watched medically. And as the weeks passed, Emma has seen Donny interact with her daughter, her sons and the grandchildren and had to accept that he was indeed a nice steady buck. Plus, the fact that he was single, educated, and gainfully employed, although, truth be told she wasn't sure a gun toting "G-man" was her idea of *safe* gainful employment. However, as the weeks passed, she was also becoming aware that the relationship between Megan and Donny was slowly moving from doctor/patient into more intimate territory. Emma wasn't dead from the neck up either. She could see that her daughter and the handsome young man had feelings for each other that they obviously hadn't intended in the beginning. She was somewhat alarmed by the change in the relationship at first. Fearing that when he no longer needed help he would quit the place and her daughter without a backward glance. However, when it became obvious that Donny was well on the mend and no longer needed to stay for medical reasons, he was now staying for her.

"I have eyes Meggie and when I have my shots I can see just fine." She lit a cigarette and continued. "It's obvious that you two have formed an attachment to each other. I just wonder where you two think this is going to lead."

"Lead?" Megan faced her mother, "What do you mean?"

"You're not deaf, dumb, or blind either, Megan. You know precisely what I mean." She waited for her daughter to take a seat at the table with her before she went on. "The reasons for him being here in the beginning are no longer valid. Now that he is no longer in need of your professional aide, what will he do? And," she reached across the table and laid her hand on Megan's arm, "what will you do when and if he leaves?"

"I don't know. I have no answers for you mom. We haven't talked about it. Not really. Give me one of those." She reached for one of Emma's cigarettes, lit it and took a long drag. "You know it's not like we planned this." She looked up into her mother's eyes holding back unshed tears.

"I know honey." Emma leaned back in her chair and cleared her throat. "I have a pretty good indication of how you feel about him. You love him don't you?" when Megan's eyes widened, Emma continued. "You don't need to answer. I can see it. How does he feel about you?"

"Oh mother." Megan grabbed a tissue from the box on the table and blotted her face. Then she threw her head back and laughed. "I don't know. Do I have to? Do either one of us need to lay our hearts and feelings down on the table at this stage? We like each other. I think we both have strong feelings for one another. Do you really need more than that right now? Do I?"

"No, I suppose not." Emma sighed. "Things seem to be moving very fast for you anyway, and I worry."

"I know you do, but honestly you don't have to. Donny and I are just taking this as it comes. And so far it is working for both of us. So please don't worry."

"I'm a mother dear, that's my job." She patted Megan's hand. "Well, I think I have given your father more than enough time alone with your Donny. And we can start dinner." Megan gave her mother a rather exasperated look as both women rose, but before leaving the room Megan gathered her mother in a hug.

"Thanks for your concern, mother."

"You're welcome." Emma rubbed Megan's back. "And for what it's worth, he's a much better catch than David what's-his-face."

"Mother!" Megan groaned. Megan just loved the way everyone referred to David as "David what's-his-face". Somehow it made it worse on him and more cathartic for her than calling him names.

"Well, I'm just saying." Emma shrugged. "I seriously doubt that you'd catch Donovan MacKay boinking your maid of honor the night before your wedding."

"I love you mom." Megan pulled back slightly and kissed her mother on the cheek.

"I love you too, Meggie."

With that settled Megan and Emma collected the vegetables, and put plates, silverware, wine glasses and napkins on a second tray. Megan carried the meat tray, and Emma the other, and they joined the men on the deck. As the women came through the door Donny jumped up and took the tray from Megan, while Patrick took Emma's and carried them to the table.

"I lit the grill for you, want some wine?" Patrick asked as he began to pour himself a glass.

"Yes and thank you." Megan took the offered glass and took a sip. "Mumm, this is good, what is it?"

"It's Coppula Cabernet Sauvignon, your Uncle Edward recommended it. Since he and your Aunt June along with Uncle Michael and Aunt Tonia are coming here in a few weeks I thought we could give it a tray."

"Are they all coming?!" Megan was so excited. "None of them have been here for so long."

"Not since last fall." Patrick remarked.

"How come ye never told me ye had uncles and aunts?" Donny asked as he took a piece of cheddar cheese from the try Emma and Patrick had brought over.

"Huh?" she looked over at Donny. "Oh I don't know, I guess it never came up. Oh this is fantastic." Uncle Edward can sure pick 'em. She always loved to be around her aunts and uncles. She could sit back and listen to the stories that flew about the brothers when they were kids and the trouble they would get into. "You said a few weeks?" she asked her father.

"Yeah Michael and Tonia are in Ireland now looking at another piece of property to buy."

"Good god at this rate they'll own half the country." Emma chuckled.

"The Irish can never have enough land, me girl." Patrick smiled at his wife.

"What about Edward and June?" Megan asked as she put the meat on the grill.

"Well, they're in England."

"Why?" Megan scrunched up her nose, while snickering on the inside. Shunning the English part of their heritage was always a way to get Emma's back up.

"You know," Emma piped up. "You and your brothers do have English blood running through your veins young lady."

"Yes dear, they do." Patrick rubber her knee. "But you know as well as I do that we try to keep that nasty bit of information secret." He laughed as Emma swatted his hand away. He knew it was always a sore spot for his wife that their children considered themselves Irish and nothing else. He could remember once years ago when the kids were young, Emma's family were going to have a family re-union out of state and their son, Morgan piped up to say, "Mom, you have relatives too?" Patrick chuckled at the memory and rejoined the conversation at hand.

"What a treat to have all of the brothers and their wives here at one time." Megan said to her father as she moved two of the steaks to the higher rack. "How do you like your beef Donny?"

"Rare, luv." He rose to join her at the grill. "Is everything ok, lass?"

"Yes, why?" she asked quietly as she moved three of the ribeyes to a plate and covered them with tin foil. Her father preferred his meat dead as a doornail.

"How did yer talk with yer mother go over?"

"Oh fine, she was just being motherly about you and me."

"Seems both mother and father are runnin` on the same wave link." He murmured

"What do you mean? You know what? Never mind, I think I already know."

"Och, I'll tell ye later. But I think you have the right of it." He kissed her forehead as she placed her father's steak on a plate.

Through dinner, conversation ran pretty much to the upcoming visit of Megan's aunts and uncles and where Patrick's brothers came in line with him according to oldest and youngest. After dinner was over, the torches were lit and with the wine flowing stories and laughter filled the star lit night.

With the dishes done, the leftover food put away, Megan and Donny waved her parents off before retiring to bed for the night.

"So," Megan began as she slid between the sheets and assumed her spot with her head on Donny's shoulder. "What did my father have to talk to you about?"

"Yer father is a verra clever man." He chuckled while gently rubbing Megan's back. "He got me talkin` aboot us before I knew tha` was what he was after."

"What did he want to know?" She figured it was on the same lines as her mother.

"He wanted ta know, now tha` me wound seemed ta be all mended, what I was goin ta do next. Whether I would be goin back ta me job."

"And what did you tell him?" She had to give her father credit. He was able to ask Donny the question she had been dying to, but was basically afraid to hear the answer. She realized once the Gavin threat was no longer hanging over their heads, Donny's case would be finally closed, and there would be no reason for him to stay.

"I said I wasn't sure what the answer ta tha` was." He had told her father more than that, Donny admitted to himself. He told Patrick that he was getting pretty tired of his current lifestyle. He'd seen enough of back alleys and watched too many ugly situations. He'd like to have a real life and a family close by. He also told Patrick that over the last few weeks he'd come to care a great deal for the lass and would like to stay with her if she'd have him. Donny wanted more than anything to stay here with Megan. He wanted to create a normal life with her. He admitted to Megan's father that he and Megan had not really discussed what he would do when he was able to leave. Donny was afraid it might be soon to have such a talk and didn't want to push her. He wanted to make sure she wanted him to stay as much as he wanted to.

"Oh." Megan felt as if a brick had dropped on her heart. "I see." She cleared her throat and decided to take the high road. "Well of course Mom and Dad don't know about Gavin being on the loose." God, what was she going to do after Gavin was caught, and there was no real reason for keeping Donny here? She hadn't realized her hand laying on his chest was balled into a fist, but Donny had.

"Meggie," he took her fist in his hand, straightened out her fingers and lacing them together. "What do ye want, luv?"

"I don't know what you mean." *Can it, you idiot girl!* Megan's head and heart screamed. *You know what you want, and here he is asking you to tell him at long last. Don't be stupid, tell him you want him to stay.* "Ok." She untangled herself from his embrace and sat up to face him. "I know we both agreed you would stay until Gavin was caught."

"Aye." He raised himself up in the bed and leaned back against the headboard.

"Well what then? What will happen when he is finally caught?"

"Happen?" He wouldn't normally play dumb at a time like this, but he wanted her to lay her cards on the table so to speak. He needed to know what she wanted from him before he was willing to open himself up to admit what he wanted.

"Yes, Donny," she reached to the nightstand and turned on the bedside lamp. They needed to have this conversation. It was time. And she needed to see his face when they talked. "What'll happen to you, to me?" *Oh hell just say it* "To us?" Her heart was pounding but she was determined to not look away. She continued to stare into his jade eyes and almost willing him to give the answer she wanted.

"What would ye like ta happen, luv?" *I guess it's no` ta soon ta have this talk after all,* he thought.

"Arg," she threw her hands up in aggravation. "Are you being evasive on purpose?"

"Nay, luv, I'm no tryin` ta be evasive'" He chuckled softly. "Mayhap a wee bit self-protective." He took her hand in his again, brushed his lips across her fingers and spoke in earnest. "But I would like ta know what ye want. How long do ye want me? Until the threat is done, or..." He took a deep breath. "How long do ye want me wi` ye, Megan?" Without planning to, he had placed his future in her hands, and he was terrified. There was a slight tremble in their joined hands, and he wasn't sure if it was his or hers that made the movement. "Tell me luv, wha` do ye want? Wha` would make ye happy?"

"Donny," she whispered. She could hear the uncertainty in his voice and saw the emotion reflected in his eyes. She knew the feeling he projected well, for she was of the same mind. "I want you here with me," she answered quietly. "Now and..." at this she finally did lower her gaze from his probing eyes to their joined hands.

"And?" he prompted. Freeing her hand he gently lifted her chin to bring her violet eyes back to his. "I need ta hear the rest luv."

"Is forever to long for you to stay?" She asked as a single tear escaped her eyes and trailed down her cheek.

"Nay, luv." He reached forward and gathered her into his arms. "Tis nay' tae long." He wanted to say it now. He didn't think he'd ever say it again to anyone, but he needed to say it now. To tell her how deeply and desperately he loved her. They lay in each other's arms, neither of them wanting to let go. "Meggie there is something else I need ta tell ye."

"What's that?"

"I love ye." He felt breath rush from her mouth against his chest, then felt her tighten her arms around him before lifting her face to his. There he saw shining eyes and a tremendous smile.

"Oh Donny, I love you too." She smiled into his eyes. "I didn't think I ever wanted to love anybody ever again. I never wanted to risk that kind of trust in another man. I created what I thought was the perfect life for myself. I had work and friends and family. I thought I could live without the entanglement and emotion and everything that goes with loving someone. And then you literally fell into my life, and you showed me how wrong I was. I do love you, so desperately." He took her mouth, pride swelling inside him. Here was this woman. She was smart. She was sassy. She was funny. She was gentle. She was caring of others. And she loved him.

"Donny?" Megan said as she drew their passionate kiss to a close.

"Humm?" he said against her neck.

"What about your job?" She eased back to look at him. "How can you stay here and still do what you do for a living? Won't that be difficult?"

"Well, I may as well tell ye now. I ha` been givin tha` a fair amount o` thought over the last months."

"You have?"

"Aye, the thought crept inta me mind some time ago when I was wi` Ian and his Madison back in Philadelphia. And it's been on me mind even more since I ha` the good fortune as ta meet ye." He leaned forward to place a tender kiss upon her lips. "How would ye feel if I left me work behind?"

"Left it behind?" She sat straight up and gasped. "You mean quit?"

"Aye." He smiled at her reaction.

"Give up the sleuth business?"

"Aye. Tha`s wha` I said, lass." he chuckled.

"But Donny, you can't." She ran her hands through her hair. "I can't ask you to do that. You love your work."

"No` as much as I used ta, luv." He smiled.

"But what would you do?" she couldn't sit any longer. She clambered out of bed only to trip over Max. "Sorry baby." She told her dog as he jumped up to find a new spot to settle himself.

"What do ye mean 'do'?" he asked as he himself moved to the edge of the bed and watched her pace around the room.

"Well, let's face it. You're not the kind of man who can sit around all day waiting for the little woman to come home from work. Besides," she rounded to face him. "how would you live?"

"Oh, I've been considerin` tha` and I just figured I'd live here wi` ye. Ye're a physician and nay doubt make enough money ta support us both." He watched her mouth gape open as she stopped pacing and stood absolutely still. Then he burst out laughing at her expression.

"Are ye worried aboot me finances lass?" He laughed. *Mayhap I should tell the lassie aboot me wealth,* he said to himself.

"Donny be serious." She put her hands on her hips and glared at him as he got off the bed and cleared the short distance between them in two steps.

"I am, luv, come here." He took her hands from her hips and drew her into his arms. Locking his hands at the base of her back he explained. "Ye're right aboot me no` bein` the type o` man who can sit on his arse all day and do nothin. But havin some time off will be a welcome change. Now as ta me financial situation. I ha` made some verra good investments wi` the money I've earned o're the years. I ha` fairly low expenses and I get verra large fees fer me time. I've managed ta save some and build what I feel is a tidy sum ta hold me ov'r fer a time. I admit I havena looked in a few months, but the last time I checked I was sittin` on o're fifty and a half million.." He watched as her face went through several changes, recognition of what he said, and maybe disbelief, and then to his amusement, utter shock. He unlocked his hands from her back and cupped her face. "Are ye alright Meggie?" he smiled.

"Well, a 'tidy sum' won't...Did you say over fifty and a half million?" She could barely draw in enough breath to speak.

"Aye, luv, I did."

"Dollars?" she squeaked.

"Aye." He chuckled. "Are ye gonna tell me now tha` ye only want me fer me money?" he accused teasingly.

"I need to sit down." *Well, this has been a full night of admissions,* she thought. Her knees turned to jelly and if not for Donny holding her, she would have ended up on the floor instead of sitting on the edge of the bed. "Well it's safe to say you don't need to worry about income." She said almost to herself. "If you had that much, why the hell didn't you quit before?" Not allowing him time to answer she plowed on. "That's quite a bank role. Your time, although I know is valuable to those who hire you but... how did you...how could you...?"

"I saw no need ta quit me jobs. And although I realize the Scots ha` a reputation fer bein tight fisted wi` money, I seem ta ha` a knack fer investin` well." He sat next to her on the bed, both turning to face each other. Donny took her hands in one of his while he traced his fingertips over her jaw line with the other, gazed into her vibrant violet eyes. "Until now." At this she threw her arms around his neck then captured his mouth with hers. She never thought that she could be this happy in her life. She finally had the man she wanted, and he wanted her. She didn't have to worry about having his male sensibilities threatened because of her successes. *Unlike "David-whats-his-face. Oh hang it girl, why should you think about that slimy scum sucker at a time like this.* she thought. Donny pulled away from her lips and wanted to make love to her, but then he glanced at the clock on her nightstand and saw it was now well past one o'clock in the morning.

"It's after one, luv," he kissed her again. "And ye have ta go ta work in a verra few hours this morn. Do ye think we should finish this later?"

"Oh hang work!" she blurted out causing Donny to laugh. "I can call and have one of the other doctors cover my caseload." Megan placed her hands on either side of his face and kissed him. "You're really going to stay here with me?"

"Aye, luv," he kissed her back, "I will." He drew her into another hug. "The rest we'll make up as we go along." He whispered in her ear. "But ye canna 'hang' work as ye call it. Ye ha` patients and other doctors countin` on ye ta be there. And ye're right I'll ha` ta find work ta do. Mayhap I'll write a book and use me years o` 'sleuthin`' as a backdrop. Mayhap I'll find a job in construction. I helped me brother build his house on Skye. I know me way around a hammer. Mayhap I'll join yer local law enforcement as I'm already used ta carryin` a gun. I could get a job washin` dishes in yer cafe across from yer office. Then we could see each other ev'r day fer lunch. It doesna really matter what I do ta keep me busy durin the day, lass, as long as I get ta be wi` ye at night."

"Donny," she kissed his neck before pulling back to look in his eyes. Yes, this was the man for her. "Make love to me." He lowered her to the mattress, deciding not to turn out the light so he could see her. And did in fact make love to her, slowly and tenderly.

Outside among the trees Gavin stood and watched the two bodies move on the bed. Though the curtains were closed he could watch their silhouettes as they clung to each other. He knew the good doctor would be leaving to go to work in the morning and he would be free to make his move on that mother fucker. As he watched the silhouettes move, his anger began to build.

That son of a bitch is sitting pretty good, enjoying the high life, while I've had to skulk around in the shadows. Because of that asshole I've lost hundreds of thousands of dollars. He really needs to pay, to suffer, Gavin's mind screamed.

I'll make you suffer for what you cost me. Gavin thought of the pretty doctor and Sam, or Donny, whatever the asshole was going by. He watched as the bastard was clinging to her now. "Oh yeah you fucker, I'll make you suffer." He thought about how he could cause Donny pain, and what would do it. As he heard the soft moans of the woman through the open windows he knew what he was going to do.

"I'll make her moan," he was growing hard at the thought. "I'll make her scream." He took himself out of his pants and began to stroke. "I'll make you watch while I fuck her up. Then my friend, you'll be begging me to end your fucking life." He continued to pleasure himself at his own words. When he had finished and was sated he saw the lights emanating from the little house had been turned out. He waited a few more minutes to make sure they were both asleep and crept through the creek to the back of the big gray barn next the road. He'd been hovering around the property for days and knew that the FBI agents made a sweep of the buildings at night. Knowing that they'd made a sweep of the barn, he crept in and found an old 1949 Buick parked next to a large support post. Gavin decided to hold there for the night. He could move around in the underneath part of this barn during the day to avoid detection. Then at night when they were at their most comfortable, he would strike.

He settled down in the old bug infested car and began to plan. As he decided what he would do to the good doctor, Gavin was once again becoming aroused. Before he allowed sleep to find him, he took matters into his own hands once more. Knowing that the next night he would find himself with the pretty doctor. While he imagined fucking her bloody, and Donny being forced to watch, Gavin's arousal needed more attention before he was finally sated enough to allow sleep to find him for the night.

Chapter Twenty-Three

The next morning a very tired Megan rolled out of bed to shower and dress for work. She and Donny sat at the table and ate cereal.

"Why don't ye take Max ta work wi` ye." Donny suggested as he took his bowl to the sink to wash it.

"I can," Megan rose and did the same with her bowl. "But then you'll be here all alone today."

"Och, well I was thinkin` I would drive ye ta work and then I'd head inta town." He ran his hand over her still damp auburn hair. "Tha` is if ye ha` nay objections ta me takin yer car, lass."

"No I don't care about that, but what do you need to go to town for?" She dried her hands on the hand towel then threaded it back through the fridge handle.

"Well, if ye ha'na noticed luv, but I could stand ta ha` a few more articles o` clothin ta call me own." He looked down at the sweats and T-shirt he was wearing and smirked.

"Oh, god," Megan laughed, "you're right. Are you getting a little tired of the pajama look? Although, technically, lounge pants aren't strictly pajamas." She hooked her arms around his neck. "By the way, do you have a place of your own somewhere? You know, like a home base you would go in between jobs."

"Aye," Donny roped his arms around her back and drew her closer to his body. "I ha` three. One in London, one in Rome, and one in Chicago." He chuckled at her wide-eyed expression. "I was thinkin o` sellin` them, unless ye'd rather I dinna?"

"Umm," she cleared her throat. She needed to get used to his stockpiled wealth. But the staggering amount was something that just didn't seem to have the right ring to it. He didn't act like a multimillionaire. On the other hand, she didn't really know how multimillionaires acted as he was the first one she's actually met. "Well that's up to you. I'm not very knowledgeable about European housing, taxes, or rents."

"Och, lass, I donna rent them. I own them outright. Rents are high in London and Rome as well as Paris and Stockholm and most o` the large cities o'er there. Much like New York, Las Angeles and Chicago and San Francisco here. It would ha` made little economic sense ta rent. I'm no` in any o` those cities often enough or long enough ta be payin` rent fer all the months tha` I'm no livin in them."

"But if you don't live in them often, why...?"

"The properties are as much an investment as they are places ta hang me hat."

"Oh." She said. "Well how often do you live in any of them?"

"Often enough tha` the purchases were worthwhile. When I'm no workin, I canna be continually spongin off me relatives in Scotland and the locations make travelin` from one case ta another convenient." He grinned at her. "As an example. If I ha` no decided ta stay wi` ye, I 'de probably go from here ta me place in Chicago ta await me next job offer.

And cry in me soup because ye dinna wan me ta stay wi` ye. And then I ha` already made up me mind which job I was goin ta take on."

"You get that many offers?"

"Aye, lass. Crime is a big healthy goin business."

"Yes, so it seems. Well, I don't really know what to tell you. As I said, I'm not up on European travel and the need for multiple housing. But I think if it were me, I'd lose the one in Chicago and hang on to Rome and London." She took a deep breath.

"Does me wealth bother ye, lass?" he looked at her. "I'm no` that wealthy, ye know. There are many who are a lot richer. I've just invested well and as I said, me expenses are low."

"I don't think 'bother' is the right word. It's just not exactly what I expected. I've heard the term 'multimillionaire'. I've just never met one. I assumed you had an apartment of your own somewhere. I wasn't expecting three owned homes in multiple European cities and also in the U.S. It'll just take some getting used to." She kissed him lightly. "How come you don't have a place in Scotland or hell Ireland for that matter?"

"Tae close ta me family. In addition, tis safer fer me family fer me ta have me own homes a distance from them. I dinna have family connections ta any of the cities I chose. Besides when I go home ta Scotland, I stay wi` me mam." He kissed her forehead.

"Safer for your family for you to live far enough away from them in case—"

"Aye, luv," he interrupted. "and it gives me a good reason ta be stayin wi` me mam when I do go ta Scotland. And by stayin wi` her, I'm no spongin off me brothers and their families or disruptin` their routines. And me mam likes fer me ta be stayin wi` her at the family seat."

"Oh, that must be nice." She smiled as she brushed her lips over his. "Holy Shit!" Megan looked at her watch, "I need to finish getting ready for work." she grinned at him. "You certainly do a good job of distracting me." She chuckled.

In the bedroom she brushed her hair and put on a little make-up. *When he goes home he stays with his mother, that's so sweet.* She thought. *It must be nice to go all over the world and see new places. Then have a family seat to go home to,* she thought, then she stopped, *My god,* she realized. *He's not traveling around all those places to see new things. He's traveling around all those places so people can shoot at him! Of course that's all over now. He's going to be here with me and he's going to be doing something else and nobody is going to shoot at him anymore.* Megan shut her makeup drawer with emphasis. *You don't need to dwell on that stuff anymore. Think about the nice stuff.* She encouraged herself. *His family has a 'Seat' interesting.* Megan knew she would always have this place to come home to and she loved it. She knew that she had family all over this country, hell some were all over the world, that thought of this place as *their* family 'Seat', although she had never used the term. It was 'home' and she wouldn't have it any other way. She thought about the parties, weddings and reunions that had taken place on this land over the years, over the generations really. Her grandfather was born on the farm. Although her great grandfather was born in Ireland, he raised his family and died on the land that was now hers. Right up in that house. Her own brothers were both married here. She had planned to be married here herself, but that wedding never took place. As she thought about the weddings that had and had not happened, Megan remembered Donny told her about his brother Ian and Madison were to be married at Ian's house in Lusta.

"Hey Donny?" she called and waited for him to come into view in her mirror. "Didn't you say your brother's wedding was coming up soon?"

"Aye, in aboot a month. They're havin an engagement party in aboot two weeks" He smiled at the thought. He was so glad Ian and Madison had found each other. He was even happier when he thought of the couple making him an uncle again. Donny had gotten word that his brother Tommy and his Sara had welcomed a baby girl at last. He knew Madison had been told she was unable to have children. He smiled when he thought, how *shocked and thrilled she must ha` been ta learn her daily sickness was no` some virus but a new babe growin` inside o` her*. He would like to be there for the party and the wedding, *but I willna leave here until I know me Megan is safe and out o` danger.*

"Well, aren't you going?" Megan asked as she polished off her make-up and turned to face him.

"No` until I know it's safe ta leave here."

"Oh Donny you can't miss your brother's—" he cut her off with a quick kiss and rested his hands on her shoulders.

"I willna leave here until I know it is safe and Gavin is either dead or behind bars. Despite yer personal arsenal." Donny's voice was absolute, but also carried a grin. Megan knew there was no way to change his mind and nodded her head. "Do'na fret, luv, Ian knows the kind o` work I do and knew I might no` be able ta be wi` him on the day he weds his bonnie lass."

"If it weren't for me you would be able to go." She sighed.

"If it weren't fer ye, luv, I would either be on another job by now, or dead fer bleedin` ta death behind somebody else's car."

"Well that's a cheery thought." She said sarcastically. "I really wish you wouldn't miss their engagement party. Or the wedding for that matter. I know," she paused as she saw he was getting ready to argue.

"You've made up your mind and that's that. Ok, change in subject." She smiled "What are you going to buy when the little woman is off at work?" She laughed as he gathered her in his arms and kissed her warmly.

"Ye ha` ta wait and see. Come, off ta work wi` ye. What is it ye Americans say? You need ta be bringin` home the bacon." He took his wallet off the top of dresser in the guestroom and grabbed the key fob to the Wagoneer.

"You're a nut. Come on Max, you're coming to work with me today." Both Megan and Donny laughed as Max scrambled to his feet and all but bowled Megan over to get out the door.

"Well, I guess we know how he's felt aboot stayin` wi` me." Donny chuckled as he opened the way back door of the car allowing the dog to jump in.

"Don't take it personally." Megan soothed as they settled into the SUV. "He just knows he gets to go for a ride."

They chatted on the way to her office. When they arrived, Donny got out to let Max out of the back and gave Megan a long kiss before she went in. Jess and Hannah heard the car pull into the parking lot and were both looking out the window when the couple emerged from the Wagoneer. Both women watched with glee when Megan and Donny said their goodbyes.

"Holy Toledo!" Hannah said as she watched Megan and her man outside. "That must be him."

"Yup," Jess said. "Wow. No wonder she kept him to herself." She looked him over. "If I were straight and unmarried..."

"Jess!" Hannah laughed.

"What? I may not drink the water, but I can admire the scenery." She watched as Megan waved him off and turned to come in the office.

"Good morning." Megan sang as she opened the door for her and Max who sailed in ahead of her. She figured by the expressions on the two women that her arrival didn't go unnoticed.

"Morning." Jess took another sip of her coffee before putting her mug on the counter. "So, I assume *that* was him?"

"Yes, that was Donny." She cleared her throat. "Shall we get to work?" She made a move to go to her office when Jess skirted the reception desk and blocked her path.

"Oh no you don't!" Jess said. "Spill it."

"What?" Megan should have known better than to think she could get passed without some conversation.

"You know damn well what." Jess said. "Come on Meggie, give us some details."

"What would you like to know?" Megan sighed. She had known Jess for years and recognized when it was better to just give in to her.

"Well, is he staying?"

"Yes." Megan beamed. "He's staying. Next question."

"With you?" Jess smiled.

"Yes."

"At the cottage?" Jess asked as she rubbed her hands together.

"Yes." Megan laughed. "At the cottage. With me. Anything else?"

"One more question?" Jess rested her hands on Megan's shoulders and sobered a little. "Do you love him?" Megan nodded her head. "Does he love you?"

"That's two questions." Megan grinned at her friend.

"Yeah, so ok it's two questions. So answer them both." Jess laughed.

Megan nodded her head yet again.

Jess clapped her hands together and gave Megan a tight hug and a sloppy kiss on the cheek. "Well hot damn and holy fucking shit!"

"Ok!" Hannah laughed. "This is a professional office, Doctor, and you have pried into the girl's private life enough for now." Hannah said warmly. "The office will be opening soon, and we all have things to do before that happens, don't we?" As if right on cue, Sara, the other doctor and one of the nurses came in. With the office starting to buzz with activity Jess had to release her friend and begin their day.

Donny decided to head to Wal-Mart to get himself some more clothes. He was grateful to Megan for the clothing she had purchased for him. And at the time sweats, lounge pants and pajamas were fantastic things to have. However, Donny decided if he never saw another pair of those baggy coverings it would be too soon. He picked up several pairs of jeans, more T-shirts, shoes, socks, and underwear. He took a pair of jeans into the dressing room, removed the tags, and slipped them on. *God it's nice ta be in jeans again,* he thought. Making sure he had the tags on the top of his heap he decided it would be a good idea to do some grocery shopping as well. Since he'd moved in, Megan had been doing all the shopping. Although Donny never really did more than buy the essentials when he went shopping on his own, how hard could it be? He decided to start with breakfast food.

"It's the first thing ye eat in a day." He told himself when he found the cereal aisle. After he found the Fruit Loops, he chuckled at Megan's comment about kiddy food. He tried to remember what she had for herself. "She likes adult stuff." He looked at the choices and decided on Raisin Nut Bran. "Tha` looks like grown up stuff." At least there were no cartoons of silly animals on the front of the box. He put the cereal in the cart and moved on for lunch type foods.

He moved through the store in much the same fashion. It was working fairly well for him and hadn't been too difficult so far. Then he moved further down his mental meal choices to dinner food. He stood in the middle of the produce department and wasn't sure what to do. He tried to think of things that she'd fixed for dinner since he'd been there. In the beginning dinners were brought in mostly, but lately she or he had been cooking. *What the bloody hell have we been eatin`?* He looked down at the display next to him.

"Potatoes!" He smiled and grabbed a bag. "She's Irish, they like potatoes." He moved around the produce department and picked up some onions, lettuce, cucumbers, squash, and other vegetables that he recognized. Next was the freezer section. "Why the hell would ye buy frozen vegetables when ye can have fresh?" Deciding to ignore the frozen section on principle he moved to the meat. "Now this is more like it!" As Donny moved down the display sections of beef, chicken, and pork he picked packages of meat and tossed them into the cart at random. Not really paying attention to how much he had already thrown in. By the time he made it to the cheeses he noticed he no longer had room for even the single bag of shredded cheese in his hand. He stood surveying the mass of food he had collected.

"You look a bit lost young man. Could you use some help?" Donny turned in the direction of the voice but saw no one. "Would you like some help?" there was the voice again and Donny glanced down. Barely as big as the cart she was pushing was a tiny little older lady with a sweet smile and laughing eyes.

"Hello." Donny looked over this silver haired rail thin woman and smiled. "I think I should be askin ye tha` question, lass."

"Oh aren't you a nice one." She chuckled. "But don't you worry I may be small but I'm strong as an ox. I take it this is your first shopping experience without your wife?"

"Och, I'm no..." Donny meant to correct the woman on his marital status, but then saw no real reason to. On second thought he just couldn't deceive the woman. Besides if she was really offering to help, why not tell the truth. "I'm nay married, but I will admit shoppin` isna what I would normally be doin`."

"Oh, I can spot the ones who are left to their own devices for the first time." She laughed. "My name is Sister Virginia O'Neil."

"Donavon Mackay, nice ta meet ye." He clasped the small hand gently and shook. *She wasna foolin`*, he smiled, *she has quite a grip. Sister? I'm glad I came clean aboot being married. And mam would skin me bald if she learned I'd lied ta a nun.*

"Well, you're not from around these parts are you?" she grinned up at him.

"Nay, ma'am. I'm born and bred in Scotland on the Isle of Skye."

"Oh how fascinating! Are you here visiting friends?"

"Aye."

"Well let's see if we can't lighten your load some." She scanned the mounded cart. "Or at least we can rearrange and organize a little."

Between the two of them Donny had discovered that he had put enough food in the cart to feed a family of five for a month. They moved through the rest of the store together and chatted about this and that. Sister Virginia had Donny return things that she thought he didn't need and add things she felt were necessities. She raised her eyebrows at the box of Fruit Loops, but said nothing. When the shopping was finished Donny walked her to her car and loaded her purchases in her trunk.

"Thank you young man, that was very nice of you."

"Nay, thank ye." He smiled. "I hope ta meet ye again should I e'er come here alone. Ye saved me a pretty penny, and were extremely helpful." Before turning away he thought about the bags he had loaded in the trunk. "Do ye ha` anyone ta unload yer groceries fer ye when ye reach yer home, Sister?"

"Oh don't you worry about me; I'm visiting some of my family this summer and the place is crawling with young bucks to unload and put away."

"So ye donna live here all the time then?"

"No, I live at the convent on Long Island. But once a summer I come out to Rileyville to visit family and sit at the lake with the ladies and the children. There is a passel of us here now. As a matter of fact I better get going. If we don't head down to the lake before midday," she whistled and looked up at the sky. "The little ones you see, they need the water." She laughed.

"I understand. Thank ye again fer all yer help today, Sister." He shook her hand again before heading to where he parked. After he'd transferred all his bags into the way-back he made the trek back to the cottage.

Donny had unloaded the SUV, and stood in the middle of the room and surveyed the damage. The amount of bags filled with food, and such was astronomical. Now he had to put it all away. At least there he had some idea of where things went. After some finagling he got everything put in its place, at least what he hoped were the right places. He finished off the job by getting his clothing purchases put away in the closet and dresser in the guestroom.

"Might need ta do somethin` about the closet space in her room." He said to himself as he walked into the room in question and looked around to see what could be done, if anything, to make the space large enough for two. As he looked around he had to admit the room was being used as wisely as it could. But Donny realized that though the cottage was perfect for one. It did need more room for two on a full-time long-term basis. He walked outside on the deck and looked for some inspiration. The foundation was sound and the concrete slab the cottage was sitting on was large enough for expansion.

"She could build out toward the lake and the creek." He said to himself. Just then a Blue Heron flew over, drawing Donny's attention up. "She could also build up." He stood looking at the structure trying to come up with ways to expand. Keeping in mind that the little building itself needed to remain basically intact. He knew Megan loved her little cottage and he had to admit, he himself was becoming more charmed by it the more time he spent there.

"Well I'll think on it." He looked at his watch and went into the laptop to check over emails and make some arrangements for his future.

It took a few hours, but Donny managed to arrange to have his apartment in Chicago packed, his clothes shipped to him and furniture put in storage. Then he contacted his broker and had the place put on the market. He also contacted the heads of the various agency's he'd worked with and let them know he was retiring. When he contacted the FBI with the same information Ted called him right away.

"What the devil do you mean you're retiring?" Ted bellowed.

"Hello ta ye tae, Ted." Donny leaned back in his chair. "I take it ye spoke ta the Director."

"You can't do this to me!" Ted stammered. "You're the best man I have."

"Ye didna ha` me." Donny reminded him "I worked wi` ye from time ta time."

"Semantics."

"I want oot, Ted."

"It's that girl, isn't it? That doctor woman." Ted grumbled.

"I told ye, ye're no` ta be callin` her tha`." Donny warned. "This was me own decision. It shouldna come as tae much o` a shock. I told ye before I was thinkin` o` leavin`."

"Yes but I never took you seriously." Donny could hear him light a cigar.

"Well, ye better start takin me seriously. And ye shouldna be smokin`. Ye know yer wife willna like it."

"Oh, fuck off." Ted was silent for a moment "What the hell are you going to do with yourself?" he asked. "You know as well as I do that retirement never goes well for people like us. You're a man of action my boy, you are not the type to sit at home or take up *golf*."

"I'll enjoy the time off fer a while and if I begin ta get restless, well I'll find somethin`."

"Listen, if you're tired of all the traveling and different agencies, why don't you come and work for the FBI permanently?" Ted hedged. "You know the director would like nothing more than to have a man of your caliber."

"Ye also know tha` yer FBI would ne'er be able ta afford me full time and I'm no interested in a pay cut." Donny was tired of this argument. "Ted, yer no` listenin`," Donny sighed. "I'm done."

"I know that tone." Ted sighed "There isn't anything I can do to talk you out of this, is there?"

"Nay." Donny chuckled.

"Well I know a losing battle when I hear one. I hope you know what you're doing."

"I do."

"Of course you know what you're giving up?"

"Aye." Donny thought of Megan and the life he knew he would have with her and felt a warm glow all around his heart. "I also know what I'm gainin`."

"I hope she's worth it."

"Ted, there is nay question. The lass is worth tha` and much more."

"Well, if that be the case, I'm happy for you, both."

The men spoke for a few more minutes before Ted needed to go on another call. Donny assured his current FBI employer that he would remain vigilant until Gavin was caught or, better yet, dead. After the call was ended Donny thought about his decision and waited for the remorse of officially retiring from his work. When after a few seconds, then minutes it still had not arrived, he was vindicated in his choice. Feeling lighter than he had in almost twenty years, Donny called Megan to see if she wanted to have lunch together.

"Are you kidding! You silly Scot, of course I do." She told him she was planning on going to the corners and why didn't he meet her there.

When Donny walked into the cafe he found Megan at the back of the little diner at a round corner table, but she was not alone. There were three women, one of them hugely pregnant, and to his utter amazement, his brother Steven.

Chapter Twenty-Four

"Bloody hell." He mumbled before walking over to the table. With his eyes on Megan, he could tell that she had not planned this ambush and felt better for it. Leaning down to kiss her cheek. "Do'na fret, luv." He whispered in her ear before he took the empty seat next to her and took her hand in his under the table, giving it a reassuring squeeze. "Well who ha` we got here?" He smiled as she sighed.

"Donny, this is Jess, Hannah, and Liz. Hannah has taken over for Liz while she is away on maternity leave." Megan began. "Everyone, this is Donny."

"Nice ta meet ye all." Donny smiled.

"Why Megan, you didn't introduce Donny and Steven." Hannah chuckled.

"No, that's ok, Hannah." Steven answered. "Donny is my older brother."

"You don't say." Hannah smiled. "Well what a small world. I can see the resemblance now that you mention it."

"How come your accent isn't as strong as your brother's?" Liz asked.

"I came over here when I got out of school." Steven answered, "I guess I've lost it."

"So, Donny is it?" Jess piped up to spare Steven from anymore questions. "How do you like our little hamlet?"

"Verra much." Donny smiled at Jess.

"Have you been here long?" Liz asked. *No wonder Megan wasn't interested in Steven when she met him,* Liz thought. *This is one hot piece of hunk she's got.*

"Mayhap nay' long by yer standards." He smiled at the pretty lass. "I ha` been in this part o` the world fer aboot six months." He noticed how his brother rested his arm on the back of Liz's chair and every few minutes would rub her back. *Humm, wonder what's goin on there?* Donny thought. *I'll ask Meggie when we're alone.*

"Are you planning on staying much longer?" Hannah asked. All eyes at the table were on Donny and Megan.

"Aye, lass." He spared a glance at Steven and went on. "I plan on bein here fer the foreseeable future." He looked down at Megan and brought their joined hands to his lips.

"Well hot damn!" Liz laughed. "Oh god." She squirmed.

"What's the matter?" alarmed Steven straightened in his chair and laid his hand on her shoulder.

"Oh nothing. I laughed, now I have to pee." She chuckled as she gingerly rose from her chair. "Don't say anything else until I get back." The table watched as she waddled to the bathroom.

"She had a doctor's visit today for a sonogram." Steven said as he watched her close the bathroom door. He turned his attention to the group at the table. "She said everything was good. Liz didn't want to know if it was a boy or girl."

"But I bet you looked didn't you?" Megan chuckled.

"If I did I'll never tell." He smiled.

"Oh, come on." The three women said in unison.

"Nope. She didn't want to know, so no one gets to know." He glanced back at the bathroom to see if Liz was on her way back yet. He sighed; she wasn't.

"How much longer ha` she before the babe comes?" Donny asked. Steven's stunned expression at being asked a question by his brother was almost comical.

"Uh," Steven cleared his throat. "Not long now."

"So ye might be missin Ian's weddin then?" Donny would get more information from Megan later, but he figured if the lad were going to doctor appointments he would more than likely be part of the birth.

Megan, Jess, and Hannah sat and watched the men talk. Their eyes moving back and forth like they were watching a tennis match.

"Well I don't know; she hasn't said whether she wants me there for the birth."

"Ye could ask the lass." Donny said as he looked at the waitress.

"What can I get you to drink?" she asked him.

"Coffee please." He smiled as she walked away and turned his attention back to his brother. "Well?"

"I don't want to push it."

"Well Steven, haven't you been taking her to Lamaze?" Jess asked.

"The last few classes or so, yeah."

"Well bucko, I'd say tha` means yer gonna be at the birth." Donny chuckled and as Steven's face began to drain of all color Donny began to roar with laughter. This was what Liz walked back to.

"What happened?" She asked as she sat back down with Steven's help. "Guys, I said not to say anything till I got back. Now, what did I miss?"

"Oh, nothing honey." Hannah patted Liz's leg. "Steven was just filling us in on your last visit with the doctor."

"Oh. Well what's so funny about that?"

"I'm sorra lass." Donny got himself under control. He might not care about embarrassing his brother, but he didn't want to embarrass the lass. "I was just thinkin` aboot a story our mam used ta tell us aboot when she was havin` our sister Emily."

"Oh yeah? What's the story?" Liz smiled.

Well ye painted yerself inta a corner now laddie, Donny thought. *Ye better come up with something.* Donny cleared his throat, dug into his imagination, and came up with a story on the fly. And to his amazement it was even funny.

They spent the rest of the time at ease and friendly conversation. Megan was pleased that Donny and Steven seemed to be getting along very well. Donny talked and charmed everyone at the table. He and Steven talked a little more about the upcoming wedding of their brother. Donny wanted Megan to go with him to both the engagement party and the wedding, but the party was too close, and she couldn't get the time off and the wedding conflicted with the arrival of her beloved aunts and uncles.

As Donny sat at the table with Steven he watched his brother interact with Liz and could see that he cared for her a lot more than just mere friendship. He couldn't tell if Liz was aware of Steven's feelings, or if she was ready for a relationship with Steven. Or anybody else for that matter. It hadn't been that long since her husband made his announcement and departed the area. He sat back in his chair and took notice of how the locals would come into the diner and not only said hello to Megan and her staff, but would stop and speak to their local state trooper. Ask how his renovations were going on the cabin he bought, how his garden was coming along. *He gardens?* Donny was surprised. Steven knew everyone by name and asked about his or her lives in kind. Donny saw that the *man* sitting across from him was not the same *boy* he had blamed for the death of Arabella and the tragedy that befell Marie. That's what Megan had said, Steven had been a boy then and he was a grown man now. Sitting there, Donny came to realize that his bitterness, resentment, and anger he had carried with him for so many years because of the past was just that, the past. He had known at the time that the responsibility for collecting the girls at the station that night had been his own. He had basically handed over the responsibility to Steven without a second thought. Then drown Steven in blame for years because it was easier than accepting full blame himself along with his grief. *But because I was ta bloody concerned aboot talkin ta me prof aboot a paper tha` I had already turned in, I passed the girls off to someone else.* He berated himself. And because of that, because he would rather blame the boy and not the man Donny thought himself to be, a rift had been placed on the family. Their mother never saw all her children at once because Donny *needed* to place blame on Steven and not fully where it belonged. He was ashamed of himself for causing this pain and separation in all their lives.

He looked over at Megan as she laughed at something Steven had said and came to another realization, He needed to let go of the past once and for all. He had his future sitting right next to him and he needed to focus on that. He glanced back at Steven and Liz and saw another future beginning. *Aye I need to let go of the past and start fresh.* he thought. *And there was no time like the present.*

"Uh Steven," Donny cleared his throat. He waited for his brother to look his way. "Are ye on duty tanight?"

"No." Steven glanced at Megan in surprise. "I don't go back on duty until tomorrow night."

"Well, I was thinkin," Donny cleared his throat again, "if ye dinna already have dinner plans ye might stop over." He glanced down at Megan. "If tha`s ok wi` ye, luv."

"Tonight?" Megan and Steven asked in surprised unison. Jess, who was abreast of the situation between the brothers, via Megan, raised her eyebrows.

"Aye." Donny told them both. He also caught Jess's surprise. *Umm, the lass must ha` filled her friend in on the estrangement.* "Ye see I went grocery shoppin taday—"

"You did?" Megan chuckled nervously. *Oh god, what did he buy?* she cringed. *The place is probably full of Fruit Loops, Pop Tarts and god knows what else.*

"I can do tha` ye know lassie." He smiled over at Megan. "Anyway I was thinkin o` tryin one o` Ian's chicken things."

"Uhuh," Steven was dumbfounded. "I was planning on stopping in at the McGrath bar-b-que this evening." *Don't blow it boy*, Steven thought. *You wanted to patch things up with your brother and here he is handing you the chance on a silver platter.* "But—"

"Ooo," Megan cut him off. "Their parties are always so much fun, what time is it?"

"I was gonna head over about five o'clock and stay about an hour or so. But—" *Jeez, cut off again.* Steven sighed as Megan eagerly interrupted.

"Oh, well that's perfect." Megan put her hand on Donny's leg and gently squeezed. She knew what a big step this was for him. "The office doesn't close down tonight until seven so dinner wouldn't be until after that." *Ok kid,* she thought, *now you can talk. Don't blow it.*

"Ok, that sounds good." He said to Megan and smiled. "What time should I be there?" he asked Donny.

"How aboot seven-thirty?" Donny told him and Steven nodded in agreement.

"Well kids," Jess looked at her watch. "It's about that time."

After the checks were paid Steven helped Liz into his Dodge Challenger while everyone else walked across the street to the office. Donny offered to leave Megan the car and he could walk back. "It twould be a good stretch o` the legs." He told her, and was systematically shot down before the words were out of his mouth. She had some time before her next patient, and it was decided that she would drive him home then bring the car back with her. She loaded up Max and took them both home. On the way to the cottage, she told him how proud she was of him for opening the door to his brother.

Megan returned to the office with minutes to spare before her next appointment. All the doctors were booked solid for the rest of that day. However, at five o'clock Megan came out to see who her next patient was and found that it was canceled. She didn't have another patient until six, so she decided to use the free time for paperwork. At five-thirty Hannah popped into her office to tell her that the six o'clock appointment was also canceled.

"God, it's an epidemic." Megan chuckled. "I'm gonna start to take this personally pretty soon."

"Well I wouldn't," Hannah smiled. "Remember the McGrath bar-b-que has started."

"Oh yeah." Megan leaned back in her chair and laughed. "Yup, I'd rather do that than go see the doctor any day. Did they reschedule?"

"Both are for tomorrow morning with Sara. You don't have any free spots for the next week."

"Don't feel too bad Meggie." Jess said over Hannah's head causing her to jump. "Thanks to the McGrath party I lost my last two as well."

"Jeez, Jess." Hannah placed her hand on her chest. "Make some noise when you walk. I'm an old woman and can't take the jolt."

"Sorry honey." Jess chuckled. "How about if I put a bell around my neck? Would that help?"

"Yes," Hannah laughed. "Yes, it would. A right big cow bell." She continued to chuckle as she headed back to her desk.

"You know," Jess came in and sat in one of the guest chairs in Megan's office. "You and I are the only ones here tonight and since both of our patients canceled..."

"What do you want, Jess?" Megan smiled.

"Oh, come on, you know as well as I do that we aren't going to get any walk-ins. Not tonight. Not with the McGrath's party happening. Let's do us all a favor, call it a night, and blow this taco stand."

"You know we still have an hour to go." Megan reasoned.

"Spoil sport." Jess grumbled.

"Oh, what the hell." Megan laughed. "Let's close down." She began to close down her computer and put her files away.

"Hannah!" Jess hollered "The boss lady said we can pack it in for the night."

"Thank god!" They heard Hannah clap her hands making both doctors laugh.

Once the office was closed down, Megan had waved off Jess and Hannah, who were both headed toward the McGrath Party. While Megan, headed home to her *own* party.

When she walked into the cottage she found Donny in the kitchen and Max cleaning up drips and drops off the floor with his big tongue. The kitchen was covered in flour, as were Donny and Max. All the cabinet doors were open, and the sink was loaded with dishes. All Megan could do was laugh. She offered to help with the cleanup, but Donny waved her off and told her to change for a quick ride as he put a covered dish in the oven. As Donny cleaned, Megan changed and explained about the cancellations, and the decision to close down the office early. When she came out of the bedroom and walked back to the kitchen she was stunned speechless.

"Wow." She breathed. The floor, counters, stove, and Max were wiped clean of flour. The spices were put away, the cabinets and drawers were closed, and Donny was finishing with the last of the dirty dishes. "I know it might take me time to change sometimes, but I wasn't in there that long. How did you get this clean so fast?" She slipped on her boots and came in to dry the dishes that were in the rack.

"I will admit ta being a messy cook," he said as he handed her a pot to dry. "But I was always stuck with the cleanin` o` the kitchen after dinner growin` up, so I learned fast ta do it quickly and get it o're wi`." He smiled as he handed her the last dish to dry.

"How long does the chicken have to cook?" Megan asked as Donny changed his clothes.

"Aboot an hour and a half." He told her as he came out of the guestroom pulling his shirt over his head. This was only the second time she had seen him in jeans. The way the denim showcased his narrow hips, mile long leg and *simply the most biteable backside I have ever had the pleasure of, mmm well...* She cleared her throat. *Oh yeah, he is yummy.* "So we ha` aboot an hour fer a ride." He took her in his arms and smiled. "I found Jack in the barn and ask if he wouldna mind saddlin` the horses fer us."

"You did, did you?" She smiled back. "Well that was handy of you." She ran her hands down his back and over his jean clad rump. "You know I forgot to mention it earlier." She gave his butt a few gentle taps. "You look really sexy in jeans." She purred.

"I do, huh?" he smiled.

"Yeah." She went up on her tiptoes and met his lips. "Too bad you already have the horses saddled." She murmured.

"Aye, tae bad." He gave her rear end a slight tap and backed away. "Let's go ye charlatan before ye make these jeans more uncomfortable than ye already ha`." Megan laughed.

"Come on Max!" She opened the door and Max ran out and made a beeline for the barn with Donny and Megan taking up the rear.

In the dark damp spaces under the old, weathered barn, Gavin watched them as they crossed the road. When they were no longer in his line of sight he retreated further into the shadows. He slithered to the other end of the building, careful not to make a sound and alerting his prey. He knew what he was going to do now. It was a pity he had to wait for them to come back from their ride, but the waiting would only make the result taste that much sweeter. He watched as they came out astride their horses. Donny on the cowhide horse, Megan on the massive black beast while the dog pranced around them. Gavin watched and waited for them to ride out of sight. He carefully made his way to the big grey hay barn where he knew they would return to house the horses after their ride. He was careful to keep to the shadows. Fearing the horses might have alerted Donny and the pretty doctor of his presence, Gavin had stayed clear. After a few minutes of skulking the unfamiliar barn he found the perfect spot to lay in wait for the happy couple to return. In his well-concealed corner, crouched down he felt the gun he'd lifted from the good doctor's bedroom. Feeling the weight at his back, Gavin thought about going through the small grey cottage when Donny had left that morning.

From the shadows in the lowest level of the damp barn that acted as his cover, Gavin watched as the good doctor and Donny left for the morning. Breaking into the place was really very easy thanks to all the open windows. As he moved around the small building he needed to remind himself often not to ransack the place. No point in alerting them to the fact that he'd been inside the cottage while they were gone. They'd just call the cops and then his plan for the evening would be ruined. He looked through her drawers, pawed at her bras and underwear and wondered what she would be wearing tonight. He looked through her nightstand and found a lock box. In retrospect, using the hammer from the kitchen drawer to open the metal box wasn't the smartest way to go about it. But there was nothing to be done about that now. Inside he found a 45-caliber handgun. With little effort he located ammunition in the drawer above.

"Well, thank you doc." He said as he took the gun and the shells. He put back the box as neatly as he could. Gavin wanted to look around some more. "If she has this piece she's got to have others." But he had already been in the house for an hour. He had no clue how long either Megan or Donny would be away, and he didn't want to be discovered before he was ready.

Now he sat in his corner in the barn, concealed by shadows, tools, and hay. He was almost breathless with anticipation. He had a good view of the stalls and knew that unless they were looking they would never see him. Not until he was ready. Not before it was too late for them both.

Chapter Twenty-Five

As they rode through the fields Megan kept a close watch on the time while looking at the scenery. It was late in the summer with color on the leaves popping up everywhere. During the day it was nice and warm, but as the evening hours took over the air took on a cooler bite. Megan could remember as a kid she loved and hated this time. She always had a fondness for fall and the colors it would bring, along with her favorite holiday. Her mother was always saying, "Megan had a ghoulish side I could never understand. Most kids look forward to Thanksgiving with its food and Pumpkin pie. Or Christmas with Santa and the anticipation of presents. But my kid looks forward to Halloween! With its costumes of ghouls and goblins, while running around in the dark beggin for candy." But as a kid this time of year also meant the end of summer and back to school. As an adult, and now living on the farm permanently, she was once again plagued with the same torment. But for different reasons. She still loved the change in season, the colors would come out, nights were cooler, and the camps would soon close their doors. Which meant the enjoyable music from Rose Lake Camp would be gone, but so would the constant loudspeaker chatter from Rosemont. Megan would be glad to have the place quiet and tranquil at first. However soon, the empty feeling would seep in. The realization that her brothers and their families would leave for the season, and wouldn't see them again until the holidays. This feeling never really lasted as long for her as it would for most. After all she never really felt completely alone, she had her parents living on the farm and now Jake, too. But it was still always there. She glanced over at Donny as he laughed at something Max had done and wondered if the same feeling would creep over her this time, and she smiled.

"Probably not."

"What?" Donny asked

"Oh nothing, I was just thinking about how things will be different this year when the tourists and camps leave, that's all." She watched as Max spotted a rabbit duck back into its hole before he could pounce on it.

"Come on Max, leave the rabbit alone." She half scolded. The big dog barked as he ran to catch up with them.

"What were ye sayin`, luv aboot the camps leavin?"

"Oh, I was just thinking that when the camps leave I am relieved they're gone, but I'm always left feeling a little lonely for the lack of noise." She looked back at him. "But this year I won't be left alone." She smiled.

"Nay, luv, ye willna."

They were quiet for a moment and Megan's mind began to wonder again. *No I won't be alone anymore, and isn't that wonderful?* She thought. *It was so nice to come home from work and find him there. Cooking, making a mess, making plans for them before dinner.* Then she remembered when he had to go into the guestroom to change his clothes. *Mmm, now that is something that needs to change. If he is going to live here with me I think we might need some more room in that place. Starting with closet space for Donny.* She decided.

"You know I was thinking, it seems a little silly for you to keep your clothes and what not in the guestroom."

"Aye, I agree, but there is nay another place ta keep them at the moment." He wondered if it was the time to tell her he was thinking of ways to make the cottage more suitable for two.

"You know, the cottage didn't always look the way it does now." She told him. "My bedroom was an add on."

"Ye mean ta tell me tha` place used ta be smaller than it is already?"

"Yup." She chuckled. "And there were five of us in our family and only one bedroom! Of course my Dad was usually only here on weekends. But yeah, just the one bedroom"

"Chummy little group ye ha` there, luv."

"Well Nathan had a room in the big house and Morgan got the daybed in the kitchen. And of course Mom and Dad had what is now the guestroom."

"And where did ye rest yer head, lass?"

"Oh! I was the neglected child." She said in mock torment. "I had to sleep on a couch on the porch."

"Outside!" Donny hollered spooking Dolly slightly.

"No." Megan roared with laughter. "There used to be a wall separating the kitchen eating area and TV area we have now. We called that the porch and used it as a seating area. There was a couch and that's where I slept for many years in a sleeping bag. My brothers of course had beds, *with* sheets." She chuckled. "My mother would hate me telling it this way, it makes her sound so bad."

"But ye did get a bed sooner or later right?" he chuckled.

"Yes, as the boys grew older and got jobs my mother and I came up here on our own. I got Morgan's bed in the kitchen. Then later when the addition was built I got the guestroom, and my parents got the new room. But back to what I was saying before you distracted me."

"I think ye were sayin' ye wanted ta expand again." He smiled. "As it is, I was thinkin on tha' taday. Ye have a couple different way ye could go."

"We." She corrected.

"Huh?" he was confused.

"You keep saying 'you' or in your case *'ye'*." She smirked.

"Cute."

"I know. But it is no longer me. It's a *'we'*." She waited for him to nod in agreement and went on. "Ok then, now. Yes the place can go out in two directions, or we can go up. Personally, I would rather go up *and* out." She thought about all the suggestions from family members, and the plans her parents had made over the years. *Oh wouldn't it be fun to be able to take something from all the suggestions.* She thought. "We'd better start heading back."

"Aye, luv," he agreed. They changed directions and headed toward the cottage. "But I have a mind ta no change the main structure tae much. If yer wantin ta go both up and out it's goin ta take some finagling'."

"I know and it might be a little late in the year to start building now. But we can study ideas and suggestions. Have plans drawn and ready when it's time to start construction. Of course if we go up and out, more than likely we'll have to move up to the big house until construction is complete."

"Ye mean live in tha' big eighteen room Victorian." He shuddered. "Please nay."

"Oh you're funny. Really truly funny." She smiled as he chuckled.

As they came to the barn hill Megan spotted Steven's bright red Challenger coming down the hill from the direction of Duck Harbor. Instead of going directly to the barn Donny and Megan rode over to the cottage to greet Steven as he pulled in.

"Wow," Megan said when Steven got out of the car. "You have no idea how badly I want one of those." She looked over the car lustfully while still astride her steed.

"Really?" Both men said.

"Well why don't you get one then?" Steven said as he pet Max on the head.

"Have you taken a gander at the animal you're currently petting?" Megan said. "I can't have a car like that with a dog the size of Max. It would almost be like trying to get Steve in the car!" she laughed as she rubbed the black horse's neck.

"I can get one." Donny put in. "What?" he said when Megan stared at him. "I will be needin a car ta be gettin around sooner or later and why no` get one ye would like ta drive now and again."

"Do I get to pick the color?" she clasped her hands together.

"Hmm." Was all Donny said. He looked at his watch. "I need ta be getting the chicken oot o` the oven."

"Well here give me the reins and you two go on ahead." Megan said as she held out her hands.

"Will ye no be needin help wi` the horses, lass?" Donny asked.

"Yeah we can at least help you put them away." Steven added.

"*Put them away?* They're not a pair of shoes, Steven." She chuckled. "And no, I don't need any help. If I'm not back when dinner is ready, just mosey on over to the barn and see what's what."

"Are ye sure, luv?" Donny dismounted Dolly and held her rains in his hands unsure of what to *really* do.

"Yes, now give me Dolly's reins and git." She told him. She knew that even though Donny had made the offer for Steven to come to dinner and mend the fences as it were, he wasn't prepared to be alone with him yet. *Well I can't always be a buffer.* She thought.

"Yes ma'am." Donny said in perfect American. He slipped the reins over Dolly's head and handed them to Megan. "I luv ye, lass." He whispered to her when she leaned down to give him a kiss.

"I know, and I love you too." She straightened in her saddle. "Now go and play nice, children." She chuckled as she rode over to the barn leading Dolly beside her, while the men and Max went to the cottage.

Megan released Dolly's reins when they reached the barn door. She smiled and watched the Gypsy Vanner walk to her stall, turn, then graciously wait to be tended. Megan rode Steve to his stall, turned him and hopped down to the floor. Before removing his saddle, Megan made sure Dolly's door was secured and then closed herself in with Steve.

Gavin's ears perked when he heard the horses' hooves hit the floor of the barn. He silently congratulated himself in his concealment, his view of the woman as she moved around was impeccable. He noticed that she was alone and was instantly annoyed. But as he watched her move from one stall to the other he thought better of it. She took the saddles off the two horses and stored the tack on the other end of the room. *Oh yeah this is better,* Gavin thought as he adjusted himself. *I can have some real fun with the bitch before the mother fucker comes for the rescue.* As she moved around the large black horse with a brush and cloth, his eyes raked over her body with greed. The way her jeans and

T-shirt clung to her body, he was growing impatient to have his way with her, but he knew he needed to wait just a bit longer. He needed her away from the horses before he could make his move. *Then you and me bitch,* he rubbed himself over top of his jeans. *We are going to have some* real *fun.* Not knowing the danger that lurked at her back, Megan finished with Steve's rubdown then moved to Dolly following the same procedure.

"There you go girl." Megan cooed as she rubbed down Dolly's flank. "Feels good right?" She chuckled as Dolly whinnied softly. "Ok now, that's enough." Megan patted the horse and took the brush and cloth to store with the rest of the tack. She checked her watch. "Jack will be down in an hour to give you guys some fresh hay and feed." Steve whinnied and kicked at the door of his stall with his front feet. "Oh, come on," she walked over to him and took his head in her hands. "You just had a lot of exercise. You know you can't have your feed now." Steve's protests were getting more exuberant. Soon Dolly was beginning to act out as well. "Hey," Megan stepped back so she could see both of them. *This isn't normal,* she thought. "What's the matter with you guys?" Both horses were kicking at their doors and rearing up. *Maybe a snake or something got in here.* She turned to look around her when suddenly she was grabbed from behind. There was a hand over her mouth and a gun pressed into her side.

"Make one sound and you're dead." Gavin whispered in her ear. "Nod your head if you understand." Megan nodded her head. "Good. Now I am going to take my hand away from your mouth, remember, scream and this gun is going to make a real mess out of you." He removed his hand from her mouth and wrapped it around her throat. "Good, now where is Sam?"

"Sam?" *Think, Megan, think!* She screamed in her head. *Donny and Steven are in the cottage, they had to have heard the horses, and they'll come.* "I don't know who you're talking about." *Stall, Megan, stall.*

"Oh come now, you know who he is." Gavin moved the gun from her side and jabbed it under her jaw while forcing her to turn her head and look at him. "You have been fucking him for quite a while now." He watched as her eyes grew wide with recognition of the man who held her at gunpoint.

"Oh my God." She whispered as she looked at his face. The same face she had seen twice before when he came to her to patch up his knee. "You're—" she couldn't finish because he had pushed the gun harder under her jaw.

"That's right, you stupid bitch." Gavin removed his hand from her throat and wrapped his arm around her torso. "Now you know who I am," he ran his nose along her cheek. "and I am guessing Sam has told you what I have done." He whispered in her ear then running his tongue down her neck. Megan was both petrified and repulsed at the same time. With every move she made to try and get free, his hold on her grew tighter and the gun under her jaw drove deeper. "Now, I'm going to tell you what I want, and what I want is Sam. Now where is he?"

"I told you I don't know who—" Gavin cut her off.

"I think I should also tell you, there is one other thing I want. You see, while Sam, or as you seem to call him Donny..." He smiled as she went stiff as a board. "Yes I know that too. While he has been living the high life with you, I have been in the gutter, I think a little payback is in order." He ran his hand up her front. "You see," he started almost conversationally. "I haven't fucked in a long while." he pushed himself against her, just to prove how hard he was. "And I'm thinking Sam owes me." Rotating his hips so she could feel just what he had in store for her. "He has had it pretty good with you, and now I want to see what you've got." He ran his hand down her to the apex. " You feel what I got for you here?" With the pressure of his hand, he was able to grind against her even harder. She tried to get away and struggled. With every move she made he countered. "That's right, rub that ass on me. Maybe we will have ourselves a little back door action first." Gavin's hand was now roving up her body to her breasts. *I have to get away! I have to alert Donny and Steven!* Megan was chanting over and over in her head. With the repulsiveness of the man at her back, whose hands were on her, Megan's mind registered the noises Dolly and Steve made. She couldn't close her mind to the sounds, smells or feel of what Gavin was saying and doing to her body. But the whinnying, screaming and kicks coming from the stalls were a godsend, her lifeline. Megan started to struggle even harder. "That's right, baby struggle. I love it when they struggle." He was so focused on her body that he lowered the gun from under her jaw a fraction. Megan saw her opportunity, opened her mouth, and released a blood-curdling scream. It did the job, Gavin jumped in surprise allowing her more physical freedom. Megan drove her elbow into his gut and brought the heel of her riding boot down on his foot.

Chapter Twenty-Six

Donny led the way into the cottage with Steven and Max trailing behind. He knew what Megan was doing when she took both horses away. *She's forcin` me ta deal wi` me brother on me own.* He smiled, *she's a right bonnie lass.* He went to the oven, pulled out the covered dish and set it on the stovetop. He removed the tin foil and scented steam permeated the room.

"Wow," Steven smelled the air, so did Max. "That smells really good."

"Aye, It does." Donny smirked. "If I do'na say so meself. It's one of Ian's dishes." Donny stood looking at the dish. *Well now what?* He thought. *The lass meant fer ye ta be alone wi` the lad, so hop ta it.* He took a deep breath. "Steven, I wanted ta talk wi` ye aboot Arabella and Marie." He leaned against the sink and crossed his arms.

"Donny I don't think we—"

"Nay, I need ta ha` this oot." He chuckled. "Tis ne'er been easy fer me ta admit when I was in the wrong." He looked at his brother. "But I need ta now." He sighed. " I blamed ye fer years fer what happened and I shouldna. The girls were me responsibility and because o` me own wants I dumped tha` responsibility off ta ye. I knew they were comin on the train and I knew when. I was so damn focused on meself. There was no reason I couldna have spoken ta me prof after the holiday." Donny shook his head and cleared his throat.

"Donny I never blamed you for how you felt about me after what happened. You were my brother and you asked me to do you a favor. All I had to do was pick them up. I knew. I was the one who went to sleep. I was the one who didn't pick them up. I was the one who let Arabella die and Marie too, for that matter." Steven sat on the sofa and put his head in his hands. "You were right to blame me. It was my fault you lost them."

"Nay lad, it wasna." Donny said quietly as he moved to sit in the little wooden rocker across from his brother. "Aye, ye fell asleep and were late gettin there. But the man or men who attacked, who killed Bella, who took Marie, it was their fault, no` yers." Donny finally came to another realization. "Any more than it was mine. If ye had been there on time, ye may ha` been able to stop them or it may ha` been worse."

"Worse?" Steven lifted his head and looked at Donny. "How could it have been any worse?"

"If ye had been there we could ha` lost more than Bella and Marie. We could ha` lost ye tae." Donny ran his hands through his hair. "We donna know wha` weapons the men had. Givin wha` we both do fer a livin, we can guess wha` kind o` arms they had wi` them. Those men werna some kids oot fer fun tha` got oot o` hand. They were professionals. Do ye really think tha` they wouldna ha` shot ye if ye had been there?"

"I never thought of that." Steven sighed. "I am so sorry you lost Bella and Marie."

"Me tae. I loved Bella so much and I loved Marie as I love me own sisters. I thought I wouldna e're be able ta move past the loss and tragedy. And I admit tis taken me years. It lead ta the work I do now or the work I was doin until now." He smiled and thought of Megan. "I buried meself in work, and it helped fer a long time. I helped a lot o` people. Put a lot o` guys away and..." he trailed off.

"Other things." Steven knew his brother had killed, many times in his line of work, but felt no need to force him to admit it.

"Aye, other things." Donny smirked. "But it wasna until I went ta Scotland on the Gilmore case and spent time wi` Ian and his lass tha` I started ta realize the job wasna workin ta fill the void in me life as I hoped it would. Then I came here on the traffickin` case and met Megan." He smiled and leaned back in his chair. "Because o` her I began ta see the past fer wha` it was and wha` par I played in it." He looked at his brother. "I need ta let it go, and so do ye. I think tis time. Yer me brother and tis time I remembered tha` tae."

"Donny I," Steven stopped when Max jumped up and went to the door. "Do you hear that?"

"Aye the horses," Donny got up from his chair at the same time Steven rose from the sofa. "Tis the first time I've e'er heard them make a fuss like that." He looked down at Max who was whimpering, a cold feeling crawled up the back of Donny's neck. "Ha` ye a gun in tha` car?"

"Yeah in a lock box in the trunk." He watched as Donny took a hold of Max's collar and pulled the protesting dog into the bedroom and shut the door behind them. He yanked the bottom drawer of Megan's night-stand and grabbed the lock box that held the 45. When he pulled the box out he saw that the lock was broken. He dropped the box, knowing there was no reason to look in the other drawer for the cartridges. The gun was gone, he knew the cartridges would be gone too. He nudged Max out of the way so he could get through the door.

"Donny?" Steven questioned.

Donny moved to the guestroom, took down the 12 Gauge from over the door and loaded it with the shells from the closet shelf. Steven took his keys out and hit the button for his trunk. They both walked out the door and froze at the sound of a scream.

"Get the bloody gun!" Donny growled low as he ran across the dirt road towards the barn.

Steven dashed to the trunk, snatched his lock box from the back and wrenched it. He grabbed his Glock, rammed in a clip, pulled back the slide and flew across to the back of the hay barn. Steve found a door and crept inside. Donny ran as fast as he could to get to the barn. *Meggie, hold on. I'm comin.* He reached the door that opened to the old milking room. *Just a little further.* His heart was in his throat and his blood was boiling. He knew who was with Megan, and could only imagine what he was doing to her. *So help me, if one hair on her is harmed I'll rip his fuckin balls off.* Donny had been in hostage situations before and knew he had to keep his head cool. He had to turn off his emotions or people could get killed. But this was different. This time the hostage was Megan, and keeping his head cool felt impossible. He had to steel his heart to keep his emotions at bay. This was his job. He'd been doing this for years and he had to follow his path to get Megan safely out of this.

As he drew closer to where the horses were housed he could hear struggling and Megan begging her capture to let her go.

"Please stop." She sobbed as Gavin threw her up against the wall. She heard her head crack on the wood wall before she felt it. Her body went limp for a moment and her eyes glazed as she saw stars.

"I told you to keep quiet!" Gavin shouted. "Now you're gonna get it." He wrapped both hands around her throat and squeezed. "I'm gonna choke the life out of you, bitch!" Megan's lungs were beginning to burn from the lack of oxygen. She clawed at Gavin's hands and tried to no avail to pull them away. She opened her eyes and looked into the face of a madman. He kidnapped girls, raped them, sold them into bondage, and prostitution. He shot Donny and left him for dead, and he was going to kill her. That much Megan knew for certain. This man was going to kill her. She would never see her family again. She would never see Donny again, touch him, make love to him, and tell him she loved him. He was going to lose her just like he lost Arabella. *No!!!!* her mind screamed. *No, I will not let this happen, I won't allow this fucker to take someone else from him!* She opened her mouth.

"What?" Gavin moved his body up against hers. "Can't you talk?" He taunted.

He was close enough now, Megan drew her knee up into his groin with enough force that there was a resounding crunching noise. Gavin bellowed and dropped to the floor, releasing her in the process. Megan fell to the floor a foot or so away from him, coughing and struggling to get much needed air into her deflated, aching lungs. She heard a noise, fearing it was Gavin she tried to drag herself further away from him. She spared a glance and saw that the noise wasn't Gavin, but Donny. He stood in the large doorway, shot gun in hand and his face contorted in rage.

Donny made it around the corner in time to see Megan ram her knee into Gavin's groin. He watched, in what seemed like slow motion as Megan dropped to the floor. He heard her struggling to breathe. He barely spared the moaning Gavin a glance.

"Meggie." He wasn't sure he said her name out loud or not. He saw her try to crawl away. Seeing her broken was more than he could bear. "Meggie." His voice cracked with emotion, drawing her eyes to his. Eyes locked, he saw the marks on her jaw and around her throat. Shirt torn and her jeans were gaping open at the waist. He heard movement to his left and looked at Gavin as he rolled from his back to his hands and knees. A red haze washed over Donny's eyes. When he thought about Gavin putting his hands on Megan, rage Donny didn't know he had inside, simply boiled. Repositioning the 12 Gauge in his hands, Donny took aim.

"Uh uh uhhhh." Gavin, seeing Donny, rolled on the floor grabbing the stolen 45. He raised his arm and pointed the gun at Megan's head. "Drop the gun or your lady here will have another hole to breathe through." Even though Gavin was some five feet or more away from her, Donny knew he was a fairly good shot and didn't want to take the risk that Gavin might hit his mark. It was the hardest decision he had ever had to make, but Donny put the gun on the ground. "Now kick it away." Megan watched as it skidded across the floor.

"Let her go." Donny motioned to Megan with one of his raised hands. "Ye ha` nay reason ta hurt her, I'm the one ye want. No` her." As he spoke he moved marginally closer to where Megan lay on the floor, keeping his hands raised and palms open.

"You're right, you're the one I want." Gavin was so focused on Donny he didn't notice Megan inching backwards or the door behind him opening slightly. "But I kinda get a charge out of the idea of making you suffer and I sorta think the best way to do that is through her." Gavin sneered. "I knew the one way to get you where I wanted you was to use the cunt."

"Ye ha` me now," Donny continued to move inch by inch closer to Megan. "Let her go." By now he was standing where Megan had been. She had moved and was now leaning against the wall with the two men in front of her. "Come on Gavin let the two o` us finish this ourselves." Donny kept his focus on Gavin and the gun, but he also saw Steven slowly move through the back door. Steven made eye contact with his brother. Something in Donny's eyes made him stop. "Just us Gavin. Ye and me. Nay one else need interfere." With that Steven understood and nodded.

"What the hell are you talking about?" Gavin shouted. "You dumb fuck, I'm the one with the gun here." He moved the gun away from Megan and pointed it at Donny, but he was weak, still trying to recover normal breathing.

By now Megan was no longer Gavin's target. She spotted the broom that was used to sweep out the hay leaning up against the support next to her. *Maybe if I am fast enough I can grab it and knock the gun loose.* She knew it was a risky thing to do, he could see her and shoot. Or worse shoot Donny in the chest because that's where her father's 45 was pointed now. *Have to do something,* she thought. *I can't sit here and let him shoot Donny.* She slowly reached out her hand and grasped the broom. Careful not to make noise or have her movement noticed by Gavin she got to her knees. Megan got a hard grip on the broom and swung in an upward motion smacking Gavin under his wrist. As his wrist went up a shot was fired in the air before the gun flew out of sight. Donny took the opportunity and dove at Gavin.

The two men rolled on the ground punching at whatever they could. Gavin landed a few good solid hits into Donny's jaw and face. They rolled again and Donny was straddled on top of Gavin. He rammed his fist several times into Gavin's face, before taking a hold of his hair, lifting his head and with as much force as he could muster, crack-ing Gavin's head back onto the concrete floor of the barn. Donny sat breathing heavily and stared at the now unconscious Gavin. He wanted to kill him. It would be so easy. Just wrap his hands around Gavin's throat and squeeze. Choke the life out of him as he had tried to do to Megan. *Megan!* Donny thought and whipped his head around to find her on her hands and knees sobbing.

"Meggie!" Donny scrambled off Gavin and scurried over to her. "Meggie." He gathered her into his arms.

"I'm ok." She croaked out. She wrapped her arms around his middle and held on tight. "Are you alright?"

"What the hell were ye thinkin`?" Donny leaned back and took her face in his hands. "Pullin a stunt like tha`?" He wiped the tears leaking from her eyes away with his thumbs.

"Are you going to yell at me now?" She put her hands on either side of his tear-stained face. "What I have in my hands now is precious to me. And I was thinking I didn't want you shot." She took a breath. "Again."

"Yer a damn bloody fool wooman." He kissed her hard on the lips. "Donna e'er do anything` like tha` again." He kissed her again, this time somewhat softer. "What I ha` here between me hands is pretty damn precious tae ta me, and yer heroics could've taken it from me."

"Well, they didn't." She moved her hands and wrapped her arms around his neck drawing him to her in a much-needed embrace. They sat in silence for a moment, rocking. Suddenly the quiet was shattered by a single shot.

Chapter Twenty-Seven

Donny and Megan broke apart in time to see Gavin sink to the ground with a hole in his chest and the 45 in his hand. As he lay on the floor, Donny looked up to see Steven in his stance, his smoking gun still aimed.

"It might have been a good idea to let me get the cuffs on the bastard before you began your love scene, brother," Steven said as he walked further into the room.

Both Megan and Donny rose from the floor and walked to where the now lifeless body of Gavin lay. Donny watched as Steven made his advance and was caught off guard as Megan threw her arms around him.

"Ye saved our lives," Donny whispered. Steven looked over Megan's head and met Donny's eyes. "Thank ye."

"You're welcome," Steven said, returning Megan's hug. "In all honesty, I was after saving her life." Steven chuckled, "You were just a bonus."

"Oh, shut up," Megan said and kissed him on the cheek. She released Steven and stepped back, watching Donny come to Steven.

"Thank ye." He whispered. Donny grabbed Steven and held him in a bear hug. "Brother."

As Steven called in the troopers and paramedics, Donny called the FBI. Megan led Dolly and Steve to the paddock so they would not be disturbed any more than the event of the evening had done thus far. The horses stayed close to the fence to be near Donny and Megan as they waited for the police to arrive. Steve, rested his giant head on Megan's shoulder, while Dolly sought comfort with Donny. The group, which consisted of horses and humans, watched as the first of the cavalry arrived. Troopers were first followed by the paramedics, with the FBI close behind. Donny watched his brother transform into his official role and decided he should do the same. He gave Dolly one last soft stroke on the forehead before drawing Megan into his arms.

"I have ta go o'er there." He drew back and kissed her softly on her lips "Will ye be ok, luv?" He knew she was shaken but admired her for trying to hide it.

"Yeah, I'm fine." She leaned back on the fence and was flanked by Dolly and Steve. "I promise."

"Look after her." He told the horses, gave Megan one last kiss, and turned to don his official role one last time.

As Donny spoke to the FBI and the troopers, he glanced over many times to keep an eye on his Meggie. That's when he noticed that she was not only guarded by her flanking horses but now, somehow, she had Max guarding her front. He stood for a moment trying to figure how the dog managed that, considering Donny had locked him in the bedroom before running out of the cottage.

"Looks like I will be replacing a window or a door. Or both." He smiled as a paramedic approached Megan, then came to an abrupt halt as dog and horses warned him not to come any closer.

It took hours, but finally, the body of Gavin Mathew was carted away, leaving Steven and, by loose definition, Donny, the only remaining law enforcement left. Megan had assured her mother and father, who had come down, that she was fine and in good hands. She convinced them to go back home and head to bed as she would be doing the same thing very shortly.

"Be sure to have Jess look you over tomorrow." Her mother demanded before heading out.

"I will. I promise."

Megan offered the guestroom to Steven, but he told her he had to head to the barracks to write up a report and would head home afterward. He also told her that once the case was officially closed, her father's 45 would be returned to her.

"Oh, good. That one's my favorite." She looked at both men, who just stared at her. "What?"

"Ye have wha` amounts to a private arsenal, and ye da's old 45 is yer favorite?" Donny chuckled as he remembered all the weapons his Meggie had at her disposal and now that he was not stressed, remembered where they all were.

"So what?" Megan narrowed her eyes at the men. "Look here, you can't tell me that you two don't have a preferred weapon, a *favorite*." When neither answered. "You're both liars and, and... Oh I don't care." She chuckled, "It's my gun and I love it."

Being too tired for anything else after Steven left, Megan and Donny decided to climb into bed. But not before Donny jerry rigged the French door closed as it appeared that was how Max managed to escape to the paddock. Remarkably, the glass was not broken. However, the doors and the hinges were no longer one with each other. He knew that new doors would be needed. As the couple settled in bed Donny was not the least bit surprised that Max needed to be close to his Mom and crawled into bed with them. He wasn't sure how long that would last before either he or the dog was on the floor.

"It bloody well willna be me," Donny mumbled as he reached over Megan to scratch the dog's head. "ye big beast."

Megan did keep her promise and asked Jess to give her a checkup the next day. She had a mild concussion and a bruised trachea. Over the next few days, Megan rested while Donny fixed the French doors and had meetings. The only one that mattered to Megan was the one with Ted Duncan of the FBI. It was to inform them the case on Gavin was finally and forever closed.

Steven finally had dinner with Donny and Megan. Over dinner, they talked about the upcoming trip to Scotland for their brother Ian and Madison's engagement party. The brothers were both disappointed that Megan couldn't go. Because of her injuries, she had to take a couple of days off. More due to her bruising and scratches than to the seriousness of her injuries. She felt her patients didn't need or really want to see their doctor all banged up. And, of course, because she had taken time away from the office to recoup, her schedule was backed up. The office staff picked up Megan's caseload and needed to keep their scheduled appointments. But most chose to wait until Megan returned. Donny was hesitant about leaving Megan alone, but she assured him that if she needed anything, her parents were right there. Neither Donny nor her parents were satisfied, so Emma decided that while Donny was away, she would come and stay with Megan after work.7 The brothers decided to travel together to Scotland, and preparations for their trip were made.

The night before the brother's departure, Donny and Megan were awakened by the phone in the middle of the night.

"Hello?" Megan answered.

"Megan, Liz called." Steven rambled excitedly. "Her water broke."

"What!" Megan jumped out of bed.

"Her water broke."

"Holy Christ." Megan put her hand on her head and looked at Donny, who sat up and leaned toward her.

"Wha` is it, luv?"

"Liz's water broke." She told him. "Where are you now?" She asked Steven. She glanced back as Donny got out of bed, pulled on a pair of jeans, and got hers ready for her. *God, I love that man.*

"In the car, we are on the way to the hospital," Steven told her. "Megan..."

"We're on our way. Did you call her doctor?"

"Liz did right after she called me. She's going to meet us there."

"Ok," she nodded her head. "Ok, I'll call Jess and Hannah and let them know when we get in the car. Get her there as fast as you can, Steven. Oh, and Steven?"

"Yeah?"

"Get her there, but be careful about it."

"Yes, ma'am," Steven said as Megan slammed down the phone and jammed her legs into the jeans Donny handed her.

"Bra, I need a" Donny handed her the bra. "Thanks," she was all thumbs. "Shirt, I," she laughed as Donny was already holding her shirt. "Thanks again. I guess I'm a little excited." She looked around for her shoes.

"Ye think?" Donny grinned. "Yer flip flops are by the door, luv." He leaned down and kissed her. "And if ye wouldna mind, I think I'll be doin the drivin`."

"Works for me." She dashed out of the room, grabbing her purse and phone on the way to the door. "Max, you have to stay here." She told the bouncing dog as she slipped on her flip-flops. "Sorry baby." She snagged the house keys off the hook in the closet, muscled her way past the dog and out the door, and locked it behind her.

Once in the car, with Donny behind the wheel, Megan made her calls. She even called her mother to tell her about Liz and asked if she wouldn't mind taking Max out in the morning. Megan and Donny arrived at the hospital, and very shortly after their arrival, Jess and Hannah walked through the doors, followed by Megan's mother.

"Mom?" Megan hugged her mother hello.

"Your father went to the cottage to wait with Max. What? You didn't think I was going to miss this, did you?" She chuckled. "And your Dad will take Max out."

Everyone made their way to the New Beginning area of the hospital and found the birthing suite Liz and Steven were in. The staff wasn't at all happy about the number of people in the room, but Liz told them this was her family and she wanted them there.

"How are you feeling, Mama?" Megan asked when the irate nurse left in a huff.

"Half that crowd are doctors, and you'd think they'd know better!" the nurse muttered as she exited the room.

"Wired, excited, and scared shitless." Liz chuckled. She looked over at Steven, who was holding her hand. "I'm sorry about this. I know you were supposed to leave to go home." She glanced at Donny. "Both of you."

"Och! Donna, worry yerself aboot it, lass." Donny smiled.

"You can still go, you know." She told Steven. Just before her face turned red and her breath came in short gasps as her first full-blown contraction started. When the contraction subsided, she continued, "Jess and Megan are here now; they can help me."

Liz's face was red, but Steven's remained bone white after watching Liz go through the first contraction. "If you think I am going anywhere, you are out of your mind," Steven said.

"Steven, I think it's time to start your birth coach routine." Jess reminded the seemingly terrified state trooper.

"What?" Steven looked up into the crowd. "Oh! Yeah! Right."

"But your brother." Liz continued.

"It's only a party, and besides," he kissed her hand. "This is where I want to be right now."

"Oh," Jess cooed. "I think I'm going to cry."

"Don't you dare!" Emma said as she sniffled.

Hours later at eight-thirty in the morning there were new sounds in the room. The sounds of a beautiful six pound eleven-ounce red haired baby girl. Mother and baby were both doing fine but exhausted by the time everyone left to go home. Steven was going home long enough to shower change and he would be right back with Liz and the baby.

By the time Megan and Donny got back to the cottage, Donny had already missed his departure time. Fortunately, he had chartered a private plane for the trip. He phoned the pilot from the hospital to adjust his flight schedule and to let him know he would be traveling alone. He also called to have a car come and pick him up at the cottage. He knew Megan would be tired, and he didn't want her to drive him to the airport.

"One of the perks of being independently wealthy, I guess." Megan grinned when Donny ended his call.

"Aye." He said as he drew her into his arms. "Should I ask ye again if ye're after me fer me money, lass?"

"Maybe you should." She grinned. "I'm a very greedy, materialistic dame."

"Aye. I can tell by the grand house ye're livin in." He laughed.

As Megan zipped his suitcase closed she heard a honk announcing the arrival of the car. The couple and Max walked out to the Lincoln Town Car and Donny handed his bag to the driver.

"Well, I guess this is it." Megan put her hand on Max's head and looked up at Donny. "You're staying through to the wedding, right?"

"Aye, luv. Come here." He gathered her in his arms and held on tight. "I wish ye were comin wi` me."

"I know me too, but..." she buried her head in his chest.

"Ye need ta stay here fer yer work, and now ye have a new babe." He chuckled as he crooked his finger under her chin and brought her gaze back to his. "I luv ye, lass."

"I love you too." She raised on her toes to kiss him. Donny drew her closer and kissed her with all he held for her and for the misery he knew he'd feel while not being near her for almost a month. "Good god," Megan breathed when he ended the kiss. "That will either hold me until you come back, or force me to jump on the next plane and meet you there."

"It will have ta hold ye, luv, yer needed here." Donny hugged her one more time before he had to let her go and get into the car. "I'll call ye when I land."

"You damn well better." She kissed him one more time through the window of the car. "I love you Donny."

"I luv ye too, Meggie."

Chapter Twenty-Eight

Megan took a good look in the mirror and decided she didn't really look to banged up anymore. She's tired of staying home, and figured she could spend some time in the office. So, naturally, being in the middle of a very full day, Donny let her know he had arrived safely. She only had a few minutes to talk before her next patient. They talked about his flight and what she was going to do after she was done at the office. Her planned is to go home, see to Max, and then go to see Liz and the baby at the hospital.

"I will have mother come with me. She'll want to see the baby and the lights at night still bother me." She told him. She chuckled, although she was still annoyed by the situation.

Donny wished he were with her instead of manning the bumpy roads at night. He was used to dealing with time changes, but he had been in the states so long that this time his body was feeling the fatigue. He came to the signpost that gave him a choice, turn left, and go to the party, or turn right and go to Ian's. But it was after nine at night, he was tired and decided it was too late to make it to the party. Decision made, he turned his rental to the right and headed for Ian's house to wait for the happy couple to come home.

Donny sighed in relief when Ian's house came into view. He parked by the kitchen window that overlooked the driveway. The light over the kitchen sink was on, casting a soft glow over the parking area. He got his bag out from the back of the car and started up the walk. He smiled when he thought of all the planting Madison had done to the flowerbeds and the trees she had set out in the front of the house. It was too dark to really see how the flower beds were fairing, but if he knew Maddy, the flowers would be thriving. Donny stepped onto the wrap around porch, took the key from its hiding spot and unlocked the front door. Thanks to the light in the kitchen he was not walking into total darkness. Donny heard a meow and looked down to see Julie, Madison's white cat, coming to greet him.

"Hello there Julie," Donny reached down and allowed her to sniff him before petting her. "Och! Ye remember me, ye silly wee animal." Julie rubbed her cheek on Donny's hand and began to purr. "There ye go. Now will ye let me pick ye up?" He gently scooped the purring kitty off the ground and cradled her in his arms while he looked around the house. Nothing had really changed since Madison had moved in.

The stairs and railing directly across from the front door were carved logs. Old plank hardwood covered the floors throughout the entire house. Donny remembered when Ian had decided to build the house on the cliff overlooking the ocean all those years ago. All the work that went in to clearing the land of trees, then using those trees to build every inch of the structure that was now, Ian and Madison's home. It had a very open floor plan. To his left was the kitchen, which was huge, with polished flagstone flooring. The island in the center held a grill and gas stove top. All the cabinet doors were etched glass with reclaimed chestnut framing. The countertops were covered in bright copper. The copper flowed around the kitchen like built-in sunshine that dipped into a deep molded sink under the large window on the far side of the room.

"Well what do ye think? Should I make meself somethin` ta eat?" Julie gave a contented yawn. "Aye, that's what I was thinkin." He turned to survey the living room. His eyes were drawn, as they always were, to the large stone fireplace, big enough to stand in. Above the fireplace hung the framed blue, green and black plaid of his family. On the left of the large room stood a desk that overlooked the view to the back of the house. In the center of the room stood a sofa and two loveseats. Both upholstered in dark green cloth. There were no overhead lights throughout the whole of the house, except for the kitchen. Therefore, lamps were placed on small tables between the two loveseats and on the desk. Donny surveyed the room once more and chuckled about all the windows, *this house isna much for privacy*. The house was by no means lacking in windows. The caveat to this, was that with every window the viewer was graced with spectacular views.

"It's a good thing they donna ha` neighbors, huh, Julie?" Donny said to the now puddled cat in his arms. He smiled, but as he looked at the sleeping cat and then over at the sofas he gave in to his weariness. "I have nay idea how long it will take yer momma and Ian ta get back." He walked over to the larger of the two sofas. "How aboot we take a nap while we wait?" Donny stretched out on the sofa, all the while still keeping Julie cradled in his arms. Once he was settled she stood up, stretched, and curled into a ball on his chest. Within minutes man and cat had drifted into a dreamless sleep.

Much later Ian and Madison came home to find Donny fast asleep on the sofa with Julie staking claim on his chest. Madison rounded the sofa and gently awakened him. Donny didn't move, but Julie looked up at her person and meowed in protest.

"I know sweetie, but I have to wake him." She told her kitty. "Donny?" Madison called gently, and as he turned his head to look at her, she saw the bruising on his cheek and eye. "Oh my god! What happened to you?"

"Maddy darlin'," Donny rose from his comfortable position while Julie voiced her displeasure at being disturbed and gave Madison a hug and a peck on the cheek. "How're ye feelin?"

"Forget me, what happened to you?" Madison gingerly touched his face and saw Ian coming from the kitchen with an ice pack.

"Here," Ian handed his brother the cold bag and watched as Donny held it gingerly to his face. "Answer the lady. What happened?"

"Nothing much, I'm fine and on holiday." He looked at Ian, "I'm sorry I couldna get here for the party. I tried." He shrugged and looked back to Madison "So. What's new?" he grinned.

Knowing they would get no answers from him until he was ready, Madison and Ian told him their news of the coming baby. Ian knowing his brother was already aware of his and Madison's news, was proud of the way his brother simulated surprise. Ian wondered who the actor of the family really was.

Donny listened as Madison told him about meeting his mother and "The Clan Mackay".

"It was a big do, was it then? How did ye like our mam?" he asked.

"Ah thought she was perfectly dahlin`!" Maddy laughed as she mimicked Ian's mother's American southern accent. At Donny's smile the extra facial movement made him wince. He saw the concern in both Madison and Ian's faces. He knew he was eventually going to have to explain about his injuries, but not now. For now, he just wanted to listen to Madison and the joy that radiated from her.

"Aye. She is tha. The Carolina comes oot strong when she gets excited or nervous."

"Aye!" Ian chuckled. "Remember when we were young lads?" He turned to Madison and his grin covered his face. "We'd be in trouble fer somethin` and our mam would be givin us hell. Half the time we dinna know what the divil she was sayin`!" The brothers laughed and for the next hour, Donny and his brother regaled Maddy with stories of them as young boys and their mother. Eventually Ian suggested they all retire and start fresh in the morning. He retrieved Donny's bag from beside the sofa, and watched his brother gingerly inch his way up the stairs and decided to talk to him in the morning about a career change. They said goodnight at the guestroom door and Donny decided to follow Madison's suggestion to take a hot shower and pile into bed.

Even though the house only had two bedrooms, each had a private bath. After Donny finished his shower he all but fell into bed. As he snuggled down under the covers his thoughts went to Megan and her bed at the cottage. He admitted to himself; he was warm and very comfortable, but the bed felt wrong. He had too much room and it lacked the warmth of his Meggie. Donny took the other pillow and pulled it to his chest. *It's nay me Meggie,* he thought as he drifted off to sleep, *but fer now it'll ha` ta do.*

The next morning Donny dressed and came downstairs to see his brother Ian sitting at the island in the kitchen.

"Mornin." Donny smiled as Ian handed him a steaming mug. "Thank ye." He took a sip and looked up in surprise. "Coffee?" Donny knew his brother was more of a tea guy.

"What can I say?" Ian shrugged. "Maddy loves her coffee and I know ye ha` a taste fer it tea." Ian waited until Donny sat down across from him before he spoke. "So, how's yer face?"

"It looks worse than it really is." Donny squared his shoulders. He knew he was in for a lecture from his younger brother. "Wha` ha` ye on yer mind Ian?"

"I think ye know." Ian sighed and looked at the bruising on his brother's face and thought about how tired he looked. "Is this the face ye want our mother ta see?"

"Well tis the only one I ha` wi` me."

"Donny, ye damn well know what I mean." Donny watched his brother get off his stool and begin to pace the kitchen. "I know it's nay me place ta be tellin ye what ta do and how ta live yer life."

"Then do'na." Donny knew Ian was spoiling for a fight and decided to have some fun with this and give his brother the fight.

"I ha` ta. Yer job is dangerous, Donny. Look at ye!"

"Ian," Donny warned "tis nay yer concern." Donny added the edge to his voice that he knew would be there if this conversation happened only months ago. *Before me Meggie,* he thought to himself.

"Nay ye listen." Ian growled.

Donny sat back and sighed. *Might as well let the lad ha` his say.* Donny thought. But to keep the air of annoyance on his face he scowled at his younger brother.

"Yer job can get ye killed. Do ye no` care aboot tha`? Do ye really want ta get killed? Ha` ye some sort o` death wish? And wha` aboot our mam? Ha` ye thought aboot wha` it would do ta her if she lost a son?" Ian took a breath to calm down. He knew he was raising his voice and he didn't want to wake Madison. "I'm sorra fer shoutin`. I wanted ta talk ta ye aboot this calmly." Ian took his seat again. "Donovan, I'm aboot ta be a da, dinna ye think I want ye around ta meet me child. I want me child ta know ye. Tommy has a baby girl that ye ha` ne're' met yet. Wouldna ye want ta be around ta see her grow up?"

"Are ye finished?" Donny made his voice dark and angry along with his facial expression. And if this conversation had taken place months ago he would be angry. But his plans were different now. He wasn't sure how he felt about being told off by his baby brother but also, he knew Ian had valid points that Donny would have ignored those several months back. But Ian was on a roll now and Donny figured he would let it play out as it would have back then. Besides, Donny was almost enjoying his own little game and was unwilling to fill his all-knowing brother in on his plans, yet. Ian was being so righteous and getting all his feelings and frustrations out in the open, *why nay leave him ta his rant,* Donny thought. *It will make him feel better.*

"It depends on wha` ye're goin ta say." Ian grumbled.

"Has it e'er occurred to ye tha` I happen to like wha` I do fer a livin?" Donny lied quite convincingly. *Ye're not the only actor in the family, lad-die.* Donny thought. "Mayhap I'm no fer the same life ye ha` here wi' yer Maddy. Mayhap I like the action, danger, and intrigue. And, if ye're interested ta know, I am damned good at me job. There are people who can live their lives oot in peace because o` wha` I do and those who are nay able ta do so fer the same reason." All of this was true, everything he was telling Ian was absolutely true and it was for that reason he stayed with it for as long as he had.

"Yer no givin up the job then?" Ian stared at Donny's hard face. "Nothing I've said means anything ta ye then?"

"I'm goin ta see our mam." Donny said, as he straightened from his place at the counter. He could tell half-truths, but when Ian asked outright about giving up his job, Donny couldn't lie to him. So since he wasn't ready to put the lad in mind with his new life plan Donny decided to keep silent. "I'll be back." For some reason telling his mother first seemed a better idea anyway.

Donny walked out on his stunned brother with a chuckle buried in the back of his throat.

"Aye! I could ha` a new career in the field of actin`." Donny said as he got in the car to drive to see his mother and tell her the news he was bursting to tell his brother. "Delayed gratification is better." Donny laughed "I canna wait ta see the lad's face when he finds he's been had over."

Chapter Twenty-Nine

As Donny drove the few miles to his mother's he smiled as he remembered Megan referring to it as "The Family Seat". He knew his mother would get a chuckle out of that. While driving down the lane leading to the house, Donny was always struck by the beauty that befell him on the graveled lane. He marveled at how the sunlight filtered through the leaves of the Silver Birch trees that lined the drive. Donny had come to love Megan's farm almost as much as she did, but nothing could match the pride he felt when he came to his ancestral home. As he drove further up the drive, the grounds of the house slowly crept into view as if giving a teasing taste before the main course. The massive green of the manicured lawns and the fantastic landscaping that would put any royal grounds to shame. Finally breaking free of the tunnel of trees, sitting on the picturesque spot with rocky hills behind, stood the three-story stone structure that had served as the home of the Laird of Clan Mackay for centuries. Donny pulled his car around the circle drive to park near the front entry. He could see his mother, Evelyn Mackay, walking along the front of the house toward the main door. Turning off the car and getting out, he had the satisfaction of seeing her stop in mid stride when she saw her son and her expression change from one of contemplation, to beam with excitement.

"Hi mam." He said as he walked to her. She was a small woman about five feet with thick silver hair, cut into a short bob that shimmered in the sun.

"Donavon!" Evelyn gasped. Donny, like all of his brothers, wrapped his arms around her middle and whirled her in a circle, which always made her laugh. "When did y'all get hereah?" she asked when he placed her back on her feet.

"Last night." He rested his hands on her shoulders. "It was tae late when I landed, and I was tired. By the time I reached the village it was tae late ta attend the party, so I bunked at Ian's."

"Oh I'm so glad yorah hereah!" she laughed and hugged her son again. "Now whereah have you been?" She kept her arm around his back while he rested his across her shoulders. They walked to the small gazebo set off to the side of the front yard to sit.

"I've been in the states workin." He told her when they sat down.

"Gettin into fights by the look of yorah face." She gently touched the bruising near his eye. "Shame on you boy, ah taught you better than that." She smiled. "Did ya at least win?"

"Aye, I did at that."

"Whereah in the states?"

"Honesdale, Pennsylvania." He waited to see if she would make the connection to Steven.

"Honesdale? Well that's wherah..."

"Steven is? Aye it is. Mam, I have a few things I need ta tell ye. First I ha` a question. Ha` ye any idea wha` I do for a livin?"

"Well, no not really. Huh, odd ah neveah thought about it." *And he'll know that is a bold-faced lie,* she thought. "As y'all neveah talked about it and Ah felt when y'all wanted me to know, youah would tell me." She eyed her son, "Why, what do you do for a livin, Donavon?"

"Och nothin` illegal so ye can stow the evil eye yer throwin` at me." Donny chuckled. "I only wondered is all."

"Well now ma interest is peaked. Come on out with it."

"I guess ye could say I'm in law enforcement." He cleared his throat.

"You'ah a State Troopah? Like Steven?"

"No` exactly. Let's say what I do covers more ground." He watched his mother arch her eyebrow in the way all mothers do when they want more information from their children and mean to get it. It was a look Evelyn had mastered over the years. "Well I work wi` different agencies all over the world doin undercover work."

"What type of agencies?"

"Interpole, Scotland Yard, FBI," Donny shifted and cleared his throat. "To name a few."

"How...?"

"How and why are no` really important. And I canna be tellin what I was doin or fer who, lets just say," *Huh, wha` do I say now?* Donny wondered. *I'm getting off track.* "I'm getting off track here. Donna worry aboot me I'm fine. I promise."

"What were you doing in Honesdale, baby?" she raised her fingers to examine the bruising more closely on his face.

"I was there on a case workin wi` the FBI. While I was there I met a wooman, a doctor. Her name is Megan Dunnegan."

"Megan Dunnegan?" Evelyn watched as she saw a light in her son's eyes, a light that she hadn't seen there in many years. His whole body seemed to relax noticeably. It had been almost twenty years since she'd seen this, and it brought the heat of tears to the back of her eyes. "Tell me about her, son."

"She's a wonder ta be sure, Mam." he said, and Evelyn could see from the look on his face that he was finally in love. Her heart swelled with love of her own for this girl who had finally been able to chase away the ghosts from her son's heart. "She's strong and carin`. She has a love o` family tha` might even rival yer own. She's a physician and has her own practice oot in Rileyville where she is respected and loved."

"Ah notice, that with all these qualities, you have not mentioned once what she looks like." Evelyn smiled.

"Och she is breathtakin` ta be sure. Dark red hair, violet eyes, and a body that—"

"Ok." Evelyn held up her hand to halt the rest of Donny's speech. "Ah think Ah've got the picture." She chuckled and thought for a moment. A visible feeling of peacefulness settled over her face. "Now, tell youah mama how y'all met."

Bloody hell, this willna be good. "Well, I was," *Oot wit it ye bloody coward!* "I was injured in the line o` me duty, ye might say and the lass took me in."

"INJAHED!" Evelyn shouted and the peaceful expression drained from her face" Oh ma God! Arh y'all alright? How wereah you inja-hed? And why in hell didn't youah say somethin before! Arh youah alright now, dahlin`?" She reached out and ran shaking hands up his arms over his chest and around to his back. While she asked questions, her southern accent grew stronger by the second.

"Mam, shh, stop." He took a hold of her hands and pulled her in for a hug. "Now ye will be needin ta calm down. Ye're all upset and I canna hardly understand a word ye're sayin."

"Don't youah darha` try to make light of this Donavon Mackay." She pulled back and looked at her son. "Spill it, and Ah mean all of it." She saw her son was trying to come up with a softer story. "That was not a request. And DON'T call me 'Mam'."

"Aye." Donny sighed "I was shot," he paused at the sharp intake of his mother's breath.

"Wherah?"

"In Rileyville." He smiled.

"Whereah on yor'ah body, youah jackass." She chuckled. "And do not get smart mouth with me, young man. Ah'm still yorah Mama!"

Donny breathed a sigh of relief. *Tis gonna be alright*, he thought. *She's angry now and tha`s better than fear.*

"There she is." He scooted back some and lifted the side of his shirt to show his mother the scars. "It was a through and through, nay internal damage. Blood loss was the biggest issue." He let his shirt fall back into place and judged his mother. When she gestured with her hands to tell him to continue, he smiled and went on. "I donna think all the gory details are necessary, but the lass found me behind her car, called the ambulance and stayed wi` me until the emergency people came. Then she followed ta hospital and waited fer me ta come oot o` surgery—"

"Surgery." Evelyn repeated as she raised her fist to her chest and squeezed her eyes shut.

"Mama, take a breath. I'm fine. As I understand wha` the doctor said, it was more a matter o` takin films to be sure none of me vital organs were damaged and stitchin` me up than anything else. I didna even stay in hospital more than one night. I was doin well and the doctors need the beds. I was ta be released but had no place ta go ta recover fully. So, Megan took me ta her home ta stay and recuperate from me wound."

"Did ya'll eveah think of becomin` a plumbah? The money I hear is very good, and...What? Wait, this young woman didn't know y'all from Adam, and she took youah intah her home? For all she knew you could have been a—"

"That's wha` I said when she offered." Donny smiled at the memory. "But we had a few conversations, and she knew I was workin wi` the FBI." He chuckled at the memory. "She also warned me o` her verra large dog who would protect her should she need it."

"A dog."

"Aye, a big beastie!" Donny tried to illustrate Max's size with his hand.

"So what then?"

"I've been wi` her e'er since she brought me from hospital."

"Ah have been out that way a few times to visit youah brother. Whereah abouts does yorah Megan live?"

"On a lake in between two summer camps."

"Oh, Ah know that place! Beautiful spot. So, she lives in that rathah large Victorian...,"

"Nay the lass lives in the wee cottage next ta the big house." He smiled. "Thereah's more of this story to tell isn't thereah?" Evelyn asked when Donny paused. "Well, let's have it."

"I ha` seen Steven. Several times in point o` fact." He could see worry beginning to build in his mother's eyes.

Donny told her about getting reacquainted with Steven. He admitted his initial anger at learning Steven lived and worked in the area but omitted the incident of the broken door panes of glass. Then told her how both of them have decided to put the past in the past where it belongs and to start fresh from the present. He also told why Steven was unable to come to Scotland for the upcoming wedding and his obvious growing feelings for Liz.

"A baby." Evelyn cooed. "Are y'all tellin me that I'm goin to be a grandmothah again?" Her eyes brightened with excitement.

"I think ye might be puttin` the cart before the horse." Donny raised his hand to her cheek. "I know Steven and the lass ha` become good friends. She seems ta trust him a great deal and they've a strong friendship, so far. I'm thinkin` they have strong feelin`s fer each other. I ken Steven cares a good bit aboot Liz, but things might take a while. The lass has been through a lot o` late. Her life now isna exactly wha` she planned or what it started oot ta be when she married."

"Poor lamb. Ah don't even know her yet orah her story and Ah already feel for her. Is the poor baby girl not married? Is her baby out of wedlock?"

Donny smiled. His mother was a sweet southern lady down to her very bones and a caring nurturing mother from her soul out.

"She was married. I dinna ken fer how many years, but her husband, fer the first time in his life, accepted his own sexuality, fell in love wi` someone else, and he and Liz have filed fer divorced."

"Ahhhh." Evelyn breathed. "Ya'll mean he came out of the closet." Donny raised his eyebrows. "Dahlin`, Ah may live in the highlands of Scotland in the backwoods of the world, but Ah'm not exactly livin in the dahk ages." Donny hugged her but when he leaned back her expression had changed somewhat. "Well, couldn't he have come out of the closet befoha` he married her and got her pregnant, for the love of God and all the saints?" Now her dander was up in defense of a young girl she didn't even know. *She and Meggie will get along just fine*, Donny grinned.

"Mama, if the lad haddna come oot o'the closet, yer chances of becomin a new grandmama so soon would be lessened considerably." He tilted his head and looked down into her eyes.

"Hmmmm." She thought aloud. "Excellent point!" she smiled. Then she cleared her throat and patted her son's knee. "Now, what are you goin to do about yorha` lady? What is it you call her?"

"Meggie." He smiled.

"Yes, Meggie. Huh, I know that name from somewhere."

"Her mother has a fondness for the book, *Thornbirds.*"

"That's it! Great book, good mini-series too."

"After the weddin I intend ta go back and spend me life wi` her."

"Arah youah goin to ask her to marry youah?" She clasped her hands and held her breath.

"Aye, I want ta marry her." His grin widened. "Ye didna think I planned ta spend me life wi` her oot o` wedlock did ye, Mama?" he feigned a shocked expression.

"Ah've already told youah that Ah don't live in the dahk ages." She huffed. "Ah know very well how youah young people arah these days. Oh Donavan!" she laughed and threw her arms around her son. "I am so happy for y'all." She sniffled as she drew back pulling a handkerchief from her pocket to blot away her tears. "When do Ah get to meet hah? Is she hereah with you? No, I suppose not with her friend just given birth. How about the weddin, will she be hereah forah youah brothea's weddin?"

"Nay, she canna come ta the weddin either. She has her practice, and she also has her aunts and uncles comin ta the farm fer a holiday. She hasna seen them fer some time."

"Ah see. And that's how it should be. Family is the important thing. Ah am so happy for you. And I couldn't be morah pleased about youah and Steven patchin up yourah differences. Ah've prayed forah that for so long. Ah just can't tell ya'll how happy you've made me today. And Donovan, yourah daddy is also pleased with you, rest his soul. You know that don't you?"

"Aye, Mama, I know." He said as he pulled her into his arms and smiled over her head. "I know. It'll take time, but I think Steven and I are finally on the right track. There is somethin` I wanted ta ask o` ye."

Evelyn released her grip on her son and dabbed at her eyes again. She smiled up into his face. "Of course."

"Ye know grams ring?"

"Yes?" She grinned with anticipation.

"I was wonderin if I might ha` it?"

"Ma dear boy." she placed her hands on either side of his face. "*Aye, ye'ah may ha*` it. Come on into the house and we'll get it." They left the gazebo arm in arm and walked across the lawn and into the house as Donny told her more about Megan and their plans for their future. Donny did eventually fill his brother in on his new plans. Ian was impressed with Donny's untapped acting skills and tried to be angry at being fooled, but he was so happy for his brother that he couldn't pull it off.

Chapter Thirty

Megan heard from Donny every night while he was away. She laughed at Donny's story about him and Ian. She couldn't wait to meet his family and soaked up every story he told her. Their conversations were never long enough given the time change and she missed him terribly.

She was buzzing with work and helping her mother to get the Big House ready for her aunts' and uncles' arrivals. It was busy work at best, but it was also fun. Megan always enjoyed the job of preparing for family visits. It meant fun times and gatherings. Then of course when her family arrived she was happily engrossed with them. Their visits were never long enough to suit her. Megan always wished she could convince them all to live on the farm like her parents do. But the aunts will not be swayed from their warm winters in California or Florida. She missed seeing them more often than she did when she was a kid. However, like when she was kid, there were family dinners and cookouts at the lake weather permitting. There was wine, bourbon, and Irish tastings and label sharing and "leaf peeping". There was the trip to the Craft breweries that were popping up all over.

One day Megan received a phone call from Cindy, the owner of the rescue that her Steve and Dolly came from. They had two more horses and wondered if she would be willing to take them on. One was a Blue Roan Percheron Mare named Lorna and a Clydesdale gelding named Albert. They were companion horses only. Both very sweet and loved being in a herd along with having human attention. They were used for work horses and when no longer workable, the former owners sent them to a slaughterhouse auction. Cindy's rescue service found them and took them in. When Megan heard the stories of the two and how they had bonded she knew she couldn't say no.

"I think they would love it here. As matter of fact, I was going to call you anyway, Cindy. I was going to inquire about a horse so I could have three for riding." She sighed and looked at the pictures of the mare and the gelding. *Their companion only Meggie,* she told herself, *you won't be able to ride them.* But when she looked at the pictures again, she was sunk, and she knew it.

"Well now that you mention it I do have a couple of horses that would suit you and would work well with your Steve and Dolly. But I don't want to overwhelm you now." Cindy chuckled.

"No, what have you got in mind?" Megan's interest was piqued.

"I have a Spotted Draft, sixteen hands that would be a good fit I think." Cindy sent the picture of the spotted almost paint looking draft horse.

"Oh he's beautiful! What's his name?" Megan was in love "His main rider would be a rather muscular man. How is he with men?"

"His name is Sligo and he's bigger than he looks in the picture, more like your Steve, so he can handle the weight and he is wonderful with everyone he meets."

"Ok," Megan looked at the pictures again and thought about it for a full two seconds. "Ok, I have to do some work on the barn to accommodate the three of them, but I will take them all."

"Oh my God, Megan!" Cindy gasped. "I swear that was not what I expected!"

"I know, me either." *Dear God, what am I doing?* she thought. "But I wanted another rider, and I can't say no to the other two. Besides, they'll be happy here. Oh! What about Max?"

"They are all used to dogs like Max." Cindy chuckled. "Well how long do you need?"

"Give me three weeks to get everything ready and you can bring them down."

"Sounds good. Thank you so much for this."

Megan sat looking at the phone as her call ended in shock. "What have I done?" She was beginning to second guess her sanity, then she looked at the pictures again and bubbled with laughter. She got back on the phone and began making the plans to have her barn changed as well as having the paddock and the fencing around the pasture expanded.

"Well that was an odd lunch break." Megan chuckled and got ready for her next patient.

On her days off she would stop in to see Liz, and most times she would find Steven there fussing. It made her smile. She could see the mounting attraction between the two of them. She could also see Liz was keeping him at a safe distance, trying to guard against getting hurt again. Megan knew Steven would never hurt Liz or the baby, and on some level Liz knew it too. But given how her marriage ended, who could blame her?

"So when does Donny come back?" Liz asked as she rubbed her daughter's back after her feeding.

"Tomorrow. The wedding was yesterday, and he wanted some more time with his family. Ahhh, now there is a healthy burp." Megan laughed as the baby belched in a small lady-like way.

"Yup." Liz cooed. "Now I can put her down for her nap." Megan watched as Liz gently placed the baby in the bassinet.

"What are you going to do with her when you come back to work?" It was the question on everyone's mind. Everyone at the office knew it would be difficult for Liz to leave the baby for a full day, but they also knew she couldn't afford to not go back to work.

"I don't know yet. Daycare, I guess." She sighed as she and Megan went to the other room so as not to wake the now dozing baby. "It's not like I have any family who can watch her during the day. And having her right upstairs would be fine I guess. At least I can see her during working hours. But she's so young, and to have such a tiny infant to care for along with all the other children. That would make the job harder on the girls up there."

"So Jimmy still hasn't been to see her?" Megan was astonished.

"Nope he and Michael are gone. He sends a check for child support, but so far, seems to have no real interest in meeting his daughter. He's more than willing to help support her financially, but he has a new life now and that's his focus. Elenore doesn't seem to care about seeing the baby either." Referring to Jimmy's mother.

"Stupid woman." Megan was quiet for a moment. "You know my mother would love to watch Emily for you initially when you come back to work. And when she's old enough, you can put her in the daycare at the office. At least then you can pop upstairs and see her during the day"

"I know, and Emma has told me that loads of times." Liz sighed. "Well I have some time to think about it." She looked at her watch. "Oh! I better start on dinner. Steven is dropping by after he's done with work."

"Oh really?" Megan smiled at Liz's blush.

"Stop it, Megan." Liz laughed as she made her way to the kitchen.

"I never said a word, but I'd like to remind you of all the times you nagged me about men or tried to fix me up. Come to think of it, I remember not so very long ago, you tried to nudge me toward Steven." Megan laughed out loud at Liz's guilty expression, "Ok, ok, I'll get out of your hair." She gave her friend a hug and left to go home.

As Megan parked her car by the side of the cottage, she noticed the lack of cars at the big house and figured the older generation had all gone out to dinner together. She loved that they were here, but was secretly grateful that she could stay at home tonight and decompress after a long workday. She walked around toward the front of the cottage and stopped in her tracks. There sitting on her front porch was Donny.

"Donny!" She dropped her purse and ran, launching herself into his outstretched arms.

"Meggie." Donny sighed with relief when she was in his arms. He kissed her neck, cheek and finally her lips.

"God I missed you." Megan said against his lips.

"And I you, luv." Donny held her tightly and deepened the kiss. He wanted her so much and feared he would take her right there on the front step unless he broke the connection. "I fear we are aboot ta make an impression right here on the front porch unless we get in the house, luv." He chuckled.

"We wouldn't want that now would we?" Megan laughed as she ran her fingers over his lips. "I thought you weren't coming back until tomorrow?"

"Tha` was the plan, but I couldna stay away any longer. Next time I go away ye're comin wi` me. Whether ye like it or no`."

"Oh, yes! Come on, let's take this inside." She started to pull back, but Donny held her tighter.

"Wait, there is somethin` I need ta talk wi` ye aboot before we head in the house."

"Ok." She had butterflies in her stomach. "Is everything alright?"

"Aye, luv." He smiled. "Come, let's walk around ta the deck."

"Why not go through the house then? It's faster."

"If we go through the house, lass, we'll no make it passed the bedroom." He ran his thumb across her bottom lip as his eyes darkened with desire. "I've missed ye so much, luv, but I want ta get somethin` settled first."

He took her hand, backtracked to retrieve her dropped purse and they walked arm and arm to the deck.

"You know you're making me very nervous here."

"Am I now?" Donny dropped her purse on a nearby chair and advanced on the woman in front of him. As he walked toward her she backed up until she was against the deck rail. Donny put his arms around her and rested his hands on the railing on either side of her, effectively caging her between his body and the deck rail.

"Sorta." She placed her hands on his arms and gazed into his jade eyes. "What's going on Donny?"

"Well." He leaned into her and grazed his lips down her neck. "I wanted ta ask ye a question."

"If the question has anything to do with going to bed the answer is yes." She gasped when he nipped her neck behind her ear and grinned at her soft moan "I thought you didn't want to put on a show."

"I dinna, luv, but I hav'na seen ye in a while and we're nay longer on the front porch, ye ken." He took his hands away from the rail and placed them on either side of her rib cage. His thumb rubbing softly against her left breast. "I just feel the need ta indulge a wee bit."

"Oh." She squeaked and breathed in his scent. "Well indulge away." She felt his smile against her neck. "Hey." She said as he abruptly lifted his head and stared down at her. "What's the big idea? I was enjoying that?"

"I have a question." He smiled.

"Well ask it dammit, so we can get back to the indulging part." She smiled and her eyes, though darkened with desire, twinkled with mirth. She watched as he took a deep breath.

"Megan Dunnegan," he stepped back from her, and she watched stunned as he dropped to one knee. He pulled a ring from his pocket all the while holding her left hand in his right.

"Oh God." She blinked the tears away from her eyes so she could see.

"I was a walkin shell o` a man whose heart was always in the dark. But since I ha` met ye, me heart is free o` darkness. Me heart has been silent fer almost twenty years and is now finally beatin` again. I am filled wi` yer love. Me heart is yers now and will be ferever. I love ye Meggie, me darlin. Ye are me light. Will ye," he took a breath. "Well, the long and short o` the thing is, luv, will ye wed me?"

"You are one crazy man, you know that?" Megan smiled as she wiped her tears away.

"Aye, luv, I know. But ye still ha'na answered the question at hand."

"Oh Donny." Megan sank to her knees, took his face in her hands, and kissed him, long and hard. "I love you too."

"Yer killin` me, lass." He groaned against her lips. "Is tha` an aye or nay?"

"That was the most beautiful proposal any girl has ever received. And it's an aye." She smiled. "Yes, Donovan Mackay, I will *wed ye*, you crazy scot."

"Thank god." He rested his forehead against hers. "Here," he slipped the ring on her finger.

"Donny, it's beautiful!" She breathed. It was a white gold band made of intricate Celtic knotting all around, ending with two trinity knots on either side of a large emerald cut diamond that flashed brilliantly in the late afternoon sun.

"It was me Grandmother's." He told her as she admired the old ring. "She and me grandfather were happily married for o'er sixty years. While I was home I went ta me mam and asked her fer the ring ta give ye. She told me on one condition."

"What was that?"

"I had ta bring ye ta Scotland ta meet the clan." He laughed as he scooped her up and turned in circles with her laughter filling the air. "Donna worry lass, they'll love ye, as I do. Ye ha` made me verra happy."

"I love you too." She kissed his lips. "And you have made me very happy." She kissed him again. "But you know what would make me even happier?"

"What's tha, luv?"

"Donny you have been gone for almost a month, you have asked me to marry you and I've said yes." She grabbed his face in her hands, brought his lips to hers and said against them. "Take me to bed."

"Yes ma'am." He bent his head to kiss her and stopped. "By the way, why is there construction at the barn?"

"Donny!" Megan laughed exasperatedly, "I'll tell you later." Donny kissed her deeply as he carried her back into the house to begin their new and long life together.

About the Author

Nora Weirich

Nora Weirich lives with her husband and four fur babies. Since 2007 she has worked as a Teachers Aide in her local school district. She has a ferocious love of reading. You can find her most days either in her office writing or in her favorite chair curled up with a blanket, a warm cup of coffee or tea with a her nose in a book.

Cadmi Ó'Cléirigh

Over the years Nora has fallen in love with the genre of Romantasy. When the opportunity arose, she began her penname of Cadmi Ó'Cléirigh. She is currently working on Golden Realm Chronicles.

Nora Weirich

Mackay Series
Cliff House
Dunnegan's Cottage

Cadmi Ó'Cléirigh

Anthologies
Where Myths Walk

The Golden Realm Chronicles
Quelocand: Land of the Queens (Coming soon)